PURE HELL WITH A GUN!

Dombey reached to his side and drew a gun. "Listen to me, Holliday!" he screamed. "If Earp doesn't protect me, I'll talk. And I know plenty!"

McCain sat up, ready to draw his Colt. Doc sat slouched in his chair, his arms crisscrossed over his chest, hands under his jacket and tucked into each armpit.

"You pulled a gun on me," Doc said calmly. "You want to talk? Talk to this." He pulled a shiny, new derringer from under his left arm and, without even taking the time to take proper aim, pointed and fired. Dombey fell to the floor, a bullet through his heart.

McCain stared at Holliday in amazement. Holliday returned McCain's gaze and said:

"I don't like people who point guns at me. Never did."

DOUBLE CROSSFIRE

ALLEN CONRAD

ZEBRA BOOKS
KENSINGTON PUBLISHING CORP.

ZEBRA BOOKS

are published by

Kensington Publishing Corp.
475 Park Avenue South
New York, NY 10016

First printing: May, 1988

Printed in the United States of America

To my mother—
gratefully.

Acknowledgements

Many people directly or indirectly contributed to the creation of this novel, and I'd like to thank them, especially Brian Thomsen for keeping his ear to the ground and putting me on the right trail, and all my friends at the NCC WW for tolerating my strange enthusiasms, particularly Fran O'Connor for her critical eye and for being in charge of "adverb control."

Special thanks are due Scott Siegel for his patience and guidance.

And thanks are long overdue to Robert Spector, Terence Malley, and Kenneth Scott for the lectures and the discussions, but most of all the confidence they helped instill.

Finally, thanks Michelle and Michael Kupfer—once again.

"They were speaking English all about me, but I knew I was in a foreign land."

Robert Louis Stevenson
The Amateur Emigrant

Author's Note

Although the Earps did eventually make it to Tombstone, Arizona, and Robert Louis Stevenson did, in fact, cross the United States by rail in 1879, no records exist which prove that any of the other events in this novel ever occurred. It is hoped that readers will treat this tale as the fantasy it is meant to be; no authenticity or accuracy is claimed.

Stevenson's journey is described in *An Amateur Emigrant,* the writer's autobiographical account of his travels to and across the United States.

Chapter One

Dodge City, Kansas, 1879

"You cheatin' son of a bitch!"

The words were directed toward Josiah McCain, who didn't take kindly to them. With swift movements he threw down his four kings and sent a flying right fist over the table to the loudmouth's jaw. McCain heard the sound of teeth clacking against teeth. The loudmouth's eyes squinted in pain, and his cigarette, lit and red-tipped, dropped from his lips and fell under his shirt collar. The accuser wriggled and squirmed, trying to keep the cigarette away from his skin. He pulled the tails of his shirt out from under his belt, hoping the butt would fall free.

Several of the other men at the card table found this highly amusing and let out bellows of laughter; other patrons of the Long Ride Saloon, however, did not, and started to move in on McCain, now on his feet and expecting the worst.

Two men, both standing tall and alert at the distant end of the bar, watched as the gathering storm of bodies surrounded McCain. One of them—Deputy Marshal Wyatt Earp—viewed the scene with an amused grin. The other man—Sheriff Bat Masterson—folded his arms and watched the small mob move nearer to the accused cheat. Neither lawman made any motion to get involved.

Luke Adams, the saloon keeper, began to get fidgety behind the bar. He finally yelled out to his customers, "If any of you bastards draws a gun in here, I'll cut your damned ears off with a sawed-off bottle of hootch." For emphasis, he smashed a bottle of cheap whiskey against the edge of the bar and displayed the ragged, jutting edges. "If you don't think so, you try me!"

Several guns were replaced in their holsters. McCain was grateful for that, but he still had quite a task before him. At least a dozen men wanted to kick his skull in.

One of them, a man to his left, threw a punch, but McCain saw it coming, blocked it with his left forearm, and landed his fist dead center in the man's ribs, knocking the liquor-tinged wind out of him.

From behind, though, someone slipped an arm around McCain's throat. He grabbed the arm with his left hand and pulled it away from his windpipe. He jerked his body down and back and succeeded in jabbing his elbow into the man's stomach. He now had two men, one on each side of him, gasping for air.

Across the room, Luke Adams shot Earp a glance that wordlessly asked the deputy to break up the fight. Just as silently, Earp's eyes gave a negative reply. The eyes also expressed interest and more than a little amusement in the ruckus.

Then a burly, bearded man ran directly toward McCain. As he approached, the man scooped up a round, oak card table, spilling drinks, playing cards, and money onto the wooden floorboards. He tried to squash McCain like a cockroach against the wall with it. The action momentarily stunned McCain. But in one way, he was grateful for it; it allowed him a few seconds—crushed up against the wall but invulnerable to any other blows for the moment—to collect his thoughts. Finally, though, he tried to push back against the top of the table, but he couldn't budge it. The man on the other side was just too strong; he weighed 275 pounds and was built like a grizzly bear.

McCain glanced down at the floor. No boots but his own were visible, so stomping on the man's feet wasn't going to be possible. Looking up, though, he noticed a small kerosene lamp and the flickering flame within it. He forced his arm up, grabbed the lamp, and smashed it down against his adversary's head.

He heard the man scream as the table dropped to the floor, the rim just missing McCain's feet. The table-wielder slapped at his face, trying to put out his burning beard. It was McCain, however, who picked up a pitcher of beer and threw its contents in the man's face, quenching the fire.

The man—smoldering bristles and all—fainted dead away. Everyone stood quiet and motionless, totally absorbed in the sight.

"Now," McCain spoke up, "anyone else want to play? I haven't killed anyone yet, and I don't really care to, but I'll be goddamned if I'll stand by and let some bastard call me a card-cheat!"

He slowly glanced around the saloon, into as many faces as he could. Then he continued, "Want to take me on? You can all have your chance, one at a time. Try ganging up on me again," his Peacemaker was pulled from its holster as quickly and smoothly as an uncoiling rattlesnake, "and I'll blow craters in your chests, so help me God!"

He stared hard; no one moved. Then he turned to Adams, still holding the broken bottle in his hand. "That goes for you too, barkeep. I'm planning on keeping my ears a while longer."

Adams was angry and thought about calling this man's bluff. It wouldn't be the first time he'd mutilated a man with a jagged bottle. In fact, just the other day Doc Holliday had told him he used bottles like a good surgeon used a scalpel: skillfully. But Adams thought some more and put the bottle down on top of the bar.

"Fight's over, boys," Adams announced. "I don't want the place wrecked. Kill this fellow if you want to, but do it outside."

All was silent for a moment, and McCain lowered his gun.

A young kid, possibly eighteen years old, stood next to Earp at the street end of the bar. Perhaps trying to impress the deputy, the wiry young man slowly lifted his pistol out of its holster. A fat man stood midway between the kid and McCain, and McCain couldn't see his actions.

Then the gun was out, rising slowly. In a second, the barrel was pointing around the fat man, straight at McCain.

Earp's hand, in a single fluid motion, whipped from a pocket of his waistcoat and smacked the young man's face. The blow sent the youth staggering across the room. He fell into the arms of another patron, who held him by the arms.

"The owner said the fight's over," Earp said unemotionally, without even looking at the boy. Then the deputy marshal picked up his glass of whiskey, poured the remaining liquid down his throat, and spun around. He headed for the doors of the saloon, but stopped for a moment when he heard McCain say, "Thanks, Deputy. Maybe I can return the favor sometime."

Earp ignored McCain and marched out of the saloon. Bat Masterson threw Adams a silver dollar and followed

Earp out into the cool night air. The two men stood on the boardwalk outside Adams' place and lit up smokes.

"You recognize him?" Masterson asked his fellow lawman.

"Nope," Earp replied. "Should I?"

"Josiah McCain. Out of Missouri, I believe. Word has it he had some trouble with the law up there." Bat puffed on his cigarette, then exhaled a cloud of smoke into the wind-chilled air. "I also hear tell he once kicked the crap out of Custer a year or so before Little Big Horn."

"You seem to know a lot about him."

"I met him once, quite a while ago. He probably doesn't remember."

"How could he forget the famous law-keeper Bat Masterson?" Earp kidded. "After all, you're almost as famous as I am."

Bat knew he was being ridden. "If I had eight hundred brothers like you, I'd be just as famous as you are."

The two men laughed, then Bat said, "I'm goin' back in. I want to talk to that McCain."

"Yeah, do that," Earp said. "See what you can find out about him. I could use a man like that right now."

"For what?"

Earp just laughed. "I don't know, Bat. Sometimes you're very naive."

"Well, you got so many rackets goin', it's hard to figure out which one you need him for."

Earp laughed again, said, " 'Night, Bat," and climbed onto his horse.

Chapter Two

Earp rode the short distance to Katie Fisher's house, located at the other end of Dodge City. Her house was commercially known as KATIE'S to the townspeople, and it was an excellent or notorious "house" depending on who was speaking. Earp reached it in minutes, got off his horse, and knocked on the front door.

A young lady about seventeen years of age, known only as Lashes, answered the door. Again, depending on who in town was speaking, she acquired her name either for her long, curled, enticing eyelashes — or her predilection for whips.

"Why, Mr. Earp," she cooed, "won't you come in?" She opened the door wider to admit him.

"Thank you," he smiled, removing his hat as he entered. Just as he always did when entering a room, he glanced around. The room was gaudily-lit as usual, all amber and red. The furniture was made of fine leather and sturdy wood. A few men he knew were talking to several of the ladies. There were also a couple of gentlemen he didn't recognize, but they didn't worry him; neither was carrying a gun, at least not visibly.

"Can I get you a drink, Mr. Earp?" Lashes asked.

"Whiskey maybe?"

"No, thanks. But you could tell me if you've seen Doc Holliday around today. I've been lookin' for him for some time. And usually when Doc's nowhere to be found, he's here."

Lashes fluttered her outstanding facial features and smiled. "Why he's here right now, upstairs with Katie. Would you like me to escort you upstairs, Mr. Earp? I could take you right to their room . . ." Lashes' flimsy silk dress fell open slightly to reveal one shapely, dark-nippled breast, ". . . or wherever you care to go."

Earp held her arm tenderly. "I'd really like to go elsewhere with you," he said, pulling her dress closed and tightening the sash around her waist that kept it together, "but business forces me to head in Holliday's direction instead."

"Too bad. I got me some new toys to play with. I'm sure you'd really like them."

"I still got marks on my backside from your old toys," Earp laughed.

"Oh well. Come," she said, pulling him toward the staircase. "I'll show you where they are."

"I know the room. The usual one, right?"

"Not this time. I guess they wanted a change of location or something. I'll take you there."

As Lashes led him up the stairs, several of the customers elbowed each other, seeing Earp headed for what they thought would be an evening of unusual pleasures. They stared at him, and when he turned his head, he saw them staring.

"Now just what the hell are you boys lookin' at?" he asked, accompanying the question with a stern look.

The men didn't answer; in fact, they were stone silent.

"All of these ladies have prettier asses than mine," he commented, his expression suddenly changing to a smile.

15

"If I were you, I'd watch theirs."

Earp's audience laughed, and he continued up the stairs with Lashes.

When they reached the middle of the upper hallway, Lashes let go of his arm, pointed to a door and continued walking.

"Thanks," Earp said, stopping at the door.

"Bye" was all Lashes said in reply. When she reached her own room, she opened the door and went in.

Earp knocked on Katie's door. There was no answer, but he could hear sounds inside. He knocked louder.

Finally, a voice yelled from the other side of the door. "Oh, go the hell away, will ya?"

"Doc!" Earp said, knocking again.

"Hey, listen, you goat's ass," the voice yelled again, "I said git yourself lost!"

Earp exhaled in disgust. "It's Wyatt," he said.

There was no answer.

Having wasted enough time, Earp tried the doorknob but found the door locked. He took a step back, raised his right leg, and booted the door open.

There before him was a sight to behold: a naked Holliday bent over the foot of the bed. Katie lay flat on her back, her head touching the headboard.

"Hell," Holliday exclaimed, standing up, leaving behind the warmth of Katie's lap. Turning, he saw it was Earp. "Wyatt. I didn't know it was you."

"I said it was me."

"I didn't hear you."

"How could you?" Earp commented dryly. "Your ears were covered."

Katie was visibly annoyed. "At least close the goddamn door, Wyatt."

Earp complied. Katie, meanwhile, got to her feet and casually slipped on her robe.

16

"Sorry, ma'am," Earp said to her.

"Don't apologize, Wyatt," she said, still annoyed. "Things like this come with the job. They're what they call occupational hazards." She finished covering herself up and then turned to Earp and Doc. "I guess you boys got some urgent business, or Wyatt wouldn't've come bustin' in here like this." She started out of the room.

"Don't go away mad, Katie," Doc said, stroking her hair.

"Yeah, right," she retorted sharply and opened the door. But before stepping through the doorway, she turned and said, "You broke my lock, Wyatt."

Earp bowed mockingly. "Yes, ma'am. I'll have it fixed."

"Yeah," Katie answered, disbelieving, "like you did that bed you shot up." She shut the door as she left.

Holliday stared at Earp, grinning and fascinated. "You shot up one of her beds?"

"Yeah."

"What the hell for? Were you drunk?"

"No, but the son of a bitch lyin' in it—who stole my brother James's horse—was."

Holliday now understood. Earp lit a cigarette and sat down on the bed.

"Doc," Earp said, "I want you to do a job for me.

Holliday's eyebrows jumped. "Now?"

"Just set your butt down and let me give you all the details you'll need."

Naked, Holliday sat on the sole chair in the room. He too lit a cigarette and inhaled. In no time, he began coughing violently, covering his mouth with his fist. The coughing persisted for several moments.

"You shouldn't be smoking, Doc, in your condition. You sound like you're about two feet from death's door."

"Aw hell," Doc said, wiping the saliva from his mouth.

"Don't start again. I like to smoke and I'm gonna, no matter who says otherwise. He took a deep breath in an attempt to clear his lungs and then continued, still holding the cigarette. "Screw them doctors. And don't you start again, either, especially since you're sittin' there blowin' smoke in my face."

Earp held up a hand. "Okay, okay. Do what you want." He exhaled some smoke, but this time he turned his head away from his friend. "Just stay alive long enough to drop off this loot."

"Yeah, sure," Doc answered. Although he knew he was sick, Holliday didn't give a damn. He was consumptive; the doctors had told him that. And although his dental training was a bit far afield from that branch of medicine, he knew what that meant: he shouldn't be smoking. But Doc Holliday would be damned if he'd give up anything he liked.

"Why don't you fill me in on all the particulars?"

Earp stood up and faced him. "I want you to take $15,000 to Jerome Beaudine. He'll be arriving in Ogden, Utah by train in a few days. He's on his way to San Francisco, but his stops include Ogden. It seems the best place to do this. He'll be expecting you there on Wednesday. You can get there by then if you move it."

"Move it?" Holliday snorted, then hacked out another hoarse cough. "I'd have to grow wings and fly there, fer Christ's sake. I hope you don't expect me to ride all the way. That's some trip!"

"I don't expect you to ride there. Ride north to Hays City, then take the train to Ogden. You'll make it in time."

Doc thought about it for a moment. "Yeah, I guess so."

"On the way there you can check on one of our enterprises. Collect some money from the boys up by

Moods."

"They ain't been hanged yet?"

"Nope. In fact, they're doin' really well. But I tell ya it amazes me that they get away with that obvious trick. But so far they've been first-rate rustlers. You realize they've been there a year and a half in that same location and none of the locals have caught on yet?"

Doc put out his cigarette. "Okay, I'll pay 'em a visit." At first, he was reluctant to go on this rather tiresome journey, but he realized that this trip, work or not, would be good for him. The more he thought about it, the more he looked forward to the change of scenery. He even looked forward to getting away from Katie for a few days. She was smothering him. He enjoyed the sex; few women knew as many exquisite ways to please a man. But Katie was fawning all over him lately. She was a different example of what Wyatt called a "professional." Lately, though, and unprofessionally, she hung on Doc all the time, and he needed some freedom.

Earp interrupted Doc's thoughts. "A couple of other things, Doc. My brother Warren is goin' to be travelin' with Beaudine. He's with him now, as a matter of fact."

Doc's face registered surprise. "Warren?" he exclaimed. "Warren? You ain't never mentioned no brother Warren. How many brothers you got? Fifty?"

Earp crushed his cigarette under his boot. The boots were new and highly polished and made a crackly stretching sound as he pressed forward on the toes. "No. Warren just ain't been this far West yet. He's still in Missouri. I wrote to him and asked him to pal up with Beaudine; then I told Beaudine that travelin' with an Earp would bring him lots of good publicity. He went for that. We're kinda popular back East since Ned Buntline started writin' them tales about us. Anyhow, Warren's with him, keepin' an eye on him for me. You got

19

the idea?"

"Yeah, I got it. But I got a couple 'a questions. When you're dealin' with politicians, things don't always go smooth."

"Shoot."

"Suppose something goes wrong? Suppose I get to Ogden and this Beaudine won't take the money? Suppose he changed his mind or something?"

Earp laughed. "Beaudine won't change his mind. He wants me or one of my brothers to be marshal when we move to Arizona. He just wants to be paid for the trouble of arrangin' it. Don't worry about Beaudine. He's scum, but he'll do this for me. He admires me; he's got even more rackets than I do. Besides, that's one reason I wanted Warren around: so he won't change his mind."

"Warren good with a gun?" Doc wondered.

"I doubt it," Earp replied. "But he's an Earp, and everyone everywhere thinks all Earps are legal gunmen, thanks to them adventures. Beaudine's no different."

Doc was about to roll another cigarette, but thought better of it and put away his makings.

"If anything goes wrong," Earp continued, "I leave it in your hands. Your decision. You've got a good, crafty head on your shoulders, and I trust you as much as any of my brothers. That's why I'm sendin' you."

Earp stood up. He started to button up his waistcoat. "So you make the decisions, Doc. I know they'll be the right ones. Just keep me informed as often as you can. Wire whenever you can."

Earp walked to the door, opened it wide, looked both up and down the hall, then turned back to Doc. "I left the money in a satchel in the saloon with Luke. You can pick it up there."

"When do I leave?"

"Tonight. As soon as you can."

"Okay," Doc muttered, surprised he was to leave so soon. "You want me to go alone?"

Earp slapped his hat against his thigh. "Damn! I almost forgot. There's a guy in Luke Adams' saloon right now, a tough son of a bitch. He just fought off damn near the whole place by himself. If he wants a job—and he's driftin' and could probably use one—hire him to ride shotgun for you. But don't tell him what you're doing or what you're carryin' till you know just how much you can trust him."

"This guy's a drifter, and you want to hire him to tag along?" Holliday asked, startled. "That don't seem smart, Wyatt."

"You be the judge, then," Earp answered, "but later on. Something about this guy tells me he'll go along and might come in handy. If I'm wrong and it proves otherwise, kill him."

"Wyatt, I don't know if this is too . . ."

"Just do it," Doc," Earp interrupted. "You know I've got this instinct about people like him; I can smell the bad ones. He doesn't smell too bad to me. Besides, I saved his ass at the saloon. He owes me one. Bat knows him. Says he's a good man."

"What's his name?"

"Josiah McCain."

Doc shook his head. He wondered if Wyatt had lost his mind. "Wyatt, I can't believe that . . ."

"Stop worryin', will ya? I just got through tellin' you Bat said he's a good man. Knew him up in Missouri. And anyway, if Bat's given us a bum steer, or if McCain tries anything or acts suspicious, get rid of him. You can do that, right?"

"Yeah, okay." Doc realized it was no use arguing with Wyatt once his mind was made up.

Earp put on his hat. "Bye, Doc. Good luck."

21

"Bye, Wyatt."

Earp hesitated at the door for a moment. "You got it straight, Doc? Any more questions?"

"No, I don't think so. Can't think of anything. It's just a simple payoff, right? I get to Ogden where no one knows us, I hand the loot to this fancy presidential aide, and I come home."

Earp ran two fingers down the length of his blond mustache. "That's it. But remember: we have to get out of Dodge soon. This trip will insure our warm reception in Tombstone. Don't let me down."

"I wont."

Chapter Three

Bat tossed down another shot of the Long Ride's whiskey. "Christ," he muttered. "That crap'll kill you."

McCain laughed. "I've had plenty worse."

"Yeah, me too, come to think of it," Bat agreed. "Remember that wash-water they had at the Red Sky in Kansas City?"

"Sure do. If I recall, I spilled that stuff once, and it took the shine clean off my boots."

The men laughed again, then just looked at each other, smiling.

"Been a long time, Josiah," Bat reflected. "How you been?"

"Not to bad."

"I guess you heard about Custer. It's been a few years now."

McCain swallowed more whiskey. "Yeah, I heard. Got what he deserved, the bastard."

"I suppose. I remember the day you caught him with your sister. Jesus, you scared the feathers off him. You damn near knocked his head off."

McCain's face grew solemn. "I should have," he said, "but the Sioux did a better job than I ever could have."

Bat lit a cigarette. "Well, your sister's a mighty pretty girl. She . . ."

"My sister *was* a mighty pretty girl," McCain interrupted.

"Was?"

"Yeah," McCain muttered. "Mary's dead."

"Jesus, I'm sorry, Josiah, I didn't know."

"That's okay, Bat."

Masterson was at a loss for words. Finally, he decided to change the subject.

"How's that pretty wife of yours? I know if I was married to a girl that fine-looking, I wouldn't leave the house to answer a call from anyone, friend or not."

McCain sipped at his drink. "She left, Bat. A year ago."

Masterson was dumbfounded. He couldn't believe he had put his foot in his mouth twice in less than one minute.

"You gotta be kiddin'," he said.

"Wish I was."

"She just packed up and left."

"Yep."

Masterson took off his hat and slammed it on the table. "Damn, Josiah. I'm so sorry about opening these wounds."

"It's okay, Bat," McCain said matter-of-factly. "That's what happens when two friends who ain't seen each other get together and try to get up to date."

"I suppose. But I feel terrible."

"Well, don't," McCain said. "And let me tell you why I did answer your call."

"Go ahead."

"You know my folks live in Missouri not far from where the Earps lived a few years ago. Wyatt's parents are still there. Well, one night I'm ridin' home to see my folks, and I hear this wailin' from the woods. I got off my horse and there on the ground, a bloody mess, is my sister. She was dead. She'd been raped." McCain lit a cigarette. "Somehow, before she died she managed to write a message on a flat rock with her own blood. It said 'W E raped' and that's all. She couldn't finish it. At first I couldn't make heads or tails out of it. 'WE raped.' We raped who? It didn't make any sense. Then I realized that the 'WE' didn't mean 'we,' but someone's initials. Those initials mean anything to you, Bat?"

Bat thought for a moment. "Wyatt Earp," he said, horrified. "But you don't think Wyatt Earp raped your sister, do you?"

McCain wet his lips again with the whiskey. "No. He couldn't have because he's been in Dodge for some time. But he's got a brother who stayed in Missouri, and my sister knew him. His name's Warren."

"Warren Earp?" Bat repeated. "Don't recall Wyatt ever mentioning him. But there are plenty of Earp brothers no one knows, evidently. They come and go around here."

"So you never saw Warren around here?"

"Never even heard of him."

"Well," McCain continued, "I've been looking for him for some time. He suddenly disappeared after my sister's murder. When your letter arrived, I was anxious to come to Dodge anyway to look for this Warren."

Bat exhaled cigarette smoke over their heads. "But Josiah, how can you be sure it was Warren Earp? Must be plenty of men with the initials 'WE' around."

"I'll know when I find him," McCain said confidently. "You see, right near where I found my sister I found a small, bloody piece of flesh. I wrapped it up and took it to the town doctor. He told me it was a man's earlobe. My sister must've put up a hell of a fight; she bit the thing off."

Bat realized what Josiah was getting at. "So if Warren

Earp'ss missin' an earlobe, he's the culprit."

"Right."

"Sounds easy."

"I got to find him first," McCain said. "Anyhow, I *am* here to help you. What do you want me to do?"

"Let me explain it to you fast," Bat said, "because it'll work against me if I sit here with you gabbing for too long. When I first got to Dodge, I wasn't exactly a good lawman. I had a lot of things goin'. Gambling, stuff like that. Then the Earps arrived. Soon it was like I had the east side of town and they had the west. After a while I felt kinda rotten about it. I liked bein' a lawman. Maybe I'm just a sucker, but I got rid of my gambling interests. Sold them to the Earps, in fact. Now things are gettin' crazy 'round here. I want to move to Tombstone, Arizona, and take up lawin' there. Legal-like, too. But I made the mistake of tellin' the Earps about it. Like I said, things are changin' around here. The population is gettin' kinda tired of corrupt lawmen running things. And they're right, even though they still include me in that crowd. So now the Earps want to go to Tombstone too, the bastards. Only they're cookin' up some deal to make sure they get elected. You followin' this?"

"Yeah. Go on," McCain said.

"Well, one day some time back, a man from the Secret Service approaches me here in Dodge. He asks me if I'll help him crack a corruption racket involving one of President Rutherford B. Hayes' aides. I ask him how, and he tells me by keepin' a close eye on the Earps. The damn Earps, do you believe it? He tells me he thinks that this aide has ties to the Earps and is involved in some of their bullshit. Riggin' elections and that sort. I told him I'd do what I could, but I can't do too much without seemin' awful nosy. That's why I asked you to come. To keep an eye on the Earps for me."

McCain put out his cigarette in his now empty whiskey glass. "How do I do that?" he asked.

"By gettin' in with them. Don't let on that we're friends. I told Wyatt I knew you and that you were a good man to have around and let it go at that."

"So you want me to work for them."

"But really work for me," Bat said. "I need your help. I don't have no organization like the Earps. I really want that job in Tombstone, and I don't want the Earps following me there, screwin' up the deal for me. It's time people thought about me as myself, not one of a kind with them. All you got to do is play along with them and let me know what's happenin'. Will you do it?"

McCain said, "I haven't forgotten that you saved my life in St. Louis. If it wasn't for you stoppin' that gambler from slittin' my throat, I wouldn't be here now. Of course, I'll do it. I owe you one, a big one. I just hope I don't botch it for you."

"Aw, you won't," Bat assured him. "Them Earps are crafty in a way, but sometimes they're awful dumb. Can't see what's right under their noses. And I hope this don't sound crude, Josiah, but maybe your path will cross Warren Earp's here."

"That would sure be a bonus."

Masterson stood up. "I'll talk to you later, Josiah, to fill you in a little more. Let me mingle with my constituents right now before someone gets wise. See you later."

McCain watched Bat join some men at the bar. He wondered what he'd gotten into. A presidential aide! The Secret Service! But he hoped Bat was right when he said Josiah's time in Dodge might lead him to Warren Earp.

Suddenly, a tall, thin man swung open the saloon doors and coughed his way through the crowd.

Chapter Four

Doc strolled up to the bar, leaned over it, and grabbed Luke Adams' arm. "Where's the bag?"

Adams, looking squatter and meaner than ever, took a few steps down the bar and reached under it. He brought a satchel into view and placed it on the bar. "Here. Must be a bundle. It's heavy as hell."

Holliday peered into Luke's scarred, pock-marked face. One scar—it ran down his right cheek from the eyebrow to the lip—had been given to him when he was a young man. A man who was attacking Adams' mother had slashed the young man with a Bowie knife while the lad was trying to get him off her. The experience taught Adams two things: assume everyone has a weapon and trust no one, not even family. The boy had found out later that the man was his mother's lover, and she had continued to see him even though he often threatened to kill the boy if he ever interfered.

Unlike Adams, Doc was tall and thin, pale of face but dark haired and mustachioed. Two men couldn't look less alike. "Gimme a whiskey, Luke."

"Sure." Adams poured a drink, and before he could fill it, Doc snatched it away and had it to his lips.

"Again," Doc said, slamming the glass down.

"You got it," Adams said, refilling Doc's glass.

"Luke, where's this guy McCain that Earp was tellin'

28

me about? I got to talk to him."

Adams made a face full of disgust and pointed to the rear of the saloon. A lone man sat at a table with a whiskey bottle and a glass in front of him. "Bat was just gabbin' with him."

Doc studied him for a minute. The man wasn't overly impressive. He was tall, not particularly muscular; in fact, he was on the gangly side. He probably stood six feet tall, Doc figured, but he couldn't weigh more than 175 pounds. But as the man leaned back, buckling his hands behind his head, Doc got a good look at the man's face. There was an air of intelligence about him; it was an air sorely missing from most of Dodge City's population, and it stuck out in this saloon like an Arabian horse in a pig sty.

Earp, too, had that air. In several ways, this stranger reminded Doc of Earp. Perhaps that was why Earp was interested in having this man work for him. This drifter had the same composure, the same confidence. But this loner didn't have the long, straight hair or stylish mustache that Wyatt had, nor was he dressed as impeccably as Wyatt usually was.

Doc found himself intrigued with him, the same way Wyatt had. "Watch this for me," he said to Adams, gesturing toward the money. He walked back to where the man was sitting. When he reached the table, the man looked up.

"Can I help you?" the man said, expressionless.

"Maybe," Holliday retorted. "Can I sit down for a minute? I'm Doc Holliday."

"Really?" McCain said, as if he were impressed. "Sit down, by all means."

"Thanks." Holliday turned the chair around so he could rest his arms on the top of the chair's back. Then he sat silently for a moment, looking at the man before him.

"What can I do for you, Mr. Holliday?"

"Earp told me about you. How you clobbered the clientele down here. He thought you might be interested in some work."

McCain swallowed another two fingers of whiskey. Then he said, "So that *was* Earp. I thought so." He wiped his mouth with the back of his hand. Then he continued. "Why doesn't Mr. Earp do his own job of recruiting?"

" 'Cause you'll be working with me," Doc responded, taken aback by the man's cockiness.

"What kind of work we talking about?"

"I'm going to Ogden to deliver some important papers — land deeds and the like — for Earp," Doc lied, "and I could use a man riding alongside of me. There are a lot of bastards who'd like to get their hands on these deeds, if you know what I mean."

"I know what you mean. You want a gunman along for insurance."

"Right."

McCain lit a smoke. "One question: why me? Earp must have plenty of men he could send."

"Don't know," Doc answered honestly. "Maybe he sees a lot of himself in you. He admires a tough, independent man."

"That's just a polite way of saying 'drifter,' ain't it?" McCain asked.

"Look, friend, I don't know why because I ain't Earp. You want the damn job or not?"

McCain dragged on the cigarette and flicked the ashes on the floor. "Ogden's a long way off," he mused. "How much are you going to pay for my company?"

"How much you askin'?"

"Three hundred dollars."

"Earp said I could go as high as two hundred," Doc again lied. Three hundred wasn't a lot of money to Earp; several of his enterprises took in that much money every hour. But Doc saw no reason to give Earp's money away.

"Tell Earp I want three," McCain insisted.

Again, Doc was taken by surprise. This drifter, who didn't look all that sure of himself had more than his share of arrogance. "Earp said two hundred."

McCain dropped his cigarette on the floor and stomped it out with his boot. Looking straight at Doc, he said, "Then tell Earp to go to hell. I didn't ask him for a job."

Doc didn't quite know how to react to that. Few men would even think of telling Earp to go to hell; equally few would think of telling Holliday to relate the message. Doc wondered what riding with this man would be like; he also wondered if he shouldn't just forget about Earp's wishes and drop this fellow right here.

Finally, though, Holliday decided to try another form of persuasion. "Earp told me you owe him a favor."

"That's right. I do," McCain said matter-of-factly.

"Well . . ." Doc just stared at McCain, waiting to hear how he'd respond.

After a couple of minutes of silence, McCain's face broke out in a smile. Holliday couldn't understand its purpose.

"Okay, Mr. Holliday. Two hundred. I guess my life's worth a hundred dollars, although there are some people in this very saloon who'd probably disagree. I'll ride with you."

"How well can you shoot?" Doc asked. "I already heard tell how well you can fight."

"I can shoot," McCain said.

"Show me."

"In here?"

31

"In here."

McCain, still sitting, drew his Colt and shot twice practically over Doc's shoulder toward the front of the bar. The shots quieted the saloon, obviously surprising the patrons. As they all watched him, McCain replaced the pistol in his holster.

Doc grinned at McCain, looked around the saloon, then noticing nothing unusual, turned back to him.

"I guess you missed. I didn't hear nothin' break," he said.

McCain poured himself another drink and grinned back at Doc. "I didn't shoot at anything breakable," he said. "But take a good look at the picture over the bar."

Doc turned his head. He couldn't see anything unusual about the painting from that distance, and the expensive portrait of a naked reclining woman was still there, hanging as usual. Doc got to his feet and walked to the bar, looking closely at the painting. Then he started to laugh.

Luke Adams, who had heard the bullets whiz over his small frame, turned around behind the bar and lifted himself until he was sitting on it. Then he noticed it too. "Why that son of a bitch!" he yelled, looking at Doc. "It ain't funny, Holliday. He shot her goddamn nipples off."

The place nearly burst with the sound of men's laughter. Adams wondered how he'd get even with the bastard who'd been showing off and wrecking his place for the last couple of hours.

"I'm gonna kill that asshole," Adams said angrily. He reached under the bar for his gun.

Doc grabbed his wrist and stopped him. "Okay, Luke, okay. Take it easy."

"But he's wrecking . . ."

"I know. But let me ask you a question."

"What?"

32

"Who you working for?"

Adams made a face. "Wyatt. You know that. Why are you wastin' my . . ."

Doc squeezed his wrist tighter to cut him off. "Well, so is he now. Earp won't like it if you kill him."

Disgusted, Adams pulled his arm back and walked to the other end of the bar. In all the excitement he had forgotten about the satchel. Luckily, everyone else was caught up in the action too. The satchel was still there.

Doc lifted a fresh bottle from the bar, turned and saluted McCain with it, then drank about a quarter of it down; and with that salute McCain knew he had a job. He got up, approached Doc, and extended a hand. "The name's McCain. Josiah McCain."

Doc took the hand and shook it. "We ride in an hour."

"Goin' somewhere?" Bat Masterson asked.

"Hi, Bat," Doc said. "Where the hell you been?"

"Oh, I just stepped outside for a while. Sometimes it gets a bit gamey in here after a while."

"I hear you know McCain."

"Met him a few years ago," Bat responded, patting Josiah on the back.

"I just gave him a job," Doc said. "Think I made a wise choice?"

"A really smart choice. Too bad, though. I was gonna offer him a job myself. I ain't had a deputy in two months."

Then Doc turned to McCain. "I'll meet you in an hour outside." He took the satchel from Adams and left the Long Ride.

"Come to my office in five minutes," Bat said to McCain. "I've got to talk to you."

Chapter Five

"Hi, Josiah, come on in," Bat said. He was sitting at his desk in his completely darkened office.

McCain located a chair in the darkness.

Bat leaned forward on his desk. "I heard Holliday say you two were leavin' soon. That's good. It's usually Holliday who runs Earp's errands for him. Something's definitely in the works, and I'm glad you'll be there. You're still willin' to go through with this, ain't you?"

"Sure," McCain answered. "I'll be able to tell my grandchildren I rode with the famous Doc Holliday. Assuming I ever have any grandchildren."

Bat wondered if McCain was smiling. He doubted it; that last remark sounded like a reference to his wife.

"You want some coffee?" Bat asked.

"No, thanks."

Bat poured himself a cup. "You won't be able to keep me informed, Josiah, while you're out of town. Earp's got the telegraph operator in this town on his payroll. So let me give you some more background, real quick." He sipped his coffee. "You already know my personal reasons for all this. Let me tell you more about the government's interest. This presidential aide or whatever you call its name is Jerome Beaudine. Ever hear of him?"

"No."

"Me neither, until I heard it from this Secret Service agent. What they want is evidence because President Hayes hates the guy. He inherited him — if that's the right word — from Grant's administration. Couldn't let him go for some reason. Anyhow, Hayes wants to string him up by his privates, but he needs evidence to do it. So anything you can get your hands on will be appreciated."

"I'll try."

"Good."

"Anything else I need to know?" McCain asked.

"Just one thing. Watch out for Holliday. He's a real friendly fellow if he likes you. But don't trust him too much. He has only one loyalty and that's to Wyatt Earp."

"Understood."

Bat swallowed the rest of his coffee. "I'm probably forgettin' to tell you all kinds of things, but that'll have to do. It ain't much, I know."

"I'll be okay. And anything you haven't told me, well, I'll just have to figure out for myself."

"Well," Bat said, "I'll see you soon, I guess. Sorry our reunion was cut so short."

The two men shook hands, and Josiah opened the office door.

"Good luck, Josiah," Bat called after him. "I appreciate what you're doin'."

Josiah waved and closed the door behind him.

Chapter Six

The well-dressed man in the office couldn't be persuaded, but this foreigner was persistent.

"I absolutely insist that you allow me to speak to Mr. Pinkerton!" said the man with the Scottish accent. "I simply must."

"You simply must get your tail out of this office before I throw it out," retorted the obstacle to Pinkerton's door, mimicking the man's accent.

"Your behavior, sir," the Scotsman continued, "confirms my suspicion: you are an unfortunate sufferer of cretinism!"

The guard did not know what this meant, but correctly assumed it had to be insulting. He grabbed the thin, young man by the lapels of his jacket and swung him around.

At that moment, the door to Allan Pinkerton's private office opened, and there stood an obviously annoyed Allan Pinkerton.

"What the deuce is going on out here?" he asked. "Lawrence, why are you assaulting this man?"

36

Before Lawrence could answer, the Scotsman answered for him. "Because he is a brute, a creature lacking the intelligence of the very lowest representative of homo sapiens."

Pinkerton laughed at the remark, then raised his eyebrows in surprise. "Sir, is that the accent of a Scotsman that I detect?"

The young man smoothed the lapels of his jacket and replied proudly, "It is indeed, sir. And since I have just made the voyage from my homeland to this city of Chicago, I wanted to greet a fellow countryman, Mr. Allan Pinkerton."

"Well, then," said the man at the door, "please come in."

The young Scotsman picked up his suitcases, gave Lawrence a satisfied sneer, and marched past the man holding the door open.

"Please sit down," said the man, extending his hand. "I am Allan Pinkerton, and if no one has done it yet, let me welcome you to the United States of America."

The young man stood up again and shook the extended hand. "Mr. Pinkerton?" said the Scotsman, "I'm somewhat surprised. Your accent . . ."

"Is all but gone," Pinkerton said. "I know. When I first arrived in this country, I thought it was the Americans who had the accent. Now I must sound quite a bit like them."

"Well, yes," said the visitor, "but you are clearly a Scotsman in your behavior and refinement."

Pinkerton laughed again. "There are many in this country who would argue with that statement, my friend. As the head of the Pinkerton National Detective Agency, I've had to behave somewhat less refined on a number of occasions."

The traveler smiled, then said, "I'm being terribly rude. Allow me to introduce myself. My name is Robert Louis Balfour Stevenson."

"A pleasure," Pinkerton said. "Now what can I do for you?"

Stevenson stared at him, embarrassment clearly showing in his face.

"I assume this isn't strictly a social call," Pinkerton said.

"No, sir, it isn't," Stevenson owned up. "I'm afraid I have no one else to turn to."

"What is it?"

"Sir," Stevenson explained, "I left for America with no family support and little monetary support. I am on my way to San Francisco to meet my fiancée. I now finance myself only halfway across this vast nation, with less than three American dollars in my purse. Perhaps I am being presumptuous, but I felt I could turn to a fellow Scotsman for assistance."

"You need money," Pinkerton said.

"Yes, sir, but not much. I don't eat much. I simply need enough to reach San Francisco, at which point I will return your loan, should you be gracious enough to grant me one."

Pinkerton reached into his pocket and pulled out a wad of paper money almost the size of his fist. "No problem," he said, counting out fifty dollars and placing the bills face up on his desk.

Stevenson protested. "That's far too much."

"Take it," Pinkerton insisted. "You might need it. And besides, if you don't repay it, I'll find you. I run a detective agency, remember?"

Stevenson took the money and put the bills in his right pants pocket. "You are a saint," he said, taking the burly, balding man's hand.

"Not quite," Pinkerton laughed. "Now I have quite a bit of work to do, so if you don't mind, I'll ask you to leave."

"Thank you, sir, once again," Stevenson repeated, picking up his suitcases. "Your kindness will never be forgotten."

"Just don't forget my fifty dollars!" Pinkerton said. "Good luck to you."

"Thank you." Then the young man left, walking past a snarling, muttering Lawrence and several other tough, grim hooligans dressed in business suits. When he was back on the street, Stevenson swore to himself that he would repay his loan as soon as possible. God forbid that one of those hoodlums who worked for his benefactor should come looking for an overdue payment!

Stevenson glanced up and down the street, trying to recall the location of the train station. Finally, he remembered where it was and slowly walked in that direction, a suitcase in each hand and the brown satchel wedged under his left arm.

Chapter Seven

"All aboard!"

The call rang through the train depot like a church bell, loud, clear, and with a note of finality. People of all descriptions pushed to board the train. A quick glance from a discerning eye would notice the different nationalities, colors, and styles of dress of the crowd. They all massed together, swirling like a pool of water, headed for the car doors.

Stevenson swallowed the last of his tea. Quickly running out of the nearby cafe, he grabbed his two suitcases and his brown satchel. They were all that he owned, aside from the clothes he had on and the money that Mr. Pinkerton had given him.

"All aboard! Union Pacific to Ogden, Utah! All aboard!"

Stevenson reached into his pocket. He felt no train ticket in it. He reached into his other pants pocket and felt the folded paper money and a few coins there, but no ticket. Panic began to set in. Then he remembered: he had been using the ticket as a bookmark. Putting down the satchel and the suitcases, he pulled the book from under his arm. He opened it. There was the ticket, marking the page where he had stopped reading Tobias Smollett's *Humphry Clinker*.

Relieved, he replaced the book under his arm, picked up his baggage, and blended into the crowd. In front of him stood two men, both big and brawny. They spoke some tongue he didn't understand but recognized as some Slavic variation. Behind him stood two other men, both huge. And since each was wearing a Stetson and a gunbelt, he felt sure they were Americans. They seemed to him typical American cowboys, strong and somehow menacing.

Beside him stood a beautiful young lady. He hadn't noticed her before, but found the sight of her a treat for his travel-weary eyes. She was a brunette, beautifully-shaped, and stunningly dressed in a blue cotton dress. Clearly, he thought, this was a woman of considerable style.

As he gazed at her, she quite unconsciously made loud tching sounds with her mouth and shook her head, apparently in disgust. Stevenson tried to see past her; he couldn't. Then his curiosity and his overwhelming desire to speak to this charming young lady finally forced him into asking her a question.

"Is there anything wrong?"

"Yes," she answered, turning to him. "Look at the way that train conductor is treatin' those Chinese folks."

Again he tried to see past her and the rest of the crowd, but again his line of vision was blocked. "I'm afraid, dear lady, I can't see. But please describe what you see."

"He's treatin' them like cattle, herdin' them onto the car and smackin' them as they go by, that's what I see," she snapped. "I hate seein' that. It's so unnecessary."

"Indeed," said the Scotsman, taking her word for it that her vision of what was happening was the truth.

41

"There's no need for that."

The crowd pushed forward then and both Stevenson and the lady were crushed against the side of the train.

"Glad you agree, mister," the lady said. "Most people don't. But I don't think the Chinese deserve that. They're not savages like most of the Indians we have roamin' 'round this country."

For a moment her eyes studied his. Then they really looked him over, very quickly, very indiscreetly. She noticed that this young man of about thirty was quite trim and attractive and looked lost somehow. It was something in his eyes.

"My name is Sara Hillyer," she said. "I'd be happy to shake hands, but as you can see, they're carrying bags right now."

"My name is Robert Louis Stevenson," he replied. "My friends call me Louis. I'd take your hand and offer to carry your bags for you if I could . . ." he grinned. ". . . but I too am holding my belongings."

Sara found his accent amusing. "Are you English?" she inquired.

"Scottish," he answered.

Again the crowd moved, and a conductor helped Sara onto the train car. Stevenson followed behind her and stepped up. When they actually turned into the passenger car, Stevenson said to her, "Miss Hillyer, I hope you won't think I'm being exceeding bold, but may I sit beside you on this journey? I'm afraid I'm quite in need of companionship and conversation."

It was what she had been hoping to hear.

"Please do," she replied. Then she noticed two seats together and hurried to one of them. "Please," she said to Stevenson, gesturing to the seat beside her.

When Stevenson was seated, she said, "I do hope you'll tell me more about yourself and Scotland."

"I will," Stevenson agreed, "if you'll help me get more accustomed to your country."

Suddenly, three men across the aisle burst into laughter, slapping their knees and holding their sides. They were watching something occur outside the train.

"Something is amusing them," Stevenson said, placing his and Sara's bags in a compartment under the seat.

Then one of the merrymakers said to his companions, "Did you see the way that guy pulled that Chink around by his pigtail?"

"Yeah," replied another of the trio. "Looked like a Chinee hog bein' dragged outa the sty."

Again the three men men exploded into laughter.

Stevenson turned to Sara. "What is a 'chink'?"

Sara shook her head and replied, "It's what some fools call the Chinese."

They looked at one another, and Sara noticed the lack of amusement — and the scowl of displeasure — on Stevenson's face.

"Yes," he nodded, "I've quite a lot to get accustomed to in your country."

Then the train began to move, jerkily at first, but slowly getting more tolerably rhythmic in its sound and motion.

Chapter Eight

Near the Kansas-Nebraska Border

The ride had taken all night and most of the next day. But finally the two riders pulled their horses to a halt.

"We have to make a stop there, McCain," Doc said, pointing to a ranch house in a shallow valley about a quarter of a mile ahead of them. This was a breakthrough in their working relationship; it was the longest sentence either man had said to the other since they had left Dodge.

"Right," said McCain. "Mind tellin' me what for, so I'm prepared?"

"We have to collect some money for Wyatt from these boys. Wyatt sorta finances that ranch and every so often he collects the interest."

McCain bent his head to one side and spat on the ground. "Earp in the money-lendin' business too?"

Holliday removed a shining silver flask from his beat-up leather saddlebag and took a long gulp of whiskey. His roan twitched its ears and snorted. With his free hand, Doc stroked the horse's thick black mane; with the other he offered the flask to McCain, who passed on it.

"Actually, Earp owns this place," Doc said. "The men

here work for him and raise his cattle. He pays 'em handsomely too, McCain, so don't be badmouthin' him."

"Just asking." McCain eyed the satchel Doc had securely tied to his saddle. He knew the satchel was full of cash, even though Doc had told him differently.

"The deed to this place in that bag of yours?"

"Huh?" Doc muttered, caught off guard. He had forgotten the cock-and-bull story he had told McCain, but quickly remembered it. "Oh . . . yeah, I think so." He took another pull at the whiskey and replaced the cap on the flask.

"Don't be so concerned with this bag, McCain. It ain't your business."

"Just askin', Doc. Curious, that's all. Must be a lot of deeds in there, though. That bag looks awful heavy."

Holliday looked coldly at his companion; then he broke out laughing. "Ah hell, man, you know what's in the bag. Let's stop this here stupid game. It ain't necessary."

"That's fine with me."

"The bag's full of money, as if you didn't know. But it's Earp's money. If you're dumb enough to try anything stupid, I'll put a bullet in your gut, and in the unlikely event I don't, Earp will, before long. You understand?"

"I understand. I'm not about to steal it." McCain took off his brown, weather-beaten hat and let a cool breeze relieve his sweaty brow.

He replaced the hat after a few silent seconds. "Since you're levelling with me, Doc, let me level with you. I'm not after Earp's money or anything he has. It was no accident that I came to Dodge when I did. I was hoping to get in with Earp's outfit, and now that I sort of am, I'm not gonna ruin it." McCain was impressed with his own half-lie.

Holliday put away his flask. "I ain't surprised. That's

kinda how I had it figured. You ain't the first to want to enter Earp's circle."

Doc's right hand suddenly let go of his reins and rose to cover his mouth. He coughed half a dozen raw, violent coughs, and by the time he stopped, his hand was covered with saliva made a pale pink from blood.

"Goddamn!" he yelled, wiping his hand on the blanket between the saddle and the roan.

"You okay?" McCain asked.

Holliday didn't answer. Instead, he gazed across the valley to the hill opposite them.

"C'mon," he said and rode ahead slowly and quietly. McCain followed.

When they were considerably closer to the ranch, they stopped. McCain now saw what Doc had seen: a group of about twenty-five men on horseback, armed to the teeth with sidearms and rifles. Most of them were on the uppermost point of the opposite side of the valley, practically above the ranch. Slowly, some of them descended on it, apparently unseen by the ranchers. Now and then a rifle reflected the sunlight.

"Looks like trouble," Doc said calmly. He removed his Colt from its holster and checked to see that it was fully loaded.

"I take it those men don't work at the ranch."

"Not the last time I was here."

Doc put away the Colt. He let the band of men progress a little farther toward the ranch house, surveying the situation carefully. Then he drew his carbine, and without a word, took aim and fired a shot. Across the valley, the lead rider's hat flew off and with it a chunk of the man's head.

Two things happened. The men on horseback pulled their horses to a halt; at the same time, half a dozen men appeared—handguns and rifles drawn—from various locations around the ranch. One of them stood on the ranch house porch and fired three shots in rapid succession. Another of the attackers took the shots in the chest and was thrown backward off his steed.

The attackers divided, some riding to one side of the house, the others to the opposite side. They fired their weapons constantly, often haphazardly. The ranchers scattered, positioning themselves behind whatever was available. They ducked behind water troughs and barrels. A couple of them went back into the house and pointed their guns out open windows.

A minute later, however, there weren't many windows left. Glass shattered all over the house, and the flying splinters of wood and glass were almost as numerous and deadly as the barrage of bullets flying everywhere.

Doc and McCain advanced only a few yards closer to the ranch. Then they stopped and fired their rifles from their vantage point; they were, in effect, visible snipers.

Three riders tore away from the rest of the group and charged up the hill toward Doc and McCain. A bullet whizzed by McCain's ear. He cocked his rifle and fired at one of the approaching riders. Doc fired a shot so close after his it could have been an echo of it. A huge hole was blown in the front of the lead rider's shirt, and a crimson spot quickly spread. The man riding next to him fared no better. Doc's shot burst through the man's wrist. Doc fired again at the third attacker, but much to McCain's surprise, missed. The man fired back and shot a hole in Doc's saddle bag. His horse jerked and whinnied, but seemed unharmed. Amber-colored liquid flowed out of the hole in the saddle bag and down the side of the horse.

"Son of a bitch!" Doc yelled when he saw the whiskey spilling out.

McCain already had his Winchester pointed at the

man. He fired, and the bullet tore through the man's chest, sending him flying to the ground, face down. A circle of blood was visible on his back.

"Nice shot," Doc said calmly.

The sound of gunfire continued to echo through the valley, but it seemed to McCain to be tapering off. Doc's first shot had robbed the attackers of the element of surprise; the ranchers in the house had had enough time to prepare. Now, nearly half of the attackers were dead, their bodies scattered around the ranch, some still attached to badly-wounded or dead horses.

Then a high-pitched whistle sounded, and the now seriously-lessened ranks of the band of riders rode up the opposite side of the valley, the way they had come. Several of the ranchers continued firing at them until they were almost out of sight.

Doc and McCain rode down their side of the valley toward the ranch. As they rode, Doc tied a bright yellow bandana to the barrel of his carbine and waved it. The ranchers took notice, several of them pointing at the approaching duo.

McCain noticed something move on the roof of the ranch house. There was a man there, positioned behind the chimney. He was pointing a pistol at a rancher standing about a dozen yards in front of the house.

McCain aimed his Winchester at the man and squeezed the trigger before Doc realized he had done it.

"What the hell you doin'?" Doc asked, but before McCain could answer, Doc saw the man on the roof fall flat on his face and slide down one sloped side of it, directly onto another dead attacker's body below.

"I wonder if those two were that close in life," McCain joked.

Doc didn't laugh. Instead, he said, "You're pretty damn good. I didn't even see that feller."

They continued toward the ranch house. Doc waved the yellow bandana again.

"That a pre-set signal?" McCain asked.

"Yeah. A yellow flag."

"Why yellow? Ain't that the color of a coward?"

Doc spat on the ground. "Suppose it is. Never gave it a thought, really. Anyhow, I'd rather think of it as the color of gold. That's a better way of thinkin', ain't it?"

McCain nodded. For this trip, though, he thought green, the color of the money in Doc's satchel, would have been a more appropriate choice.

Chapter Nine

A short, stocky man of about forty years advanced on foot and welcomed the riders as they approached.

"Doc! Good to see ya again," said the man. "You sure timed this visit right. Thanks for the help."

"Don't mention it," Holliday answered. "Had Wyatt been here, none of those bastards woulda got away."

The rancher turned to McCain and studied him.

"Oh, sorry," Doc said. "This here's Josiah McCain."

McCain tipped his hat. "Nice to meet you."

"Yeah," the rancher grunted. "The name's Dombey. Charlie Dombey." Neither man made any attempt to shake the other's hand.

In McCain's estimation, Dombey stood about five and a half feet tall and had to weigh about two hundred pounds. He might have once been a handsome man, but now his face was covered with scars that looked like railroad tracks running up and down his face from his forehead to his neck. He was extremely well-dressed for a rancher; his light brown shirt and dark brown jacket barely had a wrinkle in them, and his new, sharply-creased dungarees were spotless. Two things, then, were obvious to McCain: Dombey was paid well by Earp, and he didn't do any heavy physical labor around this ranch. Doc's next words confirmed the latter fact.

"Charlie heads up this place. He's the . . . er . . . supervisor here."

Neither McCain nor Dombey responded. In fact, there was an awkward silence all around. It was clear Doc and Dombey had business to conduct, and it appeared they didn't want to conduct it in McCain's presence.

The impasse ended when the ranch supervisor suggested the two visitors come into the house for some coffee.

Once inside, Dombey pulled out a chair and sat down at a large, rectangular oak table. He turned to one of his men who was standing in the room. "Carl, pour us some coffee, will ya?"

As Carl marched over to the stove, Doc and McCain also sat down at the table. McCain looked around the room, and no matter where he looked, there was a common sight: guns. They were hanging from the walls on hooks, mounted in cases, strewn on the furniture. It reminded him more of an army barracks than a ranch house room.

"Admiring the hardware?" Dombey asked, noticing McCain's interest.

"Yeah. You must get attacked a lot. Or do you just collect them?"

Dombey laughed out loud. "Doc, is this guy new?"

"Very."

"I can tell." Dombey snorted.

For some reason—one he couldn't really explain—McCain already disliked Dombey. He turned to Doc and said, "Want to let me in on the joke? Or do I have to sit here listening to this steer's ass laugh at me all day?"

Suddenly, the supervisor stopped laughing. He stared into McCain's face. "What did you call me?"

51

Both men started to rise from their chairs, but Doc spread his arms, pushing each man down with one hand. "Okay, okay, let's cool off. We're all on the same side here."

"He's got a damn big mouth for a new man, and I ain't . . ."

"Okay, relax," Doc repeated, cutting him off and turning to McCain. "And you gotta watch your temper. Dombey here was just havin' a little fun with you, that's all. Why don't you go outside and cool off?"

McCain recognized this gesture as Doc's diplomatic way of getting rid of him. He decided to take Doc's suggestion and stood up. As he did, he shot Dombey a look which, had it been a fist, would have knocked him clean across the room. Then he turned, went outside, and remained on the porch, standing near an open window, which would allow him to hear what was being said inside.

The first thing he did hear was Dombey's voice.

"Where the hell did you get him from?"

"Dodge. Earp told me to hire him. He's one hell of a shot, I'll give him that. And I hear he damn near kicked the crap out of half a dozen men at the Long Ride all by his lonesome."

"Can he be trusted, though? He seems like an ornery son of a bitch."

"He's showing off for me, that's all. He's new and he wants to impress me with how tough he is. He's been no trouble up to now. Of course I don't plan on tellin' him too much about Earp's dealings until he's really proven he can be trusted. If he wants to, Wyatt can tell him all that when we get back."

The coffee was ready, and Carl poured some steaming black liquid into two of the three cups he placed on the table.

52

"I still think he's a bad one," Dombey continued.

"Yeah, well, forget about him and give me one of them smokes." Doc pointed to a bunch of cigars on the table. Dombey handed him one, and Holliday lit it.

"How's the ranchin' business been?"

"Not bad. You here to make a collection?"

"Yep."

"For the church, of course."

"That's right," Doc responded. "For the church of Wyatt Christ."

As the two men laughed at their private joke, Dombey walked across the room, slid a small rug from its place on the wooden floor, and lifted a two foot square concealed door. He reached into the compartment and withdrew a cloth bag. He then closed the door, replaced the rug, and returned to the table, handing Doc the bag.

"There's fifty-nine hundred dollars in there," Dombey said proudly.

Outside, McCain sat down on the wooden porch so his ears would be level with the window. He didn't want to miss a word.

"Damn!" Doc commented, "you boys been doin' all right!"

"I'll show you why." Dombey again called to Carl, who seemed to have had the unfortunate luck to have kitchen detail that day. The man didn't look like a cook, and he was unmistakably uncomfortable puttering around the house. "Bring me them brandin' irons, will ya?"

Carl opened a drawer in the kitchen. He picked up a tray that contained the house's silverware and placed it on a small table beside him. He then reached into the drawer again and took out about half a dozen branding irons, carrying them over to Doc's table.

"You know the Triple O Ranch about fifteen miles north?"

Doc puffed on his cigar, smiling. "Yeah."

Dombey held the iron so Doc could see the brand end of it. On it were three Os.

"What you're tryin' to tell me,' Doc said, "is that you got a new set of irons for, shall we say, modifying brands."

"That's right. And Deke Robert, our blacksmith, can whip up new ones any time we need them."

"That's great, Charlie, but don't you never get caught with all these brands flyin' around?"

"Not really. First off, we got thirty-two . . . no, make that thirty-three hands now. The neighboring ranchers have a hell of a time even gettin' on our property, let alone checkin' our cattle. And then we don't keep the rustled ones around very long. We send them out usually before the owners even known they're gone."

The supervisor sat back confidently.

"Still sounds screwy to me," Doc said, sipping his coffee. "You say it works, though?"

"It does. You tell Earp that."

Doc stuck the cigar back in his mouth. "Well, it looks to me like you almost got caught before. Them ranchers looked pretty steamed up about something. And how did that raiding party get so damned close to the house if you got this ranch so well protected?"

Dombey sat up straight, nervously fingering his coffee cup. "I think you'll find that . . ."

"I think you'll find . . ." McCain said, bursting into the room, "that four men are coming down the east side of the valley. One of them is alive."

Doc and Dombey rose to their feet and ran outside after McCain. Four horses approached, three of them carrying corpses.

The one man still alive was wounded. Dried, crusty blood dotted his hair, and one arm was a grisly mess

54

with a badly-constructed tourniquet tied to it.

Dombey rushed up to him and helped him down from his horse. Several other ranch hands gathered around.

"Pete," Dombey said, addressing the wounded man. "What the hell happened?"

"The ranchers . . ." Pete gasped, ". . . they ambushed us. Killed them. Tried to kill me."

The supervisor's face turned red. "I'm gonna get the sheriff. I've had enough of this."

"The sheriff," Pete forced out, "was with them."

"It can't be," Dombey said, looking at Doc. "I've been payin' him off for years."

"Maybe he turned honest," Doc said casually.

"There's a lot of that goin' 'round," McCain blurted out. "Or maybe he wanted a bigger cut of your cattle sales."

Doc turned to McCain. "You were listenin' in on us, weren't you?"

"Nope. You were just talkin' too loud."

The man named Pete coughed violently, inhaled with a loud wheeze, and stiffened like a plank. Then his head sagged over Dombey's arm.

"Damn," the supervisor exclaimed, standing up. "He passed out."

One of the ranch hands walked up to Dombey. "What are we gonna do now?" he asked nervously.

Before Dombey could answer, Doc did. "I'll tell you what you're gonna do. You're gonna get on your horses . . ." Doc's arm swept around, indicating that he was talking to all the men present, ". . . and get the hell out of this state. Split up and head west."

"Why west?" another of the hands asked.

"Because west is the smart way to go. The law's less organized out there. Now enough crap! Get on your horses and go!"

"After Dombey pays us," the same hand answered.

Doc turned to the supervisor and pointed to the crowd of men. "Pay them."

Dombey sidled next to Doc and said, "I will. But we gotta talk. What am I gonna do now?"

"Whatever you like," was the curt answer. "Pay the boys and then we'll talk."

The supervisor marched back to the ranch house and the group of men followed him to the porch. Doc and McCain remained outside.

"I ought to blow your brains out for eavesdropping," Doc said.

"But you won't," McCain responded, scratching his forehead, "because you like me so much."

"Dombey was right, you know. You do have a big mouth."

McCain spat on the ground. "I thought you were gonna level with me, Doc. That's what you said before."

"Yeah, well, now you know about this, so what's the difference? I trust you'll keep your mouth shut. Earp don't like his business discussed in public, and he especially don't like his shining reputation tarnished. Back East they think he's Sir Galahad."

McCain smiled. "Doc, I didn't know you were such a literate man."

"I'm a man of many talents, McCain. I've even read a few books. So have you if you can use a word like 'literate.' "

All of the men mounted their horses and set out, evidently paid up and satisfied. After the last man rode out, Dombey appeared at the door of the house.

Doc and McCain marched right past him, went into the house, and took the chairs they had occupied earlier.

Dombey followed them to the table, looking flustered. "What do I do now?"

Doc looked at him coldly. "I don't care what you do. You're on your own."

"On my own? You can't just drop me like that. I been working for Earp for four years now."

"Well, your four years are up."

"You can't do this to me, Holliday. I'm a good man, a valuable man. . . ."

"You're a failure, Dombey, and Earp don't tolerate no failures."

The supervisor—the *former* supervisor—was visibly upset. Sweat poured off him, and one of the scars next to his mouth began to twitch. He spasmodically opened and closed his fists.

"You can't do this to me. I want to talk to Earp myself."

"Earp don't want to talk to you."

"Listen, you bastard," Dombey screamed, hurling a coffee cup across the room, "if Earp doesn't protect me, I'll talk. I'll talk to the governor, the newspaper. And I know plenty. Plenty about his doings. Including his whorehouses and crooked gambling joints. I know plenty.

McCain sat still, trying to act indifferently.

Then Doc said, "You won't talk, Dombey."

"I will."

"You won't. You're a failure, and you're a goddamn coward as well."

The supervisor reached to his side and drew his gun. McCain sat up attentively, ready to draw his Colt. Doc, on the other hand, sat slouched in his chair, his arms crisscrossed across his chest, hands under his jacket and tucked into each armpit.

Dombey shakily pointed his pistol at Doc's head, then McCain's, and then back to Doc's.

Finally, Doc said, "You pulled your gun on me, Dombey."

Ignoring Holliday's words, the supervisor repeated, "I'm gonna talk. I'll goddamn talk."

Calmly Doc said, "Talk to this," and pulled a shiny, new derringer out from under his left arm; quickly, without taking a second to aim, he pointed and fired. The bullet went clear through Dombey's lung. For a second just a black, seared hole appeared on the man's shirt; then blood spilled out of the hole, dribbling down his shirt. The supervisor's gun fell to the floor, and, after a sound like air escaping a balloon left his mouth, Dombey fell to the floor, dead.

McCain stared at Holliday in amazement. He was surprised not because Holliday had shot the man—because he certainly had it coming to him—but at the ease, speed, and fluidity with which Doc had done it.

Holliday reloaded the derringer and replaced it in the shoulder holster under his arm. Then he returned McCain's gaze and said, "I don't like people who point guns at me. Never did."

Chapter Ten

Doc's flask was dry, and he was annoyed that he had to resort to his canteen full of water for liquid to soothe his scratchy throat.

"How long we been riding?" asked McCain.

"About three hours," Doc answered between gulps of his water.

McCain was still amazed at the man he was riding with. Doc had dismissed a crew of cattle rustlers, added several thousand dollars to his satchel, and shot a man for threatening to reveal Earp's dealings without giving any of these activities a second thought. Was this, McCain wondered, typical of a day in the life of Doc Holliday?

Doc interrupted his thoughts. "That there," he said, pointing ahead, "is Moods, Kansas. Ever hear of it?"

"Nope."

"Well, you'll never forget it, I promise you that."

They lazily rode into the town. Their horses were tired and dry. And the two men riding them were even more weary.

The southernmost building in the small town was a blacksmith's shop. Just ahead were the other common sights of a recently-settled town: a general store, a sheriff's office, a very small church and a very large saloon. Unlike most other towns, however, there weren't men sitting about outside the saloon or other establishments. In fact, McCain noticed, there weren't many men at all. Women, on the other hand, were everywhere, walking back and forth across the town's main street or lingering in doorways.

"Hey Doc," McCain asked. "Am I crazy or are there no men in this town?"

"You're not crazy. There are some men here, though."

"Where?"

"You'll find out soon enough."

The sun was just about down, but its last reddish beams covered the town in a sultry light. Shadows loomed long, and a crisp breeze blew dirt along the streets. The town seemed bathed in a crimson haze.

Doc stopped his horse in front of the Black Sheep Saloon. He secured his horse to the hitching post and walked inside. McCain remained outside for a moment and looked at the front of the saloon. It was a building three stories high, standing far taller than the town's scanty church steeple. He could see dim lights on in some of the rooms on the upper floors, and the curtains had been pulled in every window.

McCain got off his horse, tied its reins to the post, and followed Doc inside. The atmosphere of the place almost overwhelmed him. The first floor had a large mahogany bar with several men hunched over it, smoking, drinking, and clutching women. One man had his hand under a woman's dress in full view of the public. No one seemed to notice; if anyone did, no one cared. McCain looked around the saloon, trying to act nonchalant. It was a madman's dream of brown oak, red velvet, and pink flesh.

Doc sidled up next to McCain, thumbs tucked in his lapels. "Nice place, ain't it?"

"I feel like I walked into a dream."

"You did. All your dreams will come true in here, my friend, believe me. This is the best damn cathouse in the state. The whores account for about three-quarters of the town's population." Doc lit up a smoke and continued. "I've known men to come here from far and wide to sample the wares. And, of course, the surrounding good citizens, the local ranchers and farmers, etcetera, provide the place with a steady source of income too, much to the disapproval of their wives."

McCain laughed, then noticed Doc pulling out a wad of twenty dollar bills from his inner jacket pocket.

"You got any money?"

"Not a hell of a lot."

"Well, here," Doc said, giving McCain half the bundle. "Live it up. Just remember we've got to be out of here by dawn. That gives you enough time to get drunk, get a woman or two, and get sobered up."

McCain took the money. Turning to his left, he noticed something he hadn't seen since he left St. Louis: a billiard table. He walked over to it, admired it for a moment, and then ran his hand across the smooth green playing surface.

A man in an apron approached him. In his hand was a bottle of whiskey.

"Your friend there sent this over."

"Thanks. And tell my friend thanks, will you?"

"Yes, sir," said the mustached bartender. He put the bottle down on the edge of the table, set a shot glass next to it, and left.

McCain found the cue and walked around the table to find the balls and rack. Then his eyes wandered to the far end of the bar. Doc stood there with a girl in each arm. McCain casually racked up the balls, all the time watching as Doc and the two girls started their journey upstairs.

When they were out of sight, he placed the cue ball and bent over the table to make his shot. He pulled the stick back, and felt it hit something. Annoyed, he looked behind him. There stood a young woman smoking a cigarette.

"I'm sorry," he said, straightening up.

"My fault for creepin' up on ya," she answered. "Besides, I don't mind gettin' poked every now and then."

She was quite stunning. Her black hair was swept over her head and held by a tiara. Her eyes were a soft green-blue, the color of a clear stream. The dress she wore was a pale blue, clinging one, adorned with lace and graced with a swooping neckline. Had the lace not been there, she would have had nothing covering her breasts. McCain couldn't help but look, and she noticed that he did.

"Pretty dress, isn't it?" she asked sarcastically.

"Uh . . . yeah," he answered. "I kinda like what's in it too."

"Thank you."

"Do you play billiards?" he asked.

"Not very well, I'm afraid. But I have been known to sink a few balls now and again."

She smiled and approached the table. She walked past McCain and took a cue in her hand.

"Would you like to go first or should I?" McCain asked.

"You go first," she said, leaning forward on one side of the table so her breasts nearly tumbled out of her dress. "I like to see how a man shoots."

Jesus, McCain thought, this woman has a way with words. He positioned the stick and shot the cueball across the table. He sank two balls, one in the corner and one in the right side.

The woman stood directly in front of him now, looking up at him. He could smell her perfume; it was making him light-headed.

"Two balls," she said, grinning. "Just the right number."

Four double entendres and two nearly exposed breasts was McCain's limit. He lifted the woman into his arms and started to carry her up the stairs.

"What's your name?"

"Georgette."

"Well, Georgette," he said, "I hope you're not tired tonight."

Chapter Eleven

When McCain reached the second floor, he asked, "Down the hall here?"

She shook her head.

"Third floor?"

She nodded.

"Christ!"

"It'll be worth it."

He carried her up the next flight of stairs.

"Number fifty-six," she said.

McCain looked down the hall. "They got fifty-six rooms in here?"

"Sixty to be exact."

"Must do some business."

"Quite a lot. That's because there are a lot of men around here whose wives think babies are supposed to come out of them, but nothing is supposed to go in."

McCain reached room 56 and put Georgette back on her feet. She pulled up the hem of her dress, revealing a shapely leg, and removed a key from her garter. Then she unlocked the door and swung it open.

It struck McCain odd that he and Doc had mentioned Sir Galahad earlier because Georgette's room reminded him of drawings he had seen of King Arthur's Court. Tapestries hung on two of the walls. They were far from medieval—in fact, they were unmistakably Indian, although he didn't know what tribe. And the room was decorated with velvet and lace. It was a fantasy world. And for a few hours anyway, it was exactly what he wanted.

"Are you going to come in or admire the decor all night?" Georgette asked, interrupting his thoughts.

"Sorry," McCain smiled. "But I was admiring the room. It's . . . unusual."

"Miss Alice lets us decorate them. Each girl has a very different room. She feels the girls will be happier that way and therefore perform better."

"Sounds good to me," McCain said, sitting on a plush red velvet chair. "Miss Alice, I take it, is the owner?"

"I guess you could call her that. She's a good woman. Takes care of her girls. Everyone likes her."

"That's good," McCain said, knowing full well he was running out of small talk.

"Well," Georgette said, "shall we stop talking and put our mouths to better use?"

Before McCain could answer, Georgette had unfastened her dress and let it slip to the floor. She stepped out of it, picked it up, and placed it on a chair. Then she turned toward McCain. She still had on a corset.

"Should I take all this off, or leave it on?"

He didn't answer. Instead, he got to his feet, moved toward her, and lifted her in his arms. Still standing, he leaned over and kissed her mouth. Her lips opened and her tongue darted into his mouth.

And something sparked in McCain, something that had not sparked for a long time.

Chapter Twelve

The night had been long and energetic. McCain hadn't experienced a night like that in a long time, and certain parts of the night contained activities he had never experienced before.

Now, in the small hours of the morning just before dawn, McCain was sitting up against the headboard of the bed, a bottle of whiskey in his hand. Georgette sat next to him, seemingly deep in thought.

"You're awful quiet."

"Even a girl in this line of work needs a breather once in a while," she said. "You got any tobacco?"

"No, but I could sure use a cigarette right now. It'd help kill the taste of this whiskey."

"You don't like it? It's supposed to be the best in the house."

"It's pretty bad."

"Oh, well. It's not really the liquor that the Black Sheep is famous for." She got off the bed and stood up, throwing a robe over herself. "I'll go downstairs and get a different bottle."

"Don't bother. It's drinkable. No need to go to any trouble."

"No trouble. Besides, I want to get some cigarettes for us."

"Okay. But do come back. I might get lonely."

"I'll just be a couple of minutes."

Georgette reached for the doorknob, but before she turned it, she looked back at McCain in an odd way, and remained silent.

"Something the matter?"

"No," she said. "But I'm just a curious kind of girl and maybe I'm just plain nosy, but I gotta ask you just the same."

"What?"

"That man you came in with—that was Doc Holliday, wasn't it?"

"Yeah. You know him?"

"Know of him. Most people do." She ran her fingers through her long black hair, which hung around her shoulders. "Anyhow, thanks. We get a lot of well-known people through here. I just like to keep kind of a record. You know, it's like a hobby."

"Sure."

She turned and went downstairs for the whiskey and tobacco. McCain took a swig of the whiskey bottle he held and lay back, looking at the ceiling.

McCain was satiated. He was also exhausted, and his mind wandered. He closed his eyes and thought about everything. Doc. Masterson. This woman he had just spent the night with. Other women. And Alexandra . . .

Alexandra, his beautiful wife, stood there, her face just inches from his. Her fingertips stroked his cheek. He bent slightly, she raised herself, they kissed tenderly. Then the vision blurred.

Alexandra stood to his left, walking, her hand in his.

She wore a pale blue chiffon dress, a lacy light blue bonnet, and over her head a matching parasol shaded her. Then the vision blurred.

McCain ran out the front door of his house, panic-stricken. McCain couldn't see well, but well enough. A horse-drawn coach rolled away, and he recognized one of the two passengers. Alexandra, sitting up, looked straight ahead, the man next to her looking back at McCain. McCain ran back into the house, found the note from her, then the man swung the rifle, hitting him in the forehead, everything spinning, everything going black, going to hell and back . . .

McCain's arm hung off the side of the bed. The whiskey bottle, nearly empty, fell the short distance to the floor and rattled around. The sound revived him. He had drifted off, he realized, for only God knows how long, although it seemed like only a moment. Then he realized he had been dreaming about Alexandra again. He spotted the bottle and knew he needed the last remaining drink in it. Sliding off the bed, he got onto his knees on the floor next to the bed to reach for it.

Suddenly, the door flew open and shots rang out fast and sure. Feathers and pieces of wood and mattress sprayed the room. Next to him lay his gunbelt where it had remained since Georgette had removed it. Instinctively, he reached for it.

From the side of the bed, McCain pointed the gun at the doorway and fired. His first shot caught a man in the collarbone; the force of the close-range impact drove the man backward and into another assassin standing behind him. A third gunman, already in the room, rushed McCain and was going to leap over the bed at him. There was no time to aim and fire. As the man's body flew over the bed, McCain lifted the whiskey bottle in his other hand and shattered it on the man's head. Shards of glass covered the bed and the now unconscious man on it.

The gunman in the hallway was now back on his feet. He pointed his pistol at McCain. But McCain got off the first blast of lead, one which burned a bloody hole in the man's forehead. The lifeless body with the blood-spattered face stood erect for a moment, then crumpled like a scarecrow without support.

McCain quickly put on his pants. From the hallway he heard a familiar female voice screaming hysterically, "You bastard. You filthy bastard." It was Georgette's voice. Then he heard the sound of boots — many boots — thudding against the floorboards. McCain was in no mood to find out if they were friend or foe, so he scooped up the rest of his clothing and possessions in his arms and opened the window. It was two flights down, but he thought he might make it without breaking a leg if he was lucky. He lifted his legs out the window and sat on the sill. Then, ducking, he leaped.

When he landed, stunned, a shower of broken glass fell over him. Had he remained another second above, the bullets that shattered the window would have splattered his guts onto the street.

It was blessedly dark in the back alley. Luckily, Georgette's window faced the rear of the Black Sheep instead of the better lit main street.

McCain got up, grabbed his things, and ran down the street into even greater darkness. He stopped in a shadowy corner for a second and looked back at the window. A man peered out of it; he was angry and swearing at the top of his lungs. In surrounding windows lights went on and other faces gazed out into the night.

Then McCain realized how cold he was. The night air

raised goosebumps on his flesh, much of which was exposed to the wind.

He saw two horses approaching. One of them had a rider; the other was being led by the reins. A familiar voice called out to him.

"C'mon, McCain, let's go."

It was Doc.

There was no time to ask questions. Doc stopped the horses momentarily, and McCain hopped up on the empty one. Then, as futile curses and poorly-aimed, haphazard shots whistled around them, the two men, both naked from the waist up, rode out of town as quickly as their mounts would carry them.

Chapter Thirteen

Aboard the Union Pacific

The cool air shot through the open windows of the train, causing newspapers to crumple in their readers' hands, neckties to flap under their wearers' chins, and dresses to billow over their owners' legs. It was a welcome relief. The temperature outside was near the hundred-degree mark; inside the train, it was well above it.

"Good Lord, it's hot today," said the Scotsman.

"It hit one hundred and five the other day," Sara commented.

Stevenson fanned himself with his open copy of *Humphry Clinker,* but the hefty book produced little air flow. "I'll never complain about the weather in Scotland again," he promised.

"What's it like there?"

"Oh, often it's quite beautiful. But the chilly nights on the moors can be beastly. The dampness sinks straight into your bones."

Sara patted her damp forehead with a lacy handkerchief. Looking down, she noticed that her companion had left one of his bags open. She tried to see what it contained but couldn't make out any of the contents. She sat back.

"What do you do for a living, Mr. Stevenson?"

"Louis, please. Do call me Louis."

"Very well. Louis."

"I'm a writer."

"A newspaper man?"

"No, dear lady, not for a newspaper. I write books of travel, stories of adventure."

"You mean like those stories about Jesse James?"

"No, not exactly like those," Stevenson said. "I've read a few of them. The western half of your country sounds positively chaotic."

Sara didn't know the meaning of his last word, but figured it was something bad. "It's not so bad," she said.

"Well, I do hope not. Anyway, I hope to write tales with a bit more seriousness to them. I must admit I do find the tales of your Western lawmen exciting."

"Are you successful?"

"As a writer I am just beginning to be noticed."

"Do writers make a lot of money?"

Stevenson laughed. "Some do. Others are not appreciated until they are in the grave. And then there are those whose work goes unread forever."

"What about you?"

"My fortune is yet to come, I'm afraid. Every pound— excuse me—every dollar I own I am currently carrying with me."

"In those bags?"

Again the Scotsman laughed. "Yes, those satchels contain all of my wealth, all I consider valuable."

Sara smiled at him. He seemed well-to-do, she thought. He spoke like an aristocrat and carried himself with confidence. His clothes were elegantly-made and looked new. Perhaps he was just being humble. And perhaps his bags did contain his wealth.

The young writer then changed the subject. "I'm traveling all the way to San Francisco. How far are you going?"

"To San Francisco. Isn't that a coincidence?"

"Yes. I'm going there to meet my fiancée."

"Isn't that nice?" Sara smiled. "What's her name?"

"Fanny," Stevenson said proudly. "Fanny Osbourne."

"Well, I wish the two of you luck."

"Why are you going to San Francisco? Or am I being presumptuous?"

"I . . . er . . . I'm meeting some very close friends of my family there."

The conversation was interrupted by a gunshot that seemed to originate inside the train car. Stevenson stood up, looked behind him to the rear of the car, and saw a Chinese man exit through the rear door. Over the door was a hole in the wall of the car. And standing a few feet away from the door was one of the three loud men who had been laughing at the Chinese passengers earlier in the day. In his hand was a smoking pistol.

"And stay out, ya goddamn Chink," he yelled.

"What the hell did he want in here, anyway?" he asked his friends. "They got their own car, all to themselves. We sure don't need their stink in here."

One of the men took a drink from a bottle of whiskey. "Sit down, Jack," he said after swallowing the liquor. "Give me a chance. Let me take a shot at the next Chink who pops his ugly head in this car. I hate them bastards. They're worse than Indians."

Stevenson watched the man named Jack sit down and snatch the bottle away from his friend. The third man was laughing. Disgusted and shocked, Stevenson sat back down next to Sara, who just stared at him.

"You okay?" she asked.

"Yes, I'm fine. But I can't quite believe what I saw and

73

heard. Does everyone in your country treat the Chinese like that?"

"No, not everyone. They don't bother me."

"I can't see why they would bother anyone. And it gets me terribly angry to see that sort of ignorant racism."

Stevenson's words grew progressively louder. Several of the train's passengers turned their heads or stretched their necks to see who was speaking. Sara placed her hand on top of her companion's.

"Louis, please take it easy. Those men might hear you."

"I don't care if they do hear me," he answered, speaking more loudly than before. "Only an ignorant brute would treat the members of a culture vastly older than his own like that. And if anyone stinks on this train, it's those three witless fools, those cowboys reeking of horse manure and cheap liquor."

Then he stopped, and it seemed like all sound stopped except for the train itself.

Two second later, the man named Jack was standing in the aisle next to Stevenson, looking down at him. Behind him stood his two companions.

"You got a problem, mister?" Jack asked.

Sara tried to speak, but before she could get the words out, the Scotsman answered the question.

"No, sir, but it's clear that you do."

Jack's face turned red with anger. He bent lower over Stevenson and said, "Really? I think it's you who has one Mister Loudmouth." Then he grabbed Stevenson by the hair and pulled him up out of his chair.

"Kick his skinny ass, Jack," the man behind Jack said.

Sara stood up. "Stop it."

Jack had his fingers wrapped around the Scotsman's hair and held him up out of his seat. "Your boyfriend has to learn to keep his mouth shut. I'm gonna teach him."

"Wait," Sara continued. "You don't understand. He's new to this country. He's not used to our customs. He didn't know any better."

Jack stared at Stevenson, who didn't struggle at all. "Is that right? What country you from?"

"Scotland," Stevenson replied softly. He wondered how much hair Jack had ripped out of his head. The pain made his eyes water.

"Scotland? I thought there were smart folks in Scotland. You ain't too smart, Mister Scotland."

"Please let him go," Sara repeated.

Then Jack smiled at her. "Awright, ma'am, I will. For two reasons. I can't say no to a pretty lady. And lucky for your friend here, my folks come from Scotland."

He relaxed his grip on Stevenson's hair and pushed him back into his seat. Then he stroked the top of the Scotsman's head, flattening his hair.

"But if I hear another peep out of you," Jack said, pushing a scaly finger into Stevenson's ribs, "I won't care who you're with or where you're from. You got that?"

"Yes."

Jack winked at Sara. "I think your friend's learnin'."

Jack and his friends returned to their seats, laughing. They passed around the half-empty whiskey bottle.

Stevenson sat quietly. He felt slightly ill and his face lost the little color it had.

"Are you all right?" Sara asked.

"I think so."

"Let me tell you, you're lucky he only pulled your hair."

"Lucky?"

"Louis, I've seen men killed for less."

He thought about that for a moment. "I suppose you're right. It was a rather impulsive act on my part."

"Around here people mind their own business. They live longer that way."

Then suddenly there was another man standing next to the Scotsman's seat. The man was older, fatter, and better-dressed. Just before he spoke he planted his thumbs between his belt and pants.

"You folks having some trouble?"

"No, sir," Sara answered. "Everything's fine."

The man frowned at her. "I was speaking to the gentleman, miss."

Picking up Sara's lead, Stevenson repeated, "Everything is perfectly fine, my good man. Thank you for asking."

"Just doin' my job."

"Really? And who and what are you?"

"The name is George Wright, of the Pinkerton National Detective Agency. Who are you?"

"The name is Robert Louis Stevenson, sir, of Scotland." He extended his hand for the man to shake. But it wasn't shaken. It was sneered at.

"Scotland, huh?" repeated Wright. "Isn't there anyone on this train from this country?"

Stevenson missed the sarcasm in the question and answered, "Certainly. This young lady . . ."

"Yes, this young lady," Wright interrupted. "I believe I've met this young lady somewhere."

Sara coldly responded, "You must be mistaken."

"No. I don't think so. I know I've seen your face before."

"I can't imagine where. Maybe I look like someone you've met."

Wright studied her, while Sara looked back at him defiantly, and Stevenson wondered what this was all about.

"No," Wright repeated, "I've definitely seen that face."

"Impossible," Sara insisted.

"It's part of my job to remember faces, miss, so don't tell me what's impossible."

Stevenson was amazed at the growing ire in the man's voice. "Sir, I must say, I don't see what difference it makes. The lady says you've never met. Why do you persist?"

Wright leaned back on his heels. "Well, if you must know, it's because it's my job to protect this train and the cargo on it."

"Protect it from Indians and thieves, you mean?"

Shooting a grinning glance at Sara, Wright said, "Yeah. Thieves and all sorts of undesirables."

Sara resisted the urge to return the insult, but Stevenson couldn't resist his urge to challenge the man's affront.

"My good man, you have no right to question this lady's character!"

The Pinkerton pushed back one side of his carefully-tailored brown jacket and touched the gun and holster under it with his hand.

"My agency and this gun give me any right I want."

"Good Lord!" Stevenson exclaimed. He wondered if everyone in this country carried a gun somewhere on his person.

"Let me fill you in, mister, although I'm probably wastin' my breath," Wright said. "I know I've seen this dame you're with's picture somewhere, and I can assure you it wasn't no mail-order bride catalogue. So I'm gonna be watchin' her real careful-like. And I don't much like foreigners either. They're all a bunch of thieves."

Stevenson could remain silent no longer. "Sir, I'll remind you that Mr. Allan Pinkerton, your employer, was born in Scotland."

"Oh, is that so? How would you know that?"

"We had a discussion in his office only . . ."

"Yeah, sure," Wright cut in. "And I had one with Julius Caesar last week."

Sara stood up and was about to curse the agent, but she never got the opportunity.

"Sit down, sister, and keep your trap shut. There ain't nobody that steals nothin' from any train I'm ridin' on, gold or anything else. You got me? I'm gonna be watchin' you two. Even when you don't see me, I'm watchin' you. Even when I'm lookin' the other way, I've got my eyes on you. Mark my words."

With that, Wright returned to his seat, several in front of those of the two new friends.

Stevenson turned to Sara. "If he can see us while he's looking the opposite direction, he must have eyes on his arse."

Sara smiled nervously.

"I'm sorry, Sara. Did I embarrass you with my joke?"

"Oh, no."

The Scotsman sighed an exasperated sigh and shook his head. "I really don't understand this country of yours. It seems as though people are either intimidated or intimidating."

"You may be right."

"Sara, I simply must ask you — and I hope you'll forgive me — but have you ever met that man?"

"No. He's crazy."

"Perhaps he is. He certainly is belligerent."

"Let me ask you a question. Do you really know Pinkerton?"

"Yes, we've met."

"Are you good friends?"

"I'd like to think so."

"But you don't work for him or anything?"

"Dear me, no. The only guns I want to deal with are the ones on the printed page."

"Well, that's certainly a relief."

"Why is that?"

Sara didn't answer immediately, but then rejoined, "I . . . er . . . don't like guns."

"Well, even though it's not likely, let's pray we don't encounter any more of them this trip. Perhaps if I speak only to you, my verbosity won't get us into any more trouble."

Sara nodded and sat back in her seat. She closed her eyes. The Pinkerton man was going to cause more trouble, she thought. And this new acquaintance of hers might unknowingly add to it. She hoped he would be worth it.

Stevenson, too, had his eyes shut, enjoying the silence that he hoped would last a while. He was glad he had run into Sara; she was a welcome friend — and a beautiful one. He was tempted to open his eyes and thoroughly look her over, something he resisted doing since he had met her. He resisted again though; he reminded himself that Fanny was waiting for him in California, this westernmost state he wondered if he would ever reach. Sara intrigued him; there was no denying that. She was graceful and sensual, and there was an air of mystery about her. She was elegant and earthy. And try as he would to think of other things, his mind was clouded by her presence.

Chapter Fourteen

Hays City, Kansas

The sun was high in the mid-afternoon sky, and their shadows seemed directly beneath them. Ahead was Hays City and the Kansas Pacific Railroad. The two riders were glad to see it. They had been riding for hours, the first two with a dozen men in pursuit.

Doc lifted his hat and wiped the sweat off his brow. "There's Hays City and not a moment too soon. My horse is about to drop dead."

McCain stroked the main of his mount. "This ol' boy's gettin' a bit wobbly in the knees too."

"I still say we were lucky to get away. I thought them damn ranchers had us for sure a couple of times."

McCain nodded in agreement. "I felt a lot better once we were out of that whore town." He put a cigarette in his mouth and lit it. "That reminds me. You never did tell me how you came to have those horses all ready to go."

"Are you kidding? When I heard that first shot go off in the hallway, I was out of that bed quicker than you can say 'cowshit.' I told the girls to keep quiet or I'd wring their necks, and luckily they did. I grabbed my clothes and I was out of the window, brother, into the night."

"How'd you know they were lookin' for us?"

"I didn't. But I wasn't waitin' around to find out."

McCain exhaled a cloud of smoke. "Those bastards nearly got me, Doc. That whore I was with asked me your name and like a damn fool I told her. I should have known better. Those ranchers are probably her regular clientele."

"Probably. But don't blame yourself too much. They would have found us anyway. It was my mistake goin' there in the first place. But the flesh is weak, as they say."

"Amen, Doc."

"I hope you at least had the bitch before the shootin' started."

McCain tossed the remaining inch of cigarette away. "I'm not really sure who had who, but it sure felt nice."

Doc laughed out loud, but his laughing quickly changed to coughing. He hacked several times, leaning off to one side of his horse. Finally it stopped, and Holliday spit a wad of bloody mucus on the ground.

"You okay?"

"Yeah. It comes and goes. It ain't nothin', just one pain in the butt."

Then they heard a whistle. They turned and saw the train approaching from the east. It would pull into Hays City in just a few minutes.

"We'd better hurry," Doc said. "Let's get into town and unload these horses."

The men urged their horses forward and entered the town. It was a busy place with sizable buildings and a great deal of traffic in the street. Wagons seemed everywhere.

Doc spotted a blacksmith's shop. "McCain, leave me your horse and go get us two tickets to Cheyenne at that railroad station down the street."

"What about the saddle? Should I take it?"

"Nah. I'll try to sell it for you. Get goin', man, I don't want to miss that train."

McCain ran ahead and purchased the tickets. Then he walked up to the track and gazed eastward. The train was close enough that he could see the smoke pouring out of its black chimney. In a minute or two it would pull into the station.

Looking around him, McCain noticed there weren't very many people waiting for the train. In fact there were only four: a mother and her two young sons, both running around her in a wide circle, firing toy pistols at one another, and a tall, gangly young man of about nineteen, who was whittling a piece of wood with a huge hunting knife.

The train was now so close that McCain could make out the details on the front of the locomotive. He noticed that the front car's cow-catcher was dented on one side and no longer exactly centered. It had obviously at one time or another hit something larger than a cow.

Suddenly Doc was standing next to him on the platform. "Just in time," he said, handing McCain a wad of paper money. "I sold the horses and the saddles. We'll get new ones later when we need them."

McCain weighed the roll of bills in his hand. "This is a lot of money. How'd you manage this deal so quickly?"

"I told him who we were. The combination of nervousness and excitement gets 'em every time. I usually get more'n a fair deal."

"The blacksmith knew me?" McCain asked, puzzled.

"Sure. Everyone 'round these parts knows of Billy the

Kid."

The men laughed at Doc's swindle, but the noise of the train drowned out their laughter. The locomotive passed just feet in front of them, followed by a dark, weather-beaten coal car, a somewhat newer cattle car and a passenger car with a half-dozen passengers on it. The train screeched to a halt, spit out steam, and shuddered for a second. Directly before them stood the second passenger car, which seemed empty. Behind it, a third passenger car opened its doors, and the woman and her two children jumped aboard.

Several people left the train, and the conductor helped them on and off. He took the tickets from McCain, said "Thank you, gents," and moved down the platform to where the young man was standing.

Doc and McCain boarded the second passenger car and found it empty.

"Looks like we have this all to ourselves," Doc said, sitting in a seat facing the front of the car.

"Not exactly," McCain replied. He nodded, gesturing to the young man who boarded the other end of the car and sat several seats away, near the opposite window, facing them.

"Just a kid," Doc said. "Let him stay."

Then McCain pointed to the ground beneath Doc's feet. "I notice you didn't forget that."

Doc knew he was referring to the satchel containing the cash. "You bet your boots I still got it. And I ain't lettin' it leave my sight 'til we get where we're goin'."

The train's whistle blew again, and the conductor called out, "All aboard! Kansas Pacific to Denver and Cheyenne! All aboard." There was a loud hiss of steam, and slowly the train began to move away from the station. As it passed through the town, several children waved to it, and at least one old-timer cursed it and hurled a stone at the multi-carred mechanical beast. But the rock bounced off the side of the last passenger car, doing as much damage to it as would the bite of a mosquito on the side of a buffalo.

Chapter Fifteen

McCain put his feet on the seat opposite him. "Doc, you think we'll run into those cattlemen again?"

"Nah," Doc answered. "I think we gave 'em the slip. After we doubled back and headed south to Hays City, I think we got 'em good and confused. They probably figured we kept goin' north on the western cattle trail. Right now they're probably up around Massacre Canyon. I don't think we'll run into 'em again any time soon."

"That suits me fine."

The train rumbled along at a brisk pace. The travelers saw hardly a soul out the windows, and only occasionally did they pass a ranch, a farm, or even a house. This section of northeast Colorado the Kansas Pacific traveled through was still mostly virgin territory, untouched by eastern civilization's progress.

McCain was enjoying the view. He once spent a good deal of time enjoying country like this, but recently he more often than not had to occupy seedy hotels in different dusty towns. But once in a while, while back home in Missouri, he would ride about the countryside, delighting in pure, unspoiled Mother Nature. After his wife left him, he figured he would have more time to do whatever he wanted, but he was wrong. He wasted months searching for her, until one night, in a drunken stupor, he decided to give up the quest. He'd enjoy his freedom, he told himself.

And he did — for exactly two weeks. He had just spent a few days by himself in the woods, camping, swimming in the Missouri River, hunting and cooking his own food; when he decided to head home, he was met by the grisly sight of his sister's beaten, violated body off to one side of a road in a heavily-wooded area. The discovery had filled him with grief, with disgust, and with a renewed hatred for the brutality and hypocrisy of the civilization he tried to escape from as often as possible.

That was when the second quest began: the search for his sister's murderer.

Doc yawned loudly, breaking into McCain's reflections. "Christ, I'm tired. How about you? You get any sleep last night?"

"No."

"Well, we're just sittin' here, and we'll be sittin' here for a couple of hours. One of us might as well get some sleep. You want to rest up first?"

"I'm not that tired."

"Well, then, I guess I'll nap first."

"Go ahead."

McCain noticed Holliday staring at him. He figured out why.

"Doc, I already told you. I ain't after your money. Relax and go to sleep. I'll watch the bag."

Doc thought it over for a moment. "Okay. Wake me up if we get any new passengers in here."

"I will."

McCain again turned and looked out the window. Doc curled up in the seat, trying to make himself as comfortable as possible. When he finally found a position he liked, he tipped his hat down over his eyes and crossed his arms over his chest. In less than a minute, he was asleep, snoring loudly.

McCain was bored. He hated just sitting, not doing anything. He wished he had a newspaper, a book, anything to read. Boredom caused him to think of things he'd rather forget, particularly Alexandra. Thinking about her sent him through a gauntlet of emotions. One moment he was filled with hatred for her; the next would fill him with regret because no matter how hard he tried to deny the fact that he missed her, it was true; and then he would be full of puzzlement, wondering what, if anything, he had done to cause her to leave so suddenly, so violently.

He had to stop thinking about it.

Suddenly, he saw a reflection of light from the front of the train car. He turned his head and looked in that direction. The young man was standing up, pointing a Colt in his direction.

"Don't move," the youngster said.

"I'm not."

He approached slowly, keeping a watchful eye on McCain and Doc. There was no way McCain could get to his gun without sitting up straight, something he didn't want to risk doing just then.

"You going to rob us, son?" McCain asked.

"No."

"Then just why are you pointing that gun at me?"

The boy jiggled the gun and said, "I'll ask the questions. That there's Doc Holliday, ain't it?"

"It might be."

"It is. I recognize him. I seen his likeness in this book I read once."

"What if it is? What do you think you're going to do?"

87

"Shut up," the boy said angrily. "I told you I'll ask the questions."

"Yes, sir!" McCain responded.

He was standing just in front of Holliday now, looking at him intensely, studying him. Doc was fast asleep with his head cocked to one side.

"Wake him up," the lad ordered.

"I don't think that'd be a very good idea."

"I don't care what you think. Wake him up. I want him to be awake when I kill him."

"Kill him? Now just what would you want to do a thing like that for?"

"I want to be known as the man who got Doc Holliday. I want them to write books about me."

McCain saw a certain glint in the boy's eyes, one that told him the young man was serious.

"If I wake Holliday up, you're going to be known as the dead boy who didn't get Holliday."

"Shut yer damn mouth and do like I said," he commanded. "Just who the hell are you, mister?"

McCain casually sat up straight. "Me? I'm Billy the Kid."

"Like hell you are. I got a picture of Billy the Kid right here in my . . ."

The lad let down his guard for just a second as he reached into his pants pocket, but it was more than enough time for McCain to spring to his feet, grab the boy by the wrist, and squeeze the gun out of his hand. It fell to the floor.

Stunned by his mistake, the boy tried to pull away from his opponent's grasp. McCain pulled him closer, spun him around, and bent his arm up behind his back. He pushed upward slightly on the arm.

"Yeow, mister, yer breakin' my arm!"

"Be grateful for small favors, son."

McCain forced him to march forward, never releasing his grip. When they reached the rear of the car, McCain opened the door and forced the boy onto the narrow metal platform between the cars. The wind whooshed by them, messing their hair and causing their shirtsleeves and pant legs to billow.

"Now, son," McCain said, "I'm gonna do you a great favor."

The boy just looked over his shoulder, trying to see his captor's face.

"I'm gonna save your life. It seems to me that this train ain't going too fast right now. I'm gonna get you off this train, so brace yourself."

"You're gonna throw me off?" the boy yelled, desperate to be heard over the roars of the train and the wind. "You can't do that!"

"Can't I? Brace yourself."

"I'll break my legs."

"You could've got your head broken inside — or worse."

"I'll get you someday, mister. I swear I will."

McCain was losing patience with this ignorant farmboy. "No you won't," he said, smacking the back of the boy's head with his knuckles. "You keep admirin' Doc Holliday and gunfighters like him, and you won't live long enough to get me or anyone else. Now get ready."

"I'll break my legs, I told you."

"You'll heal."

McCain pushed the boy off the west side of the train into a field full of cornstalks. Then he re-entered the train car, bringing a gust of cold wind with him. It made Holliday shudder.

"Close the damn door, McCain," he said without ever opening his eyes. "It's freezin' in here."

McCain took his seat next to Doc, grinning at him. "Goodnight, Doc."

Holliday mumbled in return. Immediately, he fell sound asleep again, oblivious to everything.

Well, his temporary companion thought to himself, I wanted a diversion, and I certainly got one. But what do I do for the next hour?

He looked out the window to his right and observed a herd of longhorns grazing in a field. He started to count them. It wasn't much, but it was something to do.

Chapter Sixteen

When the train pulled into Cheyenne, Wyoming, Doc Holliday was fumbling through his pockets looking for his makings.

"Hell. I'm all out of tobacco. You got any, McCain?"

"Sorry Doc. Smoked the last of it some time ago."

"Well, I guess I can wait a couple more minutes. Gotta get some as soon as we stop."

"You have a nice rest?"

"Not bad. I feel better now. Could use some coffee and a drink, though."

"Sounds good."

The conductor announced the stop, the train halted, jerked, and exhaled a fog of steam, and the two men were on their feet. Doc carried his satchel and followed McCain off the train. They walked a couple of blocks until they spotted a place called Ward's General Store. They entered the store and were greeted by an elderly man behind the counter.

"Good afternoon, gentlemen," he said. "What can I do for you?"

"Need some tobacco and all the makings," Doc said. "Lots of tobacco."

The old man placed the requested items on the counter. "Anything else?"

"Yeah, where can a man get a drink around here?"

"You gents waiting for the train?"

"That's right."

"There's the Hide and Tallow Saloon right around the corner. It's the closest saloon to the train station."

"Thanks."

Holliday paid the man, and he and McCain headed for the saloon. Holliday snorted, and gave half the tobacco to his comrade.

"What's so funny?"

"Lord, 'The Hide and Tallow.' What do you think, McCain? Think it's gonna be populated mostly by cattlemen?"

"I guess," McCain said blankly.

Doc just stared at him. "You ain't got no sense of humor."

"I guess not. I thought you wanted some coffee."

"If they got coffee, I do. If they don't, I can pass on the coffee. But I never pass on a drink."

They turned the corner. Not far away, they heard a train pulling out of town. Then they entered the Hide and Tallow.

Doc walked up to the bar and dropped the satchel at his feet. McCain stood next to him, leaned on the bar with his left elbow and ordered two whiskeys from the bartender.

"You got any coffee?" Doc interjected.

"Nope," replied the rotund bartender. "Got to go four blocks east for coffee and vittles."

"In that case, give me the whiskey and leave the bottle."

The saloon was practically empty, but McCain attributed that to the fact that it was around dinner time and

92

most people were probably home sitting around the table. However, there were several tables occupied by clusters of men playing cards. They looked—and even at that distance—they smelled—like cattlemen.

Then a young man in a derby hat asked the bartender a question with a noticeable Eastern accent.

"Excuse me, would you know what time the train to Denver leaves."

The bartender shot him a nasty glance and responded, "Does this place look like the railway office to you?"

"No, but I thought since you were so close to the station that you might have a schedule."

"Well, I don't."

The derby-crowned man left in a huff. The bartender watched him go; then he looked at Doc and said, "I hate folks from New York. Wouldn't give 'em the time of day unless they paid for it."

Amused, McCain asked, "How do you know he was from New York?"

"All goddamn Easterners are from New York," was his answer. "Or from Boston, which is even worse."

McCain let the conversation end right there. He really wasn't interested in the man's opinion. Doc was even less interested. His back was to the bartender, and his attention was focused on the poker games in progress.

"Feel like poker, Doc?" McCain asked.

"Yeah. Feelin' kinda lucky."

"Suppose I head down to the train station and find out when our train is due? Where we headed again? Ogden?"

"That's right. Get passage on the next train."

"See you in a little while."

McCain left Doc standing where he was, still eyeing the game, concentrating on it. Outside, the sun was beginning to set, and it burned orange in the sky. McCain headed back to Ward's General Store.

When he entered it, old man Ward recognized him. "Forget something?" the proprietor asked.

"Yeah. Anywhere near here I can send a wire?"

"Sure. The Western Union office is behind the railroad station. The back half of the building, in fact."

"Thanks."

McCain walked the couple of blocks to the train station and asked the man behind the booth when the next train to Ogden would arrive. He was told 7:05. The clock over the booth window read 5:35.

He left the building and turned the corner. The Western Union office stood less than ten feet away. When he reached the door, he ducked into the office quickly, glancing around.

"Help you?" said the bespectacled clerk.

"I'd like to send a wire."

"Where?"

"Dodge."

"To whom?"

"Bat Masterson."

The clerk looked at McCain and raised his eyebrows. "Bat Masterson? You know him?"

McCain grinned. "I don't usually send wires to people I don't know."

"You a friend of his?"

"Yes. Now can I give you the message or not?"

"Sure. This is the first wire I've ever sent to somebody that famous."

"That's very interesting."

McCain remembered Bat's warning about the telegraph operator in Dodge: he was on the Earp payroll in addition to Western Union's. The phrasing of this message had to be short, sweet, and meaningless to anyone but Bat. But that shouldn't be hard, McCain thought, because he didn't have a lot to tell him.

"Well?" asked the clerk.

"Okay, here goes. 'In Cheyenne. Heading for Ogden. More later.' "

"Go on."

"That's it."

"That's the whole message?"

"Yep."

Disappointment was written all over the man's face. "Your name?"

McCain dare not sign his name, so he made one up. "Missouri Joe."

Again the clerk's face registered dissatisfaction. He obviously wanted to learn the man's real identity. "Fine," he snarled. "Missouri Joe."

McCain paid the man and left the office. The sun was sinking even lower in the sky, and the whole area of the train station had a brown orange glow as a result.

A train with the words Union Pacific pulled into the station. McCain wondered if this train would be leaving for Ogden in a few minutes, and he ran back to the ticket-seller's window to inquire. He was told that this indeed was the train for Ogden, but it wouldn't be leaving Cheyenne until 7:05.

As passengers departed from the cars and filled the station, McCain rolled a cigarette and made his way back to the Hide and Tallow.

Chapter Seventeen

"C'mon over and join in" were the words that greeted McCain when he re-entered the Hide and Tallow. Holliday was gesturing for him to sit at the table covered with liquor, cards, and cash. There was a fairly sizable pile of bills directly in front of Doc. The other men at the table turned to see who Doc was talking to. They all had dismay-filled faces.

"Not just yet," McCain responded. He walked up to the bar and ordered a whiskey, which the bartender immediately poured.

Doc finished his hand and laughed out loud. This one he won big. Two of the other four men seated around the table pushed back their chairs and got up. The two who remained had small, dwindling piles of cash before them.

One of the men who had just retired from the game stood next to McCain at the bar. He fished a cigar out of his shirt pocket, bit off the tip, and spit it into a brass spittoon on the floor.

"Your friend there is wipin' us out," he said. "He just won six hands in a row. That's a clear signal for me to bow out. He's either real lucky or the best card sharp I ever seen."

McCain just smiled and finished his drink. "I think maybe I'll try my hand now."

"Welcome," Holliday said as his companion sat down in a vacant chair. "But I must warn you. Lady Luck is smilin' down on me today."

"Just deal, Doc. I'm an old friend of Lady Luck's."

As Doc dealt the cards, a man with a peculiar accent entered the saloon. He was carrying several travel bags and walked as if he might stumble over his own feet. Finally, he set the bags under an unoccupied table and walked up to the bar.

"Do you have beer in this tavern?" he asked the bartender.

"Yeah," was the response, "but it ain't cold."

"That's quite all right."

The bartender filled a glass and handed it to the stranger, who paid for it. He carried the glass back to his table and was about to sit down when the bartender yelled to him, "Your change, pal."

"Oh, thank you," the man said, returning to the bar and pocketing the change.

The card players were revealing their hands. The man to Doc's left turned his cards face-up. Two pair: threes and jacks. Then McCain uncovered his hand: three sevens. The man on Doc's right disclosed a pair of queens. Finally, flashing a yellow-toothy grin, Doc showed his hand: a deuce-to-six straight flush, all spades.

"Son of a bitch!" exclaimed the man on Doc's right. He threw down his cards and got up. "That does it for me. If I lose any more money, my wife'll geld me."

"Same here," said the other player. He too left the table after scooping up his remaining cash.

Doc and McCain just looked at one another. Finally, McCain spoke.

"You're just too good for them, Doc."

"Maybe. I did win a bit, didn't I?"

"You cheat?"

"Me? No way. I swear it. It's all strategy and odds, my friend. I just understand 'em better'n most men."

"Deal the cards, Doc. I've been known to play against the odds."

Holliday shook his head. "I don't want to play against you. It'd be like winnin' my own money back."

"Maybe we can interest someone else in the game."

Just then, the man who had ordered a beer took his first sip of it. He almost choked on it as it went down.

"Something wrong?" asked the bartender.

"Is this *beer?*"

"That it is. Too strong for you?"

"Not at all. It just tastes like bog water."

The bartender's face turned crimson. "Maybe milk is more along your line," he said sarcastically. "Son of a bitch foreigner."

McCain had observed the scene with amusement, but now he could see real trouble brewing. He rose to his feet and marched over to the stranger's table.

"Relax," McCain said to the proprietor. "I'll straighten him out."

The bartender turned away and wiped a glass with a towel.

The newcomer sat nervously as McCain sat next to him and lit a cigarette, tossing the wooden match over his shoulder.

"What's your name, stranger?"

"Stevenson, sir. Robert Louis Stevenson."

"Mine's Josiah McCain. Pleased to meet you."

Stevenson shook the hand that was extended to him. "I fear I offended the tavern owner."

"Don't worry 'bout him. Where you from?"

"Edinburgh, Scotland."

"Ever play poker?"

"Poker?"

"It's a card game."

"I'm afraid I'm unfamiliar with it."

"Wanna join me and my friend? We'll teach it to you."

"I don't know . . ."

"Come on."

"I have a train to catch at 7:05."

"So do we. It'll help pass the time."

Stevenson finally relented. "Very well."

McCain grabbed one of the Scotsman's bags and carried it over to the table at which Doc sat. Stevenson followed him, carrying his other satchels.

"Doc, this here's Mr. Robert Louis Stevenson. He's gonna join us, and we're gonna teach him how to play poker." McCain winked at Doc. "He's from Scotland."

"Howdy, Mr. Stevenson," Doc said, shaking hands with the man. "Have a seat."

"Thank you."

"You never played poker before?"

"No."

"Well, relax a bit and let me explain the rules."

There followed the most concise yet comprehensive explanation of the game of five-card stud that McCain had ever heard. It took less than five minutes, but McCain couldn't think of a single thing Doc had left out. Then Holliday asked the question.

"You a gamblin' man, Mr. Stevenson?"

"I have gambled on occasion, but I really don't feel prepared to match my novice skill at this game against the skills of you two gentlemen."

Doc nodded and lit a cigarette. "I understand that, Mr. Stevenson. Why don't we play a couple of hands without any money involved to see if you fully understand the game?"

The Scotsman thought about it for a moment. "Very well. Please call me Louis."

"And you can call me Doc. Cigarette, Louis?"

"No thank you, I don't smoke, Doctor . . ."

". . . Holliday."

"Holliday." It took a few seconds for the name to swirl around and finally settle. "Holliday?"

Doc sat up straight. "You know me, huh?" Then, turning to McCain, he added, "They even know me in Scotland. Ain't that a hoot?"

"You might very well be known in my country, sir, but I first read of your exploits in a book I purchased in New York City. I believe it was entitled *Kansas Law.*"

"What did it say about me?"

"That you are a very efficient lawman, much like your friend Wyatt Earp."

Doc chuckled, amused. "Well, I ain't really a lawman, but what the hell. Anyhow, let's play cards."

McCain looked at the clock that hung over the entrance to the saloon. It was 6:30, and the Hide and Tallow was beginning to fill up with patrons and several frilly, painted women who did not come in through the entrance. He realized there had to be rooms in the back he hadn't noticed before.

The three men played a leisurely four "practice" hands; the novice poker player was "allowed" to win two of them. During all four hands, McCain and Doc glanced at one another, silently telling one another that they had a prize patsy here, just waiting to lose his money.

Then Doc said, "What do you say? Shall we play for a few dollars?"

"Very well," Stevenson said reluctantly.

As Doc shuffled the cards, McCain spoke to Stevenson.

"You travelin' alone?"

100

"I was, but I met a most charming young lady who I hope will accompany me all the way to San Francisco."

"Where is she?"

"Oh, she had to run a few errands around town. She should be meeting me here in a few minutes. Her name is Sara Hillyer."

"Let's go," Doc interrupted, dealing each man five cards, two down, three up, betting on each one.

The cards were inspected. Stevenson hoped he knew what he was doing; the other two men seemed confident in their hands. When all the money was in the ante, the hands were revealed. Stevenson had a pair of aces and a pair of nines. McCain turned over two pair also, but his were threes and deuces. Doc tossed his cards down, muttering that he had "a damn pair of kings."

"Does this mean I won?" Stevenson asked.

"That's what it means," Doc confirmed. "You deal this time."

The Scotsman attempted to shuffle the cards, but several of them dropped to the floor. He picked them up and did the best he could. Then he dealt each man another five cards.

In a few minutes, the results of this round were uncovered. Again, Stevenson won. McCain smiled at Doc, figuring he was letting the foreigner win. Doc didn't smile back, though. In fact, he seemed downright baffled.

"I can't quite believe my good fortune," Stevenson said, passing the cards to McCain. "I do believe it's your turn to deal."

All three players ordered another drink before the third hand. The bartender brought them over, and the Scotsman insisted on paying for them.

The third round, after upping the ante, ended like the first two. This time Stevenson held four kings. He pulled the pile of cash in the center of the table toward him.

Doc tossed down his whiskey in one gulp. "You sure you never played this game before, Louis?"

"Quite sure. But I must say I enjoy it."

Doc snatched up the deck indignantly. "I can understand that. Now let's get serious here."

When Sara Hillyer entered the Hide and Tallow, her traveling companion had a pile of paper money two inches thick. The pile was surrounded by little towers of silver dollars. She carried her two bags over to the table and stood directly behind the big winner.

"I see you've discovered one way Americans like to pass their leisure time, Louis," she said.

"Sara, is it time already?" Stevenson said, rising to his feet. "Gentlemen, let me introduce you to Sara Hillyer. Sara, this is the famous Doc Holliday and Josiah Mc-Cain. They were kind enough to introduce me to this wonderful game."

"It's wonderful for some of us," McCain said sarcastically.

Sara beamed, looking at the stack of bills on her companion's section of the table. Quite a sum, she thought. And God only knows how much he's carrying with him in his bags.

"I've been extremely lucky, Sara. I've won eight of the last ten matches."

"Hands!" Holliday said emphatically. "They're called hands. Not matches. Hands!"

"Excuse me. Hands."

Sara looked at the clock on the wall. It was 6:50, still time for another hand or two, but she decided it might be wise to get Stevenson out of the saloon before his luck turned.

"We'd better be going, Louis."

"Yes, you're right. Goodbye, gentlemen. It's been a

pleasure meeting you both." He stood straight up and faced Doc. "And Mr. Holliday, I can't tell you what a thrill it will be for me to tell my friends that I was instructed in the art of five-card stud poker by the renowned Doc Holliday."

"Yeah, I'm sure," was the best Holliday could respond. "Miss Hillyer, nice meeting you."

"Maybe we'll see you on the train," McCain said to Sara. She was radiant, and from the moment she stood behind Stevenson, Josiah couldn't take his eyes off her.

"Goodbye, gentlemen," she said. The words were echoed by the Scotsman, and the pair marched out of the saloon, carrying their possessions.

The losing pair swept their remaining cash off the table and into their pockets. Then they too left the Hide and Tallow.

It was dark outside, and the two men made their way to the train station. The sound of the train's whistle could be heard, and several other people hurried through the streets to the railway platform.

"Nice choice to play poker with, McCain," Doc said tauntingly. "The bastard took me for a hundred and two dollars."

McCain lit a cigarette as they walked. "He took me for ninety. How was I supposed to know he'd be that lucky?"

"Lucky! You believe he's never played poker before?"

"Yeah. I watched his face when you were explaining the game to him. For a time I could tell he didn't know what the hell you were talking about."

Doc spat on the ground. "Then that's the best case of beginner's luck I've ever seen."

They were only a few feet from the platform when the Central Pacific puffed out a lengthy cloud of steam. The conductor jumped off the train for a moment, surveyed

103

the platform, and reboarded.

"Anyhow," Doc continued, "never let it be said that Doc Holliday cheats at cards. That oughta be proof enough that I could've, but didn't."

"Or me either," McCain added.

"Let's get on this train. We still have some work to do for Wyatt."

Chapter Eighteen

Unlike the train from Hays City, Doc and McCain found this one packed with people. Many of them looked like foreigners to McCain, and the constant babble of strange languages around him confirmed his suspicions. Several of the languages he was able to identify: Spanish, French, and what he assumed to be German. But there were other tongues being spoken that he didn't know because he had never heard them before: Swedish, Hungarian, Yiddish. It was an odd assortment of people who inhabited this car.

"Christ, this train is full," Doc declared. "There's only two seats left, right over there."

The men walked to where Doc pointed and took the two remaining seats. Looking across the aisle, Doc, who sat in the inner seat, noticed Stevenson and Sara.

"Hello again," said Stevenson.

"Hi," Doc nodded unenthusiastically.

Before the conversation could go any further, the train began to pull out of the station. The noise from the departing train made any conversation impossible, which was fine with Doc. He looked down and maneuvered his satchel under his seat. While he was hunched over, a small boy ran up the aisle, bumped into him when the train rocked a bit, and knocked his hat off.

"Goddamn brat," Doc cursed, retrieving it. "I oughta slap you silly." But the child was too far down the aisle to hear him.

The train picked up speed and eventually the noise decreased. The chatter of incomprehensible languages resumed. The dim lights in the car and the darkness outside made reading impossible; there were only two recourses left to the passengers: sleep or talk.

McCain announced that it was his turn to sleep, and his companion didn't object although he wanted to because it meant he'd have to sit there doing nothing. Even worse, he might get roped into another conversation with the Scotsman across from him. But as McCain curled up in his seat trying to get comfortable, Doc figured that talking to Stevenson might lead to something beneficial. He was, after all, traveling with that woman, who was not difficult to look at. He wouldn't mind knowing her better. And maybe he'd be able to lure Stevenson into another game of cards and win some of his money back. This time, he told himself, he damn well *would* cheat.

It didn't take long for Stevenson to start talking.

"Doc, may I ask to where you're bound?"

"Ogden."

"That's in the state of Utah, I believe."

"It ain't in Africa," Doc replied sarcastically.

Stevenson found this very funny and laughed. He laughed so hard that several passengers turned their heads to see what was so funny. Suddenly the laughter turned to a raw coughing that wouldn't stop. Stevenson's face went pale and Doc observed that the muscles in the Scotsman's neck were tense and strained.

Sara placed a hand on her friend's back. "Louis, are you okay?"

106

He nodded but continued coughing. Even Doc was dismayed. Finally, with tears in his eyes and a pale shade of red in his face, Stevenson stopped coughing. He swallowed and took several deep, wheezy breaths.

"Poor Louis," Sara exclaimed. "Are you ill?"

Doc answered for him. "He'll be all right, ma'am. These things happen."

"How can you dismiss something like that so lightly?" she said.

" 'Cause I am a doctor."

"You're really a doctor?"

"Well, I'm a dentist, but I know a few things about medicine and the like."

A normal, somewhat pale complexion returned to Stevenson's face, and he was finally able to speak.

"I'm afraid I'm not very healthy."

"I know," Doc said. "But you'll be okay. Take a swig of this." He handed him a bottle which he took out of his satchel. Doc was careful to tilt the bag away from the passengers. He didn't want anybody else to notice the stacks of U.S. currency in it.

"No thank you," Stevenson said.

"Take it. Doctor's orders."

The bottle was accepted, and Stevenson swallowed a small amount of the liquid. At first the whiskey burned his throat, but then it soothed it and seemed to put out whatever fire was down there.

"Thank you."

"Don't mention it," Doc said, retrieving his bottle and setting it on the floor next to the satchel. "You cough like that often?"

"I'm afraid so. Sometimes it's worse than others."

"You've got the consumption, don't you?"

"I do, unfortunately. You're quite observant, Doc."

"I'm also consumptive. But don't spread that around."

"You are?"

"Yeah. It's a pain in the butt, but I don't let it stop me from doing nothin'."

"My attitude exactly," Stevenson concurred.

"It must be dreadful," Sara added.

"It ain't that bad, Miss Hillyer. You just try to ignore it. Right Louis?"

"Right."

Then Doc looked over at McCain, who was sound asleep. "Out like a light, ain't he?"

"Is Mr. McCain a lawman too?" Sara asked.

"No. And neither am I, ma'am. I was tellin' Louis before that we just work for a lawman. One of the best — Wyatt Earp of Dodge City."

Stevenson recalled something else he had read in *Kansas Law*. "Isn't Dodge City also the domain of Mr. Bat Masterson? I've read that he too is a great law enforcer."

"Bat's okay, but he can't hold a candle to Wyatt. Wyatt's kinda like the King, and Bat's kinda like a Jack, if you know what I mean." Then Doc's eyes lit up. "That reminds me, how about a game of poker?"

Before he could answer, Stevenson was greeted by an unwelcome voice from an unwelcome acquaintance.

"Well, well, if it ain't my foreign friend again." It was George Wright, the Pinkerton. "Howdy, ma'am. Nice to see you again too."

Stevenson said nothing, not wishing to rile the man. It backfired.

"Ain't you gonna greet your ol' friend, pipsqueak?" Wright asked nastily. "Or you, ma'am?"

Sara was not as controlled as her companion. "Get lost," she blurted out.

"Why that ain't nice. That ain't nice at all . . . bitch."

Holliday nudged McCain awake with his elbow, then stood up and faced the man. "You got a problem, feller?" he asked Wright, their faces only inches apart. "You're bein' awful rude to this lady."

"Lady?" Wright repeated and laughed.

Holliday was about to strike the man when the train lurched, and it knocked the two standing men off balance. When they recovered their footing, Wright had his gun out. McCain, awake but not quite sure of what was going on, quietly slipped the revolver out of his holster and held it under his jacket.

"Sit down," the Pinkerton said, gesturing to the seat with his pistol. Doc did as he was told.

"I recognize you, Mr. Doc Holliday," Wright continued, "but you don't scare me none. I've faced worse than you."

"Who the hell are you, man?" Doc asked.

"The name's Wright. Pinkerton agent."

"Why are you botherin' these people? It ain't your job to annoy payin' customers."

Many of the passengers on board the car were watching the commotion from their seats. Others were standing, trying to get a better view. Wright noticed that he had an audience, so he decided to make a speech.

"I know my job, Holliday, and I don't need you tellin' me what it is and what it ain't. This here foreigner and his lovely cohort were up to something on the train from Chicago, but I didn't know what it was. Now I can see what it was. They were meetin' up with you. I got a feelin' you know where I'm headin', and you plan to follow me."

Holliday looked at Wright, amazed and amused. "You must be out of your mind. I ain't never heard of you, I just met them at the last stop, and I can't think of anything I'd rather do less than follow you around."

Several nearby passengers who overheard Holliday's remarks began to laugh. Wright's face turned beet-red.

"Think you're funny, do you? I'm the law here, Mr. Holliday. And I can't be bought, which is more than you can say for yourself or those Earp bastards you hang around with."

"You're nuts."

"No, I'm not. Maybe the general public swallows that crap about the so-called heroes of Dodge, but we in the Agency know better. Lawmen? You and the Earps are scum, worse than the outlaws you pretend to arrest."

Wright had been playing with fire, and with his last words he ignited it. Doc quickly raised his leg, ignoring the gun that was aimed at his chest, and pushed forward. The bottom of his boot pushed violently against Wright's stomach and forced the man to buckle over forward. Then Doc got up, grabbed Wright's wrist, and pointed the barrel upward. A shot went off and blew a hole in the ceiling. Then Doc threw a fist at Wright's face. It hit him on the right cheekbone and knocked him backward.

Wright regained his balance and kicked at Doc. Holliday grabbed the ascending boot and held it aloft, forcing Wright to hop around on one leg while waving the gun in the air over him. Passengers all over the car ducked behind seats or hit the floor. Many of them were frightened but laughed at the comical sight of the overweight Pinkerton hopping like a jack rabbit.

Doc pushed forward on the leg, and Wright fell to the floor. McCain had been amused during the fracas, but he noticed the rage in Holliday's eyes. It was a side of Holliday he hadn't seen before, and it took him by surprise. He had seen Doc kill a man, but he had done it coolly, unemotionally. This was different.

Doc pulled his handgun from its holster and pointed it at Wright. Stevenson's jaw dropped in horror, and Sara held on to his arm and buried her face in his shoulder.

But before he could squeeze the trigger, McCain

110

jumped to his feet and wrapped his fingers around Doc's drawn gun.

"Don't, Doc."

"Let go."

"We got a job to do. Quietly. We don't need trouble with the law right now."

Doc shook off the rage within him and lowered the gun. McCain stepped on Wright's wrist and pinned it to the floor.

"I'll take this if you don't mind," he said, removing the gun from the entrapped hand. "Now get up."

Wright stumbled to his feet. "Who the hell are you?" he said, rubbing his sore wrist.

"I'm the angel of mercy. I just saved your life, and now I'm gonna save you from makin' a big mistake. Doc was tellin' the truth, and I'm pretty sure these two nice folks were too. Anyhow, you have no proof of anything, so I'd advise you to leave well enough alone. Now take your gun and go back wherever you came from."

Wright took back the revolver. "You're probably one of this gang."

"There ain't no gang."

He could see there was no point in pursuing this further, so Wright slowly walked down the aisle to his seat. The stranger was right; there was no proof of anything. But just the same Wright announced, "I'll be watchin' all of you. And I'll be ready for you next time, Holliday."

"There won't be any next time unless you make one," Doc retorted.

When everyone had retaken his seat, there was relative peace and quiet for a while. And since they now knew who was on board, mothers prevented their children from running up and down the aisle of the car.

George Wright sat in his seat, shaken up, scared, and

111

utterly embarrassed. He stared straight ahead, looking at no one and nothing. He avoided all eye contact. In his mind he just repeated the name Doc Holliday over and over. It would be a real feather in his cap to catch Holliday at something. It might even get him a promotion. He wouldn't have to ride these trains with these stinking foreigners any more. Doc Holliday. He'd get him. He'd show him that George Wright wouldn't be humiliated for long. No, not for long.

Chapter Nineteen

Due East of San Francisco, on another train

"I'm telling you, President Rutherford B. Hayes is one of the stupidest men I've ever met."

The man who spoke these words was about 55 years old, with a paunch and receding gray hair. His eyebrows were bushy, and they were set above two sunken, shadowy eyes. He looked like a cross between a bear and a raccoon, albeit a well-dressed, very fashionable one. His suit was well-tailored and his belt and boots were made of the finest leather. From his mouth hung a very expensive cigar, which he often waved around like a bandleader waves a baton.

"He can't be that stupid," said the man opposite him. "He did get elected president, after all."

The big man laughed. "So what? Elections can be fixed. You oughta know that, seeing that you're the brother of Wyatt Earp, who got elected in Dodge City because of a fixed election. And aren't you here now to help rig another one for him?"

Warren Earp didn't answer. He didn't have to; both men already knew the answer. Instead, Warren asked another question.

"If you feel that way about him, why do you work for him? Why don't you do something else?"

Presidential aide Jerome Beaudine snickered at the naivete of the youngest Earp brother's question, but answered it anyway. "First off, I work for him only when I have to. Most of the time I'm left on my own. Once in a while he wants my advice on some issue, and I give it to him. But that doesn't happen often. More often than not I'm working for myself, keeping my businesses going. When we get to San Francisco — which should be within the hour — I'll show you some of them."

Warren smiled. He forced it to his mouth. He couldn't stand this fat loudmouth braggart Wyatt had asked him to ride with. The man was pompous and gaudy. But Wyatt had said that it was important that he ride with Beaudine and, as the letter that he had received at home stated, "act like an Earp." Warren knew what that meant. It meant wear a gun and act like you owned the world.

Warren, indeed, did own a piece of the world the way his brothers owned Dodge City. He did what he wanted, took what he wanted, and threatened whoever he wanted in several Missouri counties. That had been Warren's domain. He never left home like his brothers. And unlike his brothers, he wasn't very good with a gun. He carried one, but seldom used it, and even when he did, he rarely hit anything except air. But he had gained some power in Missouri despite his shortcomings with firearms. He had something else going for him, a very powerful tool: the Earp name and the Earp reputation.

And there were a couple of other tools at his disposal: Ben Cole, a wiry, cagey man whose specialty was assassination by a slip of a knife between the ribs, and Max Fisher, an enormous bear of a man who spoke with his fists, his tongue having been cut out by Apaches when he was seventeen years old. Both men had drifted into

114

Missouri, and both were hired by Warren Earp. They were his ever-present bodyguards and did his fighting and, when necessary, killing for him.

The presence of these two men on the train with the presidential aide's entourage disturbed Beaudine. He had known from the start that Warren would be along and didn't mind that. Thanks to the proliferation and popularity of dime novels across the nation, the Earps were heroes to the general public, as close to knights in shining armor as popular heroes could get. Beaudine, of course, knew that it was far from the truth, but the average citizen didn't. And that's what counted. In fact, Beaudine welcomed the idea of an Earp traveling with him. It would put him in the company of a hero. However, he hadn't counted on the two seedy thugs Warren had brought with him.

Beaudine had two bodyguards of his own, but on the surface they looked more respectable. They wore fancy suits and were well-groomed, but under their jackets they carried weapons every bit as dangerous as those carried by Warren's men. The aide had introduced them to Warren as simply "Mr. Paine and Mr. McKelton." Mr. Paine was about thirty-eight, blond, and handsome. Mr. McKelton, on the other hand, was approaching the age of fifty, and was dark and homely. The deep scar that ran from the bottom of his left ear to his lip didn't help his looks.

Beaudine puffed on his cigar. "I'm tired of riding trains. I can't wait until we get to San Francisco. My ass hurts."

Your *fat* ass hurts, Warren thought. But he said something else. "Well, we'll be gettin' there two days earlier than planned."

"I will, yeah," Beaudine answered. "You were originally gonna ride only to Ogden, weren't you?"

115

"Right. When we get to Frisco, I gotta wire my brother. Them damn Indians upset everything. Wyatt probably sent someone to meet us at Ogden."

"Well, as the poet said, 'The best laid plans of mice and men . . .'"

Warren hadn't the slightest idea what he was talking about, but nodded just the same.

"If your brother sent a good man—and I'm sure he did—it shouldn't be so hard to track us to San Francisco. All he has to do is talk to someone at the Central Pacific Office. And when he finds out that all stops between Ogden and Reno were cancelled because of the brewing Indian trouble, he'll get in touch with your brother."

"I guess so. Those goddamn Nez Perce just can't help causin' trouble. It's in their blood."

Beaudine nodded in agreement. "Particularly the Nez Perce. Before I left Washington, I got word that a bunch of 'em disappeared off the reservation we set up for 'em."

"But did they ever rob trains before?"

"No. I must admit that's something new even for them."

"So now I get stuck goin' all the way to San Francisco. And for God knows how long."

"Don't worry about it, my boy," Beaudine said with false joviality. "I'll show you around town when we get there. Ever been there before?"

"No."

"Well, it's a hell of a town. There's everything a man could want, if you know what I mean?"

Warren understood. The leer on Beaudine's face was unmistakable.

"And now that I'll be getting there ahead of schedule, I'll be staying there for at least a week. That'll give your brother's errand boy time to get to us, I'm sure."

Warren laughed.

"What's so funny?" the aide asked.

"I think my brother's sending Doc Holliday," Warren responded, grinning. "And if he does show up, I wouldn't call him no errand boy if I was you."

"N-no, certainly not," Beaudine responded nervously. Doc Holliday! the politician thought. This time around Earp is sending his top gun.

"You ever meet him?" Warren asked. "Did he drop off the money the last time you and Wyatt had a . . . an arrangement?"

"No. When your brother moved to Dodge, he and I did business, personally, just the two of us. What's Holliday like?"

"He's an animal," Warren answered. He was trying to make Beaudine uncomfortable, just for the fun of it. "I hear he once skinned a man alive for messin' up his clothes."

Beaudine tried not to let his nervousness rise to the surface. He took two quick puffs on his cigar.

Warren was enjoying himself. He had never met Doc, had no idea what he was like, and couldn't physically describe the man since he had never seen him. All he knew was what Wyatt had told him: "Doc is like family."

Beaudine shot a glance at his two well-but-secretly-armed employees. He didn't expect any trouble from Earp—any of the Earps—or Holliday, for that matter, but if there was any dispute during these negotiations, he wondered if his men would match up to an Earp, a Holliday, and two tough-looking friends.

Through the train window, the politician, whom Rutherford B. Hayes had inherited from Ulysses S. Grant, the former president, watched the California countryside pass by. Warren's news upset his stomach. He puffed again on his cigar. Only this time it tasted like hell.

Warren watched the man as he dropped the stogie to the floor and crushed it out with his boot heel. Then the youngest Earp noticed drops of water crashing into the window and exploding into smaller droplets. It was beginning to rain.

Chapter Twenty

Ogden, Utah

When they learned the Central Pacific would be leaving in twenty minutes, Stevenson and Sara made the change of train quickly. Besides, they figured, what could they see in town in twenty minutes?

Doc and McClain, on the other hand, took their time, stretching dormant muscles and gazing about. Passengers scurried about the station around the two men. Doc held the satchel of money by the handle.

"I'm gonna go check on the train that Beaudine was on," he said.

"Who's Beaudine?" McCain asked, feigning ignorance.

Doc realized that he had never told McCain anything about Beaudine, the payoffs, or Wyatt's impending move to Tombstone.

"He's the guy I have to deliver this money to. Wyatt owes it to him. A loan or something he made long ago."

"Oh."

"Wait here for a minute. I'll be right back."

McCain did as he was told. He lit a cigarette and watched as Doc spoke to one of the railroad employees on the platform. Doc had slipped, McCain realized, by mentioning Beaudine's name. But surely he wouldn't have been able to keep it a secret forever.

McCain knew he had to get to a Western Union office as soon as possible. Both Bat and the Secret Service might want to know that it was Jerome Beaudine fixing elections for the Earps.

The railroad worker pointed to an office door, and Doc knocked on it and entered the room. McCain suddenly wondered if the payoff was going on at that very second. Was Beaudine in that office? And was the transaction taking place while he stood in the middle of the station platform smoking a cigarette?

In a moment, his fears were dismissed. Doc was walking back to him, satchel in hand, looking very perturbed.

"Goddamn it!" Doc swore when he reached McCain's side. "This is unbelievable."

"What's the matter?"

"Beaudine's train never arrived. It never stopped here at all. It went straight to Reno, Nevada."

"How come?"

"Indians. Goddamn Nez Perce been hittin' the trains."

"Attacking them?"

"Robbin' them. Stealin' cash and gold."

McCain let the statement sink in. There was something wrong with it. "That don't sound like the Nez Perce."

"Who knows? Who cares? Maybe it was some other tribe. Who gives a damn. All I know is that they changed the train schedules."

"What do we do now? Do we stay put, or do we follow them to Reno?"

Doc thought for a moment. He remembered Wyatt telling him to use his judgment if anything went wrong. It was time to exercise that judgment.

"We're goin' on to Reno."

"Fine with me. I got no place else to go."

"We might have to go all the way to Frisco," Doc added. "I just wanna let you know."

"Don't bother me. But how about a hike in my salary? This is gonna involve a few more days, I suppose."

"Don't worry about it. We can discuss that later. Right now I gotta send a wire to Earp. And I'd better do it in a hurry. We don't want to miss that train."

"Want me to do it?"

"No thanks. I'll take care of it. You make sure they hold that train 'til I get back."

Doc rushed away. McCain was quite satisfied with his acting. Asking Doc for an increase in his fee was a nice touch, he thought, perfectly in character. But there was no way he would be able to wire Bat now, not with Doc sending his own message.

Passengers began to board the train. Slowly, McCain made his way down the platform. He stepped next to the conductor and asked a question.

"How much time before you leave?"

The conductor pulled a watch from his vest pocket and looked at it. "Three minutes, on the nose."

"Thanks."

McCain gazed around, looking for Doc. He was nowhere in sight. Then the train began the usual chorus of sounds that alerted anyone near that it would soon be pulling out. There was still no Doc.

"Any chance you could hold the train a minute or two?" McCain asked the conductor, who was now hanging onto a handrail between two passenger cars.

"None."

McCain decided he'd have to wait for Doc, even if it meant letting the train go.

The three minutes were up, and the train edged forward. Suddenly, Doc raced across the platform. But the train was building up speed.

"Grab it!" Doc yelled. "Get on the goddamn thing!"

McCain ran a bit, jumped, and landed on one of the steps between two cars. He held on to a small railing with his left hand. He extended the right to try to help the trailing Doc.

"Here," Doc yelled over the noise of the chugging train. "Grab this." He tossed the satchel to McCain, who caught it and placed it on the steps between his feet. Now unencumbered, Doc picked up speed. He managed to pull up next to the steps, but couldn't make the leap onto them. Finally, he pulled a bit ahead of the steps, did a strange little skip, and flew toward McCain. Their hands connected with a firm grasp. But Doc's foot missed the flat part of the iron step, hitting the point of it instead with his boot sole. The leg slipped off the step, and before he realized what had happened, Doc's legs were hanging alongside the train, and he was holding onto McCain's hand for dear life.

The train picked up speed, and it rocked back and forth as it did. One of Doc's boot heels hit a beam on the track and the leg bounced. McCain saw the look of pain on Doc's face when it happened.

He had to get Doc up fast, or he'd never be able to. The train's speed was building by the minute. Bracing himself against a handrail, McCain yelled "Now" and yanked Doc up and forward. Again Doc's foot hit the track, but he was able to reach the handrail with his free hand. McCain got hold of Doc's arm, and eventually was able to pull him onto the steps. Doc sat on top of the satchel, trying to catch his breath.

McCain bent down until his mouth was next to Doc's ear. "You okay?"

Doc nodded but said nothing.

"Your legs okay?"

"Yeah," Doc answered, regaining his breath a bit.

"They're shakin' a bit, but I think they're all right." He sat back and raised his left foot in the air. "Damn foot hurts like hell."

"I couldn't hold the train," McCain said. "Sorry."

Doc turned his head and spat into the wind. "It ain't your fault. But I'm gonna kill every goddamn Nez Perce I ever meet!"

Chapter Twenty-one

They entered the passenger car and were greeted by the stares of incredulous customers, mystified children, and an enraged conductor.

"Are you two loco?" he screamed. "You coulda got yerselves killed."

Doc just coldly stared at the man and softly said, "Shut up."

"What did you say?"

Doc's eyes grew even more icy, as did his voice. "I said shut up. And go away."

"But you can't . . ."

"Now!"

The conductor realized his safety would be better guaranteed elsewhere, so he turned and walked up the aisle, mumbling under his breath.

Doc let him go, then followed up the aisle a bit. Six or seven seats ahead he noticed Stevenson and Sara. He didn't feel like socializing with them, so he sat down in the seat directly to his left. McCain took the aisle seat next to him.

"Jesus Christ, what a day!" Doc exclaimed.

Then, from the other end of the car, there were several

loud voices going at once. They grew louder by the second, and one of the shouters wasn't speaking English. Women all over the car were sighing and whispering "Oh my!" or "My goodness!" Everyone was trying to get a better view of the commotion.

Doc rolled his eyes in disgust. "What now?"

He and McCain stood up and saw the conductor trying to pull a man out of his seat. Even though they could only hear the man's voice and see the back of his head, they knew he was Chinese; the strange, guttural words he uttered and the skull cap and pigtail that adorned his head told them that.

"Get up, damn ya," yelled the conductor, tugging the man's elbow. "No Chinese allowed in here."

The struggle continued. The conductor had his own cheering audience: three men. They were the same three men who had forced a Chinese man out of the car on the train from Chicago.

"That's it," shouted the man named Jack. "Kick his butt off the train!"

His two companions shouted similar sentiments. Several of the other passengers joined in also.

Finally, the conductor had the man out of the seat and on his feet, but he was having great difficulty getting him any closer to the door.

Jack stepped forward and grabbed the man's pigtail. He pulled it hard enough to jerk the man's head back and make him emit a high-pitched scream. Then together he and the conductor led the immigrant to the door. Most of the passengers began to cheer. The man was led out, and the door slammed behind the three men.

After a few seconds, only Jack re-entered the car, wiping his hands on his pants. Many of the passengers applauded, whistled, and stamped their feet. Jack loved every second of it and took a sweeping bow like an actor in a traveling stage show.

"The conductor took him to the Chink car," he announced. Then he sat down, rejoining his two comrades. The noise inside the car quieted. Everyone was apparently at ease now that the heathen was where he belonged.

Everyone except one lanky Scotsman.

Just as Doc and McCain were about to sit down, Stevenson jumped to his feet. He stood in the center of the car and addressed them as a group.

"I am shocked! Outraged!" he said. "I cannot believe what I have seen. How can you treat a fellow human being that way? Yes, the man is different—he is of Oriental descent—but does that mean he is your inferior and to be treated no better than you would treat a dog?"

"Yes!" shouted one man, followed by the laughter of his fellow riders.

Doc turned to McCain and said, "I don't believe that man. I hope he don't have plans to settle in this country. He ain't gonna last long."

Stevenson continued. "No, it doesn't, my friends. The Chinese are not inferior. To be precise, they are probably our superiors. Their civilization goes back centuries before our own and . . ."

"So what?" someone called out.

". . . they have made great contributions to science, to the arts, to . . ."

The Scotsman's audience didn't appreciate his soliloquy and let him know it by hissing and booing. Then the prior performer—who had won the hearts of the audience by removing the Oriental savage—returned for an encore.

"I've heard about enough from you!" Jack yelled, stepping up to Stevenson. "You like them so much, maybe you'd like to join them."

With his two cronies behind him, Jack grabbed the orator by the lapels and pulled him toward the door. The audience cheered.

Sara screamed and began pounding on Jack's shoulders with her fists.

McCain was about to go to the assistance of the young pair, but Doc held him by the wrist and wouldn't let go.

"Stay put!" he said. "He made his bed, now let him lie in it."

"They'll tear him apart."

"That's his problem. We got problems of our own. And we've had too much attention paid to us already. Now sit!"

McCain remained standing.

"I said sit."

"I'm not goin' anyplace. I just want to keep an eye on things."

Jack had Stevenson halfway to the door when he said to his friends, "Get this dame off my back and grab their luggage."

Sara threw a left hook at one of the men, and it caught him squarely on the jaw and sent him stumbling backward down the aisle. Eventually, he tripped over and fell on a young boy who had been watching, taking punches at the air in front of him in imitation of Sara.

The boy's father stood up. "Get off my kid, you oaf," he said, pushing the man aside.

Jack's friend got up and took a swig at the boy's father. He missed, and the man got the ruffian by the throat.

Jack's other friend saw this new fight breaking out and ran down the aisle. Sara picked up one of Stevenson's satchels and crept up behind the man. Then she lifted the satchel over her head and slammed it into the back of his neck.

It didn't do the harm Sara was hoping for. The man turned and moved after her. But he tripped over the bag. Furious, he kicked the bag down the aisle in the direction of McCain.

McCain wanted to help, but he knew it would mean trouble with Doc if he got involved. And trouble with Doc could mean the end of his mission.

"Doc, we got to help," he said.

"No, we don't," was the matter-of-fact reply.

Jack's friend was still battling the boy's father, and as the two struggled, they worked their way down the aisle until they were wrestling right next to McCain and Doc. The father threw four bony knuckles into the other's face, sending him sailing past the standing McCain into Doc's lap.

"Ya asshole!" Doc yelled and pushed the man off him.

McCain stepped aside, letting the two men go at it. The father was now holding the bag that had been kicked down the aisle. He threw it at his opponent, but the man ducked, and it bounced off the window next to Doc and landed at his feet.

Doc knew he should control himself, but it was too late. It was time to get involved, at least temporarily. He stood up and grabbed Jack's friend. Turning him around so that he'd be facing him, Doc drove his fist into the man's stomach. The impact caused him to buckle over, and when he did, Doc hit the man in the back of the neck, knocking him to the floor.

Stunned, Jack's friend shook his head to clear his sight and saw two satchels inches from his face. They looked alike, and he couldn't have cared less which belonged to whom.

Doc was now standing in the aisle, turning his attention to the boy's father.

Over Doc's shoulders, McCain advised, "I'd get back

to my family if I were you."

The man took the advice, but as he did, Jack's friend rose from the floor and threw one of the satchels at the retreating father. It missed its target and thudded off the back of a seat into the aisle.

Doc turned and took Jack's compatriot by the neck. He forced him in front of him and pushed the man down the aisle.

"Get the hell away from me," Doc snarled. Then he turned to McCain. "Don't go nowhere."

McCain simply stared back until Doc regained his seat. Then he returned his attention to the activity down the aisle.

Jack had the door open and was shoving Stevenson out onto the narrow platform between the cars. "Grab the dame and their bags," he shouted to his sidekicks.

They did as they were told. One grabbed their bags by the handles and carted them down the aisle. But his way was blocked by a cane that poked out from a seat.

"That there's one of hers too," said an old lady, who was holding the cane in one hand and a corn-cob pipe in the other. "Ya almost hit me with the thing!"

It was the bag that had so far made its way up and down the aisle. It was scooped up and carried with the rest of the luggage.

McCain strained to see out the far door. However, there were too many people in the way, and Jack held it only half open.

Then there was a series of screams from the car. Sara had pulled a gun from under her dress and was pointing it at Jack's other cohort.

"Touch me and I'll put a bullet between your eyes!" she said.

Then a piercing sound ripped through the car; it was the sound of a man screaming. Sara heard it and knew it was Louis' scream.

A young girl pointed out one of the windows and said, "Mommy, a man fell off the train."

Sara tried to look out the window. It was a bad mistake.

Jack's man grabbed her wrist with one hand and removed the gun from her possession with the other. She tried to kick him, but missed. He grabbed her around the neck and forced her back to the half-open door.

"It's time to join your friend," he said.

Jack and his other accomplice heaved the bags off the train.

"The bitch pulled a gun on me!" said the man who held her. "She's goin' off too."

Doc or no Doc, McCain couldn't stand it any more. He was about to pull his Colt and shoot down the aisle, but stopped himself. There were too many passengers aboard and too many people standing in the way. Instead, he marched down the aisle as quickly as he could. But gawking, amused folks blocked his path. He had to push and step over and around bodies.

"McCain!" Doc screamed after him. "McCain, get back here!"

He kept going, inching ever forward. But when he was two-thirds down the aisle, he heard Sara's scream. It sent a chill through him, and he closed his eyes in disbelief for a second. Everything quieted down. Even the passengers were amazed that a woman had been thrown off the train, even though none had said a word nor lent a hand to stop it from happening.

McCain hated them all, but knew he was just as bad as they were. He had his reasons, but they all probably had reasons which they thought were just as good, just as justifiable, for not helping her.

He continued down the aisle, pushing people aside as

if they were bales of hay. Finally, he reached the door, pulled it fully open, and met face-to-face with the trio who were trying to get back into the car.

Without hesitation, he took a swing at Jack's jaw. The fist hit hard, and it knocked the man back into his two accomplices. When the three men recovered from the shock, McCain's Colt was already drawn and pointed at them. The car door slammed shut behind McCain.

"I oughta kill the three of you," McCain said.

"What is this, mister?" asked Jack.

McCain sneered. "You boys don't like Chinese or men who speak their mind—or women either it seems. Well, I like everyone, 'cept you."

They were all huddled together on the narrow platform. Jack was close enough to knock the gun out of McCain's hand. He decided to give it a try.

It was a bad decision. McCain, in a single motion, lowered his Colt, fired a shot, and raised the gun's barrel again. The bullet tore through Jack's right boot and foot.

Jack screamed in pain while his two friends held him up by the arms. "Ya shot my toes off!" he cried.

"Make another stupid move and the next shot will cut something off a few feet higher."

Jack's boot was covered with blood, which continued to pump out of the shredded front. Tears welled up in the wounded man's eyes, and he and his two friends watched the rhythmic pumping of blood form an ever-widening pool around the mutilated foot.

"I should make you all jump!" McCain said. "But I won't. You might run into those two folks you pushed over, assuming they're still alive. Now toss your guns over."

"Wh-what are you gonna do, mister?" asked one of Jack's men. "He's losing a lot of blood."

131

For a second McCain turned his head and peered into the next car. Kicking the three surrendered guns onto the tracks below, he smiled.

"That foot needs medical attention all right," he continued. "There ain't no doctors on this car. You'd better try the next one."

"How do you know there ain't no . . ."

"He told me," McCain said, indicating his Colt. "And he never lies. Now move it."

Jack and his men slowly and awkwardly stepped over the gap between the two cars' platforms. One of his helpers was about to open the door when he suddenly stopped, turned, and screamed at McCain.

"We can't go in there!" he insisted. "This car is full of Chinks."

McCain grinned. "I hear they're great doctors."

"I ain't goin' in there!" Jack screamed.

"Don't! But you boys either take your chances in there, or out here with me. And in five seconds I start shootin'."

Before McCain had counted to four, they were inside the car. Their backs blocked the window, so he couldn't tell what the reaction was to their entrance. He really didn't care, either. His thoughts turned to other matters, and the wind that was slapping him across the face helped him think. He knew he'd have to deal with a very angry Doc Holliday and perhaps a hostile crowd of passengers back in the car, but he was less concerned about that than the fact that Sara and Stevenson had been pushed off the train and very possibly killed—and he had let it happen. He had a new admiration for the Scotsman; what Stevenson had done took courage, although Doc would probably disagree. And Sara! What a ball of fire she turned out to be.

He began to feel even more guilty. He knew he had to

get back inside the train before the feeling overwhelmed him. Before he stepped into the car, though, he resolved one matter: he would go back and look for Sara and Stevenson when the train reached its next stop, and he could get a fresh horse. And if it meant the end of his partnership with Doc, so be it.

Chapter Twenty-two

"That ain't right, what you done, mister!"

The words were the first McCain heard when he stepped back into the car. He wasn't in the mood to hear them; he wasn't in the mood to debate, either.

"Shut up and get out of my way," he said, brushing the man who had spoken aside.

"Who you pushin'?" the man asked, grabbing McCain's shoulder.

It was the wrong thing to do. McCain spun on his heels, grabbed the man by the lapels of his jacket, and sat him down hard on an empty seat. The short, citified man offered no further resistance and appeared to be melting into the seat, loose-limbed.

"I told you to shut up. Now stay in that seat!"

Josiah could feel the eyes of most of the passengers staring at him. Defiantly, he trudged down the aisle, avoiding the eyes. But his display of anger was effective. No one else challenged him or said a word. Until he reached his seat.

Doc sat with his feet on the seat opposite him, smoking a cigarette. It dangled from his lips, and with each of Doc's breaths it became surrounded by smoke.

"Very nice, McCain," Doc muttered, ashes from the butt falling into his lap. "You're a big hero now, I suppose. To whom I don't know, but I guess that's it."

McCain said nothing, but he was boiling inside.

"Did you save the Scotch fellow? Did you save the girl? No? Then you ain't much of a hero, are ya? And you coulda upset this whole apple cart, coulda got you or me killed, coulda . . ."

"Shut the hell up!" McCain said. "You coulda done the same when you fought that Pinkerton, and you know it. So shut your mouth. There's only so much crap I'll take from you.

Doc's face turned red with anger. He was angry at McCain's insolence, and he was angry because McCain was right.

"Who you talkin' to?"

"You, and if you don't like it, do something about it!"

Doc's hand flew under his jacket, but he couldn't reach the derringer in time. Before his fingertips even touched the handle, McCain had the barrel of his Colt pressed against Doc's mustache, pointing up into his nostril.

"Don't," McCain said, "unless you want a big hole in the center of your face."

Holliday didn't move, except to slowly lower his hand away from the weapon near his shoulder. Finally he had both hands in his lap.

"You can take that gun out of my face now, McCain."

"Can I?"

"Yeah."

The gun was lowered and put away. Both men sat there quietly, eyeing each other. Doc at last removed the fragment of cigarette that still hung from his lips and tossed it on the floor. His facial expression changed then: it broke into a grin.

"Nothin' like a little danger to help a man think straight," he said. "Maybe you were right, McCain. Maybe I had no cause to get so burned up at that Pinky."

McCain sat attentively, listening, but saying nothing in response.

"But maybe you had no business gettin' involved with this ruckus either. And you *are* supposed to be taking orders from me."

"Not if they stink."

"Even if they stink. You either work for me or you don't."

"This ain't the military."

"You either do what I tell you or you get lost."

"I want to go back and look for the girl."

"You do and you're fired."

"Then I'm fired."

"You're a sucker. You could have it all. With the Earps behind you there ain't nothin' that's outta reach. You think that girl's gonna get you anywhere? Or you think you're gonna get anywhere with her? She's dead, flat as a flapjack or broken to bits, for all you know."

"It still ain't right to leave her there, dead or alive. Or that Scotch fellow either."

Doc blew air through his teeth in disgust. "Fine. Do what you want. You need me more than I need you, that's for sure."

The conversation ended. Doc thought McCain the most foolish man alive. Did he really think—given what he already knew about the Earps—that he'd be free to go? Doc knew what he had to do should McCain not change his mind. He recalled Earp's instructions: get rid of him if it had to be done. Doc would do it too, if need be. The bastard had pulled his gun on him, and very few men were still alive who had done that. McCain would have it coming to him for that alone.

In some ways, though, Doc knew he wouldn't enjoy killing him. McCain had already saved his life a couple of times, and Doc never forgot great favors like that the same way he never forgot insults. But Doc never let personal matters interfere with his business — or his bond with Wyatt Earp.

The conflict between business and personal feelings also vexed McCain. He'd be letting Bat down if he didn't stick with Holliday. But now, for whatever reason, he just couldn't shake the thought of Sara — or the thought of what he had allowed to happen to her. He had to help her now if he could. It was a necessity, a compulsion, although he couldn't say why. Perhaps it was that he'd already failed to be there when other women . . . Alexandra . . . Mary . . . needed him. He wasn't sure. But he was sure he'd go back.

Chapter Twenty-three

San Francisco

Although it wasn't the ritziest nor the most fashionable place to stay in town, the Beaudine party always stayed at the Hotel Casa Verde. There was a number of reasons for this. First, it was the most secluded hotel to be found in a centrally-located part of town; it was, therefore, convenient to government offices, yet quiet enough to offer adequate security for the government official's party. Secondly, it was near to Chinatown, where several of Beaudine's businesses operated. But there was even a more sensible reason for Beaudine to stay there: he owned it.

Although originally from North Carolina, Beaudine loved San Francisco and spent as much time there as possible. It was an ideal location for his investments. Ships arrived daily at the port, bringing needed supplies and merchandise, then returned to wherever they came from carrying Beaudine products with them.

It was a rich town with rich people who would willingly spend their money on personal pleasure, legal or otherwise. And the town was heavily-populated, far too populated for its police force to adequately monitor the

138

actions of all of its citizens. And other people from all over the country would visit San Francisco for this very reason. It was reasonably well-known that whatever you wanted, you could get it there.

Beaudine did his best to supply some of these products and services, and he was an extremely wealthy man for doing so.

Warren Earp was less enamored of the city. He sat in his room in the Casa Verde drinking the champagne that Beaudine had sent to his room.

"How can people drink this stuff?" he asked, grimacing at the long thin glass containing the sparkling wine. "It don't taste like nothin'. Just bubbly water."

Ben Cole stopped looking out the hotel window for a moment and turned to face his boss. "They say that champagne is the liquor of love. It's supposed to do something to you." He flashed a grin at Warren. His exposed yellow teeth and the way his long, wispy blond hair fell over his ears and curled onto his bony, hollow cheeks always made Cole's smile look like the smirk of a skeleton covered by a thin layer of splotchy, scarred skin. Even Warren thought the men appeared downright creepy at times.

"It does something to me, all right," Warren responded. "It makes me piss. This stuff is worse than beer."

"I like it."

"Then here, you drink it." Warren tossed the bottle to Cole, who caught it with one hand and raised it to his lips. "Only don't drink too much of it. Who knows what we'll be doin' later."

At that moment, Max Fisher entered the room and walked up to Warren. The big man was sweating heavily. The front of his shirt was drenched and stuck to his hairy chest.

"You send the wire to Wyatt?" Warren asked.

Max grunted and nodded his head.

"Did you watch the telegraph operator? Did he send it exactly the way the note I gave you read?"

Again Max nodded.

"And you gave the note and the twenty dollar bill to the man at the front desk? He'll let us know the minute an answer arrives?"

Once again the tongueless man bobbed his head in affirmation.

"Good work, Max. Sit down and take a load off your feet."

Before he could do that, there was a knock at the door. Max answered it. A young bellboy stood there, looking up at Max nervously.

"Mr. Beaudine would like to know if Mr. Earp would care to join him for dinner downstairs in the restaurant," he said.

Max slammed the door in the boy's face and turned to Earp.

"I heard, Max. Tell him I'll be . . . Sorry, Max, I just keep forgettin' . . . I'll tell him myself . . ." Warren opened the door and noticed the bellboy was upset. The kid had been obviously trying to make up his mind whether to knock on the door again—whether it would be dangerous to annoy the men inside—or return to Beaudine without an answer and possibly face his abuse.

"Tell Mr. Beaudine I'll be down in a few minutes," Warren said. He handed the boy a silver dollar. "Here. Enjoy yourself."

Then Warren closed the door and turned to his men. "Ben, I want you to come with me, so put that bottle away. Max, you stay here. I don't trust that Beaudine, and I don't want none of his men creepin' around the room while we're gone. Okay?"

140

Max nodded.

Warren looked at himself in a mirror. He spit into his cupped hand and tried to flatten out his long, straight light brown hair with the moisture. He then made a small adjustment to his string tie and shifted his jacket around until it looked and felt right.

"I hope Holliday gets here soon," Warren said. "I don't think I'll be able to stand bein' cooped up in this hotel too long. I hate bein' cooped up. I think I'd rather die than be locked up somewhere."

"You'd really hate prison then," Ben said.

"Yeah, I guess I would. I'd go crazy."

"That's why I won't ever go back. No matter what."

"How long were you in for?"

"Four years."

"Shit, Ben, I woulda gone nuts."

Earp checked himself in the mirror again. This time he thought he looked just fine. He had managed to apply enough spit to his hair to flatten his cowlick down. "I'm so hungry I could eat a whole herd of cows and still have room for dessert. Let's go."

"I'm ready."

"Max, you want us to bring you back some food?"

Max shook his head, pointed at himself and with the same hand pointed to the window.

"You wanna go out later?"

The mute man nodded.

"Okay. See you later. C'mon Ben."

Ben checked to see that his Colt .44 was loaded. Satisfied that it was, he put the gun back in its holster and followed Warren out the door.

Max watched them go, sat down in the plush brown chair that Earp had vacated, and picked up a newspaper that lay on the lamp table next to him. He studied the illustrations on the paper's pages, trying to figure out who these people were. It was all he could do since he had never learned to read. After a while, it proved frustrating, and he threw the newspaper across the room.

That's when he noticed one of Ben Cole's long, thin knives resting on a low, flat table near the window. He got up, crossed the room, and picked up the knife. It was very light, easy to handle. For a moment he considered bringing the knife down to Ben who had apparently forgotten it, but then he remembered that Ben usually traveled with four such knives concealed on his person. Warren had told Max to stay in the room, and that's just what he planned to do. If there was trouble—and there shouldn't be, he knew—Ben would just have to make do with a trio of deadly blades rather than a quartet.

Chapter Twenty-four

Northeastern Nevada

Every square inch of his body hurt. It even hurt to open his eyelids. He took a deep breath and forced himself up on his elbows. His shoulders complained about this action by shooting a sharp pain down his back. Then he realized that one of his legs was folded under him, and his body was on it. He prayed it wasn't broken. Slowly, he eased it out from under his backside. It was stiff, but it moved. It wasn't broken, and he breathed a sigh of relief.

With great effort he stood up, but did so a bit too quickly. The world swam in circles around him, as if he were the eye of some furious cyclone. Once he almost toppled over, but the dizziness began to subside, and his feet felt more securely placed on the dusty ground.

He wiped his forehead, his eyes, and his nose with his hand. There was blood on several fingers. He reached up and touched his nose again; blood was trickling down from his nostrils. He reached into his pants pocket, pulled out a handkerchief, and held it under his nose.

He wondered where he was, how he had gotten here. Looking around, he spotted a brown leather suitcase. It wasn't his, he knew. How had it arrived here in the middle of nowhere?

Then it all came back to him. The small suitcase belonged to Sara. Sara! he thought. Her suitcase here. Why? The men on the train. The falling, falling, the noise, the sudden blackness . . . Had those horrible men also thrown Sara off the train? He had to know. He had to search for her . . .

He walked to the suitcase and picked it up. He was tempted to open it but refrained. He searched the immediate area with his eyes. The land was flat here, dotted with brush and a number of broad, tall, leafy trees. And, in every direction, the flatness of the land ended with mountains not too far off in the distance. It was beautiful country, but he couldn't appreciate its magnificence; to Stevenson, a stranger, the region seemed lonely, bleak, foreboding.

Something seemed out of place before him. He squinted his eyes and focused on the object. It was another satchel, about fifty yards in front of him. It looked like one of his. He marched forward to get it.

It was his, he knew as he got closer; it was the brown cloth satchel he had been carrying his books in. It was filthy, but appeared not to be damaged. He hoped the same would hold true for the books inside. Several of them were favorites of his and very hard to replace.

He knelt down next to the bag and opened it. But instead of finding his copy of Tobias Smollett's *Humphry Clinker* or the various books by Shakespeare, Sir Walter Scott, or the American poet Walt Whitman he had heard so much about, he found the satchel contained nothing but stack upon stack of American paper money. It was a shock to him. He had never even dreamed of this much money. How did it get there? Who put it there? Why? And where were his books?

These questioning thoughts were interrupted by the

sound of a distant voice. Stevenson could not make out the words, but the voice was clearly female. Sara! It had to be Sara. His heart raced, and he left the satchel where it was. He stood up, walked forward, and tried to locate Sara.

He heard the voice again. It seemed to be coming from an area directly ahead of him, an area more heavily-wooded than his immediate surroundings. He headed for the trees.

"Sara!" he called, edging ever forward. There was no answer.

"I say, Sara, is that you? Are you all right?"

Still there was no answer. At last he entered the tree-shaded expanse of land. The absence of light forced him to slow down for a moment, and he seemed to be almost temporarily blind as his eyes adjusted to the change.

He stepped forward and saw someone. But it wasn't Sara. It was a man. A man with long, black, flowing hair. A man wearing feathers on his head. A man clothed in animal-skin pants. A man carrying a rifle in one hand and a knife in the other.

It was the first time the Scotsman had seen an Indian face to face. The man didn't move. He just stared at Stevenson. Frightened, Stevenson was about to turn and run, but an arm encircled his waist from behind, and another went around his neck, its hand covering his mouth.

He couldn't speak, and he couldn't move. The hand below his nose smelled musky, and the voice that spoke behind his head uttered some unintelligible words. Everything that Stevenson had ever read or heard about American Indians flashed into his mind. He would be stripped, tortured, scalped, sent through a gauntlet. He would be killed slowly, skinned alive perhaps, bit by bit. His fingers would be pulled out of their sockets, ripped or cut off at the knuckle, and fed to animals.

Oh, Fanny! he cried silently, why have you summoned

me to my death in this land of savages and violence?

The Indian who held him said into his ear, "Remain silent. Do not try to escape."

He speaks English, the Scotsman thought. Can these savages be reasoned with?

Then the grip was released and Stevenson could breathe more freely. He was too frightened to even turn and look at the Indian who had held him. He directed his stare to the fierce-looking brave who stood before him, still holding the rifle and the knife. He had barely moved. His face seemed frozen in a scowl.

Then the Indian behind him again spoke. "Your friend?" he asked.

Stevenson hadn't the slightest idea what he was talking about, so he didn't answer.

The Indian repeated the question, grabbing the writer by the shoulders and physically turning in a clockwise direction. "The woman is your friend?" he again asked, pointing to the women who was approaching, accompanied by an Indian brave on either side.

"Yes," he managed to say, forcing the word from his throat.

Sara's dress was torn from one shoulder. The tear revealed the whiteness of the top of her left breast, a sight that at another time Stevenson might have found quite stimulating. Right now he was afraid the Indians might find that sight just as stimulating, and want to see more.

"You come with us," the Scotsman's captor said.

Stevenson finally screwed up enough courage to look the savage in the face. He was somber-looking and wore several more feathers than his fellow braves. Some adorned the top of his head, and others hung from braids down around his neck.

"Where are you taking us?" he asked.

"You come. No ask questions."

Then Stevenson noticed that Sara had been tied and gagged. A cloth of some kind had been shoved into her mouth.

"Why have you restrained her?" Stevenson asked angrily.

The leader did not appreciate the anger in the Scotsman's voice nor the question itself. He stared defiantly at his prisoner and said, "Woman tied because she no stop talking, no stop asking questions. You get same if you ask more questions. Now go!" The brave gestured to the edge of the wooded area.

When he passed her, Sara pushed into Stevenson, who held her for a moment. He looked into her eyes. She seemed frightened, but relatively unhurt. There was a bruise, though, over her right eye. It was small and was beginning to turn bluish-green. He wondered if she had received the injury from the Indians or from the fall from the train.

He put his arm around her, and together they walked forward, surrounded by the Indian braves. They were led to horses. Sara was taken from Stevenson and placed upon a handsome palomino with the leader of the party, who sat behind her. Stevenson was lifted onto a brown horse behind one of the braves. Then the rest of the party mounted their steeds, and the band galloped off toward the mountains.

Chapter Twenty-five

Although it was still early in the afternoon, and the sun's rays gave the mountains a gray-gold shine, a fire burned in the center of the clearing. Around it stood several Indians, poking the deer that was being roasted above the flames. When the horses carrying the two white people entered the camp, one of the men attending the fire left his post and went into a nearby cave.

Stevenson watched the man disappear into the mountain, and a moment later come back out, followed by a dozen other braves and a man wearing a truly regal, flamboyant headpiece of feathers. The Scotsman figured this had to be the tribe's chief, perhaps the most savage of the bunch. Wasn't that, after all, how one became chief? Didn't one have to prove his savagery, his cruelty, his ferocity? He was already worried, but at the sight of the statuesque man with the multi-plumed head decoration, the Scotsman's heart felt as if it was about to shatter inside his chest.

The riders stopped. The man standing next to the chief approached the party and signaled to the braves to dismount with their captives.

When everyone was standing, the chief pointed to Sara and Stevenson, and two braves held them by the arms and

148

walked them nearer to the chief. The chief gestured again, and Sara's ropes were untied and the gag removed from her mouth. Both white people stood silently as the chief inspected them with his eyes.

After a quiet couple of moments, he spoke. "You do not look like a white man of this area," he said to Stevenson in a deep voice that spoke surprisingly good English. "Are you from the East? Have you been sent by the white leaders in Washington to find me?"

Stevenson was amazed, both at the question and the savage's ability with the language. "No. I am from another country. I am not seeking you. I don't even know who you are."

The chief's face grew distressed and appeared angry. His bushy brown eyebrows pivoted, giving him the look of a scowling owl.

"And the white woman?"

"She is from the East, but she is not seeking you either. We were captured by your men and brought here. We mean you no harm."

The chief stared at Stevenson and then at Sara.

"You speak the truth?" he asked.

"I do."

"I believe you," the chief said. "You carry no weapon. You speak the language different than most whites."

One of the braves who had captured the pair stepped forward and handed the chief a pistol. He spoke a few words, then stepped away from the chief and returned to his horse.

"The woman carried this weapon beneath her clothing in a place where no white man would look. It is a woman's weapon, small, weak, good for shooting nothing but rabbits."

He walked up to Sara and, to Stevenson's surprise, handed the small caliber pistol back to Sara.

"Where are you bound?" the chief asked Sara.

"San Francisco," she answered.

The chief said nothing, but he made no secret of the pleasure he was getting looking at Sara's half-exposed breast. He raised his hand toward the unconcealed flesh.

"Keep your filthy hands off her, you barbarian," Stevenson shouted at the chief.

The chief's hand stopped just short of touching her. He turned his head to look at his male captive and said, "I was about to tell the white woman that her dress will be repaired for her. Why then do you call me a bar . . . barbar . . . ?"

"Barbarian," Stevenson gulped, realizing that once again his quickness of mouth may have gotten him in more trouble.

The chief lowered his hand. "What is this word . . . barbarian?"

"It's just a word," Stevenson said lamely.

"Yes, I know. And its meaning?"

"It means . . . warrior," Stevenson croaked. He prayed the chief would accept his lying answer.

"Tell me, white man," the chief repeated, drawing closer to the Scotsman. "Tell me the truth. You would not call me a warrior if you thought I was about to harm your woman."

He knew it was time to tell the truth even if the truth got him killed; he might be killed anyway for lying.

"Savage. It means savage." Stevenson lowered his eyes to the ground, distressed.

"Yes," the chief smiled, "savage . . . barbarian. The white man's favorite word for us. I must remember it . . . barbarian!"

"What are you going to do with us?" Sara asked, interrupting the chief's amusement with this new addition to his vocabulary.

"Yes. We must do something." He turned to one of his aides and pointed to his right. "Into the cave."

Stevenson and Sara were marched into the cave. It was dimly-lit and blankets were spread across the floor. The chief took his place and sat down. Then, palms up, he spread his arms wide, and everyone else sat down. The two captives remained standing.

"Sit," the chief said to them. "You have nothing to fear. You will not be harmed."

The captives did as they were told, although neither believed the chief's assurances of their safety.

"What do they call you?" the chief asked Stevenson.

"My name is Robert Louis Stevenson."

"And you?"

"Sara Hillyer."

The chief smiled. "They are good names—for whites. They sound good. My name is . . . the whites call me Joseph."

"Joseph?" Stevenson repeated. "A Christian name?"

"The name missionaries gave my father, and then was given to me."

"Are you a Christian?"

"I am a Nez Perce!" he said proudly.

"A what?"

"A Nez Perce!" the chief repeated. "You have never heard of my people?" He seemed somewhat insulted, but quickly changed his mind. "I forgot. You are not of this country."

"But even those words cannot be Indian words," Stevenson declared. " 'Nez perce' is a French term."

"That is true. The name was given to us by white men who spoke a language different in many sounds."

"I see."

"What do you see?"

"I don't see anything, really," Stevenson said. "I mean I understand."

"Then why do you say 'I see'?"

"It's just another way of saying 'I understand.' "

Joseph smiled and shook his head. "I will never fully understand this white man's language. It is a language that says one thing, yet means another."

"Are you trying to learn it? You speak it rather well."

"Thank you. I can speak the language and be understood, but it is different from my language. The language of the Nez Perce says what it means, and it means nothing else."

Sara was still visibly nervous and could not get comfortable sitting on the blanket. Stevenson, however, felt somewhat relieved. He was amazed at the chief's command of English, even with its limitations, and hoped that Joseph was a man of his word and would not harm them. He planned to keep the conversation going a while longer; perhaps he could reason with the chief and persuade him to let them go.

"Do you live here, Joseph?" he asked.

Suddenly, one of the braves inside the cave stood up. Angrily, he announced, "He is a great chief. Do not call him Joseph."

Stevenson looked at the man, and then turned toward the chief. "I meant no disrespect."

Joseph nodded and waved his arm for the brave to retake his seat. "Call me Chief Joseph. It is the way of my people, and they will be upset if you do not."

"Again, I apologize, Chief Joseph."

The chief turned his attention to Sara. "You are the woman of this man?" he asked, pointing at Stevenson.

She grabbed Stevenson's hand before he could say anything. "Yes. He is my husband."

Joseph, however, was observant, and spotted the look of surprise on the Scotsman's face. For a moment he simply stared at his two guests, then he began to smile. "It seems that your 'husband' does not agree with your answer."

Sara grew nervous, while Stevenson's face filled with the crimson hue of embarrassment. He tried to remove his

152

hand from her grasp, but she had a good grip on it and wouldn't let go. Then they both just sat still, not knowing what to say.

Joseph spoke for them. "You are not married. I know this. And I know why you spoke the lie. You are afraid, woman, that I or one of my tribe will force himself on you." His smile developed into a hearty laugh. And as he laughed, the other members of the tribe in the cave laughed also.

"I don't see what the humor is in that," Stevenson said.

The chief stopped laughing and repeated, "See?"

"I mean I don't understand."

"You must forgive the laughter," Joseph said. "It is a common belief of the whites that my tribe, and all others, live only to pursue white women." The smile faded, and in its place came a somber, serious expression. "It is not so. The Nez Perce do not kill mercilessly, do not torture, do not rape. Especially those who follow Joseph. I speak not for all tribes, but for the Nez Perce the words are true."

The captives sat quietly. Stevenson studied the chief; Sara stared at the ground between her and Joseph.

Then Joseph smiled again and continued. "If we wanted you, white woman, did you think the laws of the whites would stop us? They would not. What the whites call matri . . . matri . . ."

"Matrimony," Stevenson chimed in.

". . . that has no meaning to us. We have tried to live by the white man's rules. When we do not obey, we are treated like the buffalo, hunted, shot. When we obey them—and we have tried to live by white law—we are still hunted like the beasts. The whites want what is ours, and for many winters and summers we let them take, hoping that the Nez Perce and the whites could live like brothers. But it is not to be. To the whites—to you—we are savages. And we will always be savages. Nez Perce or Crow, Cheyenne or Sioux, savages all. We are not so foolish. We know that some white men are evil, some aren't. We do not kill all, fight all."

Stevenson was fascinated by the chief's words. He wanted to know more. "Why then did you capture us and bring us here?"

Joseph sighed. "Even now, we are being hunted by the white men. My braves mistook you for those who hunt us. We must be careful."

"But one man and one woman? Would one man and one woman hunt alone for a large group of Nez Perce warriors?"

"The white man has many ways of killing," Joseph went on. "With guns and knives, but other ways, ways that are strange to us. At this very sunset, members of my tribe still on the Okanogan Reservation . . ." the name was spoken with great distaste, ". . . are dying from sickness unknown to us before the coming of the whites. Chief Moses, my brother, remains there, watching our people die . . ."

Suddenly, Joseph stopped talking. His teeth were clenched in an effort to prevent the tears from welling up in his eyes. He swallowed with great difficulty.

Sara and Stevenson both knew to remain silent and respect the man's grief. The cave's silence was overwhelming; Stevenson had the eerie, inexplicable feeling he was in the midst of some religious service.

Joseph swallowed again, looked at the members of his tribe and then at the two outsiders. "Enough," he stated coldly. "We shall speak more tomorrow. Now we must eat and sleep."

He quickly stood up and left the cave, followed by all but two of his braves, who were evidently appointed guards. One of them gestured that the couple should also leave the cave.

Stevenson stood up and helped Sara to her feet. She was trembling slightly.

"I guess we're stuck here for the night," she said quietly.

"It seems that way," Stevenson agreed. "Don't be afraid. I can't quite explain it, but *I'm* no longer afraid. I trust Chief Joseph. He's the very embodiment of what Rousseau referred to as 'the noble savage.' "

"Rousseau who?"

"I'll explain later, Sara. But briefly, he was a great French philosopher who maintained that men who were close to a natural state were good until they were corrupted by the trappings of civilization."

Sara shook her head. "Louis, I don't know what you're talkin' about. All I know is I'm still scared, and now that the chief's given my gun back to me, I'm not sleepin' a wink tonight, and I'm not lettin' this gun out of my sight."

"You must be more trusting, Sara."

"Trust Indians? You trust them," she said. Then she jiggled the pistol a bit. "I'll trust this."

Again the guard gestured for them to leave the cave and join the meal outside. The sun was beginning to set, and the sky's orange tint was close to that of the fire. Another brave, one they had not seen before, one with a very young face and a derby hat on his head, handed each of them a juicy chunk of deer meat.

"Eat!" he said.

Simultaneously, they both took bites of their dinner. Stevenson privately thanked God he had lived to see another meal. Sara wondered if she would live to see breakfast.

Chapter Twenty-six

On the Central Pacific

The train screeched like a thousand buzzards screaming all at once. Everyone and everything on board the train was thrown forward. Women and children screamed, and the sounds of human beings crying blended with the metallic shriek of the braking train scraping along the steel tracks.

Doc picked himself off the floor. "What the hell is going on?" he cried.

McCain managed not to be thrown out of his seat. He held on to an arm rest and had time to brace his feet.

The screech continued and the train began to take a slight turn to the left. Doc got back into his seat by one of the windows on the train's left side, and, balancing himself, managed to open the window and poke his head outside.

"Jesus!" he said. "The track's torn to hell up ahead."

McCain maneuvered next to Doc and could see the bent rails, curled and pointing up to the sky. "This doesn't look good. Only dynamite could've done that damage. This smells like a holdup."

"It sure does. But right now I'm hopin' this train can stop in time. That torn up track ain't too far ahead."

The screeching continued, as did the human cries inside the car. People clutched their children, their baggage, each other. It sounded like someone had opened the gates of hell.

Finally, the train stopped, not more than fifty feet from the destroyed track. All was silent except for the wailing of the several children on board.

Doc continued to keep vigil at the window. After a moment, he nudged McCain with his elbow and said "Look!" He pointed to a hill less than a quarter of a mile away, a hill that marked the end of the flatlands they were crossing.

It took a minute for McCain to locate what Doc was pointing to. But then he saw them.

"Indians."

"Yeah, Indians," Doc repeated. "Probably them damn Nez Perce we heard about at the train station."

"Yeah, but something ain't right."

"Huh?"

"I never heard of the Nez Perce being so good with explosives."

"So they learned. Who gives a damn?"

Doc stared at the Indians, who were descending the hill, making their way to the train. There were about twenty of them that Doc could see; he wondered if there were more attacking from the other side of the train. All of them were carrying rifles.

Doc checked his Colt and his carbine and found them both fully loaded. "I'm ready for the bastards," he said. "Let 'em come."

McCain walked across the train and looked out the windows on the right side. He could see no Indians at all.

"Looks like they're all comin' from this side," he said, retaking his seat. "That ain't right, either. The Nez Perce are smart. These fellows ain't too bright if they're attacking from one spot."

Doc looked at McCain with an expression of anger and bewilderment. "I don't give a coyote's ass who they are. Maybe they're Iroquois out here for a vacation. I really don't give a good goddamn. I just want to protect my money here. Understand?" He wiped away the saliva that had built up in his mouth during his tirade. "Anyhow, what makes you such an expert on Indians?"

"I used to be a cavalry scout," he said.

Doc was truly fed up with this know-it-all. "Maybe you shoulda stayed in the cavalry. Custer coulda used ya, the poor bastard."

McCain grinned solemnly. "I used to be his scout."

Doc's eyes opened wide in surprise. "What?"

"Long before Little Big Horn. I got transferred to another regiment. He tried to have me court-martialed."

"Why?"

"I got tired of taking his crap. He treated his own men as bad as he treated the Indians." McCain spat on the floor of the train. "There were other reasons, too. Personal ones."

"That's real interesting, McCain. But right now . . ."

Doc never finished his sentence. A bullet shattered the window next to his face, and a second later he was screaming like a polecat. He dropped his gun in his lap and reached to the left side of his face.

McCain saw the pointed, triangular shard of glass sticking deep into Doc's cheek.

"Son of a bitch!" he screamed, trying to pull the glass out. A thin trickle of blood poured down his cheek and began to collect in the wrinkles of his neck. "Goddamn it!"

"Let me get it," McCain said.

Doc removed his hand, and McCain held the piece of glass between the forefinger and thumb of his right hand. "Hang on," he said, and jerked the glass out of Doc's cheek. He dropped the bloody shard and then tore a piece of his shirt sleeve off and pressed it to the bloody slit.

"You okay?" McCain asked.

"Yeah," he answered angrily. "But those damn Nezzes are dead men."

Chapter Twenty-seven

Several shots were fired from the other train cars, and small puffs of gunsmoke filled the air outside the windows. The train evidently had at least six security guards, McCain thought, and the usual array of employees, hopefully all well-armed.

He drew his Colt and made his way to the window behind Doc. He smashed the glass with the end of the gun's barrel and took aim at one of the approaching attackers. The bullet missed the man, but it nicked the horse the Indian was riding. It stopped short, kicked its front legs up in the air, and whinnied in pain. The man's rifle flew up into the smoky air, and he was bucked off the steed; then he crashed down onto the dusty ground. His foot was still caught in the right stirrup, and when the horse bolted forward, it dragged him along the ground, twisting, trying to release his foot.

McCain watched the man struggle. Then he noticed something quite interesting, something that confirmed his suspicions. The man's headdress was coming apart, and eventually it was wrenched off when the back of his head was dragged over a rock. The feathers had concealed a head of close-cropped blond hair.

This man was no Nez Perce.

Holliday, still holding the bloody piece of cloth to his face with his left hand, pointed his pistol out the window and fired four shots in rapid succession. At least one of the shots connected; an attacker less than a dozen yards in front of Doc took a bullet in the side of his neck. The flesh opened up like a second screaming mouth, vomiting blood that sprayed out onto his right shoulder and drenched his arm, his leg, and the horseflesh underneath the leg. After a few seconds, the body slid away from the saddle and off the horse.

Suddenly, a man opened the door of the train car and stepped inside. The passengers were already in a frenzy, running, ducking behind seats, or lying on the floor, trying to avoid the bullets of the marauders. This newcomer, stylishly dressed in a red and white flannel shirt, black rope tie, and blue jeans, proceeded to frighten the carload of people even more.

"There must be a hundred of 'em!" he announced loudly, and pushed forward into the car, waving his pistol for emphasis.

Doc heard what the man said and took a long look out the window. There weren't even half a hundred men outside, at least not that he could see. He turned and studied the man; after he was satisfied, he raised his Colt and fired a shot over the seats. A black hole surrounded by a rapidly-spreading blood stain formed on the man's shoulder. The gun he had been waving fell to the floor, and he placed his other hand over the wound. Unable to stand any longer, the man toppled into a seat and unsuccessfully tried to stop the flow of blood. Then, silently, he passed out.

"You villain!" a woman shouted at Doc. "Why did you do that?"

Doc wasn't going to bother answering the woman—a pretty one, he noticed, about forty years old with extremely big breasts that even her loose-fitting calico dress couldn't hide—but he figured it might help prevent his getting a slug in the back if his fellow train-riders understood his action.

"He's one of 'em," Doc said quickly. "That's a real old trick, panicking the passengers into thinkin' there's more of 'em out there than there really are so they'll surrender."

"But how can you be so sure?" the woman asked, unconvinced.

"Lady, neither you nor I got time to be sure of anything. Now stay down on the floor and shut yer trap 'fore it's too late."

He resumed firing out the window and noticed that the ranks of the attackers were thinning out. He also realized they were starting to pull away from the train. Not really retreating. Just shying away, still firing, edging slightly and slowly away.

"I don't get it," McCain said. "What the hell are they doing?"

Doc leaned forward and stuck his head out the window, stretching his neck, trying to gaze up the track. Since the train had stopped on a slight curve to the left, he was able to spy what he was looking for: a thin, steady wisp of smoke coming from beneath the cargo car.

He pulled his head back inside. "Brace yourselves!" he yelled at the top of his lungs. "They're gonna blow the freight car!"

Doc barely had the words out when a thunderous explosion rocked the entire train. The wind blew a giant fog of dark smoke, pieces of steel, and splinters of wood past the windows. When the smoke cleared a bit, Doc put his head outside the train and looked down the track.

"Jesus!" he hollered. "They knocked three cars off the track."

Most of the braver passengers on board made their way to the left side of the car and craned their necks to get a peek at the destruction. Those who could see saw the freight car sitting almost sideways on the track. The coal car in front of the freight car and the passenger car directly behind the freight car—the one carrying the Chinese—were also partially jerked off the track.

"Look what the bastards done!" Doc exclaimed.

"Never mind that," McCain chimed in. He was staring out the window, but at the so-called Indians and not the badly-out-of-joint train. "Here they come again."

The fifteen or so remaining attackers spread out, most heading for the freight car containing the train's safe and any other valuables. Several of them posted themselves parallel to the other cars and systematically fired through the windows, not caring who or what they hit.

Bullets sprayed the car near the windows where Doc and McCain sat. The latter heard a shot whiz by his ear; it was so close he could feel the heat of it. It was too close for his taste.

"They got our number, Doc," he said. "Let's move. One of those bastards seems to have chosen these two windows for target practice."

"Good idea," Doc responded. "I don't hear a hell of a lot of shots bein' fired from the train. They musta got most of the guards."

"Sounds that way."

"Prob'ly got 'em with that explosion. Musta rocked the hell outta them."

"I'm gonna make my way outside the car. Feel like getting some air?"

Another two windows shattered farther down the car. Several people screamed. One of the passengers—the woman who had cursed Doc for shooting the intruder—was struck between her huge breasts by a passing bullet. She slid backward, then silently dropped to the floor. The screams of the other passengers alerted everyone that she had been hit. She died without uttering a sound.

When Doc shook his head, a few pieces of broken glass fell out of his long brown hair. "No, sir. I'll change my seat, but I'm stayin' on this train with this satchel under my feet.

Them bastards ain't gettin' it; I ain't lettin' it leave my sight."

McCain nodded and started to move away. Doc grabbed his arm just over the wrist and restrained him for a moment.

"Try to make your way up to the freight car. I'll cover you best I can from here."

Again McCain nodded. Then he cautiously stepped toward the rear of the car. He had to step over several people who lay on the floor, huddling together, as out of the way of the barrage of bullets as they could manage. One of the men on the floor lay apart from the rest. Not a soul touched him. As McCain stepped over his legs, he noticed that the man's head was wedged in the space between two seats. The part of his face that he could see was covered with blood; a part of the scalp had been peeled back, exposing the bone underneath.

It was a sight similar to ones McCain had seen many times. They used to make him nauseous when he was younger; now, however, after the sights he had seen with Custer . . . the sight of his sister with her throat cut and her guts damn near pulled out onto her stomach and in her lap . . . these sights lost their impact. There was still a feeling of nervousness, a tightening of the knot in his gut, and a rush of adrenaline within him. But instead of making him sick, these reactions heightened his senses and made him a far more dangerous man to those who threatened him. He turned away from the gory display and pulled open the rear door of the car.

McCain waited a moment before leaving the train. Then he pulled the door open and poked his head around it. He wanted to get off the car unseen. Luckily, someone on board, perhaps Doc, fired at the Indian most likely to spot him. The Indian fell back off his horse, and his body tumbled to the earth. McCain stepped out of the car, leapt to the ground, and moved out of sight.

The battle raged on, all on the left side of the train. He was correct in assuming these train robbers were amateurs and rather lacking in strategic skills; there were no men to be seen on the right side.

He crawled under the car he had just left and lay there for a moment, studying the battle. No one appeared to notice him. It seemed, therefore, that all he had to do was walk down the track on the right side of the train, and he would be shielded from gunfire. It was too good to be true.

He moved out from under the car and stood up, the train itself protecting him from the battle. The gunfire increased, but it sounded like it was mostly coming from the Indians. Carefully, he marched forward until he reached the front of the passenger car carrying the Chinese. From inside he could hear the utterances of the Orientals, although he couldn't understand a single word. He stopped for a moment, then peered around the edge of the car. Six attackers, all mounted, fired from atop their horses. They were shooting into the freight car, the door now partially open from the force of the blast.

It was clear to McCain that at that moment the Indians had the upper hand in this battle. He could hear someone firing from within the car, but the shots were infrequent and ineffective. Whatever the Indians were after was still in the freight car, and it seemed that perhaps only one man inside kept them from attaining it.

It was time to even up the odds a bit.

McCain checked his Colt; it was nearly empty. Quickly, he snatched five cartridges from his gunbelt and placed them one by one into the weapon. Then he leaned around the end of the car, enough so that he could aim, but still have the car in front of most of his body for protection.

He fired once, hitting the Indian farthest from the train in the hip. Blood sprayed from the creased flesh at the top of the man's right leg. Then the Indian fell forward onto his horse's neck. His limp arms tried to hold on, but there was no strength in them. After another second, he fell, and his lifeless body kicked up a cloud of dust.

The other attackers' eyes searched for the assassin. Before they could locate him, though, McCain squeezed off another shot, one that took a man's hand off. The Indian screamed as blood dripped like water from a very leaky pump.

Finally, one of the attackers spotted McCain. He pointed at him, and before McCain could fire again, the band of four divided. Two headed for the rear of the train; one headed for its front; and the man who had seen him remained where he was, firing alternately at McCain and the man or men in the car.

Damn, thought McCain, at least they knew to split up and try to surround him. But he was ready for them, if and when they showed up on this side of the train.

It would be a shorter ride to the front, he knew, so he kept a watchful eye in that direction. Sure enough, one Indian turned the corner near the locomotive. He steadied his horse, raised his rifle, and took aim at McCain. But before he could pull the trigger, the man on foot fired. The bullet must have hit the rifle because the gun went flying out of the man's grasp, and he held his hands aloft as if they were burned. The second bullet from McCain's Colt hit the man squarely in the chest, and he flew off the back of the horse.

The volume of gunfire increased toward the rear of the train. Quickly, McCain looked in that direction, but the two Indians had not made it to this side of the cars yet. Then he turned back to check on the Indian near the freight car.

Suddenly, something grabbed him around the ankles and pulled, sending him face-first into the dirt. It was the man he had been looking for. He was under the train car, a knife clenched in his teeth.

The Indian removed the blade, crawled out from under

166

the car, and leaped at McCain. There was no time for him to aim, but McCain managed to get to his knees, and with an upward swing of his arm caught the Indian under the jaw with the barrel of his gun. The blow sent the brave crashing to the ground on McCain's right. The knife flew from his hand. He lay there on his back, unable to focus on anything.

But he did hear McCain's voice.

"Don't move a finger, or you're a dead man!"

And he felt the cold metallic tip of McCain's Colt pressed against his left cheek.

Still in a kneeling position, McCain saw a motion from the corner of his eye. Another man walked toward him, but he recognized the rather portly man as George Wright, the Pinkerton agent.

"They're pullin' out," Wright said. "The bastards are leavin'. We warded 'em off."

It was then that McCain noticed that the gunfire had almost completely subsided. A stray shot or two could be heard now and then, but the battle sounded over.

Wright stepped closer to McCain. "Got yourself a prisoner, do ya? Nice work. They'll string this Indian up for sure."

McCain gave the Pinkerton a look of disgust. "This man's about as much Nez Perce as you are." He pulled his captive forward until he was sitting up. Then he yanked at his hair. The brown, braided wig came off with little resistance.

Wright stared at the prisoner and then at McCain. He tried to hide the look of surprise on his face, but didn't do a very good job of it.

"White men!" he said. "Son of a bitch! I thought so all along." McCain stood up and pulled his prisoner by his now-shortened dirty blond hair until he too was on his feet. "Sure you did. I shoulda known they'd never be able to fool a well-trained agent like you."

Wright recognized the sarcasm in McCain's voice and wanted to respond, but he knew this wasn't the right time or the right place. Instead, he said, "I'll take the prisoner now."

Before turning him over, though, McCain spoke to him. "Don't you have anything to say, Indian? How's twenty years of hard labor sound to you?"

The man snarled and said. "Damn you!"

"What language is that?" he shot back. "Sounds more Shoshone than Nez Perce to me."

The Pinkerton grabbed the "Indian" by the arm, covering him with his agency-issued pistol. "Let's go." Slowly, the two made their way back into a passenger car.

McCain looked around for a moment. Everything was quiet except for the chattering of the passengers and crew and the snorting of several riderless horses whose owners' blood was now seeping into the grassy soil. He smacked the front of his pants legs with his hat in an attempt to shake the loose dust off them. Then he turned and headed back to see how Doc was faring.

Either Doc or someone else must have hit those two Indians who had headed for the rear of the train because neither of them ever made it to the other side. Or perhaps the pair had been two of the gang who escaped, McCain reasoned. He really didn't care much; either way, they were gone.

Many of the passengers began to step off the train onto the tracks and surrounding area. Some were simply stretching their legs. Others had a more somber purpose; men were carrying the bodies of the unfortunate railroad employees and the innocent passengers who had been killed. Since the disabled train wouldn't be going anywhere soon, it was an appropriate time for burying the dead.

As McCain passed their car, a group of Chinese men stepped off the car, and in five separate groups of two or three carried the corpses of four men and a woman. Mc-

Cain glanced at the face of the first body as it moved past him. The group of three men carried a Chinese woman of about thirty, her light unbleached cotton garments spattered with blood stains. One of the three men—her husband, McCain guessed—had tears in his eyes. The second group carefully, respectfully carted the body of a very old Chinese gentleman. His body seemed untouched by any of the violence that had taken place; McCain conjectured that the cause of death was perhaps a heart attack. The much younger men who transported his small, frail body were grief-stricken, tears pouring from their eyes, moans pouring from their mouths. They were all dressed in garments identical to those of the elder they carried.

McCain's interest was piqued when he saw the face of the third corpse: it was an Occidental face, round-eyed and full. And it was familiar, even through the bloody, puffed gashes that marked the cheeks and the reddish-brown streaks that looked like rope burns across the forehead.

It was one of Jack's friends, one of the men he had forced into the Orientals' passenger car. McCain took another, closer look at the body. It was a gory mess, and much of the mess rubbed off on the trio who carried it. Their hands, arms, and chests—and any other parts of their persons that came into contact with the corpse—were instantly and thoroughly bloodied.

Directly behind this troupe followed another, carrying a second white man. This victim too was a grisly sight. His face bore similar markings to the previous one, but this face was even more sickening to look at: it was missing an eye. McCain recognized the clothes if not the horribly mutilated face of Jack's other compadre.

The last group of four—the additional man was needed to transport the heavy body—quickly tried to pass by McCain, who had stopped in his tracks, watching the procession, partially in curiosity, partially in horror, but mostly in amused fascination. He blocked the path of the group and held up a hand indicating that they should halt. The men obeyed. McCain glanced at the dead man's face, even though he knew who it had to be. This face defied identification; it looked more like a muddy red puddle than a human face. He couldn't look at it for more than a couple of seconds, so he turned his head away a bit. He saw the bottom of the man's legs. One foot was bloodied and the front of the boot was ripped open, the shredded rim of the opening blackened from gunpowder, blood, and dirt.

It was Jack, all right.

McCain gave the Chinese credit. They had taken advantage of a perfect opportunity to take revenge on — and rid themselves of — three tormentors. No one would ask questions, even if someone noticed what they were doing in all the confused aftermath of the fumbled train robbery. And even if their actions were seen, proving that the three men weren't killed by the robbers would be difficult.

One of the bearers of Jack's body spoke. "All okay?" he asked. "We can bury?"

McCain couldn't resist asking the man a question. "Did the Indians do that to him?" He pointed at the body.

The Oriental nodded. "Yes. Indians kill. Very brave men, now dead. Indians kill."

"Yeah, very brave," McCain repeated. Then he waved on the four men.

Chapter Twenty-eight

"McCain! God damn it!"

Doc's voice rang out loud and clear, and McCain turned around and saw him approaching, dragging the brown satchel with him. All the color had gone out of his face. He looked like he had just seen some horrible apparition.

"What's the matter?"

Holliday threw the satchel down on the ground in front of McCain's feet. "Look in the bag."

"Why?"

"Just look in the damn bag, will ya?"

McCain squatted and reached inside and felt something soft. He figured Doc put the cotton shirt in the bag to cover the piles of bills.

Then he reached in again, wrapped his fingers around a rectangular object and raised it into the sunlight. It was a book. A heavy, thick one. He turned the book so he could read the slightly worn embossed lettering on the spine. Tobias Smollett it said at the top. The words *Humphry Clinker* appeared in bold lettering a bit farther down on the spine.

"Books!" Doc said angrily. "Fuckin' books! Where did they come from? Where's the money? This ain't my satchel. Where the hell is mine?"

Still hunched down, McCain said, "Slow down, Doc. Take it easy."

"Take it easy? How can I take it easy? I been robbed, man! Some sidewinder . . ."

McCain opened the book. "Well, here's part of the answer, although I can't put the whole picture together yet." He pointed to three words that had been handwritten in red ink on the inside cover: Robert Louis Stevenson.

"Stevenson?" Doc exclaimed, after reading the name. "The Scotsman? How the hell did he pull this off? That son of a bitch robbed me."

McCain reached back into the satchel. He pulled out another book. This one read *Don Juan* by George Gordon, Lord Byron. Then he put his hand in again, felt around in the bag, but there was nothing other than books in it.

"I'll kill that bastard. Somehow . . . somehow he took the money."

McCain took off his hat and scratched his head. "I don't think so, Doc. He was hardly the type."

Doc thought for a moment. "Maybe you're right. But that woman he was with—Sara Whatever-her-name was. She mighta done it."

"I doubt it."

"That Pinkerton fella thought she was up to no good."

"If you remember, he also thought we were up to something too."

Doc spat at the dirt near his feet. "Then how did this happen? How did I wind up with this bag full of books—like a God damn schoolboy? And where the hell is my money?"

"I don't know, Doc. I just know there has to be a reasonable explanation. So let's stay calm and think about it."

Doc lit up a cigarette in an attempt to calm his frazzled nerves. "I'm calm, but I still don't see how this could be."

"When Stevenson and Sara were thrown off the train," McCain mused out loud, "their baggage was thrown off

172

with them, right?"

"Yeah, I think some of it was."

"Maybe your bag got mixed up with their stuff some-how."

"Nah," Doc responded, shaking his head. "I had it the whole time."

"And nobody got near it?"

"Nobody but you."

"What's that supposed to mean?" McCain asked angrily. "You think I took it?"

"Could be."

"And you think if I had it I'd be talking to you? Brother, I'd be long gone. Anyhow, I don't have it, and as I told you before, I don't want anything except what's comin' to me."

Doc was reasonably sure McCain didn't have it. But he felt like taking his anger out on someone, and McCain was convenient. "Go on."

McCain thought about it more. He tried to recreate the time aboard the train in his mind. There was Wright and Doc's scuffle with him. But no one got near the bag then.

"Well, I don't hear nothin' now."

McCain ignored Doc and went on with his thoughts. There was the fight between Stevenson and Sara and the . . .

"Maybe . . ." McCain thought aloud.

"What? What?" Doc asked. "Speak up, for Christ's sake."

"That fellow during the fight . . ."

"What fellow? Which fight? Jesus, will you talk to me, man?"

"When that fellow fell on you during the fight on the train, somebody—Sara, I think—threw a satchel at him."

"So?"

"It landed right near you. Right near your bag. Then he threw one, I think."

Doc thought silently for a second and took a deep puff

on his cigarette. "You think he threw my bag?"

"Maybe. And if that was your satchel he tossed, then it woulda got mixed in with their other bags."

"It can't be," Doc countered. "How come neither one of us noticed that then? Them bags look that much alike?"

"I don't know," McCain replied, shaking his head. "I never really noticed it before." Then he pointed at the satchel full of books. "It does sorta look like yours. Same color, same shape, even beat up like yours."

"Son of a bitch!"

"You know what this means, Doc?"

"Yeah, I think I know. The goddamn bag is either in Stevenson's hands, or Sara's, or it's lyin' by the side of the track forty miles back, or . . . shit! Let's stop jawin' and head back."

"I hope I'm right," McCain said, beginning to doubt his own theory.

"You prob'ly are. I searched that train car from top to bottom, and the bag ain't on it."

Doc stomped on the inch of cigarette butt that he threw in the dirt. "Let's get us some horses."

McCain gestured with his head toward a couple of dead robbers' bodies. "We can take theirs. They won't be needin' them."

Chapter Twenty-nine

Dodge City

Even from inside his musty office with the doors closed, Bat Masterson could hear the dulled tramping of the hooves of the incoming horses and the occasional loud yell of one of the riders barking orders to his troop.

Bat put his half-empty cup of muddy, black coffee down on a pile of papers he should have been looking at. Paperwork bored him — it was more appropriate for a banker, he thought — and he always left it until the very last possible minute. The racket outside was in one way a welcome disturbance: it provided him with an excuse not to pick up his pencil and lessen the height of the pile.

He walked to the large front window of his office. Outside, dust flew everywhere. He could hardly see down the street. But he didn't have to. Several of the horsemen pulled up to his office and sat on their mounts, while others rode farther down the street, hollering and shooting off their guns indiscriminately. A few dismounted in front of the Long Ride Saloon. Bat noticed many of them had their guns drawn, and one or two entered the saloon.

When he opened the door and stepped outside, most of the dust had settled, and he could survey the situation better. The new arrivals numbered twenty-five or thirty. A good number of them were loudly yelling out the names of two men.

"Earp!"

"Holliday!"

"Get your asses out here!"

"You can't hide forever, Earp!"

Bat sucked in a deep breath and let it go, accompanied by the word "shit" in a whisper. Whoever these men were, they weren't here for a mere visit. Bat wondered what Earp or Holliday had done to rile them up. He didn't wonder long, though; the possibilities were endless. Hardly a day went by in Dodge when someone wasn't irked at the Earps for something.

A grizzled, haggard man in his sixties got off his brown gelding and stepped up onto the boardwalk in front of Bat's office. He stared at Masterson for a moment, then spoke.

"You're Sheriff Bat Masterson, ain't ya?"

Bat pointed backward over his shoulder. "That's what the sign there says. Why are you boys runnin' 'round like wolves on the prowl?"

A younger man, dressed in a red and white cotton shirt and blue jeans filthy with cow manure, brashly answered for the older man. "We're lookin' for that damned Earp. Where is he?"

Bat smiled at the brazen lad. "Now which Earp is the 'damned' Earp? I'm afraid I get 'em all mixed up."

"None of the men found the sheriff's jest amusing. The young cowboy tried to speak again, but his words were cut short by the older man.

"Shut up, Jed!" he said. "I'll do the talkin', 'specially since you can't control the filth that flows from your mouth."

He turned toward Masterson and continued. "Sheriff, we got proof that Wyatt Earp's men have been rustlin' cattle from our ranches for the last few years. My men here—all honest Kansas ranchers—want justice done. And that means we want Earp's head."

This was the first time Bat had heard the Earps accused of cattle rustling. He knew most of their businesses, but this one was a revelation even to him. It didn't really surprise him much.

"What kind of proof are we talkin' 'bout?"

"Don't tell him nothin'," Jed said. "He's one of Earp's friends too."

"I told you to shut up," the old man repeated, then turned back to Bat. "Sheriff, believe me, we got proof. We'll be happy to show it to you after we find Earp. Now do you know where he is or not?"

"What might your name be?" Bat asked. "I don't usually supply folks with information like that until I know who they are."

"The name's Keyes. Mike Keyes."

"Well, Mr. Keyes, I suggest you and your boys settle down and have a drink. As far as I know, Earp ain't in town." Bat knew that Wyatt *was* in town, but he was buying time for Earp—and himself. "I'll go have a look-see around if that's what you want."

"We don't want no drink," Jed yelled. "We want Earp, mister."

Masterson stroked his dark, thick moustache with the thumb and forefinger of his right hand and stared at the young man. "Son, Mr. Keyes told you to shut up. Now I'm tellin' you the same thing. And I ain't as friendly or as tolerant as Mr. Keyes. Understand me, boy?"

Jed saw the icy glare on Bat's face, and any response he might have had was blocked by the lump that formed in his throat. He looked away in an attempt to hide the fear he suddenly felt.

"Now, Mr. Keyes," Bat continued, "as I was sayin', why don't you boys go have a drink across the street." He pointed to the entrance of the Long Ride. "Some of your people are already there. Why don't you go join them? I can't have you shootin' up the town 'cause you're lookin' for Earp."

"Just tell us where he is."

"If I knew, I might tell you, but I don't. And ridin' 'round like a lynch mob ain't gonna bring him out if he is around. There's at least two dozen of you men. Earp can count, you know. The odds ain't exactly in his favor."

Keyes ran his fingers through his long, stringy, graying hair. "How do I know you ain't gonna find him and help him organize a bunch of his men against us? Or maybe you'll hide him someplace."

Bat smiled. It was a good question. He wouldn't have helped Wyatt fight these men; however, warning him to go underground for a while was another matter.

"Look," he said, "I don't need Earp turnin' this town into a battleground either. If you don't trust me to do my job, you or one of your boys can come with me."

Keyes thought about the proposition for a moment. Then he said, "Fine. I'll go."

Before Bat could nod his head in agreement, the shouts of the men in front of the Long Ride distracted him. The men were watching a brawl that had made its way from the interior of the saloon to the boardwalk outside. One of the men involved in the skirmish was Luke Adams; Bat didn't recognize his opponent, although he guessed it was one of Keyes' men.

"We ain't goin' anywhere right now," he said, "except across the street."

"It's Bruford," Keyes said. Then he yelled the man's name out, but Bruford either ignored it or didn't hear it because he continued to roll in the street with his hands around Adams' thick, sweaty neck.

"Kill him!" one of the men on horseback screamed to Bruford.

Bat was close enough now to notice the blue rising to the

178

surface of Adams's face. The short bartender was trying to break free of Bruford's hold, but not having much success. Suddenly, he jerked his body, reached up, and grabbed hold of a handful of Bruford's hair. He yanked hard and managed to pull his opponent off-balance. The grip around his throat loosened, and Adams sucked fresh air into his lungs.

The oxygen — and the cheers of several of the Long Ride's regular patrons — helped. With a sudden burst of energy Adams threw a clenched fist into the side of the head he still held by the hair with his other hand. Bruford fell off him to the left.

"Stick him!" a man standing in the doorway of the saloon encouraged. "Gut him like a pig!"

Adams knelt over the man, and Bat saw the bartender's hand slip inside his boot and draw out a long hunting knife. He also saw many of the spectators on both sides reach for the guns strapped to their hips.

Bat quickly drew and fired his Colt Peacemaker into the air. "Nobody move!" he commanded. "Or the next one hits more than sky. Luke, get off him. This has gone far enough."

Luke had the knife just inches above the frightened man's face. He stared defiantly at Bat, the blade wavering in his shaking hand.

"I said get off him, Luke," the sheriff repeated. Then, with a more threatening tone, he added, "Now!"

Adams looked around at the faces of the men surrounding him. Even in his rage he knew if he killed this man who had come into his saloon and threatened him, he would never leave the street alive. There were too many men. And there was Masterson, whom he never trusted either.

He pulled the knife away from Bruford's face and slowly stood up. He held the blade by his side and turned to Masterson. "Happy now?"

All eyes turned to Bat, waiting for the next act to begin,

but it was Keyes who spoke first.

"Everybody inside," he said, gesturing toward the Long Ride. "Let's cool off with a beer. The sheriff and me are goin' to have a talk with the famous Mr. Wyatt Earp—if we can find him, that is. Ain't that right, Sheriff?"

"Right."

Adams's eyes opened wide with anger, and he puffed out a breath of indignation. "These bastards ain't steppin' foot in my place. They threaten me in my own place, and then I'm supposed to welcome 'em with open arms?"

"Just let 'em sit a while and cool down," Bat responded. "You don't got to welcome no one; just let 'em have a drink."

"They stink of cowshit."

"Just let 'em in, Luke."

"No."

Calmly, Masterson approached Luke and threw his arm around him. Then he whispered in his ear. "Let 'em in or I'll break your damn neck. And after I'm done, Earp will break the rest of you."

The crowd could hear nothing that was said, and all they could see was the broad smile on the sheriff's face.

"Fine. They can come in. We'll talk more about this later."

"That a boy, Luke. Now you're bein' reasonable."

"Soon, Bat. Real soon we'll talk."

The implied threat was clear to everyone, but it didn't seem to faze Masterson at all. He turned his back on Adams while he was still talking and faced Keyes. "Shall we go?"

Keyes nodded. As the two men walked away, the crowd outside the saloon made its way inside.

Chapter Thirty

It took a while, but finally Keyes was convinced. Earp wasn't around.

Masterson had taken him to various spots in Dodge, most known as hangouts for Earp and his cohorts: Moore's General Store, run by Mark Moore, a second or third cousin of Earp, a store that sold as many illegally-acquired Army-issue weapons as bags of flour; the marshal's office, where neither he nor the marshal were; and Katie's house at the other end of town. When the two men entered the house, Katie herself greeted them. She told them Wyatt hadn't been around for a few days; in fact, he had gone out of town with his brother James, who was half-owner of Katie's business.

"We could spend all day sight-seein', Sheriff," Keyes said after a while. "That ain't exactly what I got in mind. Maybe I should go back to the saloon and send my men out to look for Earp like I was gonna when we rode in. We're just wastin' time like this."

"That ain't a good idea at all," Bat commented, following Keyes as he made his way from the front door of Katie's back toward the Long Ride. "You'll be wastin' your time like that too. Earp ain't in town. I told you that an hour ago. Everybody else has told you the same thing. And as for Holliday, he left for up north somewhere a few days ago."

Keyes stopped walking. "Well, that's true, because I seen Holliday myself up north of here."

"See? I ain't lyin' to you."

"He had someone ridin' with him. I didn't recognize him. Know who he might be?"

Bat knew. It had to be McCain. "It coulda been anybody."

"I suppose."

"Now what are we gonna do? Do you plan to tear the town apart lookin' for folks who ain't here? Or are you gonna be logical and let me handle this."

"What do you intend to do, Sheriff?"

"Well, I can't do anything now. If you leave whatever proof you got with me, and it checks out, I'll arrest Earp when he returns. If you don't show me no proof, all I can do is talk to Earp and get his side of things. So, what'll it be?"

Keyes laughed. "You must take me for a damn fool, Masterson. You think I don't know you're hooked up with Earp? Hell, man, everybody knows that. If I leave the proof with you, you'll prob'ly either destroy it or give it over to Earp. And if I show it to you, you say you'll just talk to him? Well, isn't that just dandy?" Keyes laughed again, even harder than before.

His laughter stopped when Bat grabbed the front of his plaid flannel shirt and pulled the man close to him. Keyes was surprised by the action—and suddenly very nervous.

"I'm not here to amuse you, Keyes," Bat said through lips that hardly moved when he spoke. "I'm tryin' to do my job, hard as that may be to believe. It's true that I used to be quite friendly with Wyatt. It's also true that in the past I haven't been the territory's most upright lawman. But all that's changed. I don't owe nothin' to Earp, and I get mighty agitated when people—especially people who don't live in this town and don't know about what goes on here—call me one of Earp's employees."

Bat realized his temper was getting the better of him and let go of Keyes's shirt. The old man stepped back a few feet and brushed off and smoothed out the badly-creased shirt.

"So," Bat continued, now better composed, "you gotta make a choice. You can trust me and leave town real peaceful-like and wait for me to send word to you. Or you can just leave. What's it gonna be?"

Keyes wiped the dryness from his lips with the back of his left hand. "That ain't a lot of choice, Sheriff. I got twenty-seven men back there in that saloon. We could do a lot of damage."

"And I could kill a good number of them while you're doin' it, but is that what you really want? It won't help you get Earp. And the next time you come in town, he'll be ready and waitin' for you. Right now, there are only two Earp brothers livin' in Dodge. How would you like to face all of 'em? Mark me, Mr. Keyes, they're a loyal clan. They'll all be here the next time you come to town if there's any more violence today."

Keyes didn't like what he was hearing, but if Earp wasn't in town, there would be more bloodshed today, and it would be for nothing, as Bat said. He shook his head.

"I don't know, Sheriff. You're askin' a lot of me. You want me to just trust you and leave." The head went on shaking from left to right and back again. "And even if I did trust you, what can you really do? Can you take on Earp and his men all by yourself? That seems hardly possible, even for Bat Masterson."

"I wouldn't take him on alone. I got my own set of friends in this town, you know, including my brother George, who owns the other saloon." Bat worked up a wad of liquid in his mouth, then spat it out away from Keyes. "I ain't a fool, Keyes. But I can take Earp if I have to. But I'd like to avoid a war in this town if it's at all possible, whether it's between you ranchers and the Earps or me and the Earps. Either way, a lot of innocent folks will get caught in the middle."

Keyes continued walking silently for a few moments. When he and Bat reached the doors of the Long Ride, he made his decision.

"Sheriff, I may be a blamed fool, but I'm gonna give you forty-eight hours to arrest Earp."

"Give me a reason to arrest him. You haven't shown me any proof yet."

"You're right. Step over here."

Keyes crossed the street and Bat followed him to the old man's horse, which was tied to the hitching post in front of the sheriff's office. The rancher patted his mare on the backside, then untied a package wrapped in paper and fastened to the saddle horn. The old man unrolled the paper, and as he did, the objects inside clanked together. When the paper was completely unfurled and removed, Keyes handed Bat two blackened branding irons. Masterson inspected them for a moment.

"We found those irons on the Double E spread, run by Charlie Dombey. Everybody up north there knows that the Earps own that ranch."

Neither of the irons in Bat's grasp would imprint the Double E mark. One would burn a two-inch tall V on a steer's hide; the other would burn a B.

"I ain't good at guessin' games, Keyes," Bat said. "What are these supposed to tell me?"

"They're supposed to tell you that Dombey was changing brands on our cattle. I use the V to mark my cattle. Dombey used that brand to change the V into a W. He told me once that he bought some longhorns from a Texan who used the W brand. He was lyin' through his teeth. Paully Baker, who's in the saloon right now, uses his initials: PB. But use that other iron you're holding," Keyes said, pointing to the B iron in Bat's hand, "and you turn a P into

184

another B. And . . ."

Bat interrupted. "And Dombey told you he got cattle from a Double B ranch somewhere."

"Right."

"Sounds like you boys are downright gullible."

"Maybe so, Sheriff. But we had no reason not to trust Dombey. For a while he was right friendly, even helpful to us. Then our cattle kept disappearing, little by little. A couple from one spread. One from another. Two from this ranch; three from that one. We suspected Dombey after this kept up, but we had no proof. Then we caught one of his men with these two brandin' irons in his hand."

"Sounds like Dombey's the man you should be lookin' for."

"We already found Dombey. He's dead and buried—shot through the gut—and there ain't a goddamn soul on the Double E now. They left the cattle, some of them ours. Left everything, includin' these."

Keyes reached into the pocket of his blue corduroy jacket and pulled out a small bunch of papers. Bat handed the irons back to the old man and took the papers. He recognized Wyatt Earp's handwriting on several of the letters written to Dombey.

He didn't even have to read the letters. Bat knew Keyes was telling the truth and that the ranchers had a solid case against Earp.

"You want these back, I take it," Bat said, holding up the letters.

"Yes, sir. As you say, Sheriff, we might be gullible, but we ain't stupid. And no offense intended, but I don't trust you *that* much right yet. Perhaps I'm bein' gullible listenin' to you and ridin' out of town now."

"You aren't. You'll hear from me before two days are up just like I said. And if it comes down to a war, I might just need your firepower. Know what I mean?"

"I do. We'll be ready if it comes to that. We ain't afraid

of Earp or anybody else. We damn near got Holliday and that other feller a couple of days ago."

That means he got away, Bat thought, and McCain with him. It was good news.

"Well, I hope it don't come to that," Bat continued. "Maybe Earp's got a good explanation for all this. But even if he don't, and there is some show of force needed, I don't want it happenin' in Dodge."

Keyes extended his open right hand to Bat. "Then I'll be hearin' from you, one way or another."

Bat shook the hand. "You will."

Keyes walked back across the street to gather his men. Bat stepped into his office, closed the door, pulled down the dusty window shades and sat in the darkness. He reached into his pocket and found his tobacco and papers. Calmly, he rolled a cigarette and popped one end of it between his lips. When he struck the match, the flame illuminated the office. His eyes focused on the framed document that hung on the wall next to the door, the document that officially proclaimed him sheriff of Dodge City.

He sucked in smoke and let it linger inside him.

Earp, he thought, you greedy son of a bitch! I should have let them find you and saved myself a lot of aggravation. Now I have to find some middle ground, some way of saving your ass and my credibility. You're everything I dislike, Earp, yet I can't help admiring you. I remember some wild times we had when we were friendlier, before you got so damn greedy. We saved each other's butts plenty of times. Maybe that's why I don't want to see you dead now.

The sheriff continued staring at the document, but he had the eerie feeling it was staring back at him somehow. Smoke escaped from his lungs and momentarily clouded his vision.

The sounds of the ranchers leaving town drifted into his office from outside. He decided he needed a drink to help him think clearly. There was a bottle of whiskey under his desk, so he reached for it, opened it, and poured a couple of ounces down his throat. The liquor burned and soothed at the same time. It made its way to his head and washed the cobwebs from his mind. It helped him reach a conclusion.

The Earps had the choice: leave Dodge forever and start over somewhere else, or face the wrath of the ranchers—with Bat Masterson riding with them.

Chapter Thirty-one

Bat went out the back door of his office and walked down several narrow, quiet alleys. He couldn't be sure that all the ranchers had gone, and, to be safe, he took the less populated route back to Katie's.

This time a young girl answered his knock. He couldn't remember seeing her before. She was blond and had the greenest eyes he'd ever seen.

"Hello," she said. Then she noticed his badge. "Oh, hello, Sheriff."

"Hi. Where's Katie?"

"I don't . . . er . . . know . . ."

"It's okay, Molly," Katie's voice called out from inside. "The sheriff's a friend. Let him in."

Molly smiled at Bat and pulled the door wider. "Please come in."

"Thanks." He stepped into the parlor, which was unusually quiet with the absence of men. Four women sat around smoking cigarettes and talking. Bat recognized them all from previous visits.

"Sheriff," one called out. "Nice to see you again."

He removed his hat and said, "Nice to see you, too."

Then Katie interrupted the small talk. "What can I do for you, Bat?"

Stepping nearer to her, he answered. "I think you know, Katie. Where's Wyatt?"

"He ain't here. I told you that before when you were with the stranger."

"The stranger's gone, so you can drop the act. I know he's here. So run along and get him."

Katie gently held Bat's arm and looked at him with her very appealing blue eyes. "You're tired. Maybe you'd like to relax with Janie for a while."

The sheriff didn't try to pull his arm away, but said, "Being with Janie isn't exactly my idea of relaxin'."

She laughed. "I know what you mean."

"Katie, can we please cut this game? You know he's here. I know he's here. And if I have to search every damn room to find him, I will."

A voice boomed from the top of the stairs. "Like hell you will." It was James Earp, Wyatt's oldest brother. "As long as I run this place, you're gonna get no special treatment, sheriff or not. And I don't let anybody prowl around."

"Nice to see you, too," Masterson said sarcastically. "Why don't you come down here—and bring your brother with you—so we can talk eye to eye."

James held the bannister and slowly limped down the stairs. The four women who weren't working rose from their seats when they saw him descending. Quietly, they left the room through a red beaded curtain that led to another part of the house.

Katie moved to the foot of the stairs. "Want some help?"

"No, goddamn it. I don't need no help."

It was taking him forever to get to the bottom of the stairs. Bat realized that James's bad leg—the one he almost lost in the War Between the States—must be hurting like hell again. He almost felt sorry for the man. Almost. It was difficult to pity someone as mean-spirited as James; even his brothers considered him a nasty bastard.

"Now, what the hell do you want, Masterson?" James

asked, reaching the ground floor.

"Where's Wyatt?"

"He ain't here. He's out of town."

"I've already heard that from Katie. But she told me he was out of town with you."

James shrugged his shoulders. "She made a mistake."

"You're makin' one now, James. It's in your and Wyatt's interest to let me see him."

"He ain't here. Tell me what you got to say."

"I want to talk to Wyatt."

"You ain't talkin' to Wyatt 'cause he ain't here. How many times I got to tell you that? Tell me what you got to say. I can give him the message."

Bat turned to Katie again. "Tell me where he is. Talkin' to this feller's like talkin' to a stone wall."

James's face turned beet red and his hand moved closer to his hip. Bat grabbed his arm at the wrist.

"Don't even think about it."

"Get yer damn hand offa me!"

Suddenly, Katie spoke up. "Enough! For God's sake, enough! He's upstairs in room seventeen. I don't want to be cleanin' up blood for the next hour."

James jerked his arm free and turned his anger on Katie. "You bitch! How dare you cross me! I run this place, and as long as I do, you'll do what I tell you."

Katie laughed. "Oh, you run this place? You think so? Just because your brother made you half-owner don't mean you run it, and I ain't takin' no orders from you. The shingle outside says 'Katie's.' That was its name 'fore your brothers showed up, and it'll be its name after they leave. I run it, not you."

Katie had hit a nerve. She did run the place, James knew, and Wyatt had made him half-owner basically to give James something to do. The war wounds kept him from doing more useful things. And they made him bitter.

Had Masterson not been standing there, James would

190

have slapped Katie across the room. But he was there, so James tried to ignore the woman.

"Okay, Sheriff, now that you know, I'll go get Wyatt."

"I think I'd rather go get him," Bat said. "Not that I don't trust you."

Then Bat noticed Wyatt coming down the stairs. As always, his hair was neatly combed down around his neck and his clothes were pressed and creased to perfection. However, he wasn't wearing his boots; instead, he carried them in his right hand.

"What's all the commotion about?" he asked, smiling broadly. "You lookin' for me, Bat?"

"Yeah. And I think you know why."

"Maybe I do at that," he responded. When he reached the floor, he opened a door and waved his hand. "We can talk in here."

Bat walked into the room, which was used for gambling. There were three card tables, a roulette wheel on another table, and chairs everywhere. Bat pulled out a chair at the roulette table and sat down.

Wyatt said something that Bat could not hear to his brother, then closed the door.

Even with the door closed, the loud, angry voices of Katie and James could be heard. Then they drifted away.

"Those two are gonna kill each other one of these days," Wyatt laughed.

"I'm not in the mood for small talk," was Bat's response. "You know what I want to hear."

"What's that?"

"Those ranchers want you bad."

"They don't have no proof, Bat, of whatever they're accusin' me of. What am I supposed to have done this time?"

"You tell me."

"Well, they're ranchers, ain't they? Must be cattle rustlin'."

"How'd you know that?"

"I guessed. Don't take a lot of brains."

Bat sat up tall in his chair and leaned forward. "Wyatt, you know a man named Dombey? Charlie Dombey?"

"Don't recall the name."

"You should. Those ranchers have a bunch of letters and wires that you sent him. They also got a few mighty strange brandin' irons."

Earp tapped his forefingers on the armrests of his chair. "Well, I guess we're talkin' in circles here. You already know about it. The question is what are you gonna do about it? I see you got them to leave town. I'm mighty grateful to you for that."

"Save your gratitude. The real question is what are *you* gonna do about it?"

"I don't know. Haven't had a lot of time to think about it."

"I done your thinking for you."

"And?"

"And you either give yourself up to me—you know you'll get a fair trial, probably with one of the judges you own—or you pack up and get out of Dodge. You and your brothers and all your friends."

Wyatt's fingers stopped tapping; they curled around the armrests and squeezed.

"You must be jokin'," Earp smiled.

"I'm dead serious."

"I thought we were friends, Bat."

"We are. That's why I persuaded them to give me two days to find you. They think you're out of town. And since I'm your friend, I'm givin' you this friendly advice: you were plannin' on leavin' Dodge anyway, sooner or later. Make it sooner. Make it tomorrow."

"I can't do that," Wyatt said, rising to his feet. "I can't leave under these conditions."

"You think conditions'll improve if you hang around?

You'll either be responsible for a bloodbath, or you'll be found guilty of cattle rustlin'. Neither one of them sounds too good to me."

"I can't leave now," Earp repeated. "Not till I hear from Doc. Certain arrangements are bein' made right now. I can't move to Tombstone till they're all set."

"You still plan on goin' to Tombstone?" Bat asked. "I thought I told you that's where I was goin'. I don't want to run against you for office in Tombstone."

"Then go somewhere else."

"The hell I will," Bat shot back angrily. "you know I was plannin' on movin' there."

"Too bad, Bat. It's a big country. Why don't you head north? Try Cheyenne, or better yet Hays. I hear Hickok could use an able deputy."

The debate was getting Bat furious, but he realized he was angry for the wrong reasons. Wyatt's moving to Tombstone would foul up Bat's future plans, but they could be changed in time. What wouldn't change was the return of the ranchers.

"Fine. Go to Tombstone," Masterson snapped. "Just get out of Dodge. I've protected you as long as I'm gonna."

Wyatt's eyebrows met between his eyes in an icy glare. "Protected me? I don't need your damn protection, Masterson. Me and my brothers do just fine without you."

"But how will you do against me?" Bat said, his patience long gone.

"Just try me, lawman," Wyatt mocked, dragging out the word lawman. And without thinking, he reached over, spun the roulette wheel, and with his other hand grabbed Bat's lapel.

Bat removed his hand and slammed it down on the roulette table. Then he threw a fist over the table. It connected with Earp's face, just next to his left eye.

If it did any damage, Earp didn't let on. Instead, he moved around the table toward Bat. He moved his left fist like he was going to strike with it, but quickly pulled it back, and shot out his right in its place. The maneuver worked, and Wyatt's clenched hand caught Bat in the center of his face. The blow sent Bat sailing back until his back hit one of the card tables.

"You never were much good with your fists," Earp taunted, moving closer.

Bat quickly regained his footing. He could feel the blood running out of his nose onto his lips.

"You're right!" he said, lifting up his leg, pressing it against Earp's stomach, and pushing. It knocked the wind out of Earp who stood a few steps away from him now, holding his stomach.

Then Bat advanced, but Wyatt was ready for him. Each man had the other's throat in his grasp. In a few seconds, they were both gasping for air. Bat felt Earp's grip loosen for a second. It was all the time he needed. He jerked his head away, bent low, and released his right hand from Earp's neck. The freed hand balled into a fist and slammed into Earp's chest just below the ribs.

Wyatt curled up and his torso rested on the edge of the roulette table, jarring it enough that the spinning ball dropped into a socket.

The door opened, and Kate and James entered the room. Before they realized what was happening, Bat had his Colt out.

Wyatt was still leaning over the table, struggling for breath. Bat walked up behind him and stuck the end of the Colt barrel against Earp's back.

"I think you know the story now, Wyatt," Bat said. "You decide how you want it to end." He noticed into what slot the ball had fallen. "The winnin' number is two. That's how many days you got left."

Then he walked past a bewildered Katie and a very angry James Earp and made his way out of Katie's. He headed for his brother's saloon, the Varieties Dance Hall. He needed a drink, and his brother George would provide friendlier service than Luke Adams, whom he had seen enough of for one day. And George might prove useful if any of Earp's men came around looking for an opportunity to put a bullet in his back.

Chapter Thirty-two

Somewhere in Nevada, West of Battle Mountain

"I can't believe this is happenin'," Doc Holliday said for at least the thirtieth time that morning. "We've been ridin' all night — it's daybreak, for Chrissakes — and we ain't seen hide nor hair of them. You'd think they'd light a fire at least. Maybe they're dead. They couldn't have been thrown off this far back. We musta rode thirty miles. My ass is killin' me."

McCain was tired of listening to Doc's complaints, but he couldn't ignore them any longer. They were getting close to the stretch of land where Sara, Stevenson, and the satchel had been tossed off the train. Something about the landscape — its flatness, perhaps, in the midst of mountains, or its barrenness, interrupted by clumps of treed areas — was familiar, though in all honesty McCain wasn't sure exactly what it was. He was relying on instinct, the same instinct that had been honed and refined and served him so well as one of Custer's scouts for many years.

"We're close," he announced.

Doc looked ahead along the railroad track, which was easier to see now that the sun was moving up in the sky and illuminating the area. But he could see nothing that he wanted to see. No sign of Sara or Stevenson. No satchel

196

anywhere in sight. Not a damn thing but steel rails, wooden ties and grass.

"Man, I'm about to turn around and head for the nearest town," Doc said. "I would if I knew where the hell we were."

McCain gently pulled the reins and his horse came to a halt. Doc pulled up beside him.

"Why are we stoppin'? You wanna turn around too?"

McCain removed his hat and fanned his sweaty face with the brim. "About two hundred yards away, to your left, in a clump of trees, is an Indian. Don't turn and look, though. We don't want him gettin' anxious."

"Great! Just what we needed! What tribe? Not that it matters."

"Looks like a Nez Perce, but I can't be sure from this distance. Odd if he is, though; they've been moved to a reservation far north of here."

"Maybe he's a Sioux."

"He ain't."

"How do you know?"

"You really want an explanation now? I suggest we keep ridin'."

With that, the two men causally moved on. After they had traveled another quarter of a mile, McCain turned around. He could no longer see the Indian, but that didn't surprise him. He could be hiding anywhere, or he might have gone.

Then Doc spotted something moving in a thicket of bushes. "McCain. Over there."

McCain saw the movement too. It was no Indian, he knew. It was making too much noise. "Probably a mountain lion."

A scratching noise came from the thicket. It was a sound very out of place in this environment. It sounded like the cat was checking out something with its paw. Something made of a heavy, rough cloth.

McCain urged his horse on a few steps. The cat instinctively reacted to the motion of horse and rider. It hissed loudly and bolted away through the underbrush.

"The cat found something for us," McCain said as he neared the spot where the lion had been. "Come and take a look."

Doc rode up to McCain, looked where he pointed, and jumped off his horse. There sat a beige canvas satchel on its side, filthy and half-opened. Doc knelt down next to it, set it up right, and stuck his hand in the bag. He grabbed something and pulled it out.

A white, lacy corset dangled from his hand.

"We're in luck," he said. "This has got to be hers."

McCain nodded. "Looks about her size."

Doc was so pleased they had finally found a clue to the missing pair's whereabouts that he drew the corset to his face and kissed it. When he removed it from his face, he said, broadly smiling, "Jesus, it smells good. Smells like a woman."

McCain laughed. "What'd you expect it to smell like, a buffalo?"

Holliday wasn't amused. "Very funny, McCain. You're a regular Eddie Foy, ain't ya?" Then Doc suddenly stopped himself and changed the subject. "Hey, what about that Indian? You see him? I'll bet my breeches they got Sara and the Scotsman."

"You're probably right."

"You think they killed them? Took their stuff?"

"Not if they're Nez Perce, but I don't really know."

"What do we do now?"

"It might be a good idea to split up. We can scout the area better separately."

Doc climbed back on his horse. "No way. That's a real bad idea."

"Why?"

"What's to stop you from disappearing if you find the

198

money?"

McCain rubbed his forehead with this right hand. "How many times do I have to tell you I don't give a damn about your money?"

"I know you keep sayin' that, but since you ain't workin' for me no more, I can't take no chances."

"So hire me on again."

"Just like that?"

"Yeah."

Doc sat back as far as he could in the saddle and laughed out loud. The laughter grew raspier and after a few seconds turned to coughing. Doc's face turned pale as the fit grew worse. He bent his body forward over the horse's neck and held on to the saddle horn. A drop of spittle shot out of his mouth onto his shirt sleeve.

McCain noticed the liquid was red with blood. He wanted to help, but didn't know how. "Doc, anything I can do?"

For an answer Doc just waved his hand to indicate "nothing." At last, the fit seemed to slow down, the rough heavings in his throat growing farther apart. He began to take slow, deep breaths, and the color returned to his face.

"Drink this," McCain said, handing him his canteen.

Doc took the tin canteen and swallowed some of the water. Then he just sat on the horse, trying to clear his throat.

"Thanks," he said, handing the canteen back. "But water just don't do the trick like a shot of whiskey."

"If I had any, I'da given it to you."

"I know. Thanks anyway."

"So how about it? Am I rehired?"

"I really got no choice," Doc said. "Now that we're out here in the middle of Nevada somewhere, and considerin' the fact that if we do run into Indians, I'm gonna need your help . . . well, I guess I got to rehire you."

"Thanks. I appreciate it."

"Don't thank me, buster. Just find that money and get me out of here and back on the next train."

As Doc finished speaking, McCain noticed something move over one of the hills in the distance. It moved quickly, but not so quick that the sight couldn't register in the former scout's mind. It was a brave on a horse. Maybe the same one they saw before, maybe not. It didn't matter.

"C'mon, Doc," McCain said, jerking the reins on his horse to make him turn. "I think I know the way."

"Huh?"

"I just saw our friend, the brave, dash over that hill over yonder."

"So?"

"So maybe he's goin' back to his camp."

Then McCain saw Sara's bag still on the ground. He jumped off the horse and grabbed it. Then he climbed aboard the animal again.

"Let's go," he said, and spurred the horse on.

Doc followed, scratching his head, thinking about this man he'd rehired. He'd never really met anyone he couldn't figure out at all. McCain, however, was just as big a mystery to him now as when he first met him in Dodge. And here he was, following this ex-army scout around like his future depended on it. Which to some degree, it did.

Chapter Thirty-three

"We must leave tonight," Chief Joseph told his two white captives. "At that time we will release you."

Thank God, Sara thought, but remained silent. Stevenson, on the other hand, verbalized his thanks.

"But you must promise not to reveal our location to any other white man," the chief continued. "Will you do this? You have my word that no Nez Perce will take the lives of any whites unless our hands are forced."

"I will," Stevenson agreed.

"Sure," Sara nodded, not as convinced as her traveling companion of Joseph's promise. She would have agreed to almost anything to get away from the Indians and be able to turn her attentions to her Scottish friend. "But why don't you let us go now?"

The chief sipped at the clay cup of water he held, then continued. "You might be seen leaving. When night comes there is less chance. And we will be gone too. For now, we enjoy this day."

Joseph spread out his arms and took a deep breath. The day was perfect; the sun was high in the sky without being overbearing, and a lilting breeze wafted through the air, carrying the scents of pine and grass. And from his location atop a hill at the beginnings of a small mountain range, Joseph could see far into the nearly cloudless sky and far across the plain before him.

Stevenson, even though he realized that Fanny Osbourne had summoned him with some urgency from Edinburgh to San Francisco, looked forward to spending a few more hours with this noble Indian leader and his people. There was so much to know, to learn, to understand. While in the company of such a man as Joseph, he didn't want to waste a single moment.

Then Joseph pointed down the hill. "One of my braves brings news."

Stevenson and Sara looked where he was pointing. They saw a brave on horseback quickly making his way up the rocky hill toward the camp the tribe had made in the recessed area between two hills.

"He must be bringing important news," Stevenson said. "He's driving that horse terribly hard."

Joseph answered without taking his eyes off the brave. "He brings bad news."

Stevenson looked again at the approaching Indian. "How can you tell?"

"A chief knows these things about his people. His face is grim. That is not like Pierre."

"Pierre?" Stevenson repeated, dumbfounded. "His name is Pierre?"

"It is the name the missionaries gave his family. He prefers Smoking Arrow. That is what his true name means in English. He thinks it is more fitting for a man."

"Smoking Arrow!" the Scotsman said again. He stared off at the mountains, deep in thought.

The brave reached the top of the hill on which Joseph stood and jumped off his horse. Then he spoke a few sentences in a language rich in guttural sounds that neither Sara nor Stevenson understood. Joseph nodded, then said something to him. Smoking Arrow walked away, pulling his black and gray roan behind him.

"More whites come," Joseph said. "You must return to the cave and wait inside."

"I hate it in that filthy cave," Sara complained. "Why can't we see the white men? Perhaps they . . ."

Joseph ignored Sara completely, but spoke further to his other guest. "You must bring the woman into the cave. There may be violence. Your presence may cause it, or you could be killed. In the cave you will be guarded and safe."

Stevenson nodded and grabbed Sara's arm. "We must go."

"Louis, don't you want to get out of here?" Sara asked, disgusted.

"Yes," he answered. "But I want to stay alive also."

She finally relented and walked beside him back to the cave, mumbling under her breath. Two braves followed them, and when they entered the cave, the two men stayed outside by the entrance.

Stevenson sat not very far inside the cave, which was empty except for himself and Sara. His seat gave him a good view of the area outside the cave. If there was going to be a battle, he wanted to see it, the noble Indians fighting the civilized yet ruthless white Americans. It would be something to tell his children about; it would also be something he could relate in a book some day.

Sara sat deeper inside the cavern, near the satchels and baggage the Indians had carried inside the cave for them. She lay on a beautifully woven blanket and pulled one of the satchels under her head to use as a pillow. She closed her eyes and sighed and wished she were on her way to . . . somewhere . . . anywhere.

Stevenson stood up, then sat down; then he repeated those actions. He kept waiting for something to happen, waiting for the gunfire to begin, waiting for the war whoops of the braves and perhaps even the blaring of a cavalry trumpet or the booming voice of a cannon. But nothing, it seemed to him in the cave, was happening. The anticipation was making him edgy.

"Why doesn't someone do something?" he asked.

"Why don't you sit down, Louis, and relax," Sara snapped. "They're playin' for keeps out there, you know. This ain't a game of horseshoes."

Stevenson had no idea what a game of horseshoes was, but he wasn't much interested. His attention was still focused outside.

Finally, from the musty darkness of the cave, the Scotsman saw Joseph and two of his braves talking together about twenty yards from the mouth of the cave. One of the braves walked toward the cave.

In a moment, they walked past the two guards and stepped inside. Stevenson stood up eagerly. The chief and his brave stood next to him. Sara, on the other hand, remained stretched out on the ground.

"Two white men come," Joseph said. "Do you and your woman travel alone?"

"We're alone now," Stevenson answered.

"Does anyone look for you? Hunt you?"

"I . . . I don't think so."

Joseph crossed his arms on his chest. "There are only two. They may not know we are here and may not seek us. But we cannot be sure. They may be a scouting party. Bluecoats may follow behind. We must be ready."

"What will you do?"

"For now, we hide and let these men ride in. Then they may ride out. My braves hide all trace of our being here. The fewer whites that know our place, the better for us."

Stevenson correctly assumed that by "place," the chief meant "position" or "location."

"Now we remain here. You and the woman must remain silent as the bats within this cave, or my braves will have to silence you—perhaps forever."

Sara sat up and looked fearfully at the blackness of the

cave that extended into the earth. "Bats," she said. "Bats, too!" Then she lay back down, face-up, with her arms crisscrossed over her head to prevent any stray, flapping bat from getting caught in her long brown tresses.

"Silence!" Joseph commanded. Then he pointed to the side of the cave and lowered his finger to the floor. Stevenson sat in the spot. The brave and his leader knelt on one knee, facing the brightness outside and waiting. The two guards at the entrance took a few steps into the cave and kneeled in a similar fashion, their rifles pointing upward between their legs.

All remained silent in the cave. Everyone stayed completely motionless, watching, waiting, listening for the sounds of the two strangers. Stevenson craned his neck in order to see out the entrance of the cavern. A crow flew down and alighted on the ground out in the bright sunlight. It bent its neck and pecked at the grass at its feet. It was the only motion any of the cave dwellers saw for some time.

Then the black bird took a few steps backward, flapped its wings a couple of times, and flew away. Its presence was replaced by that of two horses, each with a man on its back.

Stevenson turned his gaze away from the entrance of the cave and toward the leader of the Nez Perce. Joseph stared intently at the new arrivals. He said nothing, and his face betrayed no emotion. It was as if he were suddenly part of the cave, part of the mountain range. He no longer seemed completely human: his facial features seemed carved of stone, and his poise and concentration on this new potential enemy reminded the Scotsman of a great wild feline determining whether the intruders were hunter or prey or merely fellow animals with only survival as their goal.

One of the horses outside snorted, and the sound attracted Stevenson's attention. The two men had stopped outside the cave. One of them lit a cigarette.

Stevenson's face brightened when he recognized the two

men. The man with the cigarette, the man who leaned forward over his horse's neck like he was exhausted from riding, was Doc Holliday. The other man, the tall one with the look of concern on his face, was McCain. The Scotsman was thrilled for a moment, but his thrill quickly turned to worry. What if the braves started shooting at them, thinking them men who meant them malice? What if Holliday and McCain were indeed hunting the tribe? After all, they had never said where they were headed or what they were after. Or had they? He couldn't remember. He did remember that they both were men capable of violence. He knew that from their actions on the train.

When Stevenson again turned his eyes to Joseph, the Indian was watching him. In the quietest whisper he had ever heard, the chief asked, "You know these men?"

He nodded, afraid even to silently speak.

"Do they seek us?"

Stevenson thought about the question for a moment. He couldn't be absolutely certain of his answer, but it seemed to him just too coincidental that Holliday and McCain should wind up in the same clandestine Indian camp as he and Sara. And the two men could not have known before their expulsion from the moving train that he and his beautiful American friend would be captured by the Nez Perce tribesmen.

He shook his head to mean "no."

"Do they seek you?"

Again he thought about the question. That had to be it: Holliday and his partner were searching for Sara and himself.

He nodded.

Joseph stared at the two men sitting on their mounts at the mouth of the cave. He weighed the responses of this curious white man in his mind and considered the various courses of action he might take.

Then Holliday spoke to his companion. "Well," he said,

puffing on the slightly bent cigarette that dangled from his lips, "why are we just sittin' here? What the hell's the matter with you?"

"Something tells me," McCain answered, sitting straight as an arrow atop his horse, "that my army skills have slipped a bit."

"What do you mean? We lost them?"

"No. I mean I think we just rode right into the middle of a trap."

The last word McCain spoke set off an instant reaction from Doc. His hand lowered to the Winchester strapped to the horse.

"Don't!" McCain warned. "Don't do a goddamn thing except smoke your cigarette."

"Jesus Christ! What do we do now?"

"Just keep talking. Act natural. I need time to think."

"You need time? I think you need a damn doctor, boy! I don't see no sign of no Indian anywhere in sight."

"You notice that cave to my right?"

"Yeah. So what?"

"You see that patch of ground a few feet ahead?"

"There was a fire there not too long ago. Someone's tried to hide that fact, but they either do sloppy work or they were pressed for time. There's ashes all over the place."

"I see 'em."

Holliday sat back in the saddle, sighed, and said, "Shit. What do we do now?"

McCain made a decision quickly. "We do this. We slowly draw out our guns and throw them on the ground, so our red friends know we come in peace."

Holliday sat forward again and grabbed the saddle horn with both hands. "That seems mighty risky, McCain. Suppose it is the Sioux we've run into? They'll take our scalps for sure."

"If it was the Sioux, they'd already have our scalps."

"I don't know 'bout this."

207

"I thought you were a gamblin' man, Doc."

"Yeah. That's what I hear."

The two men peered at one another, but neither went for his weapon. Finally, McCain said, "I don't think there's any other way. I can't see them, but I know this place is crawlin' with Indians."

So he drew out his rifle and gently let it fall to the ground next to his horse. Then he drew his Colt and let it drop next to the rifle. Immediately after, Doc did the same with his guns, taking even more care to draw the weapons slowly, carefully, peacefully.

They sat there, looking around. Nothing. No one. Not a movement, save the leaves blowing in the breeze.

Nothing until they saw the shadows moving inside the cave. The shadows grew larger, less black by the second until the edge of the sunlight hit their feet and rapidly drew the curtain of darkness up their bodies to reveal animal hides, sandals, leather lashes, and beads. And finally the faces of two Indians.

"I could hear you," the older of the Indians said. "I accept your gesture of peace."

"Thank you," McCain said. The smile on his face could not adequately express the relief he felt. He had made a mistake riding into this set-up, and perhaps had made another by not investigating the brave they had spotted earlier. He was delighted to learn that he had also been twice correct this day. The gesture of friendship was accepted. And these *were* Nez Perce.

"Can we get down off these horses?"

The chief nodded, and the two white men climbed down. Holliday stepped up next to McCain, who was closer to the two Indians.

"I am glad you come in peace," Joseph declared. "My braves will not have to kill you now." He swept his hand in an arc in the air before them. Holliday surveyed the surrounding area. Braves were everywhere, behind rocks, in trees, on the rocks jutting out from the mountainside. A moment earlier not a single one could be seen.

"I'll be damned!" he exclaimed.

Joseph smiled, then he turned his head slightly and yelled a command into the cave. In a moment the two braves within marched into the sunlight, Stevenson standing between them, shielding his eyes from the bright sun with his hand.

"Stevenson!" McCain said.

"Good day, Mr. McCain," he answered. "Good day to you too, Mr. Holliday."

Holliday merely nodded hello. He was absolutely delighted that the odds of his getting the satchel back were constantly growing.

"Where's Sara?" McCain asked.

Before the Scotsman could answer, Joseph spoke up. "The woman is safe within the cave. No harm has come to her. She will remain in the cave until our words are done. A woman has no place here among men who speak of war or peace."

Sara heard the chief's comment and sat up, muttering rude words. Her hand rested on the satchel that she had been using as a pillow. She looked at it and realized it was one of Louis' bags. She also realized that while the men were engaged in negotiations — or whatever men talk about in these situations — she was completely alone in the cave.

Quickly, she opened the bag, and when she spied what was inside, her jaw dropped, and she knew that this would all be worth it soon. All the time, all the trouble, even this uncomfortable last day sleeping in a disgusting, dark, rodent-filled cave with Indians. The bag contained beautiful green paper money, solid U.S. currency. She had been right all along. This young writer was rich, and evidently he was carrying his fortune with him to his bride-to-be.

Now that she was sure of that fact, she resolved to turn on the charm even more than she already had. This Scotsman would succumb to her charms soon, she was confident, and she would share in his fortune. She would make him fall in love with her, and the thousands of dollars in the satchel would be partially hers.

Either that, or she would steal it later.

Chapter Thirty-four

Holliday was glad to be out of the saddle. Even the hard ground on which he sat felt soft. And the taste of this Indian liquor—whatever it was—was damn good, and it seemed to soothe his throat and warm his chest and belly.

Chief Joseph pointed to the three people farther back in the cave. "You have strange friends, Doc Holliday."

The weary traveler looked at McCain, Sara, and Stevenson, who were standing in a huddle, talking about something—he didn't know or care what at the moment—and smiling like they were happy to see one another. Doc had been happy to see the missing satchel, although he hadn't yet checked its contents. He didn't want to reveal to the Indians what was inside it.

"You're right, Chief," he answered politely, "they are kinda weird." Then, changing the subject he added, "I gotta tell ya, I'm mighty happy to be sittin' here all friendly-like with the great Chief Joseph. I've read all about you in the newspapers."

Joseph nodded and smiled. "And I have read all about the famous Doc Holliday of Dodge City. You too are a great man."

Doc was surprised. "You've heard about me? Ain't that something?"

Sara, Stevenson, and McCain broke up their private

conference and joined the half-dozen Nez Perce and Doc and Chief Joseph who were sitting in a circle on the cave floor.

"Everything is well?" the chief asked.

"Quite well," Stevenson responded.

Doc wanted to return to one of his favorite topics of conversation: himself. "The chief here's just told me that even he's heard of me," he said to the newcomers. "Ain't that a hoot?"

"This is true," Joseph confirmed. "I have read about the men of Dodge. They are great lawmen."

Stevenson's eyes grew wide. "Chief Joseph, sir, I mean no disrespect, but are you telling us that you can read?"

"I have learned to read your language. But much of it is still strange to me."

"Then you read of me in the newspapers, too?" Doc asked.

"No. I read a book of your adventures." Joseph gazed at one of the braves and pointed to a blanket that was rolled around several items. The brave opened the blanket, removed an object from it, and handed it to the chief. "This is the book," Joseph said, handing it to Holliday.

The work was entitled *Doc Holliday — Dodge Gunfighter for Justice* by Ned Buntline. Holliday almost laughed when he looked at the illustration of himself on the cover of the dime novel, but he choked the laughter down. Bless that Buntline, he thought. A man couldn't ask for better stories.

"Did the missionaries teach you to read?" Sara asked.

Joseph was in a good mood, so he answered the woman. "Yes, but I have taught myself much."

"Good Lord!" Stevenson said. Then, when he noticed everyone was looking at him, he explained his remark. "I'm sorry. It's just that in England we seem to think that the Indians can do little more than hunt, ride, and kill. I find this all quite remarkable."

Joseph sighed. "It is true that all white men in this country think that is true. It is also true in other lands?"

"I'm afraid so. If you'll allow me to get a book from my bag, I'll read something to you."

Joseph waved his hand, and the Scotsman headed for the satchel. McCain shot Doc a quick look, and Holliday got the message.

"I got your satchel here, next to me," Doc said. He was glad he decided to unhitch it from the saddle and bring it into the cave with him.

"Oh," Stevenson said, confused. "How in the world did it get over there? I thought that was it." He pointed to a very similar bag that sat with his and Sara's other bags.

"Nope," Doc repeated. "I got it here."

As Stevenson stepped over to Holliday to retrieve the bag, Sara resisted showing her shock. The bag wasn't his. It was Holliday's. She might have wasted her time, might have put up with this man's antics, might have risked her life, might have given herself to him completely—and all for nothing. The money wasn't his.

But maybe he has other money, she thought. Perhaps in his other bag . . .

No. It was too risky, now that she knew there was a man here who *did* have money, real money in his possession. That's why they came back after us. It wasn't for us. It was for the money.

Then she looked at Doc for a moment and had a further thought. She wondered what a woman would have to do in bed to please a man like Holliday and get him to . . . share.

Her meditation was interrupted by Stevenson's voice. "Just let me find the page," he said, leafing through his copy of *Humphry Clinker*. At last he found what he was looking for. "Here it is." Then he remembered how the passage had positively sickened him the first time he read it and wondered what had gotten into him to suggest reading it to Joseph. He was about to attempt to get out of reading

213

it when Joseph extended his open hand.

"I would like to try to read your book."

"Er . . . excuse me, Chief Joseph, perhaps reading this isn't a good idea. It was foolish of me to . . ."

Before he could finish his statement, a young brave snatched the book from Stevenson's hand and gave it to Joseph. The chief felt the weight of the cloth-bound book and smiled. Then he looked at the pages before him. His eyes moved up and down the page, finally stopping at some words that made him squint and arch his eyebrows in an expression of displeasure.

He began to read. " 'After the warriors and the matrons had made a hearty meal upon the muscular flesh which they pared from the victim, and had applied a great variety of tortures, which he bore without flinching, an old lady, with a sharp knife, scooped out one of his eyes, and put a burning coal in the socket.' "

Joseph stopped reading and stared angrily at Stevenson. The sense of friendship among the people in the cave seemed to disappear. One of the braves next to Joseph moved his hand reaching for the knife at his side. Holliday slipped his hand inside his jacket in order to facilitate drawing the derringer under his arm should the need arise.

The chief continued reading. " 'The pain of this operation was so exquisite that he could not help bellowing, upon which the audience raised a shout of exultation, and one of the warriors stealing behind him, gave him the coup de grace with a hatchet.' "

Joseph slammed the book shut and tossed it into the dirt in the middle of the circle of sitting bodies. Everyone else remained nervously silent and motionless. They stayed that way for some time.

Finally Joseph spoke. "It is sad if that is how the white man speaks of us. It is not true of the Nez Perce. It is not true of many tribes, although there are some who enjoy treating the white man as they treat them."

Holliday was astounded. "What the hell's the matter with you, Scotty?" he said to Stevenson. "You out of your mind insultin' the chief here like that?"

Joseph held up his hand. "He has not insulted me. He has taught me. He has showed me the words that poison the young whites, make them fear and hate us. It makes me sad, but I am not insulted."

"I'm terribly sorry," Stevenson said humbly.

"I fear it is our lot," Joseph continued, "to be hated and hunted. Even now, my brave warriors are forced to hide in caves and in trees because the white army searches for us. We have tried to make peace. I have spoken to the white leaders in the East. We have put down our weapons, have lived where we have been told to live. Still we are hated.

"This day brings no peace. Men—white men—were killed in the north. Our tribe had put down their guns. Still we are blamed and hunted. Your powerful engines, your trains, have been destroyed and robbed, and we are blamed for that."

McCain glanced over to Holliday and nodded. Doc nodded back, thinking that he had to give McCain credit for believing the Indians were innocent of the train robberies long before he had any proof.

Joseph stood up. "I grow old and talkative as an old woman. I shall leave you now. It is time for us to move on. If we remain here, more whites—those who seek us—will find us. I ask of you only to remain silent of our camp. I ask you this in the name of friendship, the friendship we have seen this day."

Then, with no further ceremony, the chief said, "I wish you safe journey, my friends," and left the cave, followed by his men.

The exit was so sudden, so regal, it left the four who remained seated speechless.

215

Chapter Thirty-five

The Nez Perce left the area quickly and quietly, leaving only the four white travelers behind. One by one they stood up, brushed the dirt from their clothing.

"Stevenson," Doc announced, "you got yourself a talent for almost gettin' yourself and others killed. And I might just come over there and knock your teeth down your throat for all the trouble you caused me." Then he turned his head and spotted his satchel. "Right after I reclaim what's mine."

Doc walked over to the bag, but his way was blocked by Sara, who stood in front of him.

"That ain't your bag!" she said.

"The hell it's not, lady."

"How do you know it's yours?"

"Well, that one sure as hell ain't mine," he said nastily, shooting his thumb in the direction of the identical bag he had brought with him from the train. "I don't go totin' my library with me. Now step aside."

Sara moved out of the way. Doc reached the bag, noticed it was open, and looked inside. "I hope you ain't been helpin' yourself to what's in here, folks."

Stevenson picked up his book from the ground. "What *is* in there, Mr. Holliday?"

Doc closed the bag. "Oh, you don't know, huh?"

"No."

"Well, that's real fine. Keep it that way." Then he turned to Sara. "And you, ma'am, you don't know what's in here either, right?"

"Right."

"Well, nothin' seems to be missin' so we'll just forget about it for now." He stepped toward Stevenson. "However, I think you oughta learn a few things about how America operates, Mr. Scotty."

Stevenson took a few steps backward. "Keep your hands off me," he ordered.

"Well, ain't we gettin' spunky?"

As he stepped past McCain, Doc felt a hand on his shoulder. He stopped, looked at it, and pulled it away.

"Leave him be," McCain said.

"Oh, bullshit, McCain!" Doc answered angrily. "He's got it comin' to him."

"You got what you came for." McCain gestured with his eyes toward the satchel. "Leave him be."

"You don't understand," Doc went on. "Everythin's goin' wrong. The trains. The bags. The day's ride back. I'm goddamn fit to be tied, and I wanna beat the livin' hell outa somebody. And that dopey Scotty's got it comin' to him, I tell ya."

"No, he don't. He's a victim of circumstances."

"A what?" Doc asked. "Oh, never mind. I just wanta break his jaw, so he won't open that fool mouth of his."

McCain shook his head. "I can't let you do that, Doc."

"Let me? Let me? You don't have to *let* me do nothin'. Now stay outta the way."

But McCain chose to do the opposite and grabbed Doc's shoulder again. Doc clenched his hand into a fist, spun around, and hit McCain on the cheekbone. The blow surprised him, but McCain prepared himself for the next one, a right uppercut that he managed to avoid by stepping to his left. McCain's right fist caught Doc on the jaw and sent him whirling back.

"Enough?" he asked.

Instead of answering him, Doc rushed forward and threw a right cross at McCain's face. It never made contact—McCain saw it coming and ducked—and the velocity of the thrust made Doc spin on the sole of his boot and trip over his own legs.

"You son of a bitch!" Holliday spat. He got to his knees and reached for the Colt at his side.

But McCain's Peacemaker was already out and aimed at Doc's chest. "Don't," he said. "I don't want to go down in history as the man who killed Doc Holliday. I got enough people chasin' me as it is."

Doc realized the futility of drawing his gun. If he made a move for it, McCain could easily put a three-inch hole in his belly before he ever had it clear of the holster.

"Now, do we stop this and get back to our real business, or does our business relationship end right here, right now, with the famous Doc Holliday on his knees?"

Doc raised his hands over his head and stood up. If I were McCain, he thought, I'd shoot. This fellow has had plenty of opportunities to send me to my maker, but he hasn't done it. He's either a really handy fellow to have around when a fight breaks out—he always seems to regain his temper as quickly as he loses it—or he wants me alive for some other reason. But what could that be? It's clear he doesn't want the money; he could kill me right now and make off with it. So what the hell's he after? Because he's got to be after something.

"Well? What's it gonna be, Doc?"

From the side of the cave Sara spoke up. She had been silent as a whisper through the entire incident. "Why don't you leave him alone?" she asked.

McCain glanced over at her, thinking the question had been aimed at Doc. But it was clear he was wrong. She was asking *him* the question and glaring at him like he was the devil himself.

"I'd like to, ma'am," he answered, "but till I get Mr. Holliday's word that this matter is behind us, I'm afraid I'll have to keep this gun aimed at him."

"Who do you think you are?" Sara yelled.

"Ma'am, I think you're forgetting that it was Mr. Holliday here who threatened to beat the daylights out of your friend there." He cocked his head in Stevenson's direction.

"Well, he's not now," she countered, "so why don't you put that gun away."

McCain was thoroughly confused. Sara had no reason to be siding with Doc unless she and Stevenson had had some kind of fight. Anyway, he thought, this isn't the time to worry about that.

"So can I put my gun away?" he asked Doc.

"Do whatever you like," Doc responded, slowly lowering his arms. "The fight's over, far as I'm concerned. I been thinkin', and maybe you're right. Maybe Scotty over there just somehow got mixed in with all this. Anyhow, that fight, short as it was, cleared my system. I feel a lot better."

"I'm so glad," McCain said sarcastically.

"So you can put that Colt away now."

"You're sure about that?"

"As sure as I'm standin' here."

"And there's no hard feelings?"

"Of course there's hard feelin's, 'specially since you won. But we'll deal with them when this job is over. Right now, we got to be on our way."

McCain reholstered his pistol. "Fine. Let's get going."

He turned away from Doc and walked out of the cave into the sunlight. He was beginning to feel the closeness, the confinement of the cave and needed some fresh air. As he walked, he prayed it wasn't a mistake turning his back on Holliday. Maybe all that agreeableness on his part just now was a ruse to get him in this position.

The sunlight, still bright but beginning to fade slightly, felt good on his face and his arms. It also felt good to know that if Doc was going to shoot him in the back, he would have done it by then.

Stevenson joined McCain in the open sunlight. He stepped up next to him and shielded the sun from his sensitive eyes. "I want to thank you for your intervention. You probably saved my life; at least you saved me from a good drubbing."

"Don't thank me," McCain said. "But take these words of advice. You aren't in Scotland anymore. This is a very different, very wild country, in case you haven't noticed. Folks here are suspicious of anyone who looks, speaks, or even thinks differently than them. I guess you don't mean no harm to anyone, but for your own safety, I'm advising you to keep your opinions to yourself. You're a writer? Write 'em down. Just don't speak 'em to the wrong people. Democracy works a hell of a lot better back East where there's laws and lawmen to help it along."

"I understand. And I'm sorry for all the inconvenience I've caused you. I seem to have disturbed your friendship with Mr. Holliday."

"Holliday and me are lots of things, but friends ain't exactly one of 'em." McCain lit a cigarette and tossed the match to his side. "Seems like you and Miss Hillyer ain't exactly close now either."

"It does seem that way," Stevenson agreed, rubbing his left hand with his right, "but I'm incapable of telling you the reason for her change of attitude toward me."

"Did you make a move on her?"

The writer's eyebrows rose over his eyes, and his face turned red with embarrassment. "If you are referring to a sexual advance, I should say not!"

"She make one on you?"

"Absolutely not."

"Well, something must have happened. You've got no

idea what?"

Stevenson thought about it for a moment. "I simply can not imagine what has caused this change in her."

"Don't get yourself in an uproar about it. There's no way in hell to figure women out."

McCain took a few steps forward and saw his and Doc's horses grazing, chewing up a patch of nearby grass. Much to his surprise, though, the horses had been joined by two healthy, perfectly rideable bays.

"Look at that," McCain said.

He and Stevenson approached the horses, and McCain stroked the reddish-brown mane of the better-looking of the two. Around its neck was a thin rope with a message written on tree bark attached. Stevenson took the message and read it aloud.

THE HORSES ARE FOR MY WHITE FRIEND AND HIS WOMEN, the note began. Stevenson smiled at the misspelling of the singular "woman." THEY ARE GIFTS OF PEACE FROM JOSEPH.

The Scotsman read the message to McCain, then added, "What a truly wondrous man he is!"

"Yes," McCain agreed. "Too bad all Indians ain't like him. Or all white men for that matter."

Chapter Thirty-six

"Are you okay, Doc?" Sara asked.

"Yeah, I'm just fine." There was a clear note of disgust in his voice. His patience was used up, completely gone. He wanted McCain's protection and battle-prowess on this journey, but now he also desperately wanted to be rid of him. This time the man has gone too far, knocking him down and showing him up in front of the woman and the Scot.

"I wish you'd knocked Louis around a bit. He deserves it."

"He's an honest-to-God pain in the ass."

"Yes, he is. He lacks the common sense, the cunning of a man like you."

Doc picked up the satchel by the handle and looked at the entrance of the cave. He wanted to be outside in the sun, in the open, not in this hollowed-out hole in the mountain with this woman any more. He felt rotten, and the dust and dampness of the cave were irritating his throat and chest.

"What's your game, lady?" he asked Sara, shooting a look of doubt and suspicion her way.

"Game?" she repeated, affecting a hurt tone of voice.

"You heard right."

"There's no game. I'm flattered that Doc Holliday, a man known from Washington to California, is even speaking to me. Is that so strange?"

"No," Doc answered. "Lots of women take an interest in me — for one reason or another. But the way you hardly said two words to me before now, and the way you suddenly decided your beau out there ain't worth your attention is strange."

Sara frowned. "He's not my beau. I just met him a couple of days ago. Anyhow, he ain't my type. I'm far more attracted to men like you, who act instead of talk and ain't afraid of anything."

"Really?" He stepped closer to Sara.

"Yes," she said, adjusting her ripped dress, which the Indians never did get around to repairing. The adjustment was far from the innocent movement it could have been: Sara pulled the garment tighter against her, and her breasts seemed to threaten the survival of the buttons down its front. At the same time, she gazed at the nearing gunfighter with her best seductive look.

Doc stopped inches in front of her, his right hand still holding the bag by the handle. He looked down into the brown, beckoning eyes and immediately felt a jolt of passion surge through his groin. Then his left arm whipped around Sara's back and pulled her close to him. He felt the touch of her ample breasts against his torso, even through her dress and his shirt. The passion grew within him, awakening dormant desires, inspiring heated thoughts. Then, more easily than blowing out the flame of a candle, he expelled it.

"Listen, Sara — or whatever your name is," he purred, but the sound more closely resembled that of a bobcat than a Siamese. "You might have fooled the Scot and that Pinkerton and God knows who else, but you don't fool me. You ain't the least bit interested in me. It's what's in this bag that's making your juices flow."

"I don't know what's in it."

"Don't bullshit me, lady." His grip grew tighter around her. "I don't like bein' treated like a fool."

"I'm telling you the truth."

"Like hell you are."

His hand crept up her back and grabbed the long, soft tresses of her brown hair. He pulled down on them, forcing her face to rise and her eyes to look directly into his. He moved his face even closer, close enough that his dry, parched lips brushed against her eyes and cheeks. Her skin was smooth and delicate. But he went on talking.

"If those two weren't outside right now, I'd show you just what kind of man I really am . . . and what I do to women who think they can get the better of me."

Sara figured that Doc's threat was serious and genuine, but with Louis and especially McCain just outside—they could be heard if not seen from inside—the chances of Doc actually carrying out his threat were very slim.

"Do what you like, Doc," she said in a voice that blended defiance and lust.

But Doc released her and turned away. "I ain't buyin', lady."

This isn't working, Sara thought. Time for a different strategy.

"Okay, Doc, I'll level with you," she said, trying to sound sincere and honest. "I do know you have a bag full of cash in your hand. I thought it was Louis' bag, and I opened it. But I've been telling you the truth about everything else. I really want you. It's been a long time since I've met up with a man like you."

"Really?" Doc asked doubtfully.

"I'd do just about anything for you. Anything. Why don't we leave those two losers behind—kill them both for all I care—and ride off and enjoy ourselves and that money you're hanging on to. You won't find a better woman to spend it on. I know how to earn it."

"I'm sure you do. But the money ain't mine. It's kinda in my care right now."

"Whose is it?"

"A friend of mine."

"Well, the hell with him too. There's got to be enough money there for two people to live like kings for a long, long time. If your friend's fool enough to let other people carry his money around, then he deserves to have it stolen from him."

"My friend's name is Wyatt Earp, lady," Doc said, staring at her angrily. "He makes a habit of living longer than folks who call him a fool."

"I didn't know it was his money, and I really didn't mean anything by it," she cooed cagily.

"Lady, I ain't interested, and I'm tellin' you that for the last time. You keep away from me, and you double the distance between yourself and this satchel. If I see you anywhere near it, I'll break both your arms. And here's something else you might want to think about. If and when I'm interested in you, I'll take what I want when I want it."

Then, once again, he turned away from her and made his way out of the cave.

Sara watched him as he stepped into the brightness of the afternoon. She picked up one of her own valises and slowly walked to the mouth of the cave.

The son of a bitch, she thought, is as tough and cunning as the dime novels say, although he ain't the law-abiding gentleman they portray him as. He didn't fall for it. None of it. And, unfortunately, unlike plenty of other men, the way to his fortune was not through the fly of his pants.

Chapter Thirty-seven

"Where'd you folks get the horses?" Doc asked, stepping up to Stevenson and McCain.

The Scotsman held up the message from Chief Joseph. Doc took it, read it, and said, "I guess the chief wanted to unload the excess baggage. Although why he'd give away two perfectly good horses is beyond me."

"He probably figured we could use 'em more than he could," McCain chimed in. "Anyhow, now Louis and Sara can ride easier with us."

Doc was about to tell McCain to go to hell, that no way were they riding with them, but the look on McCain's face convinced him not to say anything. Another fight wouldn't solve anything.

"That's just fine," Doc said with more than a note of sarcasm. "Now we can be like one big happy family."

Sara joined the group near the horses. "Did I hear right? The chief left us two horses?"

"Yep," McCain confirmed.

Then she noticed the bare backs of the two animals. "He didn't give us any saddles."

McCain laughed. "You can't have everything now, can you?"

"You sure can't," Doc agreed, looking at Sara, letting her

know that his remark applied to things other than saddles.

"I can ride without, ma'am," McCain said. "You can take my horse if you like."

"I'm afraid I'm going to require a saddle also," Stevenson said. "I'm not much of an equestrian, I'm afraid."

"Wanna let him ride your horse, Doc? Or is that asking too much?"

"It's askin' too much," Holliday replied without missing a beat. "I need the saddle to fasten this here bag to. And as long as this bag's attached to this horse, I'm gonna be attached to it, too."

McCain knew better than to push the issue. He sized up the situation, then suggested that Stevenson take his horse, and he and Sara could ride double on the bare horse. That way he could help her stay on and not lose her balance.

"That won't be necessary," she retorted. "Give Louis your horse. I can ride bareback all by myself."

"Are your sure?" Stevenson asked.

"Yes, quite sure, I've been ridin' since I was a baby."

"Okay then," McCain said, "why don't we get these bags attached and get on our way?"

"Sounds good to me," Doc commented. "We wasted enough time already."

In a few minutes, the various bags, satchels and one rather hard, clumsy suitcase were fastened to the saddles of the two horses by means of ropes and lashes. Doc looked at the two burdened beasts and shook his head.

"This is gonna slow them down somethin' fierce," he noted.

"It would have been a lot slower if we only had two horses, and we had to ride double," McCain said. He knew the remark would rile Holliday, and he was correct, although Doc didn't say anything in reply. The look on Holliday's face said plenty though.

With an impressive amount of skill, Sara climbed on to the unsaddled bay and sat on it like she belonged there. The

Scotsman, on the other hand, had trouble getting into the saddle, even with the aid of the saddle horn and stirrup. Twice he tried to boost himself up, and twice he could not make it, awkwardly stepping down to the ground again.

"Let me give you a hand," McCain said.

As he helped Stevenson mount up, McCain thought about the group's next move. It should be easy: all they'd have to do is retrace their steps back to the railroad tracks and head westward until the next train passed. They'd either hit the next train station—and with any luck it wouldn't be too far down the track—or he and Doc would cook up some way of making the train stop between stations so they could board it. At worst they should be on a train in a few hours.

The gangly writer was finally sitting in place atop the bay, so McCain mounted the other of Chief Joseph's gifts. Ahead, Doc was already on his way down the hill.

"Let's go," he said. Sara and Stevenson pushed forward down the incline, and McCain followed behind. From the rear, it seemed that with every other step, the Scotsman was in danger of sliding out of the saddle. McCain had seen people who looked completely out of place on the back of a horse before, but no one looked more unsuited for riding than Stevenson.

"You'll find things a lot easier," McCain said to the man in front of him, "if you stick your feet in the stirrups, Louis."

The Scotsman peered over the left side of the horse and almost fell off doing so. But he managed to hold on and put his feet where they belonged. Instantly, he stopped swaying from side to side.

"Ah, yes!" he called back. "That's much better."

When all four riders hit level ground, they could hear Doc yell back, "The train line's that way, ain't it?" He was pointing northwest.

"That's right," McCain shouted back. "Should be about

228

half a mile."

"Thank God!" Doc declared. Besides missing Beaudine, and being days behind schedule, and having no liquor or tobacco left, and no food or water, and only a few bullets, Doc felt lousy. Real lousy. His chest was burning, and it hurt like hell when he took a deep breath or swallowed. He was also wet with sweat, and the sights before him were beginning to get blurry. Pretty soon, he knew, his dryness of mouth and throat would lead to one of his coughing spells.

"McCain, you got anything to drink?" he called, trying to ignore his other two companions.

McCain shook his canteen, but he couldn't feel anything swishing around in the tin container. "Sorry, Doc, not a thing."

Holliday didn't even bother asking the Scotsman or Sara. He knew they didn't have a canteen between them and doubted they were packing liquor among their belongings. Neither of them said a word when he asked McCain for a drink, so he accepted the fact that the dryness, the raspiness, would get worse until they hit a town, got a train, or found a creek or river somewhere.

"Shit," he mumbled to himself, and accepted the fact that his illness was going to get worse before it got better. He just hoped it wouldn't get bad enough that it would delay their mission any longer.

Chapter Thirty-eight

The sun was merely peeking over a hill, providing a dim, purple-orange light to the area. Trees no longer looked brown with green leaves; they stood like black silhouettes against the oddly-colored sky.

Not a single train had passed on the track. The four travelers hadn't seen a soul since they left the cave. And very few words had been spoken. McCain had asked Sara how she was faring a couple of times, and she had curtly answered him; Stevenson had made an occasional observation about the landscape or had asked the former army scout a question about the land, the Indians, or the railroad; and Doc had said little, but had coughed and cursed a great deal.

They were all tired. Hunger was causing rumblings in their stomachs, and all of them wanted to get off their horses.

Then McCain saw something ahead, something crossing the track perhaps two hundred yards away. The dim light made it difficult to see, but he squinted and managed to focus on the moving object.

It was a wagon, and in it were two people.

"Doc," McCain called, urging his horse forward until he rode next to Holliday. "There's a wagon up there. I'm gonna ride ahead and talk to those folks."

Doc was wobbly in the saddle, and he seemed to have trouble lifting his head from its craned-over position. His arms drooped at his side, the left one holding the reins in the limp fingers.

"I'll go with you," he said, then coughed, trying to clear his throat.

McCain got a good look at his face. Doc was pale as paper, and had it not been for his brown hair, eyes, and moustache, he would have seemed to have no facial features at all. The color had even gone out of his lips.

"Doc, you okay?"

"Yeah. Just tired, that's all. Need a drink."

"We'll get one soon," McCain said, thinking he'd never seen Holliday look worse. "Let me go up alone. If we all ride up, we might scare those folks."

"Fine."

Then McCain turned around, told Sara and Stevenson where he was headed, and rode off. The wagon had crossed the track and was standing motionless. As he neared it, he realized the two people on the wagon had seen him coming.

He stopped his horse a few feet shy of the wagon. An elderly couple sat in the carriage. McCain tipped his hat to the lady and addressed them both.

" 'Scuse me, folks, I was wondering if you could help me out."

"Sure," the old man said jovially, a big smile on his face. "What's the problem?" His thumbs were tucked under the straps of his overalls, which were about two sizes too big for him.

"We — my friends back there — and I have been waiting to flag down a train if one came by, but we haven't seen one all afternoon. Would you know how often they run past here?"

"Usually a few times a day," the old man replied, "but I hear they're shuttin' down the line in these here parts for a day or two. I hear tell some Injuns blowed a train apart —

231

right off the track, as I hear it told — 'bout thirty or forty miles down a piece. So's if you're waitin' for a train, it's my guess you got a mighty long wait. Ain't that right, Lucy?"

Lucy, a slightly-overweight, middle-aged woman, pulled her woolen shawl closer to her and replied, "That's what we heard."

McCain removed his hat and ran his fingers through his curly brown hair. "Well, that's mighty bad news for us. Is there a town anywhere near here. My friends and I could use some food, and I think one of them could use a doctor."

"There's a doctor in Piercetown, 'bout eleven miles from here. That's where we live. A couple 'a miles north of it actually. We're headed that way now, if'n you care to follow along behind us." The old fellow patted his wife's knee, and she looked at him as if she were getting an unspoken message of some sort.

"That's right kind of you," McCain said, "but my friend seems to be gettin' sicker mighty fast, and I think we'd better ride ahead. He might be needing a doctor real soon. Would you mind just pointing the way to . . . Pierceville?"

"That's Piercetown," the old man corrected and pointed. "It's 'bout eleven or twelve miles northwest of here." He sat up taller in the wagon and pointed again. "If you look ahead there a bit, you'll notice a road. Just follow it till it ends."

"It ends in Piercetown?"

"No, it just sorta ends . . . in the middle of nowhere in particular, up in them hills." The man began to cackle. "Hell, I oughta know. I helped make that road. Me and a bunch of other men. There was no way to get into that town when it first came to be. That's a hell of a place for a town anyway, far as I'm concerned. Up in them hills! Well, that's neither here nor there. If you keep a'goin' northwest for a couple of miles after the road stops, you'll see the town sticking out of the hills like an ugly pimple on a woman's ass." Then the man turned to his wife. "Sorry, dear."

The other three riders reached McCain and the two kindly people in the wagon. The old man and his wife studied the new arrivals and greetings were exchanged. Doc, however, said nothing; he just sat there on his horse, looking terribly wan.

"You must be the sick feller," the man said to Doc. "Well, don't you worry none, they got a darn good doctor in town. He'll fix ya right up."

Doc didn't answer. He looked like he was about to pass out.

The elderly gentleman turned to McCain. "He gonna make it?"

McCain was about to answer, but Doc suddenly revived a bit and spoke for himself. "I'll make it. I ain't *that* sick. How far?"

"Eleven miles," McCain answered.

Doc's eyes got watery and a coughing spell erupted. His body jerked so violently that he had to hold on to the saddle horn to prevent himself from coughing himself off the horse. Finally it ceased, and with his lower lip dotted with watery blood, he said, "Let's get goin'." With no further pleasantries, he urged his horse on.

"He's welcome to ride in the wagon with us if'n he wants," the old man said. His wife looked at him nervously as he said it.

"Thanks," McCain replied, "but I think he'd rather ride."

"How 'bout you, ma'am?" Again, the fellow's wife turned to him with a disturbed look.

"No thanks," Sara said politely. "I think I'd prefer to ride with my friends. We're sort of in a hurry."

Then McCain turned and stared at Stevenson. He figured the Scotsman might prefer to ride since he had been having such a difficult time riding the animal. But the old folks didn't ask him, perhaps figuring that most men in those parts had to ride to get around—after walking it was the second thing children learned—and Stevenson said nothing.

"Thanks, but we all best be moving," McCain said, once again tipping his hat to the elderly, genial locals. "Good day to you both."

As the three riders caught up with Doc, who was several hundred yards away, Lucy looked at her husband and breathed a sigh of relief. "Finally!" she said.

"They're gone now," he replied. "I told you when I first seen 'em there wouldn't be no trouble. You're too suspicious of everyone, my dear." Then he patted her on the arm and said, "You can put that away now. I doubt if they'll be comin' back. That feller there looked awful sick."

Lucy opened her shawl a bit and placed the sawed-off shotgun she had concealed under it at her feet in the wagon. Then she reclosed the shawl and pulled it tight.

"Maybe I am too careful, Owen, but you never know who these strangers are. They coulda been the law, like that other feller before. And if they was and they got a gander at the sixty-five jugs of corn whiskey we got covered up back there in the wagon, they mighta got suspicious."

"Oh, nonsense!" Owen snorted. "How would they know we was goin' to sell it to the Injuns? We coulda told them we was takin' it to town to sell."

"Just the same, I think you're crazy, offerin' them folks a ride."

"I knew they wouldn't take it. I just wanted to seem polite."

"Well, I think you . . ."

"Enough!" Owen shouted. "Nothin' happened. For God's sake, let's git goin' and unload this stuff. There's lots of thirsty Paiutes waitin' to drink this stuff. And the Paiutes don't like to be kept waitin'."

"Fine," Lucy agreed, but she managed to get the last word in. "But I still think you're crazy. Be more careful, will

234

you? Don't you ever learn? I already had to blow one feller's insides out today with that ugly-looking gun. That's enough blood on my hands for one day."

Owen frowned at his wife, shook the leather reins in his hand, and the wagon moved onward to the rendezvous point where they would turn over the liquor to the Paiutes, and the Paiutes would give them gold and guns.

Chapter Thirty-nine

McCain first spotted Piercetown from about a mile and a half away. It looked like a series of amber dots against the black hills. As he approached, the dots grew in size, and several new lighted spots appeared. Then the spots lost their roundness and turned into squares and rectangles. Eventually, these rectangles were revealed to be windows, light pouring from inside the rooms to the blackness outside.

McCain and his company rode down the only street they could find. It passed through the town, which seemed to be only a few blocks. At the very end of the street stood a two-story building, brightly lit. It was the only edifice in town with people standing outside in front of it. The sound of a piano could be heard inside, and the smell of tobacco and liquor wafted down the street.

"The saloon!" Doc said. "Thank God!"

"Maybe we should find the doctor, first," McCain suggested.

"No," Doc replied bluntly. "I'm okay. I need a drink. That'll cure my ills."

Without further ado, Doc pulled ahead of the rest of the group, secured his horse to the hitching post outside the saloon, and walked in, pushing a couple of customers who were lingering outside out of the way.

"Lord, the mere aroma of liquor seems to have revived him," Stevenson commented.

"Not completely," McCain added. "He left the satchel tied to his horse."

Sara said nothing but had noticed that, too. It would have been real easy to lift that bag when all the travelers were inside. But McCain had to be his ever-alert self. He was a nuisance. He was also the oddest man she'd ever met. He was appealing in a way she couldn't quite comprehend, but he was too quiet, too close-mouthed for her tastes. She always mistrusted people like that. They were always thinking too much, plotting too much, worrying too much to enjoy themselves and let life just happen.

"Let's go in," McCain said. "I'm sure we could all use a stiff drink. I'll even buy."

Sara couldn't resist making a comment. "My oh my, McCain, aren't we lettin' our hair down!"

"I guess," he answered, not understanding her comment fully. But he did know he was being needled. The smirk on her beautiful face told him that.

"I could go for a whiskey myself," Stevenson added, glad to be in the town, among people, back in civilization. His rear end and inner thighs ached more than he could ever believe possible. He prayed he'd never have to climb back on the horse again.

The trio dismounted. McCain stepped over to Doc's horse while the other two entered the saloon. He untied the bag and carried it into the saloon. Two men, both smoking cheroots, watched him. He nodded hello to them and tried to step between them. But instead of moving aside and letting him pass, they blocked his way.

"What's your name, stranger?" said the man on the left. He was a giant, standing almost a whole head taller than McCain, who at six feet was considered fairly tall himself.

"McCain," he answered. "Josiah McCain."

"You live in these parts?" the man continued. The dark cheroot stuck out of his face. It was the same color as the man's moustache and close-cropped beard, and had it not been for the red, burning tip might have looked like some bizarre extension of the man's hairy, lined face.

"No. I guess you don't either, or you wouldn't be asking me that question. These parts don't seem too populated."

The other man spoke up. "That skinny feller who went in a few minutes ago, he a friend of yours?"

"Which one?"

"The one who went in by hisself. That was Doc Holliday, wasn't it?"

McCain didn't like this one bit. He wasn't in the mood for any trouble right now, not after riding all day with practically no food or drink.

"Could be. What do you boys want?"

The second man spoke again. "Just askin'. Curious, that's all. Anything wrong with bein' curious?"

"No." But McCain remembered someone else telling him she was just curious a couple of days earlier. And he remembered how her curiosity almost got him killed.

Suddenly, the tall one elbowed his friend and said, "Thanks, Mr. McCain. We got to be goin'."

They marched away down the street, light from windows illuminating their forms as they strolled.

As he swung open the doors of the saloon and stepped into the smoky, boozy surroundings, McCain knew he'd have to keep his guard up this night. He'd have to be twice as alert, in fact, since Doc was so far gone he had completely forgotten about the money-filled satchel.

Piercetown! he thought. Even this damn poor excuse for a town couldn't provide a moment's peace. There are men in Piercetown who know Doc Holliday!

He looked around the saloon. There were lots of men and very few women. The bargirls were ugly. The men were even uglier. And the saloon was a pigsty, dingy, dirty, and damp. It stank of smoke, liquor, and sweat. It was a scummy hole in the middle of a scummy town.

Sara and Stevenson were sitting at a table in the corner just to the right of the doors. Stevenson seemed to be in pain and kept shifting his body, trying to get comfortable in the cheap wooden chair. Sara seemed merely bored, and sat in the chair with her arms crossed.

McCain stepped over to their table. He sat down in another chair and slammed the satchel on the table in front of him.

"What's eatin' you?" Sara asked.

"I don't know," he answered. "Nothing. Just tired. Fed up, I guess."

"With what?"

"With everything." He closed his eyes, trying to blot it all out: Sara, the two men, this town, Bat, his wife, Doc, the endless wandering, Earp, the loneliness, his sister, her bloody body, her mouth wide open, screaming even after death, calling for him. His shut eyes didn't help. The forms, the memories, the phantoms, all passed before his mind's eye.

"Mr. McCain, are you all right?" Stevenson asked, and McCain opened his eyes. "Perhaps you're ill too."

"Just beat. Doc and I ain't slept in at least a day and a half." It was the truth, but McCain knew it was only part of the truth. When fatigue set in, the seeds of doubt and anger and blame bloomed in his mind again. It was happening now. He had to stop it, had to get his mind on other things. "Let me get you two that drink I promised you. Watch this bag, will you?"

Sara looked at the satchel and then back at McCain. At first, she thought him a terrible fool, but then she realized that he hadn't been there in the cave. He had no idea what went on.

"Sure," she said. "I'll take good care of it."

McCain walked up to the bar where Doc was standing,

smoking a cigarette. He slapped Holliday on the back.

"How you feeling, Doc?"

"A little better," he answered. The color was beginning to come back into his face, and for the first time in hours, he looked alive and awake. "I told you the whiskey would work."

"You know, you left the bag outside."

Doc almost choked on the liquor he was swallowing. "Damn!" he exclaimed, and made a motion to go out and get it.

McCain grabbed his arm. "Relax. I brought it in."

The news didn't seem to take away Doc's anxiety. He looked at McCain's hands and then at his feet. "Where is it?"

"Stevenson and Sara are watching it back by that table."

Doc turned and saw the table. The satchel was sitting in its center. And right next to it was Sara's smiling face. She was grinning at Doc, and he knew it. She was purposefully trying to get him agitated.

"McCain, are you nuts or somethin'?" he asked. "Givin' that woman the bag to watch is like handin' it over to a thief."

McCain couldn't believe what he just heard. "Sara? I think you got her wrong, Doc. I thought you said you agreed with me that they were just victims of circumstance, and they aren't after your money."

"I did believe you, and I agreed with you. But that was before. Now I know better."

"What are you talking about?"

"I'm talkin' 'bout that bitch. You deaf or something? She practically told me she'd lay down and spread her wings if I'd give her some of the money. I think she knew about it all along."

"You sure you didn't read her wrong?"

"Hell, no. I was there, man. You weren't." Doc threw the rest of the whiskey in his glass down his throat, watching

240

Sara as he did. "Let me tell you something. You might be good with your fists and Indians and the like . . . but you don't know nothin' 'bout women."

McCain was speechless. What he was saying had to be true. Doc had no reason to make up such a tale. Disappointment filled McCain, adding to the well of other disturbing emotions he had been feeling.

He grabbed the half-empty bottle Doc had been working on. "Let me have this. I promised the lady and the Scot a drink." Then he marched back to the table with the bottle. In his hasty and disconcerted state, he forgot all about bringing a few glasses. Without recognizing him, he passed by George Wright, the Pinkerton agent, who stepped into the saloon.

Chapter Forty

"Here's the bottle," McCain said, sitting down and slamming the bottle on the table. "You can pour it yourself, I'm sure."

Sara was surprised by McCain's violent act. "Sure, I can pour. But I got nothin' to pour it in."

McCain moved the satchel closer to Stevenson. "Watch this while I go get the lady a glass. If she tries to even touch it, break her arm."

"What do you mean?" Stevenson asked.

"Just what I said."

"You got your nerve, McCain," Sara said. "What flea's got up your backside?"

"Hold it."

"I ain't holdin' . . ."

"Hold it, I said," McCain repeated. His voice was cold and the words seemed to force themselves out from between his tightly-clenched teeth. His eyes were focused on the bar, away from her.

She turned to see what it was that had distracted him. Then she saw the big frame of George Wright standing directly behind Doc at the bar.

McCain saw more than that. He saw Wright's hand inches away from his holster and his fingers twitching nervously. He saw the sweat that drenched Wright's pale yellow shirt.

Without another word McCain rose to his feet and stepped quickly up behind Wright.

"Hi, Wright," he said to the back of the Pinkerton's head. "I hope you're here for a social call and nothing else."

Both Wright and Doc heard McCain, and both turned around to face him.

Doc spoke next. "Well, glory be! If it ain't my friend the Pinkerton! What brings you to a God-forsaken town like this?"

Wright took a step to his left so that he would have the two men in sight, one on either side of him. "You know goddamn well what brought me here," he answered. "It's the same thing you're here for."

"We ain't here 'cause we wanna be," Doc said.

"Cut the crap, Holliday. You're after the gold and you know it. But I've worked too hard for the agency to let you ruin my career. In the morning I'll have that gold on its way back east, I promise you that. And not you or your friends there are gonna stop me."

"You still harpin' on that?" McCain said. "We told you on the train we ain't interested in your gold."

"Sure," Wright said, half-laughing, "right, I know. It's just a coincidence you're here in Piercetown."

"I guess it is," Holliday replied.

"And it's just a coincidence that you're travelin' with Sara Johnston, I suppose."

"Who the hell is Sara Johnston?"

"Her—as if you didn't know." Wright pointed to Sara, and Doc looked her way. She had a coy, sheepish look on her face, like a schoolgirl who'd been caught with her knickers down.

"Her name is Hillyer," McCain said.

"No, it isn't," Sara chimed in. "He's right. It's Johnston."

"So it's Johnston," Doc repeated. "So what?"

"So she's only the smoothest confidence woman this side of St. Louis. The agency's been after her for years. She's the lowest of women: a whore and a thief."

Instead of saying anything, Doc looked at his compadre with an "I told you so" grin on his face. McCain raged inside, although he knew he had no reason to. She'd never said much about herself to him. He hadn't asked, and she hadn't lied. But there could be no denying it to himself now. She was what he hoped she wasn't, and he was angry at himself for not seeing truth when it stared at him in the face.

"Okay, Mr. Pinkerton, so that's Sara Johnston," Doc said. "Thanks for fillin' us in on that. But all that other stuff is pure bullshit. We're here to rest and get some supplies, and then we're leavin'. You got gold here? That's wonderful. Good luck to you. You got nothin' to worry 'bout from us. But you just announced to everyone in this place that you're haulin' a gold shipment, so if I were you, I'd go protect it 'fore one of these upright gentlemen decides he'd like to relieve you of it."

Then Doc turned his back on Wright. He swiped someone else's bottle of whiskey and poured the liquid in his glass.

"Holliday, you're full of crap!" Wright said.

"Go away," Doc said calmly, without even turning around. "I ain't feelin' well, and the sight of you is makin' me even sicker."

Wright took a quick look at McCain, who was simply standing straight with his arms by his sides. Then he faced Holiday again. "And you're a damn coward too."

Doc swallowed his drink and turned around. He seemed calm and perfectly in control. But a shock of anticipation ran up McCain's spine when he saw Doc's eyes. They had that icy glare again, the same shine to them that he had seen moments before Doc gunned down Charlie Dombey.

"Now what makes you call me a coward? Didn't I kick your butt once already?"

"Where were you when the Indians attacked the train?"

Wright asked. "I seen McCain here fightin', but I don't recall seein' the brave Doc Holliday helpin' out."

At that moment, many of the patrons of the saloon finally caught on to the fact that the moustached stranger in their midst was Doc Holliday—*the* Doc Holliday. They moved away from the three men having an argument, spreading themselves to the far walls of the saloon, and, when possible, behind columns, tables, and anything else that might stop a stray bullet.

"You're a jerk, Wright," Holliday snapped coldly.

"And you're dead, Holliday," Wright screamed.

Then McCain stepped forward and grabbed Wright by the lapels. He moved quickly for a reason. He could tell Doc had been pushed over the limit, and he wanted to get Wright out of the saloon before Doc had time to go for his gun.

"And you're out of here, Wright," McCain said, pulling the big man by the lapels. A few steps closer to the door he added, "Get out and don't come back, Wright, unless you want to have worked all these years for a pension you'll never live to get." He pushed the Pinkerton, and the man went stumbling closer to the door.

Wright regained his footing, and stood still, facing the door. He smoothed the lapels of his jacket, then turned and looked at Sara, now standing behind the table.

Sara stared back at him.

Then Wright pushed open the swinging doors, stepped outside, and let the doors go. They swung in and out of the saloon and eventually hung still. Wright had disappeared into the night.

Doc poured himself yet another drink. He turned and faced the bar and tipped the bottle just above his glass. McCain walked up next to him and took the bottle when Doc was through with it.

"That man is the saddest excuse for a Pinkerton agent I ever seen," Doc commented.

"He might be back," McCain said. "You never know with fools like that."

No sooner had he spoken those words than the doors of the saloon swung open, and two men entered. They stood just inside the room and looked around. Both were holding guns at their sides.

McCain saw them out of the corner of his eye. It was an easy matter recognizing one of them. His height revealed his identity. It was the man who blocked his way earlier that evening. And the other was his accomplice.

McCain quickly swallowed his drink, refusing to look at the man eye-to-eye. But he could see them. He could also see that they were drawing their pistols.

"Look out!" McCain said, dropping his glass, taking a step back and falling to one knee. His hand was already wrapped around the handle of his Peacemaker.

Doc ducked down low and spun around on his soles. But he'd drunk too much, and he lost his balance and wound up sitting on the filthy wooden floor, facing the intruders.

The giant and his accomplice fired almost simultaneously. A bullet splintered the wooden bar just an inch above Doc's head. Another whizzed by McCain and shattered a bottle behind the bar.

McCain shot back and hit the giant in the left shoulder. A hole appeared in the man's shirt and blood oozed out of it. It dazed him and sent him reeling backward into a man who was just stepping into the saloon. McCain saw the man's face for a second. It was Wright.

Doc finally had his gun out, and he fired back at the other man. But Doc was still unbalanced, and the shot missed, hitting the wall about a foot to the right of the man.

McCain stood up and fired two shots in quick succession. The first took out the giant's friend, hitting him in the collarbone and sending him spinning until he crashed onto the floor next to Sara's chair. The other hit the giant in the forehead as he was raising his gun to fire a second time. An inch-wide black hole formed in the center of his forehead. His legs gave way, and he crumpled to the floor.

Wright watched the body fall before him, his eyes open in horror. Then he turned on his heels and fled back into the night. With the odds now in Holliday's favor, he knew he didn't stand a chance.

"Get the sheriff," the bartender yelled to no one in particular. "Will someone get the damn sheriff?"

The only person to do anything except stand around looking stunned was McCain. He got to his feet and started for the door.

"Get that son of a bitch!" Doc called after him.

But McCain was already out the door, looking up and down the street. He saw someone pass by a lit window and duck around a corner. In a second he was after him.

Stevenson was on his feet, peering out the door. He turned to Sara. "Perhaps we should help him."

She shook her head. "We'll just be in the way. And you'll probably just get your fool head shot off."

He felt insulted that she would say such a thing, but he also knew she was probably correct. He had no experience with a gun and very little in the art of fisticuffs. But he wanted to help, so he moved toward Holliday who was picking himself off the floor.

He saw the Scotsman coming and said, "I'm all right. You stay there and keep an eye on my mon . . . on your friend there." He cocked his head in Sara's direction.

Stevenson turned to walk back to the table, but he didn't watch where he stepped. He heard a sloshing sound at his feet and looked down. He was standing in a pool of blood that had sprung from the hole in the giant's forehead.

He suddenly felt dizzy, and knew he had better sit down before he passed out.

Chapter Forty-one

McCain turned the corner and stepped into the alley between two rather small buildings. He saw Wright turn another corner to the left. McCain stepped up his pace, turned the corner himself, and eventually caught up to the Pinkerton, who wasn't very light on his feet.

McCain tackled him from behind, and the two men fell to the ground. That's when McCain noticed a glint of steel. Wright's gun was out but wasn't aimed at anything; it seemed to wave in the darkness. McCain climbed forward and grabbed Wright's wrist. Suddenly, he felt a hand around his throat; the Pinkerton's grip was tight as a noose, which surprised him. Breathing became difficult. He couldn't swallow. Blood was being cut off from his head, and air cut off from his lungs.

McCain reached out with his other hand. His fingers spread across Wright's face, searching for the eyes. But he changed his mind, balled his hand into a fist, and pounded against the mouth. The body beneath him shook slightly, and the fingers around his throat eased a bit. But not much. He had underestimated Wright; the man's bulk worked to his advantage in hand-to-hand combat.

Finally, McCain could feel the gun in Wright's hand. The touch of warm skin had been replaced by the feel of cool steel. His hand grasped for the gun, tried to pull it out of his enemy's hand, but it was no good. His grip was too tight. Then Wright brought up a knee that caught McCain in the groin. It knocked some of the wind out of him, and some of the confidence also. And for just a second it caused McCain to relax his grip on Wright's wrist.

The hefty agent took advantage of that second and got his wrist free; without delay, he smashed the revolver against McCain's forehead. Waves of pain shot through Josiah's head, and he fell back off Wright. When his eyes could again focus a second or two later, the Pinkerton was just sitting up, pointing the gun at him. Instinctively, McCain kicked out with his foot. His boot slammed against Wright's wrist, causing the gun to fly into the air. It landed several feet away, out of the reach of both of them.

Wright rose to his feet, and McCain did also. The agent's right fist shot out, but McCain moved back enough to avoid it. In return, a right hook connected with Wright's jaw. Blood dripped from his lip, and the Pinkerton was forced back several steps. McCain kept up with him, and his left fist struck the other side of Wright's jaw. The agent shook his head in an attempt to clear it.

McCain studied the agent's face. Prior to this night, it had looked somewhat pitiable, the face of a poor slob who never had and never would reach that height of accomplishment he desired so badly. Now, however, the face appeared different: it was filled with rage, with hatred, with unleashed fury.

The agent rushed McCain, and Josiah cursed himself for not being ready for it. He was knocked back, and his head slammed against the side of the building. Flashes of light prevented him from seeing clearly.

Wright was searching for his gun, couldn't find it, and disappeared into the back door of a building. From all the junk behind it, McCain guessed that it was the blacksmith's shop. Saddles, blankets, and horseshoes were scattered on the ground for no apparent reason. McCain stood up and followed Wright into the shop. He saw him inside, coming toward him, armed with a pitchfork. McCain reached for his Colt, but the holster was empty. The gun must have fallen out during the fight outside. He looked behind him and spotted another pitchfork hanging from a couple of rusty nails in the wall. He quickly grabbed it and held it out to thwart the rushing Pinkerton. The man stopped short, and for a moment each pointed his weapon at the other. Then they began circling around the blacksmith's shop like two ancient Roman gladiators battling for their lives.

Wright struck out with the weapon. Its tines struck the handle of McCain's fork. He struck out again, but stabbed only air. Then he rushed McCain like a charging bull and swung the pitchfork by the handle like it was a club. It clacked against McCain's fork and forced it to one side. It also managed to smack into the side of McCain's face, cutting a bloody slash in his cheek just below the left eye. Stunned, McCain lowered the fork.

He felt the warmth of his own blood on his face, and he felt suddenly lonely and helpless.

The Pinkerton had his chance. He lunged forward, and this time the prongs bit into flesh. McCain felt a searing pain in his chest. He looked down and saw four small holes in his sweat-soaked plaid shirt. They became four bloody holes before his eyes.

The sight of his own blood made him furious. He had seen it before countless times, but this time it angered him to the point that he wanted to lash back at the man holding the pitchfork.

Wright stood a few feet away, cackling madly, holding the fork in both hands as if it were a spear. The man's twitching eyes told McCain that he was about to throw it. McCain swung his pitchfork like a club, knocking Wright's from his hand. It flew up and to the agent's left, finally landing in a small bale of hay.

The Pinkerton moved toward it, but McCain wasn't about to let him retrieve it.

"Don't pick it up again!" he yelled. But Wright's fingers were already wrapped around the handle.

"Don't, I said!"

Again his warning was ignored. Wright turned toward him, holding the pitchfork horizontally, with the tines pointed at McCain. He arched his back, his hand and forearm jerked backward, and his eyes had a murderous glaze.

But before Wright could heave the tool, McCain threw his fork with all his strength. The two center prongs dug into Wright's neck and pierced his vocal chords. The two outer tines cut along the sides of the man's thick neck, causing blood to spray onto both shoulders. The agent dropped his own weapon and tried to pull out the one penetrating his throat. He couldn't get a good grip on it, though, and a ghastly, choking moan escaped from his lips. He reached behind his head and felt the tines protruding from the back of his neck. The agent keeled over to the ground, the bloodied tool still piercing his neck.

"Very nice!" said an unfamiliar, husky voice from outside.

McCain turned to see who it belonged to.

It was a man he had never seen before. However, the tin star pinned on the man's jacket was quite familiar.

Chapter Forty-two

"If that poor bastard wasn't dead already," the sheriff of Piercetown said, "I'd have to put him out of his mercy."

He stepped into the blacksmith's shop and kicked some dried-up horse dung out of his way. The man stood about five and a half feet tall, but his lack of height was compensated for by his confident, authoritative attitude.

"I suppose you had a good reason for doin' that," he said, looking McCain squarely in the face.

McCain pointed to the four reddened spots on his chest. "Sure. It's called self-defense."

The sheriff tipped his black hat farther back on his head. A healthy tuft of thick gray hair slipped out from under his hat and hung down his forehead. "Those wounds don't prove nothing to me. You coulda started all this."

McCain was exhausted, both physically and emotionally. He didn't feel like dealing with this small-town lawman, but he knew he couldn't just walk away from him — or the body that lay near him. "There are at least thirty witnesses in the saloon that can testify that Mr. Wright here tried to gun us down."

"Us?"

"Us!" came a voice from the back entrance. Doc Holliday stood there leaning against the frame of the door, a cigarette hanging from between his lips.

"And who might you be?" the sheriff asked the new arrival.

"Doc Holliday, at your service!" he responded, removing his hat and waving it a wide arc. McCain recognized the exaggeration and sarcasm in the grandiose gesture, even if the sheriff didn't. And Doc's eyes told the whole story. They were streaked with fine red lines, and the lids drooped lazily over them.

He was rip-roaring drunk.

"Doc Holliday, huh?" repeated the lawman. "It seems you're a little out of your territory, don't it?" He pointed to the corpse at his feet. "You know this man?"

"Unfortunately, yes. He just tried to kill me and my associate Mr. McCain there." He took a step forward, craned his neck, and glanced at the bloody remains of the Pinkerton. "Dear God, McCain. It looks like he got you a bit angry. Where'd you learn to kill a man like that? All them years with Custer?"

Doc was trying to be amusing, but McCain failed to see the humor in his remarks. He kept quiet. And then he wondered if Doc had once more forgotten the satchel and left it in Sara's hands.

The sheriff interrupted his thoughts. "You two travelin' alone?"

Doc answered. "No, sir," he said, stepping aside, bowing, and extending his arm to the back entrance. "May I present Miss Sara . . . er . . . Hillyer, is it? . . . and from far across the sea Mr. Scotty Stevenson."

Sara stepped into the shop and immediately spotted the dead Pinkerton agent. She gasped, but held her ground. Behind her came Stevenson, visibly annoyed at being called "Scotty," carrying Doc's satchel. He, too, at once noticed the body and the blood that drenched its upper half.

"Good Lord!" he exclaimed and dropped the bag. It landed next to his left shoe. The queasiness he had felt in

253

the saloon returned, and his face went pale. "I must go outside for a moment," he announced, then quickly headed out the door.

"Don't go far!" the sheriff ordered, but the command was unnecessary and went unheard. Stevenson couldn't hear anything over the sound of his own vomiting.

"Why would this man want to kill you?" the sheriff resumed. "I know he was an operative for the Pinkertons. What have you folks to do with him?"

"Not a damn thing," McCain answered. "Our paths have been crossing for the last few days, and he kinda had the idea we were following him."

"And that's not the case?"

"No."

"You know why he was here?"

"Gold, probably."

"How'd you know that?"

"He told us."

"And you ain't after it?"

"No." McCain was growing restless. "Sheriff, you mind if we continue this little talk somewhere else? I think it might be a good idea to get Mr. Wright here buried. Unless you folks here in Piercetown are accustomed to treating your flies this well."

McCain was right. The buzzing was growing louder, and the insects were grouping on the dead man's neck and face.

"All right. Let's head for my office. I'll send my deputy over to bury him. But maybe I oughta have you do it."

McCain jaw closed tightly. "I don't bury men who try to shoot me in the back," he spat out.

The sheriff didn't pursue the matter. Instead, he marched out of the blacksmith's shop with the others following close behind. Only McCain stopped to see how Stevenson, who was leaning against a tree, was doing.

"You gonna be all right?" he asked.

Stevenson coughed twice, then forced the words out. "I

think so." He let go of the tree, and he and McCain followed the procession to the lawman's office.

In a moment they were there. As he entered, followed by the four travelers, the sheriff called out his deputy's name. "Adler. Get yer feet off my desk."

The young deputy had had his eyes closed, but when he heard the annoyed tone of his boss, he opened them, removed his legs from the top of the sheriff's desk, and sat up straight in the chair.

"Get out of my chair, too."

The young man did as he was told. "Sorry, Jim," he said. He looked at the small crowd of people in the office. "What's goin' on?"

Taking his place behind his desk, the sheriff answered, "I'll tell you later. Right now I'd like you to go over to Mr. Reno's and clean up the mess. There's a body that needs buryin', so you might stop by the undertakers as well."

"It's three in the mornin', Jim. He's prob'ly sleepin'."

The sheriff looked at him with amazement. "Then wake him up, Adler."

"Yes, sir." The deputy grabbed his hat and stepped outside.

"Why don't you take a seat, ma'am," the sheriff said to Sara. "There's only one other chair in here, as you can see. You gentlemen will have to stand."

Sara sat in the chair and crossed her arms over her chest. The sheriff studied her face. It was quite attractive and surprisingly calm. If the sight in the blacksmith's shop had upset her, she was doing an excellent job of hiding that fact.

McCain saw a telegraph wire message on the lawman's desk. It was addressed to Sheriff James Pierce.

"This town named after you, Sheriff?" he asked.

Pierce was surprised by the question, but looked up at McCain, who stood next to his desk, and answered it. "No. After my father. He built this place. He was a miner, a very

255

lucky one. And he and a group of other miners put up the first four buildings. He was the first sheriff of the town, too."

"That so?" Holliday commented. "That's real fascinatin'. Now can we get on with it?"

"Sure," Pierce said. "I happen to know that part of what you folks told me is true. I myself saw Wright and those two other fellers go in the saloon after you. But I don't know what brought you to Piercetown and right now I don't really care. If you are after gold—the gold that Wright came after—you're out of luck. It ain't here. It won't be here till tomorrow. But you folks aren't goin' to be here tomorrow. Do I make myself clear?"

Holliday lit up another cigarette. "You askin' us to leave town, Sheriff?"

"No. I'm tellin' you to leave."

"We just defended ourselves," Doc said.

"I know. I also know that every time a man defends himself in Dodge, someone dies. Like there ain't no other way. This is a mostly peaceful town, except when we get unwanted visitors. Then people start dyin', just like that fool Pinkerton lyin' dead across the street now."

McCain said, "I take it you weren't exactly fond of him either."

"No. He was a big bag of wind. Every stinkin' time he came to town, he thought he'd just sorta take over. Tell me how to do my job. And the man thought everyone but other Pinkertons were his enemies. But that's neither here nor there. I don't care 'bout him. What I care 'bout is this town. And as long as you folks are in it, the stink of death is gonna follow you around. So I want you out. Now."

"Can't do that, Sheriff," Doc laughed. He was still drunk.

"If you're just passin' through and not after the gold like you say, then I don't see why not."

Suddenly, Doc's mood took a turn for the worse. "Because, you penny-ante lawman, we came to get a few things, and we ain't leavin' till we get 'em."

The sheriff stood up. "Who the hell do you . . ."

"You," Doc answered, also rising to his feet, not even letting Pierce finish his question. "You, you two-bit son-of-a-bitch!"

McCain tried to move between the two men. He could see the sparks bursting into flames. But he didn't move fast enough.

The lawman's gun was already out, pointed at Doc. "You're under arrest, Holliday. You ain't in Kansas anymore. I don't have to take your crap."

The man took a step back, then glanced aside at McCain, who was trying to figure a way to cool both tempers down. "Don't do anything stupid!" Pierce said to McCain.

But the sheriff's sideways glance was a mistake. In the two seconds it lasted, Doc drew his Colt and shot a hole in the lawman's stomach as he finished speaking. The impact at such close range sent him flying backward into the wall directly behind him. He hit it hard, and the gun fell out of his hand. His knees gave way, and he fell forward, his torso slamming the top of his desk.

"Jesus!" Stevenson cried out. "You killed him."

Sara remained seated, but her face no longer registered a calm expression. She looked at Holliday with fear and disbelief in her eyes. This was the man she tried to seduce? This was the man who threatened to rape her — or worse — if she got in his way? He was crazy, she thought, truly crazy. And she swore to herself that she'd keep as far away from him as possible until the time came when she could get away from him completely, with or without the money.

McCain charged Doc. He grabbed his wrist and forced it down by his side. "You stupid son of a bitch. What did you do that for?"

Doc looked at McCain coldly. "He had it comin'," he said.

"He didn't have anything coming, you drunken fool. We've got to get out of town fast now. The whole town'll be down here soon."

"Let 'em come. I'm ready for 'em."

"You gone crazy or something?"

Doc wavered a bit on his feet, and his eyes rolled drunkenly in their sockets. "Let go 'a my arms, McCain."

"Put that gun away."

"*Leggo 'a my arms.*"

"Sure." McCain released them, then brought up a right fist that landed squarely under Doc's jaw. The blow caught the intoxicated man completely by surprise, and it knocked him over on his back. When he hit the floor, he stayed there, out cold.

"Louis, help me get him up," McCain said, taking charge. "We've got no time to waste. We've got to get out of town before these folks realize what's happened to their sheriff."

Sara stood up and coldly said, "Why don't you leave him here? Holliday shot the sheriff. Leave him. Why should we risk our necks for him?"

McCain didn't bother to answer her words, but the look on his face told Sara she'd better discontinue that line of thought. He and Stevenson each had one of Doc's arms around his neck and carried him outside the sheriff's office.

"Head for the horses," he instructed, "and keep your mouths shut. Leave the talking for me."

Stevenson was having difficulty dragging Doc along. "But we never had a chance to purchase any supplies, or see the doctor, or . . ."

"We'll have to do without them. Keep moving."

A small army of men left the saloon and stood in front of it. In front of them, in the street, McCain spotted their horses. Except for the bag which Stevenson still had in tow, their other baggage was still secured to the horses. Apparently, McCain reasoned, the folks in this town were basically honest. No one had stolen their bags. It was hard to tell in the darkness, but it seemed no one had even touched them. Folks that honest, he knew, don't just let the killers of their sheriff ride out of town nice-and-easy-like. But if they hadn't realized what had happened yet . . .

They were steps away from from the front of the saloon. The young deputy stood there with half a dozen men, one of whom was dressed in black and white with a derby hat that was entirely too small for his head. Even with the inappropriate hat, McCain thought, the man even *looked* like an undertaker.

Before the deputy had a chance to talk, McCain said, "Deputy, you'd better get down to the sheriff's office. Some of Wright's men forced their way in. They killed the sheriff; they even got Holliday here."

Deputy Adler leaned forward and saw that Doc was unconscious. "Jesus, they killed Doc Holliday." Then he turned to one of the men behind him. "I told you that was Doc Holliday. Now pay up that five bucks."

"Maybe you didn't hear me, Deputy," McCain repeated. "The sheriff's been shot."

This time the message hit home. The deputy stared at McCain for a moment, then waved his arm and the men followed him down the street.

McCain grabbed Holliday by the legs and lifted him onto his horse. He removed the rope from the saddle horn and did a quick job of securing Doc to the saddle. The rope might hold; it might not. But there was no more time to waste.

"Get on your horses, and let's get the hell out of here," McCain ordered. "Those men will be back here in a minute."

Stevenson climbed onto his horse and held the reins in one hand and the satchel in the other. "You had better take possession of this, Mr. McCain," he said, handing him the

259

bag.

"Good idea," he said. Then McCain climbed on to his horse, checked that Sara was on hers, and spun the steed around.

"We're not going to ride too quickly, are we?" Stevenson asked. He wished McCain had tied *him* to the saddle.

"As fast as these ponies'll carry us."

Then they were off, riding out of the town, into the darkness of the surrounding rocky heights. Behind them, they could hear the loud voices of the men who would be following them, determined to bring to justice the killers of their beloved Sheriff Pierce.

Chapter Forty-three

"Head for that ravine," McCain said, holding onto the reins of Doc's horse as well as his own.

As silently and quickly as possible, Sara and Stevenson followed. The Scotsman silently thanked God that his battered rear end could at last sit still. The last half-hour of fast riding had jarred his brains, bruised his thighs, and nearly turned his empty stomach.

"He still out?" Sara asked, nodding at Doc.

"Yeah," McCain answered. "Maybe I should try to wake him up. We might need his gun."

"No, don't do that!" Sara pleaded. "Give me his gun. I can shoot if I have to."

"I imagine you can," McCain said sarcastically. Then he looked out into the night, the black mountains cutting jagged peaks against the blue-black sky. He concentrated on those mountains they had already traveled, looking for signs of the men he knew were following them. But he neither saw nor heard any sign of them. No lights. No sounds of men or horses or guns.

"I think we lost them," he announced, "but we'd still

better be careful. They know these mountains a hell of a lot better than we do."

Stevenson shifted his weight in the saddle. "Would it be possible for us to rest now?" he asked. "I don't believe I could ride another step."

"Not yet. I want to get us safely above this ravine. That way we'll see them coming."

"I could use a rest myself," Sara declared. "It's been about twenty hours since any of us got any sleep. And I'd like to get some before that animal comes to."

"What animal?" Stevenson inquired.

"That one," she replied, pointing to Doc. "The quick-tempered rattlesnake."

"We can rest later," McCain said. "Let's move up this trail into that thatch of pines."

The four of them moved on. They followed a steep, narrow trail up a hillside. It was rough going for both the horses and the riders. The surface of the trail was strewn with rocks, tree stumps, and gopher holes. More than once one of the horses almost stumbled. And a lame horse was the last thing they needed.

The riders had to lean forward on their mounts to keep their balance, but it was difficult; they were working against the law of gravity. Through it all, though, Doc remained unconscious. Now and then a muted grunt escaped his lips. McCain's method of securing the gun-fighter to the horse was holding; had it not, Doc's body would have slid off the back of the animal and rolled down into the thick underbrush that covered the ground on both sides of the rarely-traversed trail.

The riders finally reached a part of the incline that leveled off. To the left, McCain could see a clearing, a patch of flat grass that would allow him a view of the last several miles they had traveled.

"Over there," he said, pointing to the spot.

As they moved onto the clearing, a couple of shots

rang out, echoing back and forth between mountains. But to McCain's surprise, the shots were being fired from above, somewhere higher up on the mountain.

"Take cover!" he said, but he needn't have. Sara and Stevenson were already off their mounts, ducking behind a wide oak tree.

"It seems we didn't lose them," Stevenson shouted to McCain, who was busy unfastening Doc from the horse.

"Can't be them," McCain answered. "They couldn't've made it up that far."

"Then who could it be?"

"That's what I'm going to find out."

McCain finally had Doc free and dragged the man behind a huge rock jutting out of the ground. Then two shots rang out. One hit the rock in front of Doc, and small pieces of stone sprayed everywhere.

"I don't know who's up there, but he's got a shotgun," McCain informed his companions. "Stay here. I'm going to pay my respects to whoever that is."

He quickly made his way out of the clearing and into the thick underbrush. He knelt on one knee, breathed as noiselessly as possible, and listened. Two more shots were fired. This time McCain was able to determine the approximate location of their origin. He drew his Peacemaker and slowly and silently progressed up the mountain.

After a couple of minutes of silence, another pair of shotgun blasts roared through the dim light of the dawning sun. The assassin was near. Perhaps a couple of hundred feet to McCain's left. He stood tall in the underbrush and surrounding trees and gazed in that direction. Ahead, he saw another clearing, much smaller in area than the one inhabited by his friends down below. He marched toward it, carefully avoiding making any sound which would give away his approach.

Then he saw him. And he heard him.

"Goddamn it. No son of a bitch's goin' get my money.

By God, they won't."

McCain stood a few yards directly behind the man. When he heard the man's constant mumbling, he understood what this was all about. The man was a prospector—he'd probably found something worthwhile—and was protecting his claim. McCain had met prospectors before; some he knew quite well. But this man did not fit the description at all. He was by far the blackest black man he'd ever seen. He looked ancient, seventy-five at least. A circular crown of thick gray hair covered the back and sides of his head, highlighting the bald center of his head. He was short, but muscular. And as he leaned against a huge stone formation, loading his gun, McCain noticed the man's missing lower limb and the peg-leg that served in its stead.

"Jesus, Lord! He'p me smite these sinners," the man rambled. "Look 'pon me with favor, Lord, so's I can kill these sons of bitches!"

There was no reason to hurt this old fellow, McCain knew, unless he got totally out of hand. McCain took a few steps toward him. The man had his gun reloaded and was pointing it over the giant rock that hid his presence from those down below. McCain decided to wait where he was until the man fired the round.

The shot was fired, and the man cackled to himself. "Ha! Take that, ya damned unholy denizens of hell. Ya won't get my claim, for the Lord's with me!"

Then the man turned, the weather-worn shotgun held loosely in his hands. He sat down against the rock, broke open the shotgun, and searched the ground for his box of cartridges. They were gone.

"What the hell?" cursed the man. "Where did them cartridges get to? Jesus, Lord, why are you doin' this ta me?"

A voice answered him. "Maybe He doesn't like you condemning folks before the Judgment Day."

The old black man looked up and saw McCain holding the box of ammunition. He dropped the shotgun and sat back against the stone.

"G'head. Ya can kill me if ya want, but y'all never find my claim. I ain't afraid ta die. I made my peace with the Lord."

"I don't want to kill you," McCain replied. "But I don't want you trying to blow my brains out either."

"Well, what do ya want?"

"I want you to quit firing that cannon. My friends and I are on the run, and we don't particularly want the folks chasing us to know our whereabouts."

"Who's after you?"

"A posse from Piercetown, I imagine."

"Piercetown? You rob somebody there?"

"No. One of my friends killed someone."

"Who?"

McCain realized he might have talked too much already, but he decided to go on. "He shot the sheriff."

The man laughed gleefully. "Pierce! Your friend shot Pierce?"

"Yeah, I'm afraid so. That funny?"

"That son of a bitch was the spawn of Satan hisself. I know. He and his gone-to-hell father been trying to catch me fer years."

"Why?"

"It's a long story."

"Then it'll have to wait." McCain stepped forward, looked down off the mountain, then squatted down next to the prospector. "If I give you back your ammunition, will you swear not to use it on me?"

"You ain't after my gold?"

"Friend, all we want to do is hide a while, then get as far away from here as we can."

"You swear by the mother of God you're tellin' me the truth?"

"I swear."

"And you killed Pierce? You swear it?"

"I swear."

Again the man cackled, and this time he clapped his hands together. "Son of a bitch! It's gonna be nice havin' company fer a change. Tell yer friends ta come up."

"Here," McCain said, handing the man back his cartridges. "I'd better go down and get them. I don't think yelling off the mountain's a good idea right now, especially since you've been making enough noise with that cannon of yours to wake the dead."

The man stood up on his one good and one peg leg. "I got some coffee cookin' over yonder."

"Well, keep it hot, I'll be right back."

McCain left the man and made his way down the mountain. Just the sound of the word "coffee" made him feel a whole lot better.

Chapter Forty-four

He had gone from the clearing, but the aroma of the brewing coffee led McCain and company to the old prospector's campsite. McCain wasn't much of a coffee drinker, but he usually downed a couple of cups when he awoke at daybreak. On this morning, he absolutely craved it; the lack of sleep for the last couple of days made him feel drowsy and depressed. The kick from the coffee would revive him, he hoped, because there was no certainty of any sleep in his near future either.

Doc walked behind him, covered with sweat. His legs barely held him up or moved him forward. His illness made even staying awake a tiring effort. But the old man's last shotgun blast had startled him out of his sleep.

Behind Doc walked Stevenson, feeling somewhat ill himself. He tried to locate a single square inch of his bony body that didn't hurt. He couldn't find one, but pushed on, thinking that even if he had to walk fifty miles on foot, he couldn't possibly feel any worse than he did at that moment.

Sara brought up the rear. She felt a bit safer when there was a body—even Stevenson's—between her and Doc. She hoped the coffee was as good as it smelled.

"Welcome, everybody," said the oldtimer. "Pull up a rock and set a spell."

They all did just that. Doc eyed the little cigar that hung out of the man's mouth.

"You got an extra smoke?" he asked.

"Sure," said the man. He reached into his jacket pocket and pulled out a cheroot. "Here you go."

"Thanks. If you got extras, I'll buy some from you."

"You don't look so good, stranger. Maybe you shouldn't be smokin' them things."

Doc lit up the cigar. "You a doctor?"

"Lord, no!"

"Well, I am, so leave the doctorin' to me, okay?"

McCain spoke up. "Don't mind him," he said to the prospector. "He's just waking up, so he's a mite cranky."

Doc frowned at McCain but said nothing. Instead, he enjoyed the cheroot, sucking the smoke in deep, holding it, then releasing it ever so slowly through his nostrils.

"I betcha he's the one that sent Pierce to his heavenly Father," the old man said. "Ain't I right?"

McCain nodded, then glanced to Doc. The gunfighter was annoyed, but too weak to do anything about it.

"What did you tell this old nigger for?" Doc said.

"Why not?" McCain responded.

" 'Cause he'll probably go shootin' his black mouth off, that's why!"

"I won't be doin' any such thing, ya' son of a bitch," the man shot back. "And is this how ya treat your host? Don't be askin' this ol' nigger for no more smokes, ya hear?"

"Hold it, everyone!" McCain interrupted. "Why are we all fighting? What's your name, friend?"

The man poured himself a cup of coffee. "John Nel-

268

son Maxwell is my real name, but I don't answer to that no more, since I ain't no slave no more. That name reminds me of them days, an' I don' like thinkin' 'bout 'em. The folks 'round here call me Silver Johnny. So call me that if'n ya like."

"Okay," McCain said, taking and shaking the man's hand. "Silver Johnny, my name's McCain. Josiah McCain. The lady over there is Sara . . . Johnston."

Sara smiled at the man. "Can you spare some coffee?" she asked.

"Why sure, miss," Johnny said, handing her the cup he had just poured for himself. "Anythin' for a lady as pretty as you."

"Thanks." She took the tin cup and held it for a minute before tasting the coffee. When she did take a sip, she found that it tasted much better than she had imagined. "This is good. Thanks."

"My pleasure," Johnny smiled. "I'm afraid you folks'll have to wait your turns. I only got the one cup."

Johnny noticed Stevenson staring at him. "Who might you be?" he asked.

"I'm Robert Louis Stevenson. Please call me Louis."

"Nice ta meet ya." Then he turned to the only unintroduced member of his guests. "And who are you?"

"I'm Doc Holliday."

Johnny nodded, then turned away from Doc unimpressed. "Wish I had me more cups."

"Doc Holliday," Doc repeated through a cloud of tobacco smoke. "From Dodge."

"I heard ya that first time, son. Ya say the name like I'm s'posed ta know it."

"You never heard of Doc Holliday?" Doc asked.

"Nope. You some kinda outlaw or somethin'?"

Doc was going to explain, but changed his mind. "Forget it."

Sara finished the coffee and returned the cup to the

old man. He took it, refilled it, and handed it to Mc-
Cain. "Here," he said.

"Thanks." McCain took a sip of the hot black liquid.
Then he asked. "How long you been up in these mountains?"

Johnny tugged at his gray whiskers. " 'Bout twelve
years, I believe. Maybe thirteen."

Doc snickered out loud. "No luck, huh? After thirteen
years, I'd think about packin' it in, oldtimer."

"No luck?" Johnny repeated, his eyes aglow with
pride. "I've had plenty a luck."

"You found gold?"

"Sure."

"Then why are you still sniffin' around for it?"

"Friend," Johnny continued, "I spent it, the Lord forgive me. I wasted my money drinkin', gamblin', and
fornicatin'. So's I had to return to git more."

"I think you're full of baloney," Doc said.

"You do, do ya? Well, take a look at this." Johnny
reached into the other pocket of his jacket and pulled
out a gold nugget the size of a billiard ball. "This ain't
baloney, son. This here's gold."

Doc sat up tall. "That thing's real?"

"Real as the nose on my face. And there's plenty more.
And not just gold. Silver too. That's how I got my
name, Silver Johnny. I'm the only blessed son a God to
strike silver in these mountains. I got plenty a that too."

"Let's see it," Doc said.

Johnny began to laugh like a madman and slapped his
good knee, the one unattached to the wooden peg. "You
must think me pretty damn stupid, son. The good Lord
gave me brains along with my pretty face. I got my
treasure safely hid. It's buried in the ground, not very
from here. Only me an' the Lord know where it is. If
you'd like to try an' find it, you're welcome to. But you
got a damn lot a diggin' ta do." Then Johnny laughed

again and put the nugget back in his pocket.

Stevenson listened to the old man with interest. He had never met a prospector, but felt like he knew the man through the books he had read about the Rush of '49. The Scotsman was fascinated by the size and scope of this American Gold Rush. And he had recently read the newspaper accounts of the decline of John Augustus Sutter, at whose mill in California gold had first been discovered.

"Why do you bury your fortune?" Stevenson asked. "Wouldn't the bank in Piercetown be a more reasonable place to keep it?"

Johnny looked at Stevenson for a moment, then commented, "You talk mighty funny, son."

"I'm from Scotland."

"Well, to answer your question, no, it's safer to keep my good fortune right near ta me. Years ago, I brought my first find down that that cursed town, an' they stole it right from me. Took it right away from me. Said no black nigger got a right to that much money. They beat the devil out a me—Lord, thy will be done—and stole my money."

"That's outrageous!" Stevenson exclaimed. "Did you turn to the law for assistance?"

Once again, the old man cackled loudly. "Young Sherriff Pierce, that unholy son of a bitch, was the one who beat me. That's why I bury it here, safe in the good ground near me, where God almighty can keep a eye on it for me."

"Well, Pierce won't be botherin' you no more," Doc commented dryly.

"You the one got him?"

"I am."

"Then I'm grateful to ya." Johnny took the empty tin cup that McCain handed to him and filled it again with coffee. Handing the cup to Doc, he added, "But call me

271

a nigger again, and you'll be joinin' Pierce in eternal damnation."

Doc took the cup and said, "Sure. I'm terrified." Then he drank the scalding coffee in one long gulp. When he was finished, he tossed the cup to Stevenson. "Here, Scotty, you're next."

The writer caught it, and rising to his feet, gave it to Johnny to refill. Then he turned to Doc. "My name is Louis! Do you understand?" His thin face was red with anger. "Even a dunderhead like you should be able to remember a name as plain and simple as Louis!"

Doc looked at McCain angrily. "What's a dunderhead?"

McCain shrugged his shoulders, pretending ignorance in an effort to once again save Stevenson from his own willingness to put his head on the chopping block.

Johnny put the coffee cup in Stevenson's hand, then stepped away. "Lord, even I know what that means."

That remarked made Doc even more enraged. He stood up and stared at the black man. "Well, what the hell does it mean?"

Stevenson, still not content at riling Doc again, said, "It means, Mr. Holliday, an addlepate, a dullard, a moron."

Sara laughed so hard she slipped off the rock she was sitting upon and crashed to the ground, where she remained, flat on her back, her legs circling the stone.

Doc's eyes squinted. The Scot's insult was bad enough. The old man's comment was worse. But Sara's mocking laughter was all he could stand. He turned toward Stevenson, drew his gun . . . but couldn't raise his arm. A strong hand was clasped around his wrist from behind.

"Forget it, Doc," McCain said into his ear.

"I'll kill you too, McCain!" Doc warned. "You let go."

"Drop it."

"You son of a bitch, you're makin' a habit of this. I'll

cut . . ."

But before Doc could finish his threat, two shots rang out. One blew the cup from Stevenson's hand, sending the Scotsman back a couple of steps in shock. The other bullet sliced the front of Holliday's forehead, leaving a bloody groove less than an inch above his eyebrows. The impact didn't shatter any bone, but hit hard enough to knock the gunfighter unconscious. He fell to the ground, his left arm wrapped around McCain's ankles.

Chapter Forty-five

"Listen, you old nigger," echoed a voice, "you're har-borin' criminals up there. We're gonna get them, and we're gonna get you too."

Doc remained unconscious on the ground. The others took cover. McCain and Johnny hid behind the rock that the prospector had used earlier for cover. McCain had his Peacemaker out, but had not yet returned any fire. Johnny was holding Doc's Colt in his right hand.

"It's that goddamn deputy," Johnny announced. "I recognized his screechin' voice."

McCain looked around, saw that Sara and Stevenson were hidden behind a tree and another stone formation respectively, and turned back to Johnny. "Sorry we got you involved. We should have kept moving."

" 'S all right. I like a good fight now and then."

"But they'll have an idea where your claim is now."

"Nah, they still got to find it now, don't they? I'd like to see 'em get it."

A few more gunshots exploded from lower down the incline. One of them splintered some bark off the tree protecting Sara. She squatted down and hugged the tree more closely.

"How many men you reckon he's got?" Johnny asked.

McCain lifted his head over the rock. "It's hard to tell. I can't see them. But he had a small army with him back in town."

A shot rang from down below, and this time McCain saw a small puff of smoke rise from a bush. He leaned on the rock, braced his arm, and squeezed off a shot. It connected. He heard the man yell out in pain.

Johnny laughed at the sound. "Got the son of bitch. You're some shot there, friend."

"When I have to be."

"Let me have a try." Johnny stood up on his mismatched pair of legs and pointed the Colt out in front of him. He pulled the trigger, but the shot went wild.

"Son of a bitch! This thing's got some hair-trigger! I'd be afraid to use this thing all the time."

Then a volley of shots rose from below. One of them ripped into Johnny's chest between his left shoulder and his heart. The old man dropped to the ground, the peg still poking into the dirt, one knee raised skyward.

"Lord Jesus!" he moaned, holding his open hand over the wound.

McCain knelt over the man. "Johnny . . ." he said. He was at a loss for words. This friendly old guy had taken a slug for nothing, taken it because McCain was too tired to keep moving.

"It's about my time," Johnny said, struggling for breath. "It's time to see my Lord."

"You'll be fine," McCain said, but he knew otherwise. The ex-slave was losing a good amount of blood.

Stevenson remained behind the rock to their left, frightened and sad. He had liked the old man, found him unique. He was a man who enjoyed living despite the efforts of men to deprive him of his freedom and his money.

Sara left the cover of the tree and made her way over to McCain. She knelt next to him and looked into Johnny's dying eyes.

"Johnny, tell us," she said. "Where's the gold? You can tell us."

McCain stared at her in disbelief and disgust. "Shut your mouth. Let the man . . ." he was going to say "die in peace" but changed his mind and said ". . . alone."

"Tell us," she continued, ignoring McCain. "You don't want that deputy gettin' it, do you?"

"I said shut your mouth!"

Sara looked into his eyes angrily. "What's wrong with you, McCain? He won't need the money where he's going. We'll get it, and then we can get out of here. You and me." Her facial expression changed abruptly to a smile. "We'll leave those two behind. With this gold and Holliday's cash we'll be rich. We can disappear. Together. You and me."

McCain was going to unleash a verbal assault, but Johnny spoke first.

"It's okay," he sighed. "You can have it." He took a deep breath, but couldn't hold the air in his lungs; it came coughing out. "The gold . . ."

"Where?" Sara said frantically. "Where is it?"

A wave of gunfire went off, but it was louder and was being fired from a position closer than it was before.

Johnny's eyes rolled up into his head, leaving only white in the sockets. But he was still breathing, still alive. Suddenly, the brown circles fell back into the eyes and the dying old man said, "Ain't no light in here, Jesus." The last breath then left his lungs.

Sara didn't want to believe it. She took the dead man's hand and held it gently. "Johnny, where's the gold?"

"He's dead," McCain said. "Can't you see that?"

"He can't be."

McCain stood up, looking down at the back of Sara's dark-haired head. "You make me sick," he said.

Then Stevenson called out. "I can see them. They're getting very close. Can we retrace our steps and reach the horses?"

McCain too saw the men slowly progressing up the slope on foot. He fired at one who wore a red shirt. The man stood erect silently for a moment with his arms outstretched. Then he toppled backward and his body rolled down the slope until its path was blocked by a tree.

"Forget the horses," he said. "We'll never make it. We've got to move it on foot. Stevenson, you carry Doc's bag; I'll drag Doc along. Ma'am," he continued, his contemptuous gaze on Sara, "you can come along or stay here and get buried along with the oldtimer's gold. It's up to you."

Without waiting for an answer, he carefully ran over to Doc and lifted the unconscious bulk onto his shoulders. He saw that Stevenson had the bag and was ready to move.

"I'm comin'," Sara said, although had the deputy and his men not been so close, she might have stayed a few minutes longer to search the old prospector's possessions for a clue to his fortune's whereabouts.

"Then follow me and keep close," McCain instructed. "And don't make a sound."

He headed for the dense underbrush he had traversed on his way up the mountain. This time he wondered if it would be dense enough.

Chapter Forty-six

"Please," Stevenson sighed, "I simply cannot walk another step."

McCain felt the same. They had been walking over and around mountains for three or four hours. The sun was intolerably hot when they walked out in the open; there wasn't a cloud in the sky. And the weight of Holliday's body on his shoulders added a great deal to McCain's fatigue.

He looked around, noticed they were on a somewhat level patch of ground surrounded by trees and other vegetation, and decided that this spot of earth might provide them with a moment's peace.

"All right. We'll rest here."

McCain gently lowered Doc's body to the ground. The sick gunfighter's face was streaked with caked blood. His face looked like that of a corpse, but he was still breathing through his raspy gullet. McCain piled some leaves under his head, trying to make the man as comfortable as possible.

"How bad is he hurt?" Sara said, standing over Doc

and the kneeling McCain.

"It looks a lot worse than it really is," McCain said. "The wound on his head's just a real deep scratch. He's stopped bleeding. It's this illness of his that's got me worried. I've never seen anyone so worn out."

"Consumption can truly steal the energy from a man," Stevenson interjected.

"Well now, don't you know it all," Sara snarled. "You ain't no doctor."

"No, but believe me, I know about consumption."

Stevenson had a strange look in his eyes, McCain noticed, and he too looked white as snow. The Scotsman stood still, staring off into space, still holding Doc's bag.

"You don't look so good yourself," McCain commented. "Why don't you sit down and take it easy."

As the frail writer leaned forward and placed the bag on the ground, his jacket hung open in the front. McCain noticed the man's shirt was almost completely soaked with sweat. Then Stevenson sat down as slowly and creakily as a man three times his age.

"You aren't getting sick on me too, are you, Louis?" he asked, kneeling before him and looking into his eyes.

"I'm afraid I am," he answered. "This has all been a bit much for me."

"Well, take it slow now and try to fight this thing."

"I'll try."

"Anything I can do? You don't seem as bad as Doc. You're not passing out or coughing up a storm."

"I don't smoke or drink like he does."

"Would food help?" McCain said, then realized what a ridiculous question it was. Of course food would help. They hadn't really eaten a full meal since they left the Nez Perce.

"It might help," Stevenson answered. He suddenly starting trembling, and he wrapped his arms around himself. "I've got to sleep. Sleep might help."

"Go ahead. I think this time we lost them. We can rest a while."

"That's what you said the last time," Sara snapped.

"You want to keep moving?"

"No. My legs are achin' as bad as anyone's. And I guess we have lost them. I haven't heard a shot in the last couple of hours."

When McCain looked down at Stevenson again, the man was already asleep. Perspiration was pouring down the sides of his face.

"He's sick, too," he said, standing up.

"This consumption thing contagious?" Sara asked.

"I don't know. Wish I could help them."

"Why don't we help ourselves?"

"What do you mean?"

"I mean help ourselves. Help ourselves to Doc's money and high-tail it out of here. It's just our luck to get stuck with two dyin' men — probably the only two men this side of St. Louis with this sickness — and a damn posse chasin' us."

"How do you know they're dying?"

"How do you know they aren't?"

"You're no doctor, either."

"No, I'm not," Sara said, shaking her head and pointing a finger at McCain. "But I ain't pretendin' I am either. And I ain't pretendin' I'm Mr. High and Mighty Do-Gooder. You don't fool me for a moment, Mr. McCain. I don't know exactly what your game is, but I know there's a game bein' played. You're after something."

"Like you?"

"Yeah, like me. I'm after the money; I ain't makin' no bones about it. I thought Louis was rich. That's why I clung to him. You think I'd be interested in a scarecrow like him if I thought he didn't have anything to offer?"

"Doc tells me your interested in lots of men."

"That supposed to be an insult? It ain't. Sure, I'm interested in all kinds of men, but they all gotta have one thing in common: they gotta have something to give me."

"Or you'll steal it from them if you get the chance."

"Why not? I've had to steal to survive. You think there's something wrong with that? What about the banks that steal people's land and property right out from under them? What about the wise old politicians, stealin' from each other? Stealin' the land from the savages?"

"I didn't know you were so concerned about them."

"I'm not. I'm concerned about me."

"Well, I'm concerned about me too, but I'm also concerned about them." McCain stabbed a finger toward Stevenson. "And I'm not gonna leave them here to die."

He stepped away from Sara and checked on Doc. He didn't look any worse, but he was now curled up on the ground, occasionally shaking and letting out a deep, resonant, throaty cough.

"I've got to hunt some food," he told Sara.

"Fine. I'll stay here and watch these two."

"Like hell you will. I'm not leaving you here with that bag of cash, and I sure as hell ain't carrying it around with me."

"Well, I'm not goin' with you," Sara insisted, sitting on a tree stump. "And you can't make me go."

McCain gritted his teeth and wondered why he had been attracted to this woman. Her outer shell was nicely-curved and pleasant to look at, but inside the shell was a personality as dark and dangerous as gunpowder.

"Can you climb a tree?" he asked.

"What?" she responded. "No. Why?"

He removed the satchel from its place on the ground next to Louis. He carried it a few paces, then began swinging it to and fro in an ever-widening upward arc. Finally, he released the bag from his grip and sent it flying into the air. It landed on a wide limb of an oak tree.

"Now you can stay," he said.

Sara watched him as he turned his back on her and walked away. "That was real smart. Suppose that posse does show up, and we've got to get out of here fast?"

"I'll worry about that if it happens," he answered, not bothering to turn around.

He continued on his way. Sara looked at the two ill, sleeping men around her and sighed. Finally, she stood up and followed McCain into the wooded area, saying, "Okay, McCain, I'll come with you. It can't be any worse than listenin' to these two snore. And I ain't a good nursemaid."

Chapter Forty-seven

Over his shoulder hung a leather strap; on each of its ends hung a rabbit, one bouncing off his chest as he walked, the other dangling between his shoulder blades. He had caught them with his bare hands. It had taken longer than shooting them would have, but gunfire could have alerted the posse that still might or might not have been in the area.

Sara had watched him as he caught them. She was amazed at the speed of the man and how he seemed to know beforehand exactly what the rabbits would do and where they would run. He was, she realized, a useful man to have around out in the wilderness. But he was still a pain-in-the-neck.

"Let's head back, McCain. Those two rabbits oughta hold us over for a while. The huntin' doesn't seem to be real good today. We've been crawlin' around for hours."

It was true. The sun was setting, and it was getting difficult to see in the woods.

"Sshh!" McCain whispered, kneeling down on a patch of grass.

"What?"

He brought his index finger to his lips and again ordered silence. Annoyed, she knelt beside and quitely said, "What is it? You hear a deer?"

He didn't answer, but instead closed his eyes in concentration. Sara kept quiet and tried to hear whatever it was that he heard.

He made the gesture with his finger again, then waved his hand in a request that she follow him. She took his cue, stood up, and followed him a dozen steps.

Again he squatted down, this time in thick, tangled underbrush. But this time she knew why. There was a trace of smoke in the air, a trace that couldn't exactly be seen, but could easily be detected with the nose.

She whispered, "You think it's the posse?"

"Could be," he quietely said. He removed his Peacemaker from its holster, checked to see that it was loaded, and replaced it. "You stay here. I'm going ahead to see."

"But . . ."

"Don't move."

She didn't want to stay there in the woods alone, but knew protest was useless; the look in his eyes told her that.

McCain dropped the rabbits in front of her and crept off around a tree. She watched as he sank to his hands and knees and disappeared into the underbrush.

The smell of smoke grew more distinct as McCain neared its source, and he could hear a man's voice. He crawled closer, paying attention only to his destination. Ahead there seemed a better-lit area of the woods, obviously a clearing that was open to more of the late afternoon sun. Finally, he stopped for a moment and lay flat on his belly, looking ahead.

He could see part of the fire through the bushes, whenever a flame shot high in the air. And the male voices were more noticeable, although he could still not make out the words.

He crawled closer, slowly, carefully. At last he was near enough to eavesdrop on the ongoing conversation.

"I swear to God, Leo, it wasn't my fault," one man was saying. "I ain't the brains of this outfit. Never claimed to be. It's Willy's fault the plan screwed up."

"Sure," answered another. "Blame Willy. He ain't here to defend himself. His carcass's prob'ly rottin' back there by that damn train."

A third voice spoke up. It was deeper than the other two. "Will you shut up? I don't give a damn whose fault it was. It's over now. The whole game's over. For four months we bust our asses dressin' up like stinkin' savages, and what do we got to show for it? Not a god-damn thing."

The first man spoke again. "Not till we get back to Willy's cabin. The money's got to be there, don't it?"

"It damn well better be!" the deep voice replied.

McCain shifted his weight to his arms and propped himself up. He could see one of the men, dressed in jeans and a green and white checkered shirt that was much too big for his skinny frame. The sleeves were rolled up around his elbows. His face was filthy. Then it occurred to McCain: it wasn't dirt under the man's eyes and on his cheeks and chin; it was a white man's poor version of war paint.

"Nothin'!" one of the voices continued. "Not a god-damn nickel. Maybe the three of us could try one more train. Just the three of us."

"Are you outa your mind?" boomed the resonant voice. The speaker moved in front of the fire, removing the tin coffee pot from its midst, and pouring himself a cup. "Just the three of us are gonna stop a train? Listen, a while tribe looks a lot more impressive." He sipped at the coffee, then continued. "Anyhow, the rest of our 'tribe's' dead. And I think this game was just about up anyway. That last train was heavily armed. They was prepared. A few of those bastards could shoot."

McCain had heard enough. The knowledge of who they were made him feel good. He could now steal their supplies, their horses, and anything else they had that he could use and not feel the slightest bit guilty about it.

However, he also knew that he'd have to do it as quietly as possible, and that meant no gunplay. The last thing he needed was for that posse to reappear.

Then, behind him, he heard dried leaves crunch beneath someone's weight. He was about to drop, roll over, and fire his Colt—even though he knew that would give him away—when he heard a familiar voice whisper to him.

"McCain. What is it?"

Without turning, he knew it was Sara. At first he was angry that she hadn't stayed put like he told her, but he realized her presence might be a blessing in disguise. If he could persuade her to follow his instructions this time.

He slid back along the ground until he lay next to her. At least the woman had the sense to stay low, he thought.

"Who are they?" she asked.

"No time to explain," he answered. "They're murdering thieves who we're gonna rob."

"We?"

"We! You still have that gun of yours?"

"Sure. Why?"

"Why do you think?"

"Oh!"

"Don't use it unless you have to."

"What are you gonna do?"

"I'm gonna rob them. You cover me."

"You're goin' in there alone?"

"Yeah. I don't want them to know you're here. Not

alone, anyway."

"Huh?"

"I'm gonna tell them I'm alone."

"Why? That sounds stupid to me."

"I got my reasons. Now keep a watchful eye."

McCain spotted the man with the deep voice. He was sitting on the opposite side of the fire, away from his two associates. McCain slowly moved in that direction. He was even more careful than before; the sun had moved lower in the sky and the amount of light was rapidly decreasing. Finally, looking out from the hedges, he could see the big man's back. He closed his eyes for a minute, took a deep breath, and marched out into the clearing.

The man never heard McCain move up behind him. And he never realized what happened to him. McCain slammed his pistol's butt-end down onto the back of the man's head, and in a second, coffee and blood were both seeping into the ground around the unconscious thief.

Neither of the other two thieves were paying attention. One was fumbling through his saddlebag, looking for a cigarette, while the other relieved himself in the underbrush, his back to the fire. McCain stood there, Peacemaker pointed at the ground, waiting to be noticed. But it didn't happen, and he grew tired of waiting.

"You boys always so rude to your guests?" he asked.

The man looking through his saddlebag dropped it and reached for his gun.

"Don't!" McCain ordered, and when the man saw the drawn and cocked Colt pointed at him, he followed his guest's instructions.

The other man stood silent and still.

"When you're done, friend," McCain said, watching him, "you turn around real slow with your hands in the air."

Then a strange sound filled the air for a moment. It

sounded like Sara. It sounded like a scream cut off mid-scream.

The sound was followed by other sounds. Twigs snapping underfoot. Branches swishing against clothing. A man yelling "Christ!"

In the course of two seconds, McCain's eyes darted from the other man to the far end of the clearing where four horses were tied. McCain bit his lip and cursed himself. Four horses! The words echoed in his skull.

The fourth man entered the clearing about six feet to McCain's right. He had his arm around Sara's neck and a gun pointed up below her chin. She stood there before him, in terror with tears pouring from her eyes.

"Drop that gun, mister," said the new arrival, "or this lady ain't gonna have no jaw no more. And that would be a real shame 'cause when we get through with you, I plan on fillin' that mouth of hers with somethin' she'll really enjoy."

McCain slowly lowered the gun. His gut ached, his heart pumped faster, and he felt possessed . . . by something. Sara's head was pulled against the man's chest, his ugly face directly above her frightened one. From the corner of his eye, he could see the other men; one stood there grinning, the other was bent over a bit buttoning up his fly.

He'd get only one shot. He knew that. Just one shot, and even that might not be enough to save Sara or himself. But it was take the chance now or surrender to Sara's rape, her death, his death.

There was really no decision to make. Instead of dropping his Peacemaker, he brought it up again. No thought was involved, no aim, no second-guessing, and very little time. He fired at the face hovering over Sara's head. One second it was grinning menacingly; the next it was a hideous, bloody half-face. The bullet caught the man in the eye and tore away the upper right side of his cheek.

Blood sprayed down on Sara's hair and face, and the hand holding the gun under her jaw went limp. The grip around her throat eased, and the arm slid by the side of her neck like a snake running off her shoulder and down her back.

She fell to her knees, screaming.

McCain was already on his. The man who had been facing the woods was spinning around, his hand already on his half-drawn pistol. The other man had no gun, but was rushing him just the same. McCain made a choice between the two men. He fired at the armed man. Through the flames of the campfire he saw the man's chest erupt like a crimson fountain. The other man was only a couple of feet away. McCain fired from the hip and the bullet ripped into the man's groin. He toppled sideways onto the fire, still alive and screaming. The combination of the smell of burning hair and the sounds of Sara's crying and the man's screaming was too much for McCain. He fired another bullet into the burning man, then using his boot, pushed the body off the flames. Smoke rose from the carcass for another moment until the breeze put an end to it.

He put his gun away and walked over to Sara. He helped her to her feet, and she sobbed uncontrollably. They wrapped their arms around each other and held on tightly. She felt good in his arms. Despite himself, he enjoyed holding her. She felt warm and gentle, more like a little girl than the hard-edged, self-serving bitch she was—or pretended to be.

She stopped crying, and with the crying the serenity of the moment ceased also. She pushed herself away from him and looked at him angrily.

"You're a maniac!" she yelled. "A damn maniac. I thought you knew what you were doin'. Was that supposed to be a plan? You almost got us killed. You didn't think about me or anything else. You just rush in like that? You're crazy. And I've got to put my life in your hands? You'll get us all killed."

The words hurt McCain, not because she was saying them, but because there was a degree of truth in them. He *had* been careless. He tried to reason with himself that it was due to his fatigue and lack of food; but true or not, he felt those reasons weren't good enough. He was getting impulsive and reckless. He felt increasingly alone with each passing day. He had nothing, wanted nothing except catching his sister's murderer. He wondered if he'd even be able to accomplish that.

Sara had calmed down a bit. "Can we go back now?" she asked, wiping the tears from her face with the back of her hand. "Your pals must be awake by now."

He had even forgotten about Louis and Doc. He shook his head, trying to jerk some sense back into it. "Right. We'll eat those rabbits, then come back here for the horses. And we'd better be quick about it. That posse — if they haven't given up on us — might have heard those shots."

He walked past her, and she stared at him as he passed. "You really are crazy, McCain. I swear I can't figure you out."

He stopped dead in his tracks, but didn't turn around. "Maybe I am crazy," he said with no emotion at all. "But right now I'm all you've got." He marched forward and mumbled to himself, "All I've got too."

She heard what he said and wondered what he meant by it.

Chapter Forty-eight

"What is that?" Sara asked, pointing to a spot of light far off in the distance.

McCain noticed it also. The pinpoint of light was moving; gradually, it bobbed its way down a hill. "It's a torch."

"The posse?"

"Could be." He turned to Sara. "I hope it is. They're heading the opposite way."

"Are you sure?"

"Yeah. They could always decide to double back, though. Or maybe they'll split up."

"Are we gonna keep movin' tonight?" Sara wanted to know. "To be honest I don't think I could go another foot. I'm havin' trouble even makin' it back to camp."

McCain resumed walking and pointed ahead. "The camp's only fifty feet ahead. You'll make it. But I know how you feel. I'm plain worn out, too."

In another minute, they were back at the patch of ground they called their camp. Both Doc and Stevenson were still asleep on the ground, practically curled up in the same positions they were in when McCain and Sara left.

"Should we wake them up?" Sara inquired.

McCain shook his head. "No, let them sleep." He gazed up at the starry blackness overhead. "Maybe we should grab some sleep too. I think we'll be all right here as long as we're quiet. But we'll have to wait until morning to eat. Lighting a fire's out of the question now."

"What'll I do with these damned rabbits?"

"I don't know. Bury 'em in some leaves or something."

"But some animal'll get 'em."

"Then we'll get some more tomorrow."

Sara laid the rabbits on a small pile of leaves and covered them over with more leaves. McCain, meanwhile, checked on the two sick men.

"They okay?" Sara asked, seeing McCain feel Stevenson's forehead with the palm of his hand.

"He's mighty hot, but he seems to be sleeping all right."

Then he stood up and walked the few steps to where Doc slept. He knelt in front of the man and touched his forehead. "Doc doesn't feel as hot, but he looks like hell."

"That don't surprise me. He always looks like hell."

McCain ignored her remark. "I wish we had some blankets or something. I didn't think to check those horses before."

"You gonna go back? That's a long walk."

"Maybe I should."

Sara looked around her. The darkness seemed oppressive to her, and the thought of being left alone with these two sickly, sleeping men made her very uneasy.

"I'll go with you," she said.

"I thought you couldn't walk any more."

"I'll force myself."

McCain headed back into the forest. "Well, come on."

Sara ran up next to him, looking through the woods ahead. "How the hell can you see where you're goin'?"

"I don't know," McCain answered honestly. "But I could always find my way around at night pretty well."

"Don't get far away from me, McCain. I'm a city girl. I hate bein' around all these animals and bugs."

"But you don't mind being around a maniac?" he asked,

throwing her word back in her face.

Sara's answer surprised him. "I'm sorry 'bout that, Mc-Cain. I was just upset before. You can understand that, can't you?"

"Yeah, I can. Forget it. Besides I was . . . I don't know . . . kind of careless."

Sara grabbed his forearm with her left hand for support as she stepped over some loose foot-long stones. But when she had made her way over them, she left her hand there. Then she slipped her arm under his and held it with the crook of her elbow. McCain looked down at her.

"You don't mind, do you?"

Her skin felt smooth, and it had been a long time since a woman had leaned on him for any kind of support. He liked the way it felt. "No, I don't mind."

Then they made their way back to the horses of the four men they had encountered a short time ago. Sara didn't want to walk through the clearing where the men lay dead; she was afraid it would get her upset all over again. So when they neared the area, they circled the clearing to the side where the horses were secured.

They found three blankets. They removed them and also took two canteens. One was full; the other was almost empty. And Sara found an unopened bottle of whiskey in one of the saddlebags.

"Look!" she said to McCain.

McCain smiled. "I could use a belt of that. Bring it."

They left the campsite and made the trek back to Doc and Louis. The night had grown quiet, except for the chattering of crickets and the occasional growl of some mountain cat. They spotted the tiny speck of torchlight off in the distance again. It was even smaller than before, flickering, it seemed, off and on as it passed under the trees.

A few minutes later they were back in the camp. Sara took one of the coarse khaki blankets and covered Stevenson with it, tucking the sides around his body. McCain threw another one over Doc, covering all of him except his head and his boots.

McCain held the third blanket and turned to Sara. "Here," he said, handing it to her. "You take this one. I'm not cold."

"Thanks."

"I think we'd better get some sleep now. We may have a whole day of riding tomorrow."

"Well, here," she said, giving the whiskey bottle to McCain. "If I get the blanket, it's only fair you get this first."

He took it, undid the top of the bottle, and took a long swig of the liquid. It warmed his insides. Then he handed it back to her.

She too drank from it, swallowing at least twice as much as McCain had. "Ahh, that's good stuff," she commented. "Wonder how whose men got hold of it?"

McCain shrugged his shoulders. "Stole it, most likely. Anyhow, good night." He sat before a large elm tree, his back resting against the tall, dark trunk. He removed his hat and placed it behind his head in an effort to make some cushion between his head and the hard wood behind it.

Sara lay at the base of another tree. She spread the blanket on the ground, lay on top of one side of it, turned and pulled the other half over her body. She lay on her side and closed her eyes.

They wouldn't stay closed, however. She stared off into the woods at nothing in particular. Then she rolled over and looked at McCain, stretched out by the tree. She still couldn't make him out, she realized, but he was certainly unique. She'd never met anyone quite like him.

Her eyes searched the trees for the bag of money, but it was impossible to see in the dark. When she thought back to McCain tossing the satchel up into the trees, she laughed. It suddenly seemed very funny to her, his going to that much trouble to keep her away from it. Perhaps it was the whiskey, she thought, that was making her feel differently about things. And perhaps it was the liquor that suddenly made the sight of McCain so appealing.

Even his looks, which she had noticed before, but thought nothing special, seemed engaging. From her spot on the ground, she could make out his profile. His nose was interesting; it wasn't too big or too small, and best of all it wasn't one of those turned-up ones she couldn't stand. His jaw was solid, and it rested below a pair of lips that seemed more suited to smoking a cigarette than kissing.

His body was lean—rather skinny, in fact—but there was a sexiness to the long legs, the trim, but full buttocks, the narrow waist. The truth to be told, she said to herself, he was nothing special to look at. But at this moment, she couldn't take her eyes off him.

She wanted to be with him.

She got to her feet, picking up the blanket with one hand and the bottle of whiskey with the other. Silently, she walked over to McCain. Standing before him, she fanned his legs with blanket.

"Can't sleep?" he asked, his eyes still closed.

"You heard me comin'?"

"Heard you get up."

She wasn't surprised. "Want some more whiskey?"

His eyes opened this time and blinked a couple of times. "Sure. Why not? Maybe it'll help me sleep."

"This is crazy," she said, sitting next to him. "We haven't slept since . . . when did we sleep?"

"I guess you slept in that cave."

"Right. How about you?"

"I don't even want to think about it."

She handed him the bottle of whiskey. "Here."

"Thanks." He swallowed a mouthful of the liquor, then handed the bottle back to her.

When she reached for it, her hand missed the bottle and slid up part of his forearm. Underneath the hair, she could feel the bumps on his flesh. "You're cold," she said, taking the bottle and setting it on the ground at her side. "Here. Cover yourself up."

She threw the blanket over him, and he grabbed an end of it and pushed it down to his waist, laying his arms on top of it.

"Mind if I join you in there?" she asked.

"No. I don't need the whole thing."

She slid under the blanket beside him and, like earlier that evening, tucked her arm under his. Then she snuggled up against his arm and placed her head on his shoulder. His body jerked a bit, and she could feel the muscles tighten in his arm.

"Want me to let go?" she asked, raising her head and looking into his eyes.

"No," he answered. But his eyes gave him away. He wasn't quite sure what was going on—or how he felt about it. "I'm just a bit surprised, that's all."

"At what?"

"At you. Why are you suddenly so friendly?"

"You think it's 'cause of the money, don't you?"

"It could be. You think me wrong to be suspicious?"

She let go of his arm for a moment and grabbed the neck of the whiskey bottle with her other hand. She took a long drink of it before answering his question.

"No, I guess not," she said, handing him the bottle. "But right now I'm not thinking about the money."

McCain swallowed another ounce of the liquid, put the bottle down, and wiped his mouth with the back of his hand. "What *are* you thinking about?"

She answered the question by kneeling up and kissing him on the lips. Slowly, she lowered herself off her knees until she was half on top of him. His whiskey-soaked lips tasted good, and she wanted more of them. Her hands met behind his head, pulling him toward her.

His hands circled her shoulders and pulled her body

closer too. But suddenly they were on her shoulders pushing her gently away.

Their lips separated, and she stared at him. "What's wrong?"

"Nothing," he said, reaching for the bottle, finding it, and raising it to his lips. "I just wonder what I'm gettin' into."

"What's that supposed to mean?"

"I don't know. Yesterday, you hated my guts. Today, I'm a crazy man, and suddenly you're kissing me. What's tomorrow gonna bring? You gonna shoot me in the back and take the money?"

Sara recoiled a bit, then slapped McCain across the face and stood up. "What about you, McCain? When I first met you, you had that lean, hungry look in your eye like you ain't had a woman in years. Don't think I didn't notice it. You wanted me to notice it. Then I wind up out here in the wilderness, bein' held by a bunch of Indians, and there you are again. And I see that look again. Then you find out that I've got an interest in that money, and suddenly that look's gone. Like I ain't a woman anymore."

"Am I wrong," McCain interrupted, "or wouldn't you do just about anything for that money?"

"I might. But it's got nothing to do with right now, with this."

"How do I know that?"

"You don't," she said, turning and walking away from him.

McCain watched her move away in the darkness. He was glad to have regained his wits before he gave in completely. She was trouble, he told himself, and tomorrow she'll turn around and try some new plan to get the money. And another woman would walk out on him, just like Alexandra.

Then he realized something. He had loved Alexandra, really loved her. That's what made her leaving hurt so much. And here he was with Sara—a woman he knew well enough only to realize that she was capable of anything—fearing she would leave him too.

He took a deep breath and knew the truth: no matter what she was, no matter what she'd done or would do tomorrow, he was in love with her. He took another sip at the liquor and threw the bottle away.

"Sara, wait!" he said.

"Go to hell!" she answered.

He stood up, knocking the blanket to the ground. Ahead, he could see her ambling about, her arms crossed over her chest. He walked up to her, spun her around, and looked into her deep brown eyes.

"You're crazy, McCain," she said.

"I know. So are you." He put his arms around her.

"You're drunk."

"Just a little."

She wiggled, trying to free herself from his embrace. "Let go of me, of I'll knee you real hard."

"No, you won't," he insisted.

She studied his face, thinking he might be turning brutal again. She'd seen him kill three men today; she hardly knew this man, hardly knew what he was all about . . . But she'd never seen him look like this. There was a tenderness in his eyes and a playfulness in his smile. He was holding her tightly, but his grip was gentle.

And suddenly she felt the attraction of the man too much to resist.

They kissed, holding each other tight. Sara stood on her toes, covering his body with hers. She felt the hands at her back pressing her up to him. Her left thigh moved between his legs, and she could feel the hardness there.

His tongue pressed against her lips. Hers met it in the chamber their mouths created, and each tongue danced around the other. His hands fell down her back, resting on her waist. Then they lowered a bit more, each cupping one

298

side of her bottom. The hands pulled her closer, then suddenly let go.

He started unbuttoning his shirt from the top, and when she realized what he was doing, she helped him, beginning at the bottom. Soon the shirt was open, revealing his dark-haired chest. She ran her fingers up the chest, through the hair, and rested on his shoulders. Under her arms, he unfastened her dress, pulling it apart to her sides. She was naked underneath from the waist up. He grabbed her wrists and pulled her arms from his shoulders. Then he bent over, burying his face between her firm, warm breasts.

They got to their knees, then fell over on their sides, holding one another for a moment. She reached for his belt and undid it; he slid his fingers under the top of her silk petticoat and slid it down over her hips. When she finished tugging the pants down past his buttocks, down around his knees, she kissed him again on the lips, her hands around the small of his back.

Then he rolled on top of her, their mouths urging each other on. Her legs opened beneath him, and he moved between them. Slowly, he entered her. They both groaned slightly. And as the rhythm of their passion increased and intensified, the world around them seemed to cease to exist for a few rapturous moments.

Chapter Forty-nine

The rays of the morning sun peeked through the overcast sky, warming the mountains and everything on them. Stevenson was the first to awaken; he was out in the open, unprotected by any shade-providing tree. The sun beat down between two clouds and nearly blinded him. As he sat up, he held his hand over his eyes. Slowly, they adjusted to the brightness, and he looked around him. Doc lay where they had left him; he was still asleep, his arms outstretched to either side of him. Stevenson turned the other way and saw McCain's head sticking out from under a blanket. But something was wrong with this particular scene. The blanket covered a great mound that Stevenson knew couldn't possibly be his body. Then he noticed the four feet protruding from the blanket's bottom.

"Good heavens!" he exclaimed, realizing that half the mound and two of those feet had to belong to Sara.

Then the mound moved, and the blanket was pulled down. Sara's head lay upon McCain's chest. She saw that the source of the words had been Stevenson and pulled the blanket up over her head again.

"Go back to sleep, Louis," said the muffled voice beneath the blanket.

The Scotsman did not follow her order. Instead, he rose

to his feet and marched into the woods.

Sara's words woke McCain up. "Where're you going, Louis?" he called out.

"Nature calls, my good man," Louis answered and disappeared from sight.

McCain felt Sara shift beneath the blanket; then he felt her warm hand move between his legs. He lifted the blanket in order to peek under it. There, Sara beamed up at him.

"Not now, Sara," he laughed. "Louis is up and about. This might be a good time to get up and dressed."

"Business as usual again, McCain," she said. "Morning's here."

He brushed her hair back over her head. "It's not like that. But we do have to move on."

She seemed a bit annoyed at him, he thought, but she got up, and the two of them quickly dressed. Sara had not quite finished buttoning up her dress when Louis returned to camp. He noticed what she was doing, but pretended he hadn't.

Then Doc stirred and rolled over. McCain stepped over to him, reached behind him, and helped him sit up.

"How you doing, Doc?" he asked. "Feel any better?"

Doc started gagging, and, had anything been in his stomach, he would have thrown it up. McCain held him by the shoulders and waited for the fit to pass. But it went on so long Louis came over and watched the man spit up the little that was inside him.

Then the coughing stopped. Doc's eyes rolled in the sockets, unable to focus on anything. Then he fell back again, and McCain lowered him to the ground.

"He's extremely ill," Stevenson commented. "We must get him to a doctor."

"He's soaking wet," McCain said. His hands had felt the sweat through the shirt sleeves.

"We've got to get him to eat or drink something."

"Right. Can you cook?"

"Me?" Stevenson remarked. "Not very well, I'm afraid."

"You, Sara?" McCain asked, turning in her direction.

"Sure," she answered. "Although there are other people I'd rather cook for than him. But I'll get those two rabbits."

She recovered the rabbits she had hidden the previous night. "They're a little dirty, but they'll be all right." Then she found the whiskey bottle they half-emptied during the night. There was still about a third of the liquor left. She poured some of the contents over the two animals. "That oughta kill any bugs that are crawling on 'em."

Stevenson's face went blank at the thought, but Sara's comment made McCain laugh. He watched as she gathered wood for the fire and made a neat little pile with them.

"You got any matches?" she asked.

McCain stood up and reached into his pocket. "Yeah." He handed them to her and said, "You seem mighty chipper this morning."

"I feel better this morning," she said with a grin. "I guess I slept well."

McCain grinned back. "So did I."

Sara lit the match and held it under a couple of thin twigs. In a few seconds the fire grew and spread to most of the branches piled above the twigs.

"I'm gonna go back and get those horses," McCain said. "There's no way Doc's gonna be able to get to them. And I'll be damned if I'll carry him anymore."

"Where did you get new horses?" Stevenson asked. "Or did you go back last night and find the Indian horses? And our luggage?"

"These are fresh ones," McCain said. "We're borrowing them. It's a long story, and I don't have time to tell it to you."

"Very well. I'll look after Doc."

"Good. See you in a while."

McCain ran off through the woods, and in a couple of minutes was completely out of sight. Sara had the fire going nicely, and with the help of two forked branches standing up on both sides of the fire and one laid across the other two, started to roast the rabbits. The whiskey dripped off them, and the drops fell into the fire, causing the flames to jump and hiss.

Stevenson pulled a notebook from his jacket pocket. Then he reached into the other and pulled out a pencil. He started to write something.

"Workin' on a book?" Sara asked. She really wasn't interested, but there was no one else to talk to. Also, she was beginning to regret the way she had spurned Stevenson. He really wasn't a bad fellow—not like Doc.

"No," he answered. "I just make observations and take notes in this pad. Perhaps at some future date they may coalesce into a book-length work."

"What have you observed lately?"

"Right now, I'm thinking about that poor old prospector, Silver Johnny. He was quite a fascinating fellow, burying his gold in the ground like that. It reminds me of tales of buccaneers I used to hear as a child."

"I'm not following you," Sara said, poking one of the cooking rabbits with a stick.

Louis closed his notebook and turned to her. "The pirates supposedly put their ill-gotten gains into a chest and buried the treasure in the beaches of the West Indies."

"That so?"

"It is. Some of the treasures are rumored to be still buried, waiting for some lucky adventurer to find them."

"You gonna write a book about pirates?"

"I might some day. Somehow, I'd like to work old Silver Johnny into it."

"Well, good luck, Louis."

"Thanks."

Suddenly, Doc propped himself up on his elbows and cried out. "Give me a drink." His voice was terribly hoarse.

Sara handed one of the canteens to Louis and said, "You

give him some of this. I don't want to go near him."

Louis took the canteen, knelt next to Doc, and poured some water into Doc's mouth. The gunfighter swallowed once, coughed, then fell back down, moaning and shaking.

"These rabbits are just about done," Sara noted. "Try to keep him awake. We'll force some of this meat down his gullet."

Then McCain returned to camp, riding a brown gelding, pulling the other two horses behind him.

"He awake?"

"Barely," Stevenson answered.

"These critters are done," Sara announced.

McCain approached the campfire and took one of the rabbits. He placed it in a tin dish he found in one of the saddlebags and brought it over to Louis and Doc. He removed his hunting knife from its sheath on his belt, and carefully, he sliced the flesh. Then he stopped and held the charred rabbit close to his eyes and inspected it carefully.

He turned to Sara and asked, "Did you skin these things?"

Sara seemed perplexed. "You mean you got to skin them?"

"Of course you got to skin them!"

"Well, I didn't know."

"I thought you said you knew how to cook."

"So I lied."

McCain started to get angry at her, but he realized how silly the whole thing was. He started to laugh and said, "Never mind. I'll skin them now."

Sara removed the other rabbit from the fire. "I told you I wasn't much good in the wilderness, McCain. I'm used to eatin' in saloons and restaurants."

Still laughing, McCain cut away the blackened skin from the rabbit and sliced the juicy flesh into strips. When he had enough, he said to Stevenson, "You hold him up. I'm gonna feed him."

The Scotsman did as he was instructed. The back of the sick man rested on Louis's arm. McCain placed a piece of the meat on Doc's lips, but they wouldn't open

"Hold him tight," McCain said. "He's gonna eat this if I have to force-feed him."

He pinched Doc's nostrils closed with a thumb and forefinger, and after a few seconds, the mouth popped open, searching for breath. McCain shoved a thin strip of meat into the mouth.

Dreamily, almost reluctantly, the teeth chewed the meat and eventually swallowed it. McCain repeated this procedure six more times. At no time did Doc show any signs of waking up.

Stevenson let the man lie down again. McCain handed him the plate with the rabbit on it.

"Help yourself, Louis. Me and Sara'll polish off the other one."

"Thanks," Louis said, accepting the dish.

McCain stood up. "By the way, how're you feeling? You weren't in too good shape yesterday."

"I feel much better, thank you. I'm sure I'll feel even better after I eat this. I'm absolutely famished."

McCain cut part of the meat from the other rabbit and ate it. Sara nibbled at some of it with him. When it was finished, McCain took a swig from the whiskey bottle.

"There's enough in here for a swig for everybody. Just leave a few drops for Doc. Maybe it'll wake him up."

The bottle was passed around, and after Sara and Louis both had taken some, the Scotsman poured the remaining ounce or two into Doc's open mouth. The man stirred, swallowed, but went right back to sleep.

"Jesus, I think he's dead already!" McCain said. "I've never seen anybody sleep that much, sick or not."

"He needs medical care as soon as possible," Louis noted. "This accursed disease can suck the life from a man. Mr. Holliday is not recovering at all; I fear he's getting worse the longer we delay."

"Then let's be moving on," McCain said.

"Don't forget your bag," Sara called, pointing up into the tree.

"Right," McCain said. He found a large, round stone and heaved it at the bag. It hit it, but didn't dislodge it from its perch. He picked the stone up and tossed it again, this time with more force. It hit again, this time knocking it from the branch to the ground below.

"Nice shootin', McCain. I bet you're a hell of a horse-shoe player too."

Stevenson watched as McCain picked up the bag and secured it to the gelding. "If you don't mind my asking, how did that satchel wind up in the tree?"

"It's a long story, Louis . . ."

". . . but we don't have time now," Louis finished. "Very well. Some other time."

"Help me with Doc again," McCain asked Stevenson.

Together, they lay the man across one of the saddled horses, and McCain tied the man into place once again. Then he said to Louis, "You can ride that one. If Sara doesn't mind riding double with me. One of them horses back there was lame."

She shook her head. "I don't mind."

They all mounted their horses, and McCain led the way, followed by the horses carrying Doc, and then Louis.

When they had traveled nearly half a mile, Sara leaned forward on the horse and lay her cheek against McCain's back. Her arms were around his waist. "You trust me now, McCain?"

"Should I?" he asked playfully.

"I don't know. You decide. Maybe I'm riding with you for the money, which I notice is within grabbin' distance. Or maybe I'm ridin' with you for this." She lowered her hand to his crotch and squeezed the bulge between his legs.

He was startled for a moment, but then he said, "Take

the latter. It's worth more."

They laughed, and he enjoyed hearing her laugh. But he still wasn't exactly comfortable with her. There was still a game being played, one where the outcome wasn't clear. He no longer had any animosity toward the beautiful, enigmatic woman whose arms were circling his waist. But he still wondered if he'd fall even more in love with her than he already was—and one day soon find her gone, with or without Doc's money.

The money didn't seem so important now.

He just wanted her, wanted to stay with her, wanted her to be his and stay with him. Forever. Not like Alexandra.

Chapter Fifty

The town of Bitter Grass, Nevada, wasn't much of a town at all. In fact, besides the railroad station, there were only two other sites of interest: McLaglen's General Store and a small but heavily-populated cemetery.

McCain had spotted the town when the band of travelers hit the steel rails crossing the country where the mountains ended. He, like the other two conscious riders he was with, let out a whoop of joy upon spotting the platform. They had been riding for close to five hours, and the post-noon sun was the hottest it had been in days. At McCain's urging, the group galloped up to the establishment ahead.

When they reached McLaglen's store, McCain dismounted and told his companions to wait outside. He opened the wooden door, and a copper bell tinkled over his head.

"Hello!" said an elderly man. "What can I do for you?"

McCain looked around the store for a moment before answering. For a general store, he noticed, there weren't many supplies in it although the selection of goods wasn't bad; there seemed to be one of everything.

"You Mr. McLaglen?" McCain asked.

"That's right." Only the upper half of McLaglen's short body could be seen over the counter. His arms dangled somewhere behind it.

"I could use a few supplies. But I've got a more important matter on my mind. Does the train stop here?"

"That it does. It should be rollin' in in about forty minutes. Goes to Reno, Sacramento, and San Francisco."

"Where do I get tickets?"

"Right here," McLaglen said proudly. "I'm the official, licensed ticket vendor."

"Fine. Let me have four seats."

McLaglen looked down at his feet for a moment, then up at McCain again. "You mean you're gonna buy four tickets?"

"That's right."

The balding man stared at his customer with a perplexed look. "You're gonna pay for them?"

"Sure. Something wrong with that?"

McLaglen raised his arms from behind the counter. In his hands was the biggest damned knife McCain had ever seen. It was a machete, but longer than any he'd ever come across; it was almost a sword.

"What the hell . . ." McCain started.

"Sorry, mister," McLaglen apologized. He laid the machete on top of the counter and moved around it until he was in front of it and standing next to McCain. Standing tall, the man only reached McCain's shoulders. "I gotta be careful. I get robbed a lot, and I'm damned fed up with it. I'm all alone out here most of the time, and it seems every criminal in Nevada and California knows it."

"Won't the railroad send anyone to help you?"

"They keep sayin' they're gonna, but they don't."

"Well, sorry about that," McCain said, removing his hat and brushing back his hair with the palm of his hand. "You oughta get yourself a decent gun. That bush knife won't protect you from a bullet."

"Nah!" the old man insisted. "I hate guns. They just put a little hole in ya. The next thief who dares come in here is gonna feel that blade. No little hole for him; I wanna see his arm cut off. Or better yet, his head!"

McCain wondered how much of what the man was saying was meaningless bragging; he certainly didn't look like the type of man to be that violent and blood-thirsty. But as he had been told before, he wasn't a very good judge of character.

"How about those tickets?"

"Yes, sir. Four you said, I believe."

"Right."

McLaglen looked out the front window of the store and spied the three other travelers outside. "They your friends?" he asked. "Boy, the lady's a mighty pretty one. And . . . say, is that there fellow stretched over the horse dead?"

"No, he's sick," McCain answered.

"What's he got? Smallpox?"

"No, not smallpox. I don't quite understand what he's got."

"They might not let you bring him on the train."

"They will."

"I wouldn't be too sure 'bout that," McLaglen warned.

"I'm sure. It ain't contagious."

"Well, if you say so. Here's the tickets. Say, how far are ya goin'? I forgot to ask."

"To San Francisco."

"Okay," McLaglen mumbled, and punched out a circle on each of the four tickets. Then he handed them to McCain. "You said you needed some other things."

"Right. You got tobacco and makings?"

"Bull Durham. Finest quality."

"Good. Let me have some shells for this Peacemaker too. And what have you got to eat?"

"Lots of canned goods. Peaches. Beans. Got some real good peppermint candy sticks too. Some beef jerky."

"Let me have some of all of it."

310

"Yes, sir."

McLaglen stepped around the store, putting together the order. While he did, McCain opened the front door. Sara and Stevenson were off their horses, stretching their legs.

"You want anything?" McCain called to them.

"Yeah," Sara answered. "Get me some kind of perfume or toilet water. Anything. I smell like a goat."

"Does he have any books or newspapers?" Stevenson asked. "I'm absolutely desperate for something to read."

McCain called to the old man in the store. "You carry anything to read?"

"Not too much," said McLaglen, who had put on his glasses to help him read the labels. "Got the latest dime novel by Mr. Buntline, though."

"It ain't about Doc Holliday, is it?" McCain inquired.

"I don't think so, no. Hold on a minute." The man ducked under the counter for a moment, then resurfaced holding the cheaply-printed, tan book. "It's called *Bill Hickok: Tough Town Tamer*."

"I'll take it."

"Fine. I think I've got everything you need here now. Will there be anything else?"

"You got anything to drink?"

"You mean liquor?"

"That's exactly what I mean."

"Just some local stuff. There's an old couple who make a pretty good liquor. They live south of here. Stuff's got a kick like a jackass with a bee up its ass."

"Let me have a bottle."

"Done," the proprietor said, placing the bottle on the counter with the other goods.

"Can you open them cans for me?"

"Sure. That'll be thirty-six dollars, includin' the tickets."

McCain reached into his pocket. He still had two twenties from the night in Moods. "Here's forty. Keep the change and get yourself a decent gun."

"Thanks." He pocketed the money. "You folks might want to sit in the cemetery and eat. Lots of shady trees there."

McCain scooped up his purchases in his arms. "You take care of that cemetery, too?"

"Yep."

"Is there anyone else in Bitter Grass? I can't imagine you'd need a graveyard for this town."

"Oh, they're not townspeople," McLaglen corrected. "The occupants of that cemetery are all fellers who tried to rob me."

McCain smiled, nodded, and left the store. "Thanks."

"Let's eat!" he announced when he stepped outside.

"You get me some perfume?" Sara asked.

"I forgot. We'll get it later."

"You eat," Sara said. "I'll join you in a minute." Then she stepped into the store.

McCain and Louis walked over to the cemetery and sorted out the merchandise beneath a large, blooming yew tree.

"A book!" Stevenson cried. "The printed word! I pray I haven't forgotten how to read."

"When you read this thing," McCain noted, handing Stevenson the Buntline opus, "You might wish you had."

He walked back to the front of the store and dragged the horses over to the cemetery. They grazed lazily nearby while Stevenson opened the book and read the title page, and McCain got Doc down from his horse.

"We'd better get him awake," McCain said. "I know he's sick, but I get tired just looking at him."

He stood up and a sweet smell wafted through the air and penetrated his senses. He turned around. There stood Sara, smiling.

"Nice?" she asked.

"Real nice, but what's it supposed to smell like?"

"Roses, McCain. It's rose water. Don't you know

nothin'?"

He shrugged his shoulders, then smacked Doc on the cheeks a couple of times. The man didn't budge.

"Louis, hand me that bottle, will you?"

Stevenson gave him the whiskey bottle. McCain opened it and poured some of it into Doc's half-open mouth. Holliday sputtered. Some of the whiskey poured out of his mouth, but some of it made its way into his system. His eyes opened. He blinked a few times. He licked his lips. Then he forced himself up on his elbows and sat up.

He still looks like he's at death's door, McCain thought, but at least the man is conscious. McLaglen was right; the whiskey did have quite a kick.

From the distance, a train whistled twice. Sara looked in the direction of the sound.

"I can see the smoke," she announced. "Should be here in a few minutes."

McCain held the whiskey bottle to Doc's lips and tilted it up for him. "Drink some more, Doc. We've got to keep you awake, at least till we get on that train."

"Train?" Doc asked, his voice raspy and weak.

"Train! We should be in San Francisco tomorrow some time. Now eat. We've got some food."

"Food!" he repeated.

"And I even have a book!" Stevenson announced to him joyously. "At last, I have nourishment for both my mind and my body. Since I had to leave my baggage behind—and all my books, some of which are irreplaceable, I'm sure—I feared I'd never again enjoy the pleasures of verse, of prose. But now I have . . . a book!"

Doc stared incredulously at the Scotsman through watery, bloodshot eyes. "Screw your book!" he said, then looked up at McCain. "The money?"

"I've got it," McCain assured him.

Then Doc's eyes caught a glimpse of Sara. "You still here?" he asked her.

She ignored him and helped herself to a can of peaches.

The train tooted again, and McCain felt a slight trembling in the earth. "Eat up," he said. "That train'll pull in any minute now."

He rolled a cigarette and looked around him. Except for his three companions and Mr. McLaglen, there wasn't a soul in sight. He wondered whatever possessed the Central Pacific people to make Bitter Grass a stop on the line. There was no water tower, no coal supply, and most of the time, he imagined, no passengers. Perhaps it was a mail stop. He didn't know. What he did know was that before much longer he'd be in San Francisco. He'd had enough of the wilds of Nevada, and the faster pace and denser population of the big city would at least provide a change of pace. And with any luck, he and Doc would be able to complete their business.

Chapter Fifty-one

San Francisco

Warren Earp read the wire message for the fourth time in two days: STAY PUT. DOC FOLLOWING. WYATT. He crumpled the piece of paper in his hand and tossed it on the plushly-carpeted floor.

"I'm goin' crazy," he said. "I can't stay another minute in this goddamn hotel room." He rose out of his chair. "Get your jackets, boys. We're goin' out."

"Where we goin' tonight, Warren?" Ben Cole asked.

"I don't know, but I need me some excitement. This hangin' around is bullshit."

"Why don't we wait a few more minutes? Maybe Beaudine'll give us another guided tour."

Warren spat on the expensive carpet. "That's what I think of his guided tours! So he's rich? I don't give a damn about his shipping companies or his other businesses. I can only kiss that man's ass so long."

Then there was a knock on the door. Ben Cole answered the knock. On the other side of the door stood the better-looking of Beaudine's bodyguards, Mr. Paine. He stepped into the room.

"Gentlemen, Mr. Beaudine has a rare treat for you tonight," he announced. "He's going to give you a night in the Chinese District, at some of his, shall we say, less reputable establishments."

"What's that mean?" Warren asked. Privately, he hoped it meant whorehouses.

"Just come along, all three of you," Paine continued in his best condescending tone.

"I don't want to eat none of that Chinese slop," Ben added.

Paine crossed his arms over his chest. "Did I mention anything about dinner? I don't think so. But when this night is over, you'll have worked up quite an appetite, I can promise you that."

"Cut the crap, Paine," Warren said. "Where are we goin'?"

"To Weng Wo's."

"That's supposed to mean something to me?"

Paine smiled. "Weng Wo's is an antique shop full of artifacts from the mysterious Orient."

"So?"

"It's also the best cathouse in San Francisco, once you go upstairs. Mr. Beaudine owns it. Now are you coming or not?"

Warren looked at Ben and then at Max Fisher and smiled. "We'll come along," he answered. "I don't think any of us ever poked a Chinese girl."

"Well, you should enjoy it," Paine said. Then he left the room, and in a few seconds was followed by three very happy men.

Beaudine sat in a carriage, puffing on a big cigar. He watched as the men cramped together on the seats.

"It's only a short ride," he said. "We probably could have walked, but what for? When you've got it, spend it, I always say." Then he chuckled at his remark.

"You do a lot of business with the Chinks?" Warren asked.

Beaudine blew a cloud of foul-smelling cigar smoke into

the carriage. "Yes, a lot. There's a lot of advantages to doing business with the Johns."

"The Johns?" Cole repeated. "What's a John?"

"A Chinese, my friend. John's a lot easier to remember than their ridiculous heathen names." Again he laughed at his own wisdom.

"What kinds of advantages?" Warren asked. "You mean you can cheat them left and right?"

"Oh, no. You can't cheat them. They are amazing when it comes to money. That's the first thing they learn when they get off the boat. They know the currency, let me tell you. But there are other things. They work on Sunday. They don't care about Sunday; they ain't Christian. But the best thing about them is this — and I'm trustin' you boys not to say a word about this to anyone. Some of my businesses aren't what you'd exactly call legal. Weng Wo's, for example, where we're going tonight. The beauty of doing business with the Johns — letting them run the place — is that should the real business of Weng Wo's be discovered, the legal testimony in court of a Chinese is inadmissible evidence."

"So no Chink can testify that you're the owner?" Warren asked.

"That's right."

Warren looked out the carriage window. "That is an advantage."

The look of the town outside the window was changing. The signs on various storefronts no longer had lettering that could be understood; instead, some scribbling replaced English words. The buildings themselves looked different; there were more balconies, more flags and streamers, more colors. And Warren noticed another difference in the area.

"Where are all the women?" he asked. "I ain't seen a Chinese woman yet on the street. The Johns keep 'em locked up or something?"

317

Beaudine laughed. "In a way, I suppose they do. It's not proper for the women to walk on the streets."

"None of 'em?"

"Not if they're honorable."

Ben Cole reached up with both of his hands and smoothed the long blond hair down the sides of his head. "These women at Weng Wo's," he interrupted. "They ain't honorable, are they?"

"Honorable?" Beaudine grinned, flicking his ashes out the window. "Son, dishonor is now the way of life for these ladies. Particularly the Chinese ones. They can do things to you that you never thought possible."

"The Chinese ones?" Warren asked, looking out the window and seeing only Oriental faces. "They ain't all Chinese?"

"No, not all. I got a few white ones, a few niggers, and an Indian, no, make that two Indians—an Apache and a Crow. Man, you should see those two fight. They hate each other."

"Why the variety?" Cole asked.

"Variety is the spice of life, as someone once said. Besides, sometimes I trade them."

"Trade with whom?" Warren asked.

"With the shippers. You have any idea what a white woman or an Indian is worth in China?"

Warren was speechless for a moment. He had really underestimated the nerve of Jerome Beaudine. Besides everything else, the man was a white slaver! "Never thought about it," was all he could say.

The carriage came to a halt outside a shop that occupied the bottom floor of a three-story building. Over the entrance to the shop hung a brightly-colored awning. In the shop's window, which was filled with lamps, vases, and what appeared to be highly-decorated knives, was a sign that read Weng Wo: Importer.

"Now before we go in," Beaudine said seriously, "I'd just

like to ask you boys a couple of favors. Please don't refer to these people as Chinks when you're inside. After all, they are my business associates. And one more thing: don't go beating up my girls."

Ben Cole smiled and said, "We wouldn't do a thing like that." Then he turned to Warren. "Would we, Warren?" Cole laughed out, and after a second was joined by Max, whose laughter sounded more like grunting.

Warren Earp, though, didn't find his associate's private joke very funny. Instead of laughing, he opened the door of the carriage and stepped out.

"Let's go," he said.

Chapter Fifty-two

There was no escaping the sickeningly sweet-smelling smoke. Even two flights up, even with the other odors — mainly those of tobacco, mildewed wood, and the musky aroma of his whore for the night — there was no way to hide from the fumes of burning opium that permeated the very walls and floors.

Warren Earp found the aroma repulsive, and he did his best to shield himself from it. But nothing helped, not tobacco, not the half-fifth of whiskey he had consumed. For a while, his servant of the night — he never quite understood her pronunciation of her own name, but it sounded like Lo Lee, so that's what he called her — took his mind off the odor of the burning narcotic. Now, though, he lay there on the bed, wishing he could shut his nostrils completely.

Weng Wo, the nominal proprietor of the shop, had asked Warren and his associates if they would like to partake of "the dream pipe." Only Ben Cole was familiar with the drug; only he had experienced its effects before; so only he accepted the offer, and he was led to a sub-street-level room.

The other five members of the entourage were far more interested in whiskey and the delights of the flesh than in delightful dreams. All had been led upstairs to the third floor, where they made their choices from the assembled collection of twenty-four women, ranging in age from about thirteen to thirty. Most of them were Chinese, but, as Beaudine had promised, the other races were also represented.

Max Fisher was the first to choose. He didn't wait to be invited. As soon as he spied the women, he marched up to a young Chinese girl and grabbed her by the wrist. Fear immediately registered on her almond-skinned face as Max latched on to her and grunted his wordless approval. She looked to Weng Wo for sympathy, but found none. He simply bowed to her, and, dutifully, she bowed back. Then she turned and led the huge, speechless man down the hall into one of the rooms.

Beaudine was obviously annoyed at the presumption and lack of manners Max had displayed. But like the others in his party, he realized that Max's massive size and threatening demeanor dictated his choosing first if that's what he wanted. No one—especially not Warren Earp, who had learned better on a number of occasions in the past—was about to reprimand Max for so trivial an offense.

The politician then offered the next choice to Warren. He took a long time to decide, but finally selected the Oriental woman with the biggest breasts. Most of them, he noticed, were rather small-chested, but one, slightly older and slightly heavier than most in the group, had nice round breasts with nipples that showed through the fine, sheer, silky fabric that covered them. Had his criteria been solely size, the lone black woman or the Apache woman would have been better choices. But a Chinese girl was something new to be experienced, something he hoped would provide much-needed amusement during his deadly dull stay in the big city.

Neither Paine nor McKelton were offered a choice, nor did they expect one. Beaudine wanted them alert and on-duty at all times. McKelton was sent down to the far end of the dimly-lit hallway while Paine remained in the room they presently occupied.

After his guests were safely tucked away in their rooms, Beaudine made his selection. He walked up to the youngest girl in the room and stroked her black hair.

"Very nice," he commented. "Very nice, indeed."

Weng Wo nodded his head in agreement. "Yes, new girl very sweet. Only thirteen year old." He smiled, revealing a full set of teeth, many of which were badly stained from smoke. "Damn hot. Damn hot."

"I bet she is," Beaudine said. Then he passed the only white woman in the group. While holding the young girl by the wrist, he eyed this crimson-haired woman and studied her from head to toe. Even beneath the silk robe she had on, he could see the curves of her body. He raised his free hand and grabbed the woman's left breast.

"I've heard that you've given Mr. Wo a hard time, my dear," he said to her. "Is that so?"

The young woman's lips began to tremble and she closed her eyes. She was too scared to speak.

Weng Wo spoke for her. "No trouble now. She good girl now. Was plenty trouble, but no trouble now. She learn. She damn hot now."

Beaudine smiled at her, squeezing the breast he still held. "Is that true, my dear?"

Again she trembled and couldn't utter a word. But she opened her eyes.

"Can't speak?" Beaudine teased. "Well, that's all right." He let go of her breast and grabbed her arm. "You come along with me, and we'll find out just how good you are now." He turned his head to face Weng Wo. "You don't mind if I take two, do you?"

"No, sir," the old man answered, shaking his head so vigorously the queue down the back of his head swayed from side to side. "Two good girls. You see. Take three!"

Beaudine laughed at his employee. "I think two will be fine."

Then he entered a room halfway down the hall and shut the door behind them.

It was quiet for the next couple of hours, except for a lot of noise coming from Beaudine's room. Warren Earp, who had the misfortune to have the room next to Beaudine, had heard the man yelling, moaning, and laughing at different times; he had even heard the sound of an occasional slap coming through the thin walls. Even during sex, Warren thought, Beaudine was a damn fool loudmouth.

He wondered what time it was; it had been dark for hours, so he guessed that it was well after midnight. He realized that he had been lying in that bed for hours, without once getting up. There had been no need to; the pretty young lady who lay on top of the sheets, her head resting near the foot of the bed, her smooth, ivory-toned bottom within easy reach, had been ever-dutiful and seemingly insatiable. He knew he had only to stroke one of her beautiful, exposed buttocks now to begin a new act of her ever-changing sexual performance.

But Beaudine wanted to get up now. The smell of the opium was getting to him, making him edgy and restless. And the room seemed to be getting smaller—he definitely felt more confined. Perhaps it was the smoke, he thought. He'd been told that the fumes of the poppy did strange things to a man's senses. Or perhaps it was simply that he'd been in the same small room too long, and he doubted that he would have the stamina to make it through the next act of this exotic woman—as pleasurable as it would probably be.

He slid his legs off the bed and stood up. He felt tired and very dizzy for a moment, and he had to place one hand on the mattress to steady himself. Lo Lee placed her hand on top of his. He looked at her and shook his head. Then he stepped to the door and opened it.

The hallway was full of men, and it startled him. They had made no noise. He tried to make sense of the scene before him. Were these men other customers? Was silence some kind of house rule? But no answers came to him; he had drunk too much, and it was too difficult to hold any thought for long.

Then one of the men approached him. He stood before Warren, but even close up it was hard to see his face in the dim light.

"Mister," the man said, "we don't want no trouble. Just come along with me."

The man's jacket opened slightly, and a metal badge reflected the little light from inside Warren's room.

For a moment Warren was speechless. His body felt numb. He managed to force out a few words. "What is this?"

He received two answers. The first was spoken. "This is a raid, and you're under arrest." The second was unspoken, but it confirmed and supported the first; Warren felt the barrel of a gun pressed against his naked chest.

He suddenly regained his wits, if not his strength. He pushed forward in an attempt to knock the law officer off-balance, but the man was prepared and Warren fell into his arms. The policeman then stepped back and let Warren fall to his knees.

Warren knelt there for a few seconds, his head the seeming center of some swirling vortex. His eyes wouldn't focus, and he was unable to get up.

Suddenly, there was no need to rise. The law officer brought the butt end of his revolver down against the side of Warren's head.

Chapter Fifty-three

The two men walked down the deserted back streets just outside the Chinese district. They were a study in contrasts. Beaudine's hair and clothes were disheveled, and he couldn't stand still. Tears were forming in his eyes, but somehow he managed to keep them from dropping onto his face. The other man was as neat and crisp as a fresh pack of playing cards. He walked along the street calmly, his hands tucked in his pockets, privately amused at the jittery man next to him.

"So, Mr. Beaudine," he said. "Do we understand each other a bit better now? Do you understand what happens when the payments are late?"

"Yes, of course," the politician answered. "I'm sorry. I didn't realize. It won't happen again."

The other man stopped walking, turned, and grabbed Beaudine by the lapels. "You're goddamn right it won't happen again. But that's not good enough. Do you realize what I've got to do now to keep your name out of the police reports? There are lots of people I'll have to, shall we say, reward monetarily for their silence."

"I understand."

"Do you?"

"I think so. You want more."

"Yes, more." He let go of Beaudine's jacket and replaced

his hands in his pockets. "I figure between the money you owe me and the money I'll need now and the penalty you'll pay . . ."

"What penalty?"

"The penalty for breaking the law, Mr. Beaudine. You break lots of them. And I'm still the assistant chief of police in this city. I can't allow lawbreakers to go unpunished, can I?"

"You're going to prosecute me?"

"You've already been found guilty in my private court. You can pay your rather hefty fine privately, or you can pay a worse fine publicly. That's up to you."

"You know I don't want my name connected with Weng Wo's."

"Very well, then. That's settled. Now let's talk about the fine."

"How much?"

"I think maybe $15,000 ought to do the trick."

Beaudine stopped walking. "I don't have that kind of money with me."

"Then get it."

"I'll need some time."

"Fine. Take all the time you need. Just remember that for every day you take, you can add another thousand on."

"That's crazy, Lodge. I won't pay it."

The assistant chief of police removed one hand from his jacket pocket and used it to count along with his remarks, popping one finger out from the closed fist at a time. "Let's see. One, drug smuggling. Two, prostitution. Three, white slavery—that should get me the promotion I so richly deserve. Four, kidnapping. Five, sodomizing a minor." He took out the other fist and popped out the sixth finger. "Six, . . ."

"Okay," Beaudine interrupted. "You've made your point."

"My point is $15,000 and you walk away from this scot-free. Plus the thousand a day if you need the time."

"Agreed."

"When can I expect the money?"

"It's the weekend, Lodge. The banks aren't open. So you'll have to wait until Monday."

"That'll make it $17,000."

Then Beaudine remembered that Earp's money was on the way. "Maybe I can have it for you sooner. I'm expecting someone in the next day or two, I hope. Someone who should be bringing about that much money."

"Really?" Lodge said. "How convenient."

"Should I send one of my men over with the cash? I assume you're letting them off as well."

"Sure, I'll include them in the price. But now that I think of it, we do have to pin this on someone." He stared at Beaudine. "Any suggestions?"

"Pin it on Weng Wo."

Lodge laughed. "No. That's not good enough. What about one of the guests you brought to Weng Wo's?"

Suddenly, fear made Beaudine's face turn pale. "No. I can't. I can't do that."

Lodge realized that he had hit a nerve. "Why? Who'd you bring? Another politician?"

"No."

"Well, who did I arrest? You might as well tell me. I'll find out anyway."

Beaudine had trouble spitting out the name. But he forced himself. "Earp."

"Wyatt Earp?"

"No!" Beaudine corrected, wiping the sweat from his brow with the palm of his hand. "Warren Earp."

"One of Wyatt's brothers?"

"Yes."

Lodge looked off down the street, thinking about this lucky catch. "Well, he's still an Earp. Let's say the operation at Weng Wo's is his."

"Why do we have to do that? I'll have every Earp after my head. And it'll shut down the operation. What'll I do then?"

"Start it up again at some other John's shop," the police official answered. "It's a minor inconvenience compared to being exposed in the newspapers, don't you think?"

Beaudine thought it over for a moment. "No, Lodge. Not Earp. Take someone else—one of his men perhaps."

Lodge shook his head. "No. The Earp name gets lots of attention. It should get me what I want, the chief's job. Think of the business we can do then."

"If I'm alive to do it. The Earps are going to hunt me down."

"That's your problem. Hire yourself more bodyguards."

The sweat rolled off Beaudine's face, soaking the collar that surrounded his neck. A sharp pain between his ribs began to eat away at his insides.

"You send one of your men to me when you have the cash," Lodge continued. "Not with the money. I'll pick up the money at your hotel. You sit tight until then. And whatever you do, don't leave town. I'd hate to have this story uncovered. The newspapers would eat it up, don't you think?"

Then Lodge turned a corner and got into a waiting carriage. "See you soon," he said, closing the door behind him. "By the way, I'd get back to your hotel as soon as possible. These streets aren't exactly safe at night."

The San Francisco Police Department vehicle drove off, leaving Beaudine alone in the street. And although the politician knew that Lodge's warning was true—the streets weren't safe—he knew that no street anywhere would be safe once the Earps learned that one of their own had been framed.

Chapter Fifty-four

On the Central Pacific, the next morning

"Excuse me, sir," Robert Louis Stevenson said to the man in uniform aboard the train, "would you be so kind as to tell me how long it will be until we reach San Francisco?"

The man took out a steel-plated watch from his vest pocket and flipped the cover open. "We'll be arrivin' 'bout 8:25. That's about two hours from now." He put away the watch and stooped down in order to see better out the window. "Pretty sunrise, ain't it?"

"Indeed it is," the Scotsman agreed.

The conductor yawned and marched up the aisle, leaving Louis to savor the sight of the rising sun and the beautiful land its rays of light uncovered. The writer jotted some notes in the notebook he had in his lap.

"What are you writing, Louis?" a weak, tired voice asked.

The question came as a surprise to Stevenson because all of his companions had been asleep moments before. But he recognized the voice as McCain's.

"Mr. McCain! Good morning!"

"Good morning. But I don't think I slept more than fifteen minutes."

"Oh, dear, yes. You've been asleep for at least a couple of hours."

"Don't feel like it." McCain felt the weight on his shoulder and looked down at his left. Sara's head lay on his shoulder, just where it had been when he dozed off. He tried not to move; he didn't want to disturb her.

Next to Louis sat Holliday, still wrapped in a blanket, still snoring. McCain noted the differences in the two men who sat opposite him and smiled. They were an even more unlikely pair than he and the woman whose dark hair hung over his arm.

"How long has he been sleeping?" McCain asked softly.

"Quite a while," Stevenson answered, looking down at Doc. "He's been in a very restless mood."

"Yeah?"

"He's been squirming around and sweating profusely. I think his fever may finally be breaking."

"That good?"

"We can only hope so."

McCain glanced down at Stevenson's notebook and noticed that the Scotsman had written quite a bit. The open page before him was nearly filled with words.

"You feeling inspired tonight?"

When Louis realized what the question was in reference to, he smiled and said, "A bit, yes. I've a wealth of material before me."

"Where?"

"Right there." The writer pointed his pencil at Doc.

"I didn't think a sleeping man would inspire great thoughts. But I guess Doc is quite a character."

"Indeed, he is. Some of the utterances that have flown from his lips tonight!"

"He talks in his sleep?"

"More like ranting, I should say, probably caused by his fever. But they're fascinating, and some are quite disturbing. I've written some of them down."

"If they're nothing but rants, why are they so interesting?"

"Well, it's difficult to explain," Stevenson said. "How well do you know him? Really know him, I mean."

"Not very well. I only met him a few days ago."

Stevenson was surprised by the answer. "I thought you were comrades-at-arms?"

"Sort of. Because I have to."

"I don't understand."

Before pursuing the conversation further, McCain attempted to glance down at Sara's face, but her down-tilted head made it impossible to see her eyes. "How long has she been asleep?"

Stevenson looked at Sara, then said, "At least a couple of hours. And she hasn't moved a muscle all night. She must feel quite comfortable."

"She still out?"

"Very."

"Good. I don't want her to hear this."

"She's asleep."

McCain took a deep breath and began. "I'm with Doc because I have to. I promised a friend I'd keep an eye on him and see who he delivers that bag of money to. The government of the United States is interested in that too, so I guess you could say I'm sort of working for the government, unofficial-like."

Stevenson's eyes widened in amazement. "You're an agent of the government?"

"Not officially."

"What is this . . . this criminal involved in?" The writer moved as far away from Doc as the bench would permit.

"Not so much him as his boss, Wyatt Earp."

"Wyatt Earp?" Louis repeated loudly.

"Want to keep it down, Louis?" McCain chided. "If Doc hears this, we're both dead."

The Scotsman regained his composure and lowered his

voice. "But I thought Wyatt Earp was on the side of the law. I thought he was a noble lawman."

"Right," McCain snapped sarcastically, "and I'm Abe Lincoln's grandma!"

It took a few moments for this fact to sink into Louis' consciousness. Then he asked, "But what about the books? All those stories about the Earps? A-are they all lies?"

"Some. You're a writer, Louis. You always tell the truth?"

"Not factual truth, but . . ."

"I rest my case."

Stevenson thought it over. He thought about his meeting with Chief Joseph. That man was far from the brutal savage the novels had described. And Holliday was far from the crusading warrior of justice he had read about. Why shouldn't the same be the case with the Earps?

"Then this man is not your friend?"

"No. I'm stuck with him for a while."

Louis leaned forward and his facial expression became serious. "Then I recommend you part company with him as soon as your business is concluded. The man is a demented lunatic."

"I know."

"No, Mr. McCain, I'm quite serious. I've done some reading on diseases of the mind. And this man is mad. He seems to have two separate personalities, one somewhat praiseworthy in its loyalty, but the other extremely dangerous and sadistic."

"I don't understand."

"Listen to this," Louis said, flipping back a couple of pages in his notebook. " 'Nobody'll stop me, Wyatt. I can do it. You and your brothers are the only friends I got. I'll find him. I will.' Then later he called out, 'Cut the bullet out, Wyatt, cut it out. That's it. It don't hurt that much.' Then again later, he yelled 'I owe you, I owe you. The rest of my days, I owe you.' "

McCain was interested, but didn't follow the Scotsman's point. "So he's loyal? That don't make him crazy."

"There's more," Stevenson noted, "and this is where it gets fascinating. Interspersed with those ravings, he also called out, 'They're all after me, Wyatt. I'll kill them all. Kill you too, you bastard. Better than me. Better than me. Want to kill me too.' " Louis turned to the next page. " 'No good. Katie. Evil. Bitches, all of them. Don't Wyatt. She'll turn on you. Don't marry her. Bitch. Kill her. Kill you too.' "

Then he stopped, and the train jerked. Holliday's head snapped back against the back of the bench, but tilted forward again. His sleep continued undisturbed.

When the writer was certain that Doc hadn't awakened, he asked softly, "Does that sound like a sane man to you?"

McCain answered. "No. But he's sick. People dream all kinds of crazy things when the fever comes upon them."

"Maybe. But I think his actions since I've known him verify my opinion. He's quite mad—and I must say I'm quite uncomfortable sitting next to him."

"We'll be in San Francisco soon. Then you'll be leaving, and you'll never have to worry about Doc again. So relax."

"Oh, I suppose you're correct. But I doubt I shall forget my encounter with Mr. Holliday. Someday, perhaps I'll write something about the conflicting personalities within a man. And these notes, I imagine, will come in handy."

"Where will you go when we get to San Francisco, Louis?"

"I hope to meet my beloved, Miss Fanny Osbourne, there. She summoned me several weeks ago to meet her there. I am hopeful that we shall soon be married."

"Is she from Scotland too?"

"No, she's an American, although I met her in France. We've been waiting for her divorce to become legal."

McCain smiled drowsily and leaned his head back against the wooden bench.

"Are you married, Mr. McCain?" Stevenson asked. Then he glanced at Sara, but when he did, he suddenly got nervous and prayed McCain wouldn't take offense at his question.

"I was," he answered. "I don't think I still am."

"I don't understand."

"Neither do I, Louis. Neither do I." McCain clutched at his eyes with his right hand and tried to wipe the sleepiness away from them. "My wife left me some time ago. I haven't heard or seen her since."

"I'm sorry. I hope some day you find her."

McCain smiled, then said, "I'm not sure I want to."

Suddenly, Doc's raspy breathing got louder and he started coughing turbulently. Small gobs of sputum shot out of his mouth onto everything around him.

The noise and fury of his coughing woke Sara up, and she lifted her head off McCain's shoulder. She sat there upright, holding his arm, mesmerized and terrified by the vehemence of the gunfighter's fit.

Doc, too, regained consciousness and struggled for breath between coughing spasms. He buckled over, his head just a foot above his knees. Watery blood shot onto his pants and hands.

Stevenson tried to give him his handkerchief, but Doc angrily slapped it out of the writer's hand. The coughing continued for a few more moments, then finally abated. Doc sat back in the seat, taking deep breaths. His face was cloud-white except for his eyes, which were streaked with crimson lines.

Regaining his breath, he snarled, "What the hell are ya all lookin' at? Ya all seen it before."

No one answered him; they all avoided eye contact with him.

"McCain, we still got the money?" he asked.

"Sure, Doc," he answered. "Right here under my legs."

Doc noticed the bag beneath McCain's seat. "Good. You

slept at all?"

"A couple of hours, according to Louis there."

Doc turned to the Scotsman. "You slept?"

"I dozed off now and then when everybody was asleep, yes."

"When everybody was asleep?"

"Yes."

Then Doc stared at Sara for a moment. "What about you, miss?"

"What about me?" Sara asked.

"You been sleepin' all night?"

"What's the difference?"

"The difference is that maybe you removed the money from the bag when everyone else was sleepin'." Doc turned back to Louis. "Or maybe you did."

"Or maybe I did," McCain said. "You're being ridiculous, Doc."

Holliday was too weak to fight, but he wasn't going to take anyone's word that the money was still in the satchel. He knew he'd been asleep for a long time. "Gimme the bag."

"Here." McCain reached down, grabbed the bag by the handle, and placed it on Doc's lap.

Doc opened it, looked into it, and stuck his hand inside. He pulled out a handful of green U.S. currency, then spread the bag apart and looked inside.

"Why don't you count it?" Sara snapped. "Maybe Louis there took a few bills to buy some new books."

A look of horror shot across Stevenson's face. "I assure you, I did no such thing."

Doc ignored the Scotsman and looked at Sara. "Very funny. Your sense of humor is almost as inspiring as your body."

Sara leaned forward and tried to smack Doc's face, but McCain held her wrist and restrained her.

"That's it, McCain," Doc said, laughing. "Hold onto her.

335

It appears you're the only one left for her to play up to. So you hold onto her real tight."

"You bastard!" Sara said.

Doc found her anger amusing, and he laughed even harder.

"That's enough, Doc," McCain said. "Lay off her. In another hour, we'll all be out of each other's hair. Let's all stay nice and calm till then."

Doc continued to laugh, and Sara ripped her arm out of McCain's grasp. Then she sat back and tried to subdue her anger.

McCain looked out the train's window. They were traveling quickly. Trees whizzed by the side of the car and even the clouds in the sky seemed to be gliding by more quickly than usual. He turned back for a moment, noticing that all three of his companions had their eyes closed, apparently relaxed now and busy keeping to themselves. Doc still had a smile on his face; the satchel lay on his lap. The consumptive fit and fever seemed to have passed because the gunfighter looked better than he had in days.

McCain turned back to the window. He didn't want to look at Sara, fearing what he might see on her face. If she was feeling affectionate, he wanted to avoid seeing it. Doc was a suspicious enough fellow, without him thinking the two of them were in cahoots. And if she was angry—angry at him, too—he didn't want to deal with that either. He'd seen that look on too many female faces in his time. On Alexandra's face. Even on his sister's face. No, it was better to look away into the gold and green California land the train traversed.

But had he looked at Sara, he would have seen the self-satisfied smile on her face, the smile she was trying to suppress. She was pleased with the knowledge that Doc hadn't really checked the bag too carefully. And she was equally pleased with the conversation between McCain and Louis she had overheard. Especially the part about Mc-

Cain's relationship with Doc. She now understood at least something about the man and could reasonably explain some of his past actions.

It was also pleasing to know that for reasons of his own he was an even better confidence artist than she was.

Chapter Fifty-five

San Francisco, that evening

The first thing Doc noticed when he stepped off the train was the odor of the place. It was unusual, but not unfamiliar. It was the scent of people.

"Can't believe we're finally here!" he said to no one in particular. "I was startin' to worry back there. Thought we'd never make it."

"I didn't think you'd live to see it," McCain added, taking the step from the train to the wooden platform. "You seem a lot better now, but you were mighty sick for a while. You have any idea how much you slept?"

"No, and I don't give a damn either. You worry too much, McCain. I've been battlin' this sickness for years, and I always win. Sometimes it just takes time."

Sara looked down at the two men. "Won't one of you two gentlemen help me down from this car?" she asked.

McCain turned and extended his arm to her. She held on to it and took the long step down to the ground.

Stevenson followed her down, and for a moment the four travelers stood together. They were all somewhat amazed that they had finally reached their destination, and, as if to let the fact sink in, stood there, surveying the train station, soaking in its sounds and sights.

"Let's move," Doc said to McCain, interrupting the reveries. "We got business to attend to." To emphasize his point, Doc shook the satchel in his left hand.

"Yes, you must go," Stevenson said, "and I shan't keep you. Just allow me to wish you the best of luck." He extended his hand to McCain, who took it and shook it.

"Good luck to you too, Louis."

Then Louis presented the same hand to Doc. "Mr. Holliday, good luck."

Doc simply glanced at the hand and said, "Right."

Suddenly, Sara touched both Louis and McCain on the arm and announced, "I really have to run. I see my friend down the platform there, and she's walking away. I don't think she saw me. So goodbye and good luck."

Then she bounded away down the platform, without looking back even once. McCain watched her go, wanting to call after her, wanting to know where she was headed.

Doc sensed this and grabbed McCain by the arm. "Let's go."

But McCain's gaze stayed on Sara until she was gone.

"C'mon," Doc repeated. "Let's go. Forget about her. I told you she was trouble. You shouldn't've let her get to you. That kind don't care 'bout no one but themselves."

McCain turned and stared at Doc with expressionless eyes. He hated to admit it, but it seemed that Doc was right.

"Gentlemen," Stevenson interrupted, "again I wish you good luck." He nodded and drifted away from them and into the crowd of people criss-crossing the station.

Doc walked into the crowd also. McCain stood silently for a moment, then tried to shake her out of his system by giving his head a quick, little jerk. It didn't work, but he stepped forward and followed Holliday into the sweltering, noisy streets of San Francisco.

Chapter Fifty-six

It took a couple of hours for Doc and McCain to find the hotel at which the Beaudine entourage had camped. The Casa Verde was the sixth hotel they checked. And had it not been for the extreme nervousness of the clerk at the desk, they might have believed that the politician's party wasn't staying there either. But the thin, foppish man blinked excessively and swallowed hard before each answer. Both McCain and Holliday knew just by looking at the man with the pencil-line mustache that he was lying through his very white, very polished teeth.

"So there ain't no Jerome Beaudine stayin' here?" Doc asked for the second time.

"No, s-sir."

"How 'bout Warren Earp? That name ring a bell?"

The man's face went white, and he spun the guest book around so he could pretend to read it and thereby avoid eye contact with Doc. "L-let me check, s-sir."

"You know who Warren Earp is, mister?" Doc continued. "He's Wyatt Earp's brother. You heard of Wyatt Earp, haven't you?"

The clerk tried to ignore the question and ran his finger up and down the list of guests' names.

"He's the meanest bastard in the West, mister. And Warren's next meanest. He'd be pretty mad if he knew you lied to me, if he was stayin' here and you didn't tell me."

"I see n-no Earp staying here, Mister . . ."

"Holliday," Doc answered, smiling. "Doc Holliday." Then he shot his thumb over his shoulder to McCain, who stood beside him. "And this here's Josiah McCain. You heard of him?"

"N-no."

"He's the guy who killed a barber in Wichita for cuttin' his hair too short. Cut the poor bastard with his own razor!"

The clerk stared at McCain, and McCain stared back, looking angry, eagerly playing along with Doc.

"Cut his throat from ear to ear," he said, adding detail to Doc's tall tale.

The clerk struggled for breath, and bent low over the desk, trying to hide the rising tears which were forming in his eyes. Doc placed his hand on the man's shoulder, then grabbed the cloth and raised the man's body until he was standing straight.

"Now," Doc said, tightening his grip and giving the man a good shake, "enough bullshit. Let's have the truth."

The man shook like a reed, and the tears broke free and ran down his cheeks. Doc looked around to see if the patrons of the hotel were watching. The lobby was almost empty, except for an old man whose attention was focused on his copy of *The Police Gazette*.

"Tell me the truth. What's Beaudine's room number?"

"I can't!" said the clerk, weeping quietly. "He'll have my job. I have a family to support."

Doc let go of the man and said, "Out with it, man. I already know he's stayin' here. You practically just admitted that. Now tell me why you lied."

The man tried to bury his face in his open hands, but Doc pulled them apart.

"Tell me, damn it. I ain't gonna hurt you."

The man realized he had no choice now but to tell the truth. "He told me to say he wasn't here. He told me he'd fire me if anyone found out he was here."

"He say anything 'bout expectin' a friend of Wyatt Earp to show up?"

"Y-yes."

"Didn't he tell you to let me in?"

"No. In fact, he told me to be on the lookout for a messenger of Earp."

"And?"

"And get rid of him."

"Why?"

The man looked away from Doc and McCain.

"I asked you why?"

Taking a deep breath, the clerk answered, "Because last night Warren Earp was arrested. I might as well tell you. You'll hear it anyway soon enough. It's all over town."

"Arrested? Arrested for what?"

"I'm not exactly certain. But the rumor is he was smuggling opium into the country and ran a . . . a house of ill repute."

Doc let the facts sink in for a moment. He knew that Warren had no contacts and certainly no business in San Francisco; he remembered Wyatt telling him that Warren hadn't been much west of Missouri.

"What's the name of this house of . . . this whorehouse?"

The clerk thought for a moment, then answered, "I heard it's called Weng Wo. I think that's the name. Those Chinese names are hard to keep straight."

"Weng Wo?" Doc repeated. "A Chinese whorehouse?"

"Yes, sir. It's in the Chinese District."

Doc looked at McCain, then turned back to the very rattled clerk. "Thanks for all the information. Now we'll need a room. No, make that two rooms—next to each other."

The man stood up and asked, "You mean here?"

"Don't mean nowhere else."

"But . . ."

"Two rooms, friend, now!"

The frown on Doc's face unnerved the hotel employee, and he figured he had pushed his luck enough already, so he turned the guestbook around so Doc could sign his name. Doc took the quill, dipped it in the bottle of blue ink, and signed his name on the blank line. Then he stepped back, and McCain signed the registry on the line underneath Holliday's signature. Before he put the pen to the paper, though, McCain noticed that his companion had signed the name I. Tooth.

"What the hell is that?" McCain asked.

"An old joke we used to pull in dental school," Doc answered. "That's just in case Beaudine takes a gander at the book. Can't sign my real name, now can I?"

McCain signed his name on the blank line. The clerk turned the registry again and wrote "Room 38" next to Doc's pseudonym and "Room 39" next to McCain's name.

"One more thing," Doc said to the clerk. "And you listen to me good. You keep this quiet. If Beaudine finds out we're here—especially if he finds out *I'm* here—I'm gonna blame you personally, and friend, you'll regret the day you ever dropped outta your momma's belly. You understand?"

"Y-yes," answered the clerk.

"You ain't seen me or my friend here, and you ain't been approached by any associate of Wyatt Earp if Beaudine asks. Am I makin' myself clear?"

"I understand," the clerk replied.

"God help you if you cross me. There won't be no place to hide."

"I won't cross you, Mr. Holliday."

"That's Mr. Tooth from now on," Doc corrected. "Now gimme the keys." He extended an open hand.

The desk clerk took the key from the hook on which it

hung and handed it to Doc. "Your rooms are on the second floor."

"Where's Beaudine's room?"

"On the third floor. Room 59."

"Did Warren Earp have his own room?"

"Yes, sir. Room 57."

Without further words, Doc turned and made his way to the stairs, his satchel in tow. McCain tipped his hat to the clerk and followed Doc up the stairs.

When the pair of threatening men were gone the clerk sat back down in his chair. He cursed the day he ever left the last hotel he worked at, the Silver Stone Hotel in Reno, Nevada. But business had been bad, and his boss had to let him go; Reno, it had seemed to his former employer, was just not a good hotel town.

So the clerk moved to San Francisco and gladly accepted the position that a representative of Jerome Beaudine offered him. Now his luck was turning for the worse again. He was caught in the middle of a feud between two powerful factions, the U.S. government and the gun-toting Earps. And he didn't know which side he feared more. What he did know was that one side was going to be after his head when all the shooting stopped.

He resolved to look for a new job when this day's shift was over.

Chapter Fifty-seven

McCain got restless. He had been sitting in his room smoking cigarettes and looking out the window for the past hour, waiting for Doc to return. When he could sit no more, he stood up and paced the room a few times.

Finally, there was a knock at the door. McCain swung the door open, and Doc stepped into the room.

"Well, that didn't tell me nothin'," he said, shaking his head, "except that Warren *was* here. I found a crumpled-up wire message from Wyatt on the floor of his room."

"So what do we do now?"

"I ain't doin' much till tonight. I ain't feelin' so good right now, so I'm gonna sit down and think things over. I gotta get Warren out of jail, and I'm gonna have to confront Beaudine 'fore too long."

"But you're not going to do that now?"

"No. I ain't up to it now. I'm gonna get back to my room and think this all over."

"Take that with you," McCain said, pointing to the satchel. "I have to get out for a while."

"Where ya goin'?"

"I thought it might be a good idea to check out this place in Chinatown where Warren got pinched. Maybe I can scrounge up something to clear him."

Doc smiled. "That's not a bad idea, McCain. But do you think the police'll let you anywhere near it?"

"I'll find a way."

"Good. I'll hang around here. Keep my ears open for any word on Beaudine."

Doc stood up, grabbed the satchel, and headed for the door. McCain put on his hat and followed Doc out into the hall. They closed the door behind them and took the few steps down the hall to the door of Doc's room.

"See you later, Doc," McCain said.

"Right. Later."

Then Doc disappeared into his room, and McCain continued down the hall. He heard the door of Doc's room shut behind him, then dashed down the stairway to the hotel lobby. The clerk behind the desk looked at him nervously, and McCain nodded to him as he made his way out of the hotel onto the busy streets of San Francisco.

He let the sunshine warm him for a moment, and he stared up and down the streets, enjoying the sights of this big city. Wagons paraded through the streets, and people of all shapes and sizes, all nationalities and races, seemed to be on their way to some appointment, some destination.

He lit a cigarette. A Chinese man dressed in a blue silk jacket crossed his path, and McCain stopped him. "Excuse me," he called after the man.

The fellow stopped and looked at McCain.

"Can you tell me which way it is to the Chinese District?"

The man pointed over McCain's shoulder, then held up four fingers. "Four streets," he said.

McCain tipped his hat and said, "Thanks."

The Chinese man bowed, turned, and continued on his way at the same quick pace as everyone in this city. McCain moved off in the opposite direction.

Five minutes later, he noticed he was the only non-Oriental on the street. He felt as if he had crossed some mysterious, invisible borderline and entered a strange, foreign nation. The people seemed friendly enough: most of them smiled at him as he walked by, or waved to him from within their shops, beckoning him to come in. He passed one doorway and could hear the sounds of musical instruments and human voices combining to make a completely alien brand of music. Looking above the doorway, he saw the sign that said "Chinese Theater." Had he more time on his hands, he might have gone in; it had been a long time since he heard music or saw a show of any kind.

But he had more important matters on his mind. Doc was interested in finding a way to clear Warren Earp; perhaps McCain would find something at Weng Wo's that would serve that purpose. It would also serve McCain's private interest. He wanted to meet this Warren Earp, and then he could settle the matter of whether Earp had murdered his sister. A simple glance at the man's ears would tell.

He stopped for a moment and looked at the buildings on the street, reading as many of the shop names as he could. He crossed the street and searched for the name of Weng Wo on any of the establishments. He saw plenty of names that sounded like Weng Wo—they all seemed to contain the letters "eng"—but the name Weng Wo was not among them.

Then a young boy of maybe six years of age approached him. The youngster looked up at him and asked, "You lost, mister?"

McCain squatted down to the boy's level and smiled. "I guess I am," he replied.

"What are you looking for?" the boy asked in near-perfect English.

"I'm looking for a place called Weng Wo's, son, but I don't suppose you'd know about a place like that."

"Yes," the boy corrected, "I know where it is."

"You do? Where is it?"

"Around that corner. The fourth store."

"Well, thanks, son. That's mighty nice of you to help," McCain said, reaching into his pocket and pulling out two bits. "Here, buy yourself some candy."

"Thanks, mister."

"You're welcome," McCain said, standing up and watching as the boy joined a group of other Chinese children and flashed the quarter at them. Then the whole group ran off into a store down the street.

When he turned the corner, McCain looked for the fourth store. The boy knew the store, and he had given him correct information. But McCain was surprised to see that the establishment was an importing company. For a moment he wondered if there were two Weng Wo's in the area. Then he noticed the policeman standing guard outside the front door and realized that this indeed must be the place.

He'd have to get past that policeman, he knew, and he wanted to manage that without raising any suspicion. He couldn't just walk up and ask the policeman to let him in. So he thought for a moment, then turned to see if the children were still playing in the streets.

In the distance—maybe a block or two away—the loud, popping sounds of firecrackers could be heard echoing off the buildings. An idea came to McCain.

The children poured back onto the street, all munching on some treat McCain didn't recognize. Slowly, he approached them, and when he was near, softly said, "Son, come here."

The youngster stepped away from his small crowd of friends. "Yes?"

"How'd you like to make two dollars?"

The boy's eyes lit up. "Sure."

"Here's what I want you to do. Take this." He handed the boy five dollars. "Buy as many firecrackers as you can get for three dollars. Keep the other two for yourself. Then I want you to light them up right there." He pointed to the corner. "You understand."

"Yes."

"Good. Now you do like I asked, okay?"

"Okay."

The boy rejoined his group of friends, and they ran off down the street whooping and yelling with excitement. McCain turned the corner again, slowly marching down the street, pretending to be interested in the wares in the shop windows. When he reached Weng Wo's shop, he studied the merchandise on display in the window. It consisted of exotic jewelry, pottery, and cutlery.

The old cop who was stationed in front of the establishment leaned over to McCain. "Place is closed, sir."

"Oh," McCain said, pretending ignorance of the fact. "Owner die or something?"

"No," the cop laughed. "The place was selling more than pottery. Selling a good time, if you know what I mean." He winked knowingly.

"Ladies?"

"And opium."

"Good Lord, what's this world coming to?"

"Don't rightly know."

"Thanks for the warning," McCain said, staring for a moment at the cop's shining badge. "I'll go somewhere else. Good day!" Then he tipped his hat and moved down the street, stopping at the next store window.

Just then, the group of boys entered the intersection of narrow streets. They gathered near the cop and made a small circle with their bodies, all facing its center. In a second, a small stream of smoke rose from the center of the circle, and the boys spread out, two of them heaving some smoking object into the air.

The firecrackers exploded before they hit the ground, and they spread to each side of the street. The noise was almost ungodly, and there seemed no end to it.

The policeman angrily shouted at the kids to stop.

Another boy heaved another dozen or so packs of fireworks into the air, and they too shot off in midair. The boys regrouped at the corner with still more fireworks at the ready.

When the cop saw this, he stepped away from his post and yelled at the children. "I told you to cut it out, damn you!"

But another long fuse had been lit, and another set of firecrackers was already flying down the street. The cop waved his nightstick and took off after the young pests.

"I'll get you, you heathen little bastards!"

When he was far enough away, McCain took the opportunity to try the door of Weng Wo's shop. It was locked, but McCain pushed up against it with his shoulder. The lock didn't feel too sturdy, so he quickly stepped back and rammed the door with his shoulder. It flew open, and McCain stepped in, closing the door behind him. He waited to see if the cop was returning, but there was no sign of him, so he moved deeper into the darkness of the shop, away from the daylight pouring in through the shop window. He pushed aside a silk curtain and stepped into a back room. Ahead of him were a door and a stairway leading up.

He heard someone's voice and was startled for a moment. But gazing out around the curtain to the front of the store, he could see the policeman standing there, smacking his nightstick into an open palm, loudly cursing the stray, delayed firecrackers that still popped around him.

McCain decided to explore the upper floor first and quietly climbed the staircase. At its top was a room that preceded a long hallway. There was nothing in the room except a small table and chair, so he pushed off down the hall.

To his left and right were doors, all closed. Might as well start with the first of these eight doors, McCain thought. He turned the knob, opened the door, and stepped inside, leaving the door open behind him.

There was absolutely nothing unusual about the room. It contained an unmade bed, a table with only a small glass on it, and a window with the blind pulled down. McCain bent over, looked under the bed, under the table, but found nothing. He left the room, closing the door behind him.

The next room was more interesting. It was identical to the previous one in size, but some objects covered the floor in this one. A pair of slippers occupied one corner, and the bed sheets were hanging down off the bed. McCain pulled the sheet, shook it, and tossed it on the bed. Something had gotten tangled in the sheet, and it fell to the floor. McCain picked it up. It was a heavy gold ring, not unlike the one he used to wear when he still had a marriage. He had thrown his ring into a creek when he realized he no longer could consider himself married; perhaps, he surmised, the man this ring belonged to felt it was morally wrong to sleep with a prostitute while wearing it.

He placed the ring on the empty table and moved on to the next room.

It was a mess. The floor was covered with cigarette butts, half-dried liquor, and articles of clothing. McCain kicked at a man's white sock, knocking it across the room. He bent over and picked up an empty whiskey bottle, setting it up on the table. A garter belt lay atop the crumpled sheets on the bed. He patted down the sheets to see if anything was concealed beneath them. Nothing.

He began to wonder if he was wasting his time, particularly since he didn't know exactly what he was looking for. But since he was up on this floor, he decided to at least poke his nose into the remaining rooms.

The next few were as uninformative as the last few, and he didn't bother going beyond the door. But then he opened the door to the second to last room, and a sight caught his eye. It was a folded-up piece of paper under the bed. McCain bent down and picked it up. When he had it unfolded, he tried to read the words on it, but only two of them were in English: Jerome Beaudine. Above those words were a series of numerical calculations and a long column of Chinese lettering written by hand.

He folded the paper up and placed it in his pocket. He had no idea what the paper meant, but it *was* found here, and it *did* have Beaudine's name on it. Perhaps it contained something incriminating, perhaps not. He'd have to find someone who could translate it for him.

McCain closed the door, and moved on to the last room. He swung the door open and gazed inside, but other than a horrendous odor that wafted into the hallway, there seemed nothing unusual about it.

Then he heard something, and he froze. It sounded like a creaking door, and it definitely came from downstairs. McCain turned toward the stairway, half-expecting to see the cop's face at the top of the stairs. He drew his Peacemaker and held it at the ready.

Quietly, he stepped forward and peered down the stairs. Nothing but quiet and shadows below. He descended slowly, taking two steps at a time, praying they wouldn't creak. When he hit bottom, he stole a glance at the window. Outside stood the cop, pacing back and forth, bored, no doubt, with his uneventful tour of duty.

In front of McCain was a door he had passed earlier. He opened it and was surprised to find a stairway leading down. It was pitch black inside, and the stairs extended farther than he could see. He stepped away from the door for a moment and searched around the shop for a candle. He spied a desk in the shop and headed for it. Sure enough, a thick white candle sat in a porcelain candle-holder atop the desk. He took it and returned to the door.

After lighting the candle, McCain moved down the stairs as quietly as possible. The stairway was narrow and long; he had descended at least twenty steps before he spotted the last step. He kept moving, one hand holding the candle over his head so the flame wouldn't blind him, the other wrapped around the handle of his Colt, his forefinger pressed lightly against the trigger.

When he moved off the final step, he heard something move across the floor. He held the candle up and waited for his eyes to adjust to the darkness. Then he heard the scratching noise again and saw what was responsible for it. A rat crawled away and disappeared into what appeared to be a small hole in the wall.

The room was surprisingly spacious. Along the walls were cots. They were uncovered by sheets or blankets, and they were obviously often-used: each of them sagged in the middle.

There was a closeness, a murkiness in the room despite its spaciousness. And at first McCain thought it was the candle's dim light, but no, there *was* a thin cloud of smoke in the room. It wasn't a foul-smelling smoke, just an unusual-smelling one, one that he had encountered only once before, and that was in New Orleans. It was the smell of opium.

He stepped forward, and something crunched beneath his boot. He lowered the candle to the floor and discovered that he had crushed a long, thin clay pipe. He picked up the bowl-end of it and held it close to his nose. It was opium, no doubt about that.

He stood up again and extended his arm, letting the light from the flickering flame spread to the far wall. In a corner sat another desk, so he headed for it. Suddenly, the solid floor beneath his feet didn't sound so solid. The floorboards rumbled more. He stopped and again lowered the candle to the floor. After a few seconds, he noticed a couple of slits cut into the boards. It did not take him long to realize that the slits provided a very crude, almost unnoticeable handle.

McCain grabbed the handle and pulled on it gently. If this was a door to an even lower room, it wasn't budging. He let go of the handle and crouched down, studying the floor. It was a door of some kind; that was certain. It took him another second to realize that the reason it wasn't opening was because he was standing right on it.

He moved off it and tried the handle again. This time the door swung up a few inches when he pulled. But the door was solid and heavy, and both hands would be required to swing it fully open. He placed the candle by his feet and grabbed the slits with both hands. He pulled up and the floor opened. The door stopped when its end pointed at the ceiling, and it remained wide open.

But before McCain could step back and look below, a shadow jumped out of the hole in the floor. It was a human shadow, except for the long, thin metal blade it was holding in both hands. The candlelight reflected on the steel, and McCain saw the horizontal arc the blade was making. He ducked and not a moment too soon. The sword whooshed over his head and knocked his hat off. Then it swished back the other way, so close to the top of his head that he felt the wind from it in his hair.

McCain's Colt rose — almost as if it had a mind, a will apart from its owner — and pointed at the man's head. But McCain knew that pulling the trigger would give away his presence here, kill any hopes of finding more evidence of Beaudine's involvement or Earp's innocence, and quite possibly land him in the San Francisco jailhouse. So instead of firing the gun, he lowered it and stepped closer to his attacker, readying himself for the next swing of the sword.

It came the second he moved up. But this time the man swung the sword down, trying to cleave McCain's skull in two. He stepped aside skillfully, and with his arm, prevented the man from raising the sword back up again. Then, stepping forward another step, McCain brought the pistol down on the man's head.

His foe staggered around for a moment, dropped the sword at his feet, knocking over the candle with it. The flame still burned, and McCain noticed the man holding the side of his face over his right eyebrow. He was moaning like a cat stuck in a fence.

McCain grabbed him by the shoulder and forced him onto one of the cots. The man sat there, tilted forward, his head between his hands. His moans grew more mournful. It seemed to McCain that the man expected death to claim him any second now.

"Shut up!" McCain said angrily, pushing the man down on the cot until the brown, almond-shaped eyes looked up at him fearfully. "Stop the wailing!"

The man stopped moaning, but lay there shaking. McCain took a good look at him. He was young. Very young, perhaps seventeen. He was dressed in a light blue cotton shirt and pants made of the same material. The clothing was way too big for him, and they hung off his thin body like a couple of nearly-empty potato sacks.

"You speak English?" McCain asked.

The man made no attempt to answer. He just closed his eyes.

McCain placed the end of the gun barrel against the sore spot on the man's forehead. "Speak up, boy. You speak English?"

"Little bit," the young man answered, opening his eyes.

"I hope you speak English better than you wield that melon-splitter of yours. Who are you?"

"My name is Seow Fong."

"You work for Weng Wo?"

"Yes."

"This your workplace, down here? You in charge of the opium?"

"No. I work upstairs."

"In the shop?"

"No. Upstairs." The boy turned his face to the wall, avoiding McCain's stare.

Upstairs? McCain thought. Then it hit him. The boy was

thin, but not unattractive. And his embarrassment at being asked where he worked all added up. He was another of Weng Wo's prostitutes.

"Why are you here?" McCain continued.

"I hide from police. No find me."

"Anyone else here?"

"No."

McCain pulled the gun away from the boy, but kept it out just in case the boy decided to get hostile again.

"You ever hear of Jerome Beaudine?"

Once again, the boy didn't answer and closed his eyes.

"Answer me."

The boy spoke up, but the agitation in his voice revealed he was upset even hearing the name. "I know. Beaudine come here often. Weng Wo work for him. I work for Weng Wo."

"Weng Wo works for Beaudine? You sure of that?"

The boy nodded.

"What does Weng Wo do for Beaudine? Do you know?"

"Get girls. Get opium too. Send girls to China sometime."

"He sends girls to China?"

"Yes. Tie them up, send girl on boat at night."

"Chinese girls?"

"All kind of girl."

McCain wondered if even the U.S. government suspected the breadth of Beaudine's activities. Bat hadn't mentioned kidnapping — or what sounded like slave-trading. Perhaps Bat didn't know. Perhaps the men in Washington — right up to the President — didn't even know.

"Where does Weng Wo keep his records?"

The lad stared at McCain, not comprehending the question.

"His records. His papers. Where does he keep them?"

The boy pointed to the desk in the corner. McCain stepped over to it, opened the drawer, and discovered a small metal box inside. He took the box out, freed the clasp, and raised the lid. Inside were several receipts, although for what he couldn't figure. Chinese characters were littered up and down the page.

"Can you read this?" McCain asked, holding up one of the yellow sheets.

The boy nodded, and McCain brought him the paper. The boy took it and studied it.

"Is an order for money plates," the boy answered.

"Money plates? What the hell is a money plate? That something Chinese?"

Seow Fong laughed, then stopped himself. He didn't want to anger this man by laughing at his stupidity.

"Well, what are money plates? Do you know?"

"I show you."

The boy stepped back into the hole in the floor he had popped out of earlier. McCain picked up the candle and held it over the opening. "Stay where I can see you," he ordered. He couldn't be sure there weren't more swords down there.

But the boy surfaced again, this time with two square metallic objects about an inch thick and several inches long. The boy stepped up to the surface and handed one of them to McCain.

McCain took it, holding it in the same hand as his gun. He held the candle over it to get a better look. It was a plate, just as the boy had said. But this plate was not used for eating or holding anything; its use was limited to pressing counterfeit twenty-dollar bills.

"Hold that one up," McCain said, and the boy held the other plate just under the candle. "That one's this one's little brother," he thought out loud. "Used for tens."

McCain studied his prizes for a moment more, then said, "Close that door and put the plate on the desk."

The boy did as he was instructed and sat in the chair in front of the desk. He stared at McCain.

The plates were useless to McCain — and, in turn, useless to the government — unless he could provide proof that they were the property of Jerome Beaudine. Then he remembered the piece of paper he had found upstairs.

"Read this," he said, unfolding the paper and handing it to the lad.

The boy read it quickly. "Some kind of letter to Beaudine."

"I know that," McCain said impatiently. "Read it to me."

"It's very long."

"Then tell me what it's about."

"It says how much opium shipped to Weng Wo. How many girl ship take to China. How many dollars make here. How many pottery Weng Wo get from China. How many jade. How many . . ."

"I get the picture," McCain interrupted. "That's enough. Give it to me." The boy handed the letter back.

McCain smiled. He had to smile. He couldn't believe the gall of these people. They did their legal business importing pots and vases right along with selling live human flesh and counterfeiting. And it all came on one handy accountant's sheet.

"Who wrote this letter? Can you tell?"

"Weng Wo. No one else write to Mr. Beaudine."

McCain shoved the twenty-dollar plate into his jacket pocket and the letter in the other pocket. Then he turned his attention back to the boy.

"Did the police take any opium? Do you know?"

"Some."

"Not all?"

The boy laughed again, and again caught himself. "Opium all over."

"Get me some."

The boy didn't have to go far for it. He reached into his pocket and pulled out two items: a tiny green bottle containing a milky white fluid, and a powdery nugget about the size of an acorn. McCain had never seen opium shaped like a nugget before, but he assumed that's what the customers smoked through the clay pipes. He took both of the items from the boy and shoved them into the pocket with the import-export record.

Now, he thought, what about this boy? He couldn't very well let him go. He might run to Beaudine or Weng Wo if he was still free; he might get help and come after me; or he might just disappear into the streets, and that wouldn't do because perhaps the boy could be persuaded to testify against Beaudine. Then a strange idea occurred to him.

"You use this stuff?" he asked the boy, patting the outside of the pocket that held the opium.

"Some."

"You like it?"

"Very nice. Very nice dream."

"Use some now."

The boy stared blankly at him for a moment, then reached into his pocket and pulled out another white nugget and a long, thin clay pipe. He struck a match and held it between the third and fourth fingers of his right hand. Then he dropped the pellet into the bowl of the pipe and ignited the substance. The boy inhaled the smoke, and each time he did, the match's flame dipped into the pipe bowl and sprang up again.

McCain watched the boy smoke the opium. The young man's eyes glazed over and a dazed smile filled his face. Then, without missing a puff, the boy pointed at one of the empty cots. McCain waved the barrel of his Colt, signaling that he didn't mind at all if the boy wanted to recline while entering dreamland.

The lad lay there for a few moments. Then his eyes closed, the pipe still stuck between his lips. McCain put away his gun and searched for something to bind the boy. In the desk drawer was a silk garment of some kind. It would have to do. McCain ripped it into long strips and tied several of the strips together. Then he walked over to the boy, took his hands and feet and bound them with the strips.

All that was left to do now was to get out of Weng Wo's. McCain blew out the candle and quickly but silently ran up the stairs. Once there, he noticed the policeman still outside, seeming more bored than ever. At the rear were several windows, much smaller than the single large one the cop paraded before. McCain opened one of them as quietly as he could and stuck his head outside. The windows opened onto an alley filled with trash and large poplin bags containing what looked like potatoes or onions.

He stepped out into the alley and saw that it led to a busy street. He noticed a small gang of children run by on that street. It might be the same street that he first met the young boy. And that gang of kids might be the same gang who had helped him distract the peace officer.

If they were the same kids, he was going to give them a bonus of another couple of dollars.

Chapter Fifty-eight

When McCain returned to the hotel, Doc Holliday wasn't in his room, and he was glad he wouldn't have to spend the next few hours with him. There were certain things he wanted to do alone.

McCain first removed the objects he had taken from Weng Wo's from his pockets and placed them under the unruffled pillow on his bed. It wasn't a very original place to hide them, but he figured they'd be safe there until he returned that night.

Then he left his room again and sent the following wire to Bat Masterson in Dodge: Still working. Good news soon. Like the message he sent days earlier, McCain made this one purposely sketchy; it would be tragic if Wyatt Earp got wind that he was even communicating with Bat. Again he signed the message with the name Missouri Joe.

McCain spent the next couple of hours in his room with a pouch of tobacco, rolling papers, a bottle of good whiskey, and a newspaper. He slid a plush chair over to the window, opened the curtain wide, and let the sun shine into his room. Then he sat back and threw his feet up on the windowsill. With a glass in one hand and the newspaper in the other, he waited until Doc called upon him.

That didn't happen until six o'clock. Then there was a loud knock at the door, and McCain answered it. Doc pushed into the room and sat in the chair that McCain had vacated.

"Where you been, Doc?" McCain asked. "I tried your room earlier."

"Been out," he answered. "Been to a police station. Tried to find out what I could 'bout Warren."

"And?"

"And he's in a cell, all right. Got more charges against him now than I ever thought possible for one man. It's just crazy."

"And you're sure he's innocent?"

"Of most of 'em, yeah. He don't have no business connections out here. He's bein' framed by that son of a bitch Beaudine. Ain't no question 'bout that."

"Makes sense to me."

"Well, I'm glad," Doc commented sarcastically. "I'm glad it makes sense to you. I see you been sittin' here for some time, smokin' an' drinkin' and havin' just a right nice afternoon. Did you go to that Chink place?"

"Yeah."

"Find anything we can use?"

McCain thought about the question for a moment before answering. He could tell Doc the truth and show him the evidence against Beaudine, but if he did, there was the possibility that Doc would use it merely to blackmail Beaudine, and then hang onto it. Then the government would never get their hands on it. Maybe Doc wouldn't do that; after all, he was supposedly here to pay off Beaudine. Doc's main reason for trailing the politician was supposed to be to insure the election of an Earp in Tombstone.

No, it was better to lie right now.

"Found some opium, but nothing that'll get Warren off the hook."

"Shit!"

"What should we do now?"

"I was talkin' before with our friend the desk clerk. He

says Beaudine's been locked in his room with two body-guards all day. Even had lunch in the room. But the fellow swears Beaudine doesn't know we're here. He also told me that Beaudine eats in the restaurant downstairs at six o'clock every day without fail. It's a little after six now. Maybe we should get ourselves somethin' to eat, too."

"You think that's a good idea? You want to confront him down there in front of all those people?"

Doc lit a cigarette, dragged on it, and coughed out the smoke. "Christ! My throat is burnin' up. When we get through with all this I've gotta get myself to a doctor. That goddamn campin' in the mountains took its toll on me. I feel like a buffalo's sittin' on my chest."

"You don't look so good either," McCain commented.

"Thanks."

"You wanna head downstairs then?"

"Have to, as I see it. I couldn't get near his room today. He's got at least two guns workin' for him. He had 'em stationed out in the hallway. Anyhow, out in the open he might be less willin' to pull somethin' stupid. He is a big-ass politician now, ain't he? Can't go blastin' people down in front of witnesses."

"Sounds risky to me. Suppose he won't deal? Then he knows we're here. He can get extra protection. Or run. Or try to frame us for something."

"Don't worry 'bout that," Doc said confidently. "If the bastard won't cooperate, I'll take care of him."

"What'll you do?"

"I'll put a bullet between his eyes. Just 'cause he can't come out shootin' don't mean I can't."

"We could wind up in jail, too."

"I been there before. Besides, Wyatt'll find a way to get us out 'fore long."

"I don't know . . ."

"You don't have to know," Doc interrupted. He stabbed the cigarette into a green glass ashtray and stood up, adjusting his vest and holster. "You just come with me, and do what I tell ya. Don't worry 'bout nothin'. Wyatt'll take care of us if we run into trouble."

Suddenly, McCain wondered if he'd made a mistake lying to Doc about not finding anything useful at Weng Wo's. Perhaps if Doc had solid evidence to barter with, the negotiations with Beaudine might go a lot more smoothly—and a lot less violently.

But not necessarily, he realized. He wished he were better at this sort of thing. Indians he knew how to deal with; politicians and criminals were another matter entirely.

He decided to keep his secret, but carry the evidence with him just in case.

"It's gettin' late," Doc said. "Let's get downstairs and give that politician some indigestion."

Doc opened the door and stepped into the hallway, checking his Colt .45. It was fully loaded, and he tucked it back in the holster. While Doc was occupied with that, McCain reached under the pillow, grabbed the plate and ledger sheet, and shoved them in his pocket. Then he joined Doc, closing the door behind him.

"By the way, Doc, where's the bag?" McCain asked.

"In my room, hidden away."

"You think that's a good idea?"

"Probably not, but I got nowhere else to put it. Anyhow, I bought some clothes and other stuff before, and I shoved all that in the bag on top of the money just in case anyone takes a look."

"Still sounds risky."

"This whole crazy mess is risky now. Anyhow, we won't be gone long."

"Why don't you bring it down with us?" McCain asked. "Maybe Beaudine will cooperate. You might persuade him if you wave the money under his nose."

Doc weighed the suggestion for a moment. "That's not a bad idea, McCain. And then I don't have to sweat about it if somethin' does go wrong downstairs."

No, McCain thought to himself, you won't have to worry about it. Because you'll have it with you, or you'll be in prison where the police will take care of it, or you'll be dead, in which case you really won't have to worry about it.

After a brief stop at Doc's room to pick up the bag, the two men headed downstairs to the hotel's restaurant.

Chapter Fifty-nine

Doc and McCain were seated a few tables away from the restaurant entrance. They both ordered meals, and while they waited for them to be brought to the table, they checked out the clientele of the Casa Verde Restaurant.

Most of the patrons seemed pretty well off. The women were dressed in expensive gowns, their hairstyles were fancy, and their faces were made up to perfection. The men were dressed in suits that all looked new and properly tailored, and they all reminded McCain of every banker he ever knew.

While they waited, they couldn't help overhearing the conversation at the next table. A middle-aged woman was speaking to her beau around mouthfuls of food.

"The room is rather packed tonight, wouldn't you say, Oliver?" she asked.

"It certainly is," her mate agreed.

"I do believe that's Miss Fanny Osbourne across the room," she continued. "Or should I say *Mrs*. Fanny Osbourne. The last I heard she was still married. That hasn't prevented her from parading around with her new paramour, though, has it?"

Oliver stretched his neck to see who his wife was referring to.

"Oliver! For goodness sake! Don't look at them. They might see you looking!"

Oliver stopped staring, but Doc and McCain couldn't resist. They both took a long look at Stevenson and his fiancee.

"Guess he's stayin' here, too," Doc said. "She ain't so bad-lookin', is she? Got a right fine body and a pretty face."

McCain nodded. "Very attractive."

"Wonder if she's a walkin' bundle of trouble like him."

McCain shrugged his shoulders. He was more interested in finding Beaudine—if he was even in the restaurant.

"Gotta give him credit, though. Never thought a dude like him would have the craw to run around with a rich, married society lady."

Doc's meditations were interrupted by the ongoing dialogue at the next table.

"Did you see who else is here?" the woman asked.

"Who's that, my dear?" asked Oliver, wiping the corner of his mouth with a napkin.

"Mr. Jerome Beaudine."

Doc and McCain sat straight up in their chairs at the mention of the name.

"Who?" asked Oliver.

"Mr. Jerome Beaudine. You remember him, don't you? The mayor was supposed to arrange a formal introduction for us, but he never did. Mr. Beaudine, I understand, is one of President's Hayes's most valued advisors."

Oliver's brow wrinkled as he tried to recall the man. "I'm afraid I don't remember, dear. Which fellow is he?"

"The one in the tan suit near the rear of the restaurant. Very distinguished. But don't turn around, Oliver. He might see you staring."

Again Oliver followed the directions given to him, and again Doc and McCain looked where Oliver was forbidden to. They spotted the portly man in the tan suit. He was forking pieces of steak into his mouth as his two companions sat with him, nervously eyeing the other diners.

"So that's what he looks like," Doc mused.

"About what I figured," McCain said.

"Shoulda known he'd be a big, fat lardass. Think I'll go pay my respects." Doc glanced at the bag on the seat next to McCain. "You keep an eye on that."

"You want me to stay here?"

"Yeah."

"I might be more useful coming with you."

"Maybe. But if we both go waltzin' over, we may panic him or his two boyfriends."

"Okay."

"You keep me covered. Keep your eyes and ears open."

"All right."

Doc walked casually across the restaurant to the table about fifty feet away. As he approached, Mr. Paine pulled his chair up close to the table. McKelton saw him coming too, but sat back in his chair, his arms folded across his chest. But when it seemed that Doc was headed for their particular table — and his sight never left Beaudine's face for a second — McKelton stood up and held out a hand that indicated Doc should halt.

"That's close enough," McKelton said. "Are you looking for someone?"

"Yes, sir," Doc answered. "I'm here to speak with Mr. Beaudine."

The politician quickly swallowed the unchewed piece of beef in his mouth and stared up at this stranger. At first he was very nervous, but when he saw that Doc was alone, he relaxed a bit. His two men were ready to protect him if need be.

"Your name, friend?" Paine asked. He was leaning forward into the table, his arms underneath the tablecloth.

"This, I believe, is Doc Holliday," Beaudine said, smiling. "Is it not?"

"It is," Doc said. "And if your man there doesn't want both his arms broken, you'll tell him to put his hands on the table where I can see them."

Paine stared up at Doc angrily, but Beaudine touched him on the shoulder and said, "It's all right. Do as he says. Mr. Holliday's just here to talk." He looked up at Doc. "That is right, isn't it?"

"That's right.

"Well, do sit down. Everyone. Sit down. We'll all keep our hands on the table."

Doc pulled out a vacant seat and sat down, and McKelton

sat facing him. Eight hands were on the table, some with fingers interlocked, some palms down.

"Mr. Holliday, I assume you have no objections to speaking in a civilized, soft tone of voice," Beaudine said. "We don't want to attract any more attention to ourselves, do we?"

"No, sir," Doc agreed.

"You've brought the money?"

"I have it."

"Then I'll take it."

"Before I hand it over I've got two words to say."

"What are they?"

"Warren Earp." Doc squinted, then smiled at the politician. Beaudine smiled back. "So you've heard about that unfortunate turn of events! It's a shame. I didn't know the Earps were involved in that sort of thing."

"Neither did I."

Beaudine and Doc silently stared across the table at each other. Paine's fingers began to tap the table in front of him. McKelton's thumbs pressed against each other.

McCain, meanwhile, was straining his neck trying to see what was going on across the room. It wasn't easy. He couldn't hear a word that was spoken; the chatter and clatter in the dining room made hearing from that distance impossible. Once in a while he could read Beaudine's lips because the man was facing him, and McCain had an unblocked view of his face. Doc, on the other hand, was facing the politician; all McCain could see of him was the back of his head.

"You set him up," Doc stated accusingly.

Beaudine didn't answer.

"Why? Why'd you do that? Did you think you'd get away with that? Did you think Wyatt would let his brother be put away like that?"

Again, Beaudine sat silently. McKelton asked, "How about I swat this insect, Mr. Beaudine? He's ruining your dinner."

Doc's hands tightened into fists on top of the table. Beaudine noticed this, and tried to break the tension.

"Let's be reasonable, gentlemen," he said. "I'm sure we can work this out."

"You want to work this out?" Doc asked. "Then get Warren out of jail."

"I'm afraid not even I can do that."

"I'm afraid you'll have to do that," Doc mocked. "Or we got nothin' else to talk about. It looks an awful lot like you framed him, and that was a big mistake. 'Cause now you got to free him."

"I told you I can't. And what makes you think I framed him?"

"Cut the bullshit, Beaudine."

Paine's attention was diverted to another man approaching the table. "This one of your friends, Holliday?" he asked, nodding to someone over Doc's shoulder.

Holliday knew better than to turn around. It would only take a second for either Paine or McKelton to reach for his gun.

"Can I join the party?" McCain asked. In his hand was the satchel.

"You stay right there," ordered Paine.

"Who is this?" Beaudine asked Doc. "Another illustrious patriot from Dodge?"

"The name's Josiah McCain," Doc answered. "He's a friend."

Beaudine looked up over Doc's head at the new arrival. "I'm afraid you're too late, Mr. McCain. I'm afraid the party's just ending."

"Oh, how disappointing!" McCain replied sarcastically. "How come?"

"Because I don't like being accused of framing somebody I hardly know."

"Then you didn't frame him?" McCain asked.

Beaudine's face turned red with anger. "That's enough. This meeting's over."

McCain ignored the politician's words and continued. "Because I've got a piece of paper in my pocket from a Mr. Weng

Wo addressed to you, Mr. Beaudine."

"Like hell you do."

"Can I reach into my pocket and get it, or will your boys get jumpy and try to blow me to kingdom come?"

"Let's see it."

Doc was interested too, and he turned his head as McCain pulled out the paper and shook it open.

"It's a fake," Beaudine said. "A forgery. That doesn't prove anything."

"It's quite real," McCain responded. "I also have a former employee of yours who'll testify in court, I believe."

"A Chinese witness? Their testimony doesn't mean a damn thing."

Doc stood up, disgusted and angry. "Then you really did frame Warren. I wasn't really sure until just now."

Beaudine knew denying the truth would do no good from this point on, so he tried the truth. "I had to. It was unavoidable."

Doc's teeth ground together, and in a rage he tipped the table over toward Beaudine. But Paine was a lot quicker than he expected; he already had his pistol out, and as the table rose, he fired his weapon from under it. The bullet went clear through Doc's left thigh, and he fell to the floor, accompanied by the sounds of the diners screaming in fear and surprise.

The fall also saved his life. McKelton too had his revolver drawn, and he fired a shot that would have hit Doc square in the face had he still been standing. The bullet whistled past McCain and blew a hole in the wall over Oliver and his wife's heads.

McCain dropped to his knees and drew his Peacemaker just as Paine was aiming his at Doc. But McCain squeezed his shot off first. Then Paine's chest collapsed from the close range of the bullet, blood pouring out onto his jacket.

Beaudine dropped to the ground, using the overturned table as a shield from McCain and Doc. McKelton stared at his fallen partner, not believing the amount of blood gushing from the dead man's chest. The seconds he wasted on his friend were fatal. From his prone position on the floor, Doc drew his .45 and shot the bodyguard in the patch of flesh between his chin and throat. The bullet traveled upward, shattering his jaw, piercing his brain, and exiting through the top of his head. The lifeless corpse fell over onto Beaudine, causing the presidential aide to scream and try to push the body off his legs.

Doc grabbed the table and rolled it to one side. It made a quarter-circle away from Beaudine to Doc's right, leaving the politician in the open. Doc pointed his gun at Beaudine's face and savored the moment: the look of absolute terror in the man's eyes was a sight he wanted to record for his own personal history.

The patrons of the restaurant were in a panic. Many of them fled through the open entrance, others held each other in fear, while some hid under or behind tables. The sound of feminine screams was constant, accompanied now and then by cries of "my God" or similar expressions, and more than once McCain heard the sound of someone retching.

Doc's moment of enjoyment ended, and he said, "Here's your payoff from the Earps." His finger tightened around the trigger; Beaudine covered his face with both hands.

Suddenly, McCain said, "Don't."

Doc didn't budge. "No way, McCain," he said without taking his eyes off Beaudine or his finger off the trigger. "He's dead."

"Don't do it, Doc," McCain repeated, more insistently this time. "I can't let you do it."

"Then shoot me in the back!" Doc yelled, propping himself up to a reclining position with his free hand. He steadied his gun hand and concentrated. "I'm sick of you tellin' me who I can shoot."

"The government wants to prosecute him," McCain announced. "Let them have him."

A look of surprise registered on both Doc's and Beaudine's face. But it was Doc who responded angrily. "The govern-

ment? What the hell do you know about the government?"
Then he realized both he and Wyatt Earp had been deceived by
the "drifter" they had hired in Dodge.

Doc let his body fall flat to the ground and rolled over,
raising his gun quickly until the barrel pointed straight at
McCain's chest. "You son of a . . ."

But Doc's epithet was drowned out by the sound of two
Colts firing simultaneously. McCain's bullet entered Holliday's
wounded thigh, but an inch or two below the first bloody hole.
Doc's shot was badly-aimed, but the bullet hit McCain's right
hand. The Peacemaker flew out of his hand and skidded under
a table a few feet away.

McCain's hand felt numb and blood poured out of the small
chunk of flesh missing from his index finger. Doc's gun now
lay on the floor, nearly under his head. The gunfighter covered
his twice-shot thigh with his hands, moaning in pain.

McCain turned, searching for his Peacemaker. He didn't
know where it was.

When he turned back, Beaudine was no longer on the floor.
The man was on his feet, running toward the door. He pushed
several spectators aside, and bounded out of the restaurant.

McCain had no time to lose looking for his weapon. He
took Doc's .45 and headed out after Beaudine.

Through teary eyes, Doc watched him go. Then he noticed
the satchel lying there a few feet away, all by itself, unprotected.
He slid his body along the floor until he could grab it and pull
it close to him. He wrapped his arms around the bag and let the
dizziness, the faintness, overwhelm him. He passed out, his
arms tightly circling the bag like the limbs of a child wrapped
around a familiar, comforting toy.

Chapter Sixty

McCain passed several shocked people in the lobby of the hotel as he stepped out into the street. He was surprised at how dark the sky had become; more time than he had thought had passed since he and Doc first entered the restaurant. He looked up and down the street, but Beaudine was nowhere in sight. However, the distraught faces on the citizens to the left of the hotel entrance told him the politician had fled in that direction.

McCain hurried down the street, shoving Doc's .45 into his holster as he ran. The streets were crowded with citizens out for an evening stroll on this warm but comfortable night. Moving quickly, McCain tried to dash around and between them, but they were slowing him down.

Finally, he crashed into a man walking with the aid of a polished wooden cane. The man toppled over, and McCain too lost his balance. He regained his footing and helped the man to his feet as stunned spectators watched.

"A man with bloody clothes," McCain said hurriedly, "did you see him?"

The man with the cane nodded. "He ran down that street there," he said, pointing with the cane.

"Thanks." McCain dashed in the direction of the less-populated street the man had pointed to.

When he turned the corner, McCain could see several shadowy figures down the street. One was moving quickly in the direction of the Chinese District. And when he heard a woman scream from the far end of the block, McCain was certain that the figure was Beaudine.

He moved nimbly for such a big man, McCain thought as his boots clomped out an echoing beat against the cobblestone streets. But that fact didn't surprise him. Beaudine was running for his life.

Turning the next corner, McCain saw Beaudine knock over a woman carrying a large object wrapped in brown paper. The package crashed to the ground. Beaudine turned down another street, still heading for Chinatown. When McCain passed the young woman, she was on her knees, looking at her destroyed prize, crying.

McCain followed him onto the next street. He was gaining on the politician, but the streets were too crowded with people, now mostly Oriental. Taking a shot at the man was out of the question; he didn't want to hit some innocent bystander.

Then Beaudine's form blended into a throng of people gathered in front of an outdoor vegetable market. Cases of fruit and other goods were piled up on the street in front of a store, and the small mob marched about, inspecting celery and squeezing melons. McCain reached the crowd in a matter of seconds, but Beaudine was nowhere in sight. Confused and dismayed, McCain studied the faces around him. All were Chinese. He looked back down the street the way he had come. All Chinese. He stepped into the interior of the market and gazed at each face. All Chinese.

He took a deep breath and resigned himself to the fact that he had lost Beaudine.

Then he felt a tug at one of his trouser legs. He looked down, and a smile forced its way onto his face when he recognized his young accomplice from that afternoon. The boy wriggled his finger, beckoning McCain to bend down.

He squatted down until his head was level with the boy's.

"You chasing fat man with gun?" the boy asked.

McCain nodded. "Did you see which way he went?"

The boy pointed to the rear of the market. McCain stood up and looked inside, but he didn't see Beaudine. What he did see was an open back door.

"Through the back door?" he asked.

The boy nodded and smiled. McCain ruffled the boy's hair in appreciation and headed for the door.

It led to a long alley which led to another street. McCain stepped over piles of rotten fruit and when the path was clear of obstacles, ran toward the street at top speed.

He looked up the street. Not a soul on it. Then he looked in the opposite direction. Nobody there either, and as dark as pitch. But he heard something from that dark side of the street: the sound of a cat squealing. Then, as his eyes adjusted to the darkness, he saw the cat quickly slink away. It seemed it magically sprang from the tall brick wall that bordered that side of the street. But more likely, McCain knew, there was a window or a vent somewhere in the wall.

He drew his gun and slowly proceeded toward the darkness. He stepped softly, not wanting to create any reverberating sounds on the cobblestones. He put a touch of pressure against the trigger with his index finger. He felt nothing, no pain, no sensation at all. He couldn't even really say if the finger was squeezing the trigger or merely touching it. The nerves had gone dead.

Still moving ahead cautiously, McCain took the gun in his left hand. For now, it was the safer thing to do. He was afraid that if he left the gun in his partially-numbed right hand, he might accidentally fire it. And the last thing he wanted to do now was give away his presence.

The gun felt awkward in his left hand. He was as far from ambidextrous as a person could get, and he wondered how well he'd be able to aim if the need arose. But at least he'd be able to feel himself pull the trigger.

McCain noticed from where the cat had sprung. It was no vent or window; it was an alley. It was no more than six feet wide, and it was covered with a darkness even blacker than that on the street.

He pressed himself against the wall where the alley began, peered around the corner of the building carefully, and tried to distinguish any shapes. But it was just too dark.

"Beaudine!" he called into the alley and carefully listened to the sound of his own voice. It didn't seem to travel far, and he reasoned that the alley was a cul-de-sac.

"You may as well come out," McCain continued, not even sure if Beaudine was in the dead end.

There was no answer. McCain again peered around the corner, his face pressed against the cool brick, the rest of his body protected by the end of the wall.

Then there was the sound of a shot, a flash of light, and a man's voice from a few feet within the alley. Something shattered an inch from McCain's face, and his eyes began to burn and sting. He clutched at his eyes and felt tiny pieces of brick and dust in his eyelashes and on his eyelids. He brushed them away and tried to open his eyes, but they stung painfully when he did. He cursed himself. This was no time to be without sight! He must get them open.

Tears built up, and McCain forced the eyelids open. The tears ran down his cheeks, fortunately carrying with them much of the painful debris. He wiped at his eyes, opened them, and there before him stood Beaudine, a .45 in his hand.

"Drop your gun, McCain, and step into the cul-de-sac."

McCain dropped the pistol and backed into the alley, still wiping at his eyes.

"You can stop right there," Beaudine said. He remained at the entrance of the alley for a moment, then stepped into it.

"I didn't know politicians carried guns," McCain said. His eyes still burned, but at least now he could see. "I thought you let others do that for you."

"That's generally true," Beaudine answered. "But being a politician is only one of my careers, as you already know. I carry this gun more for my other lines of work."

"You're gonna kill me?"

"Of course. I missed the first time. I won't now."

McCain could make out Beaudine's form in the darkness. He stood about ten feet away. It would be almost impossible for even a man inexperienced with a gun to miss a six-foot target at that range. McCain looked around him. There was nothing to hold on to, nothing to throw, nowhere to run or hide.

"Don't you have enough blood on your hands?" McCain asked. "You can't get away with all this, you know. Even if the President doesn't learn about it, even if you try to cover it all up, you'll still have the Earps to deal with. They'll hunt you down and nail your carcass to a tree."

Beaudine laughed. "I'll worry about that later. As for having more blood on my hands, I don't think I'll worry about that either. Look at me. I'm covered in Mr. McKelton's blood. It's ruined my suit, it's in my hair, it's in my lap. I don't think a little more on my hands is going to bother me."

Then McCain heard something in the distance. Then he heard it again. It sounded like someone's shoes scuffing against the cobblestones. And it didn't seem like Beaudine heard it.

"Now, goodbye McCain."

The noise ceased. McCain wondered if he'd been imagining it. His stomach muscles tightened. He could only rush the man or try to duck the shot. Beaudine didn't give him time to think about it. "I bid you safe journey on your way to hell."

Beaudine extended his arm, aimed at McCain's chest, and . . . a shot was fired from behind the politician. McCain saw the quick flash of light, saw the figure of a man pressed against the wall across the street. But he couldn't see who it was; it happened too quickly.

The politician gasped and staggered forward. The .45 dropped to the street, but Beaudine inched forward, his arms extended. As he got within a couple of feet of him, McCain saw the blood pouring out of his mouth, covering his lower lip and chin. The dull, dead eyes stared at McCain blankly. Then the overburdened legs gave way, and Beaudine lay dead, his eyes and mouth wide open.

McCain stepped over the body and quickly retrieved his gun. He looked across the street and could barely make out the shadowy figure still against the wall.

"You," McCain said. "Who are you?"

The figure moved, then stepped closer.

McCain approached the figure until he was near enough to make out his facial features.

"Louis!" McCain said in disbelief.

Stevenson gazed at the ground and handed McCain the gun he had fired. McCain took it; it was his Peacemaker, the one he had lost at the restaurant.

"How did you get here, Louis?"

"I followed you," the Scotsman answered with difficulty, forcing the words out over the lump in his throat. "I was in the restaurant. I saw what happened. I saw that Mr. Holliday was . . . hurt, and I saw you run out after this . . . this . . . despot. I thought I owed it to you to help you."

McCain saw that his friend was upset. He grabbed his arm and said, "Help me? Louis, you saved my life."

Stevenson forced a deep breath from his lungs. "But I had to kill a man to do it," he said sadly.

McCain remembered the first time he had to kill a man. It was in self-defense, but that fact didn't make it any easier to accept. The guilt and the pain had stayed with him for a long time.

"Sometimes there's no other way," he said. "It ain't easy to accept, but it's the way it is. It's the way this miserable world works."

Louis shook his head. "Makes you long for a deserted place somewhere. An island somewhere where civilization doesn't exist."

"I suppose," McCain responded, "but I wonder even about that. Most men, I think, would wind up killing every animal on the island—and then kill themselves."

Again the Scotsman shook his head. "That's a very depressing, cynical view of things, Mr. McCain."

"Is it? Maybe it is. I'll have the rest of my life to think about it now, thanks to you. Maybe I'll change my mind. Right now, we've got to get you out of here."

"Aren't you going to get the authorities?"

"Later. Now I want to get you safely back to the hotel. You're staying at the Casa Verde?"

"Yes."

"Well, let's get going. I don't want you implicated in all this. I'll tell the police I shot him if I have to."

"Why would you do that? I shot him."

"You shot a leading political figure of the United States, corrupt or not. You're not a citizen of this country; I am. Even if they find you had cause to shoot him, they might deport your backside back to Scotland. You want to risk that?"

"No, I guess not."

"Then let's go. We'll walk back to the hotel. Then you can go on ahead and enter separately. And stay in your room until I tell you it's safe to come out. Understand."

Louis nodded, and the two men took the least populated route back to the hotel.

Chapter Sixty-one

McCain had the key in the lock of his hotel room door when a voice called from inside, "It's open, Mr. McCain. Come in."

Josiah pulled the Peacemaker from his holster and held it ready. Then he pushed the door open. There sat a man he didn't recognize. His legs were crossed, his mouth held a pipe containing some pleasantly aromatic tobacco, and his hands were clasped in his lap in an obvious attempt to show McCain that he wasn't holding a gun.

"What do you want?" McCain asked.

"I just want to talk to you. Do come in. I'm quite alone."

McCain kept his gun pointed at the well-groomed, dark-haired man, but stepped into the room and closed the door behind him. He hurriedly looked around the room, and, seeing no one else, lowered the gun.

"Who are you?" McCain asked. "You from the police?"

"Not exactly, no," answered the man. "In fact, I'm from the Secret Service. You've heard of us?"

"Yes."

"Please, sit down," the man said amiably, gesturing at the other chair in the room. "My name is Michael Evans. I've been trying to find you for the last couple of hours, ever since I heard about the little incident downstairs in the dining room. Had a bit of trouble, I hear."

"A bit, yes," McCain replied sarcastically. "I think I've lost the use of this hand for a while." He held up his bloody right hand for a moment. "But I guess I shouldn't complain. Three men lost their lives tonight."

"Two men," Evans corrected. "Mr. Holliday, much to the glee of dime novelists everywhere, is still alive."

"No, three men. I wasn't thinking of Doc."

"I know about Mr. Paine and Mr. McKelton. And I heard you took off after Mr. Beaudine. Are you telling me he's dead?"

McCain took off his hat and let it sail onto the bed. "That's exactly what I'm telling you."

"Damn!"

"I had to."

Evans shrugged his shoulders. "Oh, well. We wanted him alive because I'm sure he could have helped us uncover plenty of other nests of corruption."

"Is that what the Service does? Uncover corruption?"

"No, not exactly. Mostly we're after counterfeiters, and we were really trying to get Beaudine on that charge."

McCain was about to reach into his pocket and pull out the counterfeiting plate, but he thought better of it. "How do I know you're who you say you are?"

Evans stood up and removed his wallet from his pocket. "Here's my badge," he said, "and here's my identification card."

McCain inspected them for a second. He'd never seen a Secret Service badge before, but it looked authentic. So did the card. "Okay. Now I have something to show you."

He handed Evans the plate.

"Well, I'll be damned!" Evans exclaimed, inspecting the plate much more carefully than McCain had inspected his identification. "Where did you get this?"

"From a whorehouse owned by Beaudine."

"How do you know that? Can you prove it?"

"Yes," McCain assured him. "And so can you."

"What do you mean?"

"I mean there's another one where I found this. At a place called Weng Wo's. You familiar with it?"

"Quite. Weng Wo is a drug smuggler."

"For Beaudine he is."

"Yes. I know. But we've been unable to prove that."

McCain handed the agent the ledger sheet. "Here's the proof. It's Chinese, but it spells out the whole story."

Evans relit his pipe and smiled. "McCain, you've done us a great favor, even if we'll never get to prosecute Beaudine. But I guess he's already paid for his crimes."

McCain stretched his legs and sat deeper in the chair. "Does that conclude your business? Or this case, I mean."

"No," laughed Evans. "I wish it were that easy. There's still Weng Wo to deal with. And I've had my eye on a fellow named Lodge out here. He's the assistant police chief. We're reasonably sure he's been taking bribes from Beaudine."

"How do you know?"

Evans laughed even harder. "Beaudine was no fool. He must have paid Lodge off with counterfeit bills, because about six months ago Lodge was spreading them all over town without knowing it."

Evans reached into his inside jacket pocket and brought out a shining silver flask. "Care for a drink, McCain. It's the least I can offer you. And you look like you could use a drink."

"No thanks."

The agent sipped at the liquor, then replaced the cap. "Well, what can I do for you? At least let me pay for your train fare back to Dodge. Or wherever you're headed."

"How'd you know I came from Dodge?" Or wherever you're headed."

"How'd you know I came from Dodge?"

"You were with Holliday, weren't you? Anyhow, Bat Masterson told me he was going to try to enlist your aid."

"You know Bat?"

"I asked him to keep an eye on the Earps."

"Oh," McCain nodded, "I remember. Bat told me he'd spoken to a Secret Service agent."

"That was me. And the Service is in his debt. And yours."

McCain extended his hand. "I think I'll take that drink now."

Evans stood up and handed the flask to McCain. "Keep it. A small token of my appreciation."

"Thanks."

"Well, Mr. McCain, I guess I'll be on my way." Evans headed for the door, then turned around. "By the way, you have nothing to worry about from the police. I'll take care of it for you. Part of my job is making explanations and excuses to local law enforcement agencies. Nobody from the police should bother you."

"I appreciate that."

"No problem at all. One other thing you should know: we've got nothing to get Holliday on, so he'll be walking free soon. So will Warren Earp and the two men he was arrested with."

"Thanks for the warning."

"Anytime. Bye, McCain, and thanks again."

"Goodbye."

The two men shook hands, and Evans left. McCain took another sip of the whiskey. It soothed him, but it seemed to stimulate his mind. It made him think about Doc. It also made him think about Warren. He didn't want to miss meeting Warren.

He was glad that Beaudine was out of the picture now. His full attention could be turned on Warren Earp. Warren Earp! The name was repeated over and over in his mind. And each time he thought of the name, he also thought of his sister's abused body and the piece of flesh bitten off an ear.

Chapter Sixty-two

Dodge, City. Midnight, the same night

Bat was posting the latest batch of wanted posters in his office when the door was kicked open, and six sweaty ranchers seething with anger spread out across the room.

"Sheriff, I think we've waited long enough," Mike Keyes said in his husky voice. "Where's Earp?"

Bat didn't even turn around to look at the men. He went on hammering in the posters with the butt of his Colt. "I tried to talk some sense into him," Bat said, stretching the truth a bit. "But he's a stubborn man."

"Then you didn't arrest him like you promised?"

"I didn't promise nothin'. I said I'd try. I also said I might be needin' your help to arrest him."

Another man said, "We're here. Let's go get him."

Bat finished posting the last badly-drawn ugly face and sat on his desk. He picked up a stone cup decorated with Indian symbols and gulped the last of the tepid coffee.

"You got more than six men?" he asked.

Suddenly, a barrage of gunshots went off in the distance.

"That answer your question?" the young man called Jed said.

"Where are they?"

Keyes looked at him proudly. "Masterson, they're all over town. Fifty-one of 'em."

Bat slammed his cup down, shattering it into several

pieces. "Goddamn it, Keyes, I told you I didn't want no war breakin' out."

"You get us the Earps, the war ends."

"Don't give me that bullshit!" Bat yelled angrily. "You get your men together, and we'll spread out real organized-like. I don't want no innocent people gettin' hurt."

"Since when do you or the Earps care about hurtin' innocent folks?" Jed asked. He had a cocky, smug smile on his face.

The question dug at Bat. There was the association with the Earps again. There was the reminder of his less-than-shining past.

He stood up, stepping toward the boy, poking a finger at him. "Listen, you snot-nosed son of a bitch, you say one more word—just one more—and you'll be spittin' out your teeth for the next week!"

The man who had spoken earlier spoke again. "That's mighty big talk comin' from a man who's outnumbered six to one."

Before any of the six realized what had happened, Bat drew his Colt and was waving it at them.

"Ain't no need for that, Sheriff," Keyes said, trying to calm the situation.

"No? Then I talk to you, and the rest of your men keep their mouths closed tighter than a muskrat's asshole."

The gunfire outside continued, and Bat saw several ladies run by his office window.

"Your men are shootin' hell out of this town, and I ain't gonna allow that."

"Then help us get Earp."

"I will. But first you get your men under control. You probably scared the Earps outta town already."

"We'd rather have their heads," Keyes said.

"You ain't gettin' nobody's head. If I find you killed anybody 'cept in self-defense, there's gonna be hell to pay. You mark my words. Now here's what we'll do. You take a group of men to the Long Ride. Send another group to cover my brother's saloon, up the street there. Some of them might hang around outside the hotel. That's where Wyatt's been sleepin' these days. I'll check out Katie Fisher's place. There's a good chance he'll be there, and an even better chance his brother James'll be there."

"I'll go with you to Katie's," one of the men said.

"No you won't. I want him to come with me." Bat pointed at Jed. "I want to keep an eye on this boy. God knows who he might wind up shootin'."

"One problem," Keyes said. "We all seen Wyatt at one time or another, but what's his brother look like? How'll we know him?"

"He's bigger than Wyatt—and older. And he walks with a limp."

"Okay."

"What about that crazy bartender across the street?"

"Luke Adams is in the back locked up. I arrested him yesterday for pinnin' a customer's hand to the bar with his knife. You don't have to worry 'bout him. Now get goin' before some little old lady gets killed. We'll meet back here in an hour. Sooner if you catch anybody." He pointed at Jed. "You come with me."

Jed nodded nervously. "Sure."

Then the men left his office and headed for the saloon across the street. Bat waved for the boy to follow and headed for the other end of town. He knew without a doubt that Wyatt would be at Katie's. Since the last time the ranchers rode in, Wyatt had made the brothel his headquarters, and he had hardly shown his face outside it. Either Wyatt was afraid of being assassinated, or something else was in the works. Bat hesitated to think of what it could be. He had this picture in his mind of countless Earp brothers—Earps from all corners of the country—organized as an army, armed to the teeth, just awaiting the return of the ranchers.

Bat dismissed the foolish notion and stepped up his pace. "Move it," he said to the boy. "You want to get Earp, don't you?"

Jed followed behind, staring at Masterson's back. How he'd love to put a bullet there, he thought. But now wasn't the time; there were too many people on the streets.

The sound of gunfire began to subside. Evidently, Bat thought, Keyes was getting his men under control. That was good. What wasn't so good was the fact that there'd be no more delaying a confrontation with Wyatt.

He turned down a side street, waving behind him for Jed to follow. "Move it, boy. We still got a lot of ground to cover."

Jed followed behind, but he noticed that he and Masterson were alone on this street. The shops that bordered the street were closed, the blinds in their windows drawn.

This would be a perfect opportunity to get Masterson. He'd think of a story later to explain his death. Maybe he'd blame it on the Earps.

Walking closely behind Bat, Jed slipped the battered old .45 out of the holster and held it pointed down by the side of his leg.

Bat turned to look at the boy, saw he was hiding something behind him, and stopped. Jed stopped short also. The nervous look on his face told Bat he was up to something.

"What's with you, boy?"

Jed screamed, "Stop callin' me 'boy'," and raised the gun.

Without a moment's hesitation, Bat grabbed the barrel of the gun and forced it up until it was pointing at the sky. Then he yanked it out of Jed's hand and threw it in the dirt a few feet behind him.

"What are you gonna do?" Jed asked excitably.

"I'm gonna say goodnight, son." Bat sent a right fist into the boy's face. The blow knocked him back, down, and out cold. "Sleep tight."

Then Bat continued on his way to Katie Fisher's.

Chapter Sixty-three

"For Christ's sake, Katie," yelled Masterson, "I know you're in there. Open the door!"

It was the third time he had knocked, but the first time he got any response. "We're closed, Bat," said Katie, loud enough to be heard on the other side of the locked door.

"You ain't never closed! Now open this door, or I'll bust it down!"

Bat heard the bolt slide back. The door swung open slightly, and he stepped inside. On the other side of the door stood James Earp. He closed and locked the door behind Bat, then turned to him and said, "This is all your fault, Masterson."

Bat ignored him and asked, "Where's Wyatt?"

"He ain't got no time to talk to you," James answered. He turned his back and started walking away, mumbling under his breath. "Goddamn ranchers going crazy!"

Katie stepped up to Bat and slipped her arm under his and pulled him to the other side of the room. "They're leavin'," she said. "They're leavin' right now, for good, I think. You ain't gonna try to stop them, are you?"

Bat stared at her for a moment. She looked very beautiful this evening. Her black hair, peppered with gray streaks along the sides, was swept up over her head appealingly. "They're really leavin'? You ain't tryin' to put one over on me now, Katie, are you?"

"Look at me, Bat," she said. "You ever see me look this sad?"

Her point was well made. Bat noticed the worn look on her face and the dark, etched lines around her eyes. She'd been doing some crying, plenty of it. Although there were no tears present then, the toll they'd taken on her face was evident.

"You goin' too, Katie?"

"Eventually, but not now. I'll wait to see if Doc returns to Dodge. If not . . . well, then I'll follow the boys to Tombstone."

Tombstone! The word stung at Bat's ears like someone had rammed forefingers in them. He knew, though, that it would be fruitless at this particular time to try to persuade the Earps to go elsewhere. There wasn't much time for a debate.

"Masterson," James called, "why don't you make yourself useful and keep watch at the front window? Unless you're here to arrest all of us, that is." He snickered to himself and carried a large wooden box into the back room.

Bat was about to answer him, but his attention was suddenly drawn to the sight of Wyatt Earp coming down the stairs, carrying an armful of Winchesters. Five steps from the bottom, Earp saw Bat, hesitated a moment, then continued stepping down, saying "We're leavin', Masterson. I assume that makes you real happy. I also assume you ain't gonna try to stop us."

"Not if you're really goin'. That was my offer, and it still stands."

"You'll help us?"

"I didn't say that! I just won't hinder you."

Wyatt squinted meanly at him and carried the rifles to the back room. Bat gently removed Katie's arm and followed Wyatt.

The back door of Katie's house was wide open, and

390

right outside the door stood a flat wagon. Wyatt and James loaded the rifles on the wagon's seat. The back of the wagon was filled with various possessions of the Earps too valuable to leave behind. Most of them were covered with blankets, but Bat recognized a large metal safe that sat on the wagon directly behind the driver's seat. He could only imagine the wealth in cash, deeds, and gold it contained.

Then Wyatt stopped for a second and lit a thin black cigar. He puffed on it, and turning back to his brother, said, "That's about it, James. Say your goodbyes, get your wife, and let's move. Harrison said they're workin' their way down to this end of town. I wanna be gone 'fore they get here."

James nodded and stepped past Bat as he entered the back door. He continued into the front room and disappeared from sight.

"I think you're making the right move," Bat said to Wyatt. "Although I think you took too damn long to make it. There's 'bout fifty of them ranchers spread out all over town."

"We'll get out," Wyatt said confidently. "Don't you worry your ugly head over that."

"I *was* gettin' worried. Thought you decided to stay and fight. It really ain't like you, runnin' like this."

"I ain't a fool, Bat. I can't take on that many blood-hungry, shit-kicking cowboys with just my brother James." He drew on the little cigar. "It'd be different if Virgil and Morgan were here. Together, there ain't no damn army that can stop us. But they ain't here. Even Doc ain't here."

Bat nodded. Katie had reminded him about Doc Holliday just moments before. "You ever hear from Doc? I know you said that's what you were waitin' for."

"No, I ain't heard what I've been waitin' to hear. He's in San Francisco, that's all I know."

"What's he doin' there? Bat asked, thinking for the

moment about Josiah McCain, who he knew was also in San Francisco from the wire he had received the night before.

"Gettin' fallin'-down drunk, most likely," Earp snapped.

Then a dozen or so shots were exchanged, shots that didn't sound that many streets away. Wyatt threw down his cigar, stepped past Bat, and was about to yell inside for his brother, when he saw James coming, pulling his wife behind him.

Then James helped his wife into the back of the wagon, and he climbed into the seat, taking the reins in his hand and waiting for Wyatt.

Wyatt stared at Bat for a moment. "You plannin' on comin' to Tombstone later on?"

"No, I don't think so," Bat answered. "I heard it's rough gettin' a lawman position out there."

Wyatt didn't appreciate the quip. "Not for me, it ain't, Masterson. Not for me."

More shots went off, closer than the last rounds.

Bat extended his hand to Earp to shake. "Well, I wish you luck, Wyatt. No hard feelings."

Wyatt sneered at the hand. "Damn you and your luck! And believe me, Masterson, you'll need plenty of it the next time we meet." Then he stepped up into the seat and sat next to his brother.

The wagon began to pull away, and Bat watched it roll forward. No way, he thought. There's no way he was going to let Earp have the last word.

When the wagon was several yards away, he called out to the Earps. "And please give my regards to Jerome Beaudine!"

Wyatt heard the words. His nostrils flared over his thick moustache. How the hell did he know about Beaudine? he wondered. The sneaky son of a bitch!

James Earp heard it too and pulled his revolver out. But Wyatt said, "Put that away. You wanta let them ranchers know where we are?"

James followed his brother's advice and lowered the gun.

Wyatt turned around as the buckboard progressed, but looking back at the rear of Katie's house, he saw that Masterson was gone.

"Move this thing!" he said angrily at James, who snapped the reins and whooped, urging on the horses.

Then Wyatt smiled and lit another cigar. He decided he was glad that Bat had gone straight-and-narrow, and he was even more glad the son of a bitch wasn't following them to Tombstone. Masterson was craftier, far more underhanded, and a hell of a lot more admirable than he'd ever given him credit for.

Chapter Sixty-four

San Francisco, the next morning

The sunlight poured in the window through the crack between the curtains. The shaft of bright light ran up and down McCain's face, and its brilliance and warmth caused him to open his eyes for the first time in several hours. It blinded him for a moment, and he lifted one hand to cover his eyes. Then he sat up slightly, enough that the light now made a bright stripe up the side of his jacket and ended at his shoulder.

It had been a deep but dreamless sleep, and it took McCain a few seconds even to realize that he *had* been asleep. He was still sitting in the chair he had occupied while talking to Evans. And the flask of whiskey lay cradled in his lap.

He stood up, wondering what time it was. There was no clock in the room, so he stepped over to the window and pulled the curtains apart. The sun was still low in the sky, and he knew it had to be an hour or two after dawn. Looking down into the normally busy San Francisco street that crossed in front of the Casa Verde Hotel, he was surprised to see it empty. Not a person was out yet. Not a wagon or a horse traversed it.

Until a group of four men turned the corner, heading for the hotel. McCain rubbed his eyes and studied them carefully. One of the men he recognized. He was moving slowly, a wooden crutch propped under his arm, one foot never really touching the street. It was Doc Holliday.

The other three men with him walked patiently by his side, talking to him. One man was huge. He said nothing and stared blankly ahead. In his hand was Doc's satchel. Another man was less-impressively built, but his long, very blond hair gave him an air of distinction. He seemed bored or withdrawn, hands tucked into his pockets, speaking only when spoken to.

The third man spoke constantly to Holliday as they walked at a snail's pace down the street. McCain was certain he'd never seen the man before, but there was something familiar about him nonetheless. Then it occurred to McCain: the man's face was like a younger version of a face he'd seen in Dodge. This had to be Warren Earp!

Without a moment's hesitation, McCain grabbed his hat, put it on his unkempt head of wavy brown hair, and headed downstairs. While descending the staircase, he loaded his Peacemaker, replacing the cartridges that had been fired the night before. He passed the main desk, noticing that there was a different clerk sitting there.

He waited just inside the entrance for a moment. There was a knot forming in his gut, a knot caused by nervousness, anticipation—and anger. Then he could hear them; they were close enough to the entrance that he could hear their voices although not a single word registered meaning with him. All his attention—all his energy—ran through his body, down his arm, into the Peacemaker in his hand.

He stepped out into the sun, turned to his left, raised the Peacemaker, and said, "Stop right there. Keep your hands where I can see them."

He caught all four men by surprise. They stopped in their tracks, and only Doc Holliday spoke. "McCain! We were just about to look you up!"

"Now you don't have to," McCain answered.

"Reckon not. What do you think you're doin'?"

"I got some unfinished business to attend to."

"I feel the same way. That's why we was lookin' you up."

"My business ain't with you, Doc," McCain snapped. "It's with you." He swung the barrel of his revolver until it was pointed squarely at Earp's face.

"Me?" Earp said. "Listen, mister, I just spent a day and a half in a stinkin' box of a prison cell, and I ain't in no mood for this. I don't even know you."

"The name's McCain."

"Lots of people named McCain. I even courted a girl named McCain once back in Missouri."

McCain's body tensed and he stared long and hard at Earp. "I know. That's why I'm here. She was my sister."

Earp took a step backward when McCain's words hit home. He looked at the man with the Peacemaker, and suddenly his stomach felt like there was a rock in it. "Hey," Earp said nervously, "you got this wrong."

The big man with the satchel moved his hand closer to his hip, but McCain saw the motion. "At this range, this gun'll put a hole clear through even a horse, friend," McCain said to him. Max moved the hand away.

Doc stood on one leg, resting on the crutch, utterly confused. "What the hell is this?"

"Don't concern you, Doc," McCain answered. "Earp, step forward!"

Reluctantly, Warren stepped up, his hands in the air. "I didn't kill your sister, mister."

McCain reached forward and grabbed Earp's shirt just under his neck. The top of his fist pressed against the bottom of Earp's chin, and a look of terror filled the youngest Earp. Then McCain raised the gun and pressed the barrel against the man's head, under his long hair, just over his ear. He pushed the hair back and saw a full, normal ear under the hair.

The lanky blond man shifted his weight to the other leg.

"Don't try nothin'," McCain ordered, looking at the blond for a second, "or the Earp family's number decreases by one."

The blond man stood still.

McCain moved the barrel of the gun to the other side of Warren's head. Again, he lifted the hair and . . . McCain thought he was seeing things. It couldn't be. Another perfectly normal ear.

"McCain, you crazy or somethin'?" Doc asked.

McCain didn't hear the words. He was lost in his thoughts. Had he come this far only to find he was wrong? Had he completely misinterpreted his sister's bloody message?

Then Warren, still shaken, still being held by McCain, said, "I know what you're lookin' for. But I didn't kill her. It wasn't me." He turned to the blond man, yelling frantically, "I told you, Cole. I told you she had a brother who . . ."

But Cole moved before Warren finished the sentence. Somehow he had worked a long knife out of his jacket sleeve and was advancing on McCain. Earp pushed away from McCain's grasp, finally getting free.

Cole swung the knife in an attempt to slash McCain across the face. But McCain pulled back just in time, the tip of the blade missing his eyes by an inch. McCain reached up quickly and grabbed the blond man's wrist, forcing the blade back. But Cole raised his knee and rammed it into McCain's groin, knocking the wind out of him and causing him to drop the Peacemaker. The numbed right hand just couldn't hold onto it.

Then Cole reached under his white jacket with his free hand and pulled out a second, identical knife. He slashed at McCain's chest with a backhand motion, and the blade ripped through the front of McCain's shirt.

McCain grabbed the other wrist and held it up in the air. He now had both of Cole's arms up over his head. He stared into Cole's face. The eyes seemed unnatural; there was desperation in them. They were cruel, unfeeling eyes, eyes that belonged to an animal that could maim, could kill, could rape without thought or regret.

Instead of holding the arms over Cole's head any longer, McCain yanked them forward. He tumbled back as he did so and raised his knees. Cole fell forward onto McCain's legs, and when McCain raised them, the man flew over his body, landing on the cobblestones face up.

Max Fisher watched silently. He dropped Doc's satchel and reached for his revolver. But a gray-haired man had stepped up behind him, poked the barrel of a gun in his back, and said, "Don't." Max raised his hands in the air without even turning around.

Cole still held the knives, trying to get to his feet. But McCain was already up and facing Cole. The blond man was on his knees, and McCain kicked out at the man, his boot catching Cole under the chin. The man leaned back, using the hands, still holding the knives, to brace him from behind.

Cole stayed in that position for a moment, resting on his hands behind him. The kick clearly had him reeling. His eyes looked out from his head, unable to focus on anything. Blood trickled from both corners of his lips. His long, weedy blond hair was thrown back off his face, hanging down behind his neck. It was the first moment that McCain could see all of the man's skeletal features: the small, thin nose, the pale, cracked lips, and—McCain's heart sank and his longing for vengeance rose when he saw it—the scarred, stubby half-ear on the left side of his face.

"Get up!" McCain screamed at him. "Get up, you son of a bitch!"

Cole staggered to his feet dizzily, but once on them, he seemed to regain his wits instantly. He lunged at McCain, one knife held over his head, the other down by his side.

McCain sidestepped the advance, grabbed Cole's lower

arm, and flung him into the outside wall of the hotel. Cole's back and head smashed against the bricks, and the man again fell to the ground. But this time both knives fell out of the blond's grasp. McCain stepped over him and picked the two blades up. Then he knelt with one knee on the weakened man's chest, staring angrily at him.

He wanted to stab him, to make the man pay, to make him suffer for his sister's rape and death. But for some reason, he couldn't. Something was holding him back. Some power prevented him from lowering the knife.

Cole looked up at him. Defiantly, he smiled at McCain with his bloody mouth. Then the smile opened into an audible laugh.

"Your sister," Cole laughed insanely, "was the greatest lay I ever had!"

Then he cackled wildly for a few seconds, seconds that freed McCain from his personal restrictions. Coldly effortlessly, he sank the knife deep into the man's heart.

The grin left Cole's face, and, a second later, his head turned to the left, his open eyes revealing no sign of life.

McCain stood up, feeling strangely unsatisfied. He looked around, surprised at the number of spectators in the street. Then he heard a familiar voice.

"Mr. McCain, do you have any business with *these* men?"

The speaker was Michael Evans. His gun was out, keeping Doc, Warren, and Max Fisher in line.

McCain still was in shock. He didn't — couldn't — answer right away. His whole body felt numb; it felt the way it had felt when he had come upon the body of his sister.

"You all right, Josiah?" Evans asked.

McCain fought off the numbness. "Yes." Then he looked into Warren's Earp's eyes.

The gaze startled Warren. "Max and I tried to stop him," he said. "We were just havin' a little fun. We didn't know he'd . . . do that."

McCain felt that he should make Warren and the big, silent man pay for not stopping their mad friend. But he had no fight left in him, and he had caught and killed his sister's actual murderer.

"I got no business with those two," he said. Then he turned to Doc, who he noticed was smiling at him.

"But we got business, don't we?" Doc asked.

"Do we?"

"Oh yes, McCain. We got us a big score to settle."

Suddenly, an elegantly-dressed man pushed through the crowd, interrupting the conversation. "Not here you don't," he said. "You men have spilled enough blood on these streets. You do your fighting somewhere far away from San Francisco."

Then the man turned to Doc. "Holliday, you just leave my office and already you're involved in something else."

"Now, now, Mr. Lodge," Doc responded, "we was just comin' back here to pack our bags and go. Then McCain here decided to kill Mr. Cole. You remember Mr. McCain? I hear tell he's the man who shot Mr. Beaudine . . ." Doc glanced at the satchel by Max's feet, then smiled up at Lodge again. ". . . who, I believe you were tryin' to convince me, owed you . . ."

"That's enough, Holliday!" shouted Lodge angrily. He turned to McCain. "You come with me. I want you to answer a few questions."

Before McCain could answer, Evans stepped forward. "I'll speak for Mr. McCain."

Lodge looked at the man disapprovingly. "Who the hell are you?"

"My name's Evans. I'm with the Treasury Department."

Lodge stared at him wide-eyed.

"And while I'm telling you all about Mr. McCain, I have a few questions I'd like you to answer."

Evans turned to McCain and said, "You're free to go, McCain. Let me know if anyone gives you trouble." Then he stepped into the crowd of people who had gathered, signalling to Lodge that he should follow him.

Lodge turned to a uniformed policeman and said, "Clean up that mess." He pointed to Cole's body and followed Evans into the crowd.

McCain turned to Doc. "You were saying . . ."

Doc laughed, shaking his head. "A Treasury Agent. Goddamn, McCain, I'd known all along there was something strange 'bout you. You sure had the wool pulled over my eyes." Doc moved forward awkwardly, obviously still not used to the crutch. "We still got us a score to settle, like I said. This just ain't the time or place for it. But it'll happen. Trust me, one of these days it'll happen."

As Doc hobbled near him, McCain said, "I notice you're still carrying around the bag."

"Yeah, I still got the money. Or rather, Max has it for me. That lawman Lodge wanted me to turn it over to him. Told me Beaudine owed it to him. I told him to go to hell." Then Doc shook his head. "It's hard to believe the amount of corruption in this town, ain't it?"

McCain nodded and couldn't help but smile. "Seems like no one's who they're supposed to be."

Doc laughed. "See ya, McCain. Se ya back in Dodge, I hope. You and your buddy Masterson. I shoulda known better. He's been in on this all along, ain't he?"

McCain didn't answer.

"I thought so. The sneaky bastard."

Then Doc entered the hotel, Warren Earp and Max Fisher following closely behind.

McCain watched as the policeman covered the body of Ben Cole with a sheet, much of the crowd pressing forward near the body for a better look.

He couldn't go right back to his room, so McCain walked for a couple of blocks, breathing deeply, thinking, reasoning, trying to tell himself it was all over. Cole was dead, the Secret Service seemed satisfied, Bat would be pleased — at least he thought he would — and with any luck, he'd never run into Holliday or any of the Earps again.

But he still felt uneasy. He had no idea where he would go or what he would do now. He'd never go back to Dodge, he didn't really want to return to Missouri, although what he had left of a family was still there.

He suddenly felt very alone and very lost, a man whose quest for revenge — the only quest he had had for the past year — was over.

He looked across the street and noticed two women pointing at him, talking to each other. They quickly moved on when they noticed he saw them.

He wanted to be alone, but instead he felt that he was the center of attention. He decided to go back to the hotel, get a bottle of whiskey, take it to his room, and drink until he didn't have to think anymore.

Chapter Sixty-five

McCain was halfway up the stairs, a new bottle of whiskey in his hand, when someone called his name from behind.

"Mr. McCain! Please wait for me!"

Robert Louis Stevenson dashed up the steps until he stood next to McCain.

"Hi, Louis. Anyone approach you about last evening?"

"No. Not a soul, thank heaven."

"Good."

The two men climbed the stairs together, and when they reached the second floor, Louis said, "Mr. McCain. I realize you're a very busy man, but my room is just down the hall here, and I do wish to introduce my fiancée to you."

McCain's first reaction was to beg off from the introduction, but he remembered what Louis had done the previous evening. "Sure. But call me Josiah, will you?"

"I will. Please, this way."

Louis led McCain down the hall and knocked twice on a door. It swung open, and there stood the very attractive woman McCain had seen Louis with in the restaurant.

"Please come in," she said.

Louis stepped into the room, followed by McCain.

"Josiah McCain, this is my fiancée, Mrs. Fanny Osbourne." Louis stopped for a moment. "Am I supposed to make the introductions the other way around? I never can remember."

Fanny laughed. "There's no need to stand on ceremony, Louis."

McCain took the delicate hand that was presented to him and shook it gently. He wondered if he was supposed to kiss it. Unlike Louis, McCain hadn't forgotten the ways of society people; he never knew them.

"Pleased to meet you, Mrs. Osbourne," he said. "Louis is a mighty lucky fellow, and I wish the two of you the best of luck."

"Thank you. Won't you join us for tea?"

"Well," McCain said, "tea isn't exactly my drink, and I don't mean to be rude, but it's been a long day for me."

"So Louis has told me," she said. She smiled at McCain and continued. "Louis has told me all that you did for him."

"I didn't really do anything."

"Now, now, don't be humble. Louis' ailment can get very serious, and he often needs a lot of care. You apparently gave it to him. And you protected him from that awful Doc Holliday."

"I'm sure Louis could've taken care . . ."

"Not to mention that awful woman who continually made advances on Louis. I simply could not believe the stories Louis told me about her. The nerve! Trying to force him to make love to her—in full view of a train full of people!"

McCain glanced over at Louis, who was staring behind him, blushing a bit. The Scotsman had evidently embellished the story of the past few days and now was afraid of being caught with his embellishments showing.

"Yes," McCain nodded. "That was true. I, too, was shocked. But Louis bravely stood his ground. He proclaimed his love for you, and managed to fight her off."

Fanny looked proudly at her beau.

McCain turned to Louis. "I just want to thank you for

404

what you did last night. It was a brave thing to do."

"I owed you so much, Josiah," Louis said.

"You didn't owe me anything. And if you did, consider it paid in full." McCain faced Fanny again and asked, "Would it be rude of me to ask when the wedding will be?"

Fanny sighed. "I'm afraid I'm awaiting my final divorce papers. The day after I receive them, Louis and I will be married."

"Well, I wish you both the best of luck." McCain tipped his hat and said, "I'd better be going."

"Goodbye, Josiah," Louis said. "It's been my pleasure to have known you."

McCain shook the hand the writer presented to him. "Same here, Louis. I'll be looking out for those books you're going to write."

Then a young boy ran into the room and stood behind Fanny.

"This is my future stepson, Lloyd Osbourne," Louis said.

"Hi, young fellow," McCain said.

"Hi," said the muffled voice hiding behind his mother.

McCain said, "Ma'am," tipped his hat, and closed the door behind him when he left.

He was happy for Louis, happy that he was stepping into a ready-made family, happy that he had a woman as attractive and charming as Fanny. Louis deserved it, and McCain hoped the writer would have far better luck than he had.

Then he realized he was jealous of the Scotsman. He reached his room, but before even opening the door, McCain had the bottle open and was guzzling down a mouthful of Scotch. He needed it.

Chapter Sixty-six

McCain heard a sound inside the room as he poked the key at the keyhole. It sounded like someone opening or shutting the window.

Christ! he thought, do people always enter my room when I'm out? He wondered if it could be Evans again, but decided that wasn't likely. Then he feared it might be Holliday or Warren Earp or that ape of a man who was with them. He quickly unlocked the door and threw it open.

Sara stood by the open window, the breeze blowing her dark tresses around her face. "Where have you been, McCain? I saw you down in the street with Holliday an hour ago."

He closed the door and asked, "What the hell are you doing here? How'd you get in?"

"I let myself in. I'm real good at that. As for what I'm doin' here, I got lonely."

"What happened to your friend?"

"What friend?" Then she recalled the "friend" she

supposedly met at the train station. "Oh . . . she's busy."

McCain sat down on the bed and lifted the bottle of whiskey to his lips. When he was finished, he held it up and said, "Want some?"

Sara smiled, stepped over to him, and took the bottle. She gulped down a mouthful, then handed the bottle back to him. In her other hand she held a paper bag she had had when she hurriedly left the train station. She raised the bag over McCain and poured the contents down on his head. As the storm of green U.S. currency descended on him, she asked, "You want some of this?"

McCain picked up a twenty dollar bill, inspected it, and asked, "Who'd you steal this from?"

"Holliday. Who else?"

"Holliday? When did you steal it? I saw him an hour ago, and he still had the bag with him."

"I didn't want the damn bag," she answered, smiling. "Just the money. I got about half of it, I guess."

"Half?"

"Sure," she explained. "I couldn't take it all. All he had to do then was look into the bag and he'd see it was gone. I took half of it, stuffed the bag with a lot of junk—newspapers, mostly, any ol' crap I could find on the train—then laid the money on top and spread it out so unless he looked real carefully, he wouldn't notice the missing money. I guess he never checked."

"I guess not," McCain agreed. "You're not playing with a full deck, I swear, Sara. Suppose he *had* checked?"

"He didn't."

McCain couldn't argue with the facts. "You took this on the train?"

"Yep. When Doc was real sick. I had to wait forever for the rest of you to fall asleep. I didn't think that was goin' to happen for a while."

"I can't believe it."

"Believe it. You're sittin' in the proof."

McCain took another sip at the whiskey. It was beginning to go to his head, and for the first time he noticed Sara's clothing. She had on a new dark blue dress that clung to her ample shape. Shiny black shoes covered her feet, and silky stockings ran up her shapely legs.

She noticed him eyeing her. "You like the clothes?"

"Sure," he said, pretending not to care too much about them. "Tell me what you're doing here, Sara. What do you want with me? I got nothing to give you."

"Sure you do."

"What?"

She smiled and said, "We'll talk about that later. Right now I want to do this." She bent over, took McCain's head between her hands, and kissed him on the lips.

McCain was stunned for a moment. "I don't get it, Sara. I just don't get it."

"There's nothing to get, McCain."

"Nothing to get? First you hate my guts . . ."

". . . 'Cause I thought you were workin' for that bastard Holliday," she interjected.

"Then you sleep with me . . ."

". . . 'Cause I was cold, and I wanted to."

"Then you run away from me at the train station . . ."

". . . 'Cause I thought you were a lawman. You told Stevenson you were on a case for the government."

"You heard all that? You were sleeping."

"Like hell I was. But you ain't a lawman, are you?"

"No."

"I kinda gathered that when I watched you down in

the street before. You weren't actin' like no lawman."

"I guess not. How long you been up here?"

"A while. Don't exactly know."

McCain's head hurt. "I still don't get it," he said, flopping back onto the bed.

Sara sat down on the edge of the mattress. "I tell ya there's nothin' to get, McCain. I like you, I really do. I just couldn't figure you out. But I thought it over, came up here wantin' to talk to you, saw the scene outside, and here I am. I got nobody in San Francisco—or anyplace else for that matter. I thought I could enjoy spendin' that money a lot better if I had someone to spend it with."

"And I'm convenient?"

Sara stood up angrily. "Well, if that's the way you feel about it, then you can lie there and drink yourself to hell."

She tried to move away, but McCain swung his legs around her and tightened them against her waist. Then he drew them in, and Sara fell on top of him. Her face was inches above his, and he looked deeply into her eyes.

"That isn't the way you feel about it, is it?" he asked, thinking he knew the answer. "It's not the way I feel either, Sara. I'm glad you're here. I don't think I know how to enjoy myself any more. You'll help me with that, won't you?"

She stared down at him, not knowing what to say.

"I think I love you, Sara. I've been trying to deny that to myself because it seems the people I love either get hurt or they leave me wondering what went wrong."

"At least you've had people to love," Sara countered. "I ain't never had anyone. No family. No husband. Not even a real lover. I've been with men, but it wasn't their love I was after, believe me. It was their money or whatever I could get from 'em. This is all new to me, McCain."

"This?"

"I guess I love you too. I don't know. I got nothing to compare it to."

"It feels like hell sometimes."

"Well, you're a man who's always doubtin' me, makin' me feel like hell. Does that mean I love you?"

"Yes," McCain laughed. "That's what it means."

Then he reached up and brought her lips down to his. The kiss began gently, but became wilder and more passionate as the seconds passed.

After a few minutes, they both had their clothes off. McCain rolled on top of her and lowered his face onto her chest, kissing the body that heaved beneath him. Her hands reached his armpits and she urged his body up until their lips met again, their mouths opened, and their tongues touched.

He entered her softly, and he felt her flesh surround and squeeze him as he rocked his hips. She began to breathe more heavily, though in shortened breaths. Then she rocked beneath him, pushing up as forcefully as he was moving down. She seemed to melt beneath him, her grip loosening, her muscles becoming more relaxed. Then he too melted on top of her, onto her, into her.

They remained like that for a moment, savoring the pleasure they had experienced and the warmth and comfort each body was giving the other. After that moment, McCain slid next to her.

"Are we both crazy, McCain?" she asked.

"Maybe," he answered. "Why?"

"I don't know. I just never would have predicted this."

"I know what you mean."

"Sometimes things just happen, I guess."

"As long as things like *this* happen, I can live with it."

Sara laughed. McCain had a warped sense of humor; for the first time she could appreciate it.

"Can I ask you a question, McCain?"

"Call me Josiah, will you?"

"I like McCain better."

"What's the question?"

"You ever been married?"

"Yeah. Why?"

"You still married?"

"Legally, yes. But I ain't seen my wife in a year."

"You leave her?"

"The other way around."

"Oh. Sorry."

"Why do you ask?"

"You make love like a married man."

McCain perched himself up on one elbow. "What's that supposed to mean?"

"Oh, don't get all angry! You were fine. Just a little bit . . . I don't know . . . what's the word? . . . inhibited?"

"That's how married men make love?"

"The ones I've been with."

"So you want me to get uninhibited?"

"That'd be nice."

"No problem. Give me the bottle."

She handed him the half-empty bottle of whiskey, and he gulped down a third of what was left. Then he handed the bottle back to her, and she placed it on the floor.

"That might help," he said. "And if it doesn't, I've got some opium that I found last night."

"You do? Give it to me."

He reached under the pillow and brought out the nugget and the small vial. She took them from him, inspected them for a moment, and threw them out the open window.

"What'd you do that for?"

"That junk puts people to sleep. I don't want you sleepin' just yet."

"I don't feel like sleeping."

"Good."

He kissed her again, and again the warmth of her lips made him feel excited, yet calm, aroused, yet secure.

She broke off the kiss and asked him another question. "What are you gonna do, McCain? Where are you gonna go?"

"I don't know," he answered honestly. "I really got nowhere to go. Maybe someday I'll hook up with Bat Masterson again."

"You know him well?"

"We're friends. Have been for a long time. But I'm in no hurry to return to Dodge. I've really got no reason to go there."

"I got no reason to go anywhere. 'Specially since I got about eight thousand dollars."

"Well, we can wander around together if you want," McCain said, "until we find what we're looking for. Who knows? Maybe we're looking for the same thing."

"Sounds good to me. You don't mind me taggin' along?"

"No," he smiled. "Besides, you got eight thousand dollars. I just gotta keep an eye on you. Keep you out of trouble. Think you can stay out of trouble?"

"I ain't makin' no promises."

"You don't have to."

"We really ain't suited for one another."

"You suit me just fine!" he said. He pulled her on top of him, and he entered her again. She sat on his hips and rode him feverishly.

And as the night progressed, he lost all his inhibitions, and she lost any doubt that for once in her life she had found a man who she could love — even if she was just beginning to figure him out.

BOLD HEROES OF THE UNTAMED NORTHWEST!
THE SCARLET RIDERS
by Ian Anderson

#1: CORPORAL CAVANNAGH (1161, $2.50)

Joining the Mounties was Cavannagh's last chance at a new life. Now he would stop either an Indian war, or a bullet — and out of his daring and courage a legend would be born!

#2: THE RETURN OF CAVANNAGH (1817, $2.25)

A private army of bloodthirsty outlaws are hired to massacre the Mounties at Fort Walsh. Joined by the bold Indian fighter Cavannagh, the Riders prepare for the deadliest battle of their lives!

#3: BEYOND THE STONE HEAPS (1884, $2.50)

Fresh from the slaughter at the Little Big Horn, the Sioux cross the border into Canada. Only Cavannagh can prevent the raging Indian war that threatens to destroy the Scarlet Riders!

#4: SERGEANT O'REILLY (1977, $2.50)

When an Indian village is reduced to ashes, Sergeant O'Reilly of the Mounties risks his life and career to help an avenging Stoney chief and bring a silver-hungry murderer to justice!

#5: FORT TERROR (2125, $2.50)

Captured by the robed and bearded killer monks of Fort Terror, Parsons knew it was up to him, and him alone, to stop a terrifying reign of anarchy and chaos by the deadliest assassins in the territory — and continue the growing legend of The Scarlet Riders!

SADDLE UP FOR ADVENTURE
WITH G. CLIFTON WISLER'S
TEXAS BRAZOS!
A SAGA AS BIG AND BOLD AS TEXAS ITSELF,
FROM THE NUMBER-ONE PUBLISHER
OF WESTERN EXCITEMENT

#1: TEXAS BRAZOS (1969, $3.95)
In the Spring of 1870, Charlie Justiss and his family follow their dreams into an untamed and glorious new land — battling the worst of man and nature to forge the raw beginnings of what is destined to become the largest cattle operation in West Texas.

#2: FORTUNE BEND (2069, $3.95)
The epic adventure continues! Progress comes to the raw West Texas outpost of Palo Pinto, threatening the Justiss family's blossoming cattle empire. But Charlie Justiss is willing to fight to the death to defend his dreams in the wide open terrain of America's frontier!

#3: PALO PINTO (2164, $3.95)
The small Texas town of Palo Pinto has grown by leaps and bounds since the Justiss family first settled there a decade earlier. For beautiful women like Emiline Justiss, the advent of civilization promises fancy new houses and proper courting. But for strong men like Bret Pruett, it means new laws to be upheld — with a shotgun if necessary!

#4: CADDO CREEK
During the worst drought in memory, a bitter range war erupts between the farmers and cattlemen of Palo Pinto for the Brazos River's dwindling water supply. Peace must come again to the territory, or everything the settlers had fought and died for would be lost forever!

Available wherever paperbacks are sold, or order direct from the Publisher. Send cover price plus 50¢ per copy for mailing and handling to Zebra Books, Dept. 2363, 475 Park Avenue South, New York, N.Y. 10016. Residents of New York, New Jersey and Pennsylvania must include sales tax. DO NOT SEND CASH.

POWELL'S ARMY
BY TERENCE DUNCAN

#1: UNCHAINED LIGHTNING   (1994, $2.50)

Thundering out of the past, a trio of deadly enforcers dispenses its own brand of frontier justice throughout the untamed American West! Two men and one woman, they are the U.S. Army's most lethal secret weapon—they are POWELL'S ARMY!

#2: APACHE RAIDERS   (2073, $2.50)

The disappearance of seventeen Apache maidens brings tribal unrest to the violent breaking point. To prevent an explosion of bloodshed, Powell's Army races through a nightmare world south of the border—and into the deadly clutches of a vicious band of Mexican flesh merchants!

#3: MUSTANG WARRIORS   (2171, $2.50)

Someone is selling cavalry guns and horses to the Comanche—and that spells trouble for the bluecoats' campaign against Chief Quanah Parker's bloodthirsty Kwahadi warriors. But Powell's Army are no strangers to trouble. When the showdown comes, they'll be ready—and someone is going to die!

#4: ROBBERS ROOST   (2285, $2.50)

After hijacking an army payroll wagon and killing the troopers riding guard, Three-Fingered Jack and his gang high-tail it into Virginia City to spend their ill-gotten gains. But Powell's Army plans to apprehend the murderous hardcases before the local vigilantes do—to make sure that Jack and his slimy band stretch hemp the legal way!